I Hate Tft

Heather Hill

Copyright © 2016 by Heather Hill

All rights reserved. This book or any portion thereof may not be reproduced or used in any manner whatsoever without the express written permission of the publisher except for the use of brief quotations in a book review or scholarly journal.

First Printing: 2016

Ebook

www.hell4heather.com

Ordering Information:

Special discounts are available on quantity purchases by corporations, associations, educators, and others. For details, contact the publisher/author, Heather Hill - Email: hell4heather@gmail.com

U.S. trade bookstores and wholesalers: Please contact Heather Hill

Cover design: D16.co.uk

To Stephen,
For being there.

'Let me not die while I am still alive.'
- The Prayer of Hannah

Preface

Imagine Death; a towering, darkly cloaked figure with a scythe taller than he is, sombrely following a frail, elderly gentleman as he shuffles across a busy road. Your stomach tightens. You feel desperate and afraid for the gentle, oblivious old man. You think, 'I do hope he had a happy life.' And while he makes it safely to the other side, Death gets run over by a truck.

Now you are primed and prepared.

This, dear reader, is my story about death.

Chapter One

SOMETIMES I GET SO LONELY AND SO FRUSTRATED, I BUY SEXY VEGETABLES – FLEUR BROOKES, WIDOW, 68.

In the plant-filled conservatory in her vast, luxurious bungalow in the Scottish borders, Joanna-Rose Hepple blinked at her computer screen. Her eyes were not what they once were.

'What?'

It took a minute for her to understand Fleur Brookes' Facebook post and afterwards, racing to the kitchen for a cloth to mop spat out wine off her keyboard, she decided her eyes must have been deceiving her.

'Or it's a joke,' she muttered, with a shake of her head. 'Must be that.'

Three miles away, in her dusty, ancient little cottage, Fleur rolled a wisp of ash-grey curls around her finger, grinned and sat waiting for the likes, the open arms and the flood of 'welcome to the group' messages. These were her people after all. Coming across, and then being accepted into, a closed Facebook group of local widows had been a real find. She had a window to the outside world again. Until now she had only joined, then spent three weeks' worth of days watching and reading about the lives of this small group of bereft women without comment.

Five minutes passed. Then ten. She yawned, reached into the back of her pyjama bottoms and tugged at her g-string.

'Ooh ya bugger,' she said, snapping it from the groove it had dug for itself in her skin to a place where it would soon begin digging another.

Still no likes.

As she stared at the screen, a new status update appeared, pushing hers down. It was from Joanna-Rose Hepple, with a photo attached:

REMEMBERING YOU, ROBERT. TWO YEARS TODAY.

That hit the spot with everyone. This was a support group for widows, after all. As she added a like and watched the thumbs up numbers rise, Fleur began searching the top and sides of the couch cushions with her free hand for her spectacles. What she found were kernels of popcorn, several crisp packets, some coins and copious amounts of a sand-like substance that got under her fingernails instead. The popcorn was still delicious, if a little soft. She swallowed two more salty kernels while pulling the mobile phone closer to her face, squinting to try to make out the faces of the four grinning men in the very old photograph, Joanna-Rose had posted.

'No, it can't be!' Fleur gasped. Yet there he was, large as life and younger than she remembered. He was unmistakeable; the same round, jolly face and straw yellow hair, grinning as though he'd just told his favourite startled moose joke.

'Hey, Flurry!' (Why had he always called her that?) 'Want tae see my impression of a startled moose?'

'Don't you start with that silly, startled moose impression again,' she said aloud, stealing a glance at his chair, disregarding the foot high pile of train magazines and Celtic match programmes that now sat where he once had. Yet she saw it again. The wide-eyed, feigning-surprise expression, the thumbs on his temples, fingers outstretched as makeshift antlers, ready to deliver the punchline:

'Whit the fuck was that?'

'It wasn't funny then and it's not bloody funny now,' she told the pile of train magazines. 'Smiling like you're about to guzzle that entire thing.' She tapped what she thought was a beer barrel in the photo on her screen, which rewarded her by opening an even larger one in another window. 'Look at you there,' she said to his face on the screen, 'all happy and smug like you never have the audacity to go and bloody die on me.'

Twenty-seven years of marriage had been her penance. They met when she was thirty-six, after she fell spectacularly over a broken slab in the high street, then fell again – for the plump, smiley-faced lawyer from Glasgow who had picked her up from the floor. The same lawyer who, after two years of courtship, had bowed down on one knee, begged her to be his wife and then admitted he hadn't bought a ring yet after she said yes. Tight git.

She squeezed her eyes shut, willing a tirade of pity-filled tears to fall. Nothing. She opened them again and stared, unblinking, at the pile of train magazines for sixty seconds.

'There,' she told Charlie's chair, as her stinging eyes leaked at last. 'Three tears and I thought about you, okay? Now leave me in peace.'

Somewhere in a nearby town and at the same time, resting her laptop on a pile of unopened letters, Cathy Harper clicked to open the picture Joanna-Rose had posted on the Widows Together Facebook page, before leaning in for a better look. Then, she gasped.

Fleur sniffed. Still no likes on her status; but twenty had appeared already for Joanna-Fecking-Rose's photo. Some people couldn't help gloating about knowing people. So her husband had his photo taken with the world famous psychic medium, Derek Montrose. So what? She wasn't going to be one of those braggers. Looking at the picture again, she scratched her chin and sighed. Yes, she was sure she had this photo in amongst her papers somewhere; a newsletter or magazine article she was sure, but no, she wasn't going to comment. Charlie had met a lot of people from all walks of life in his legal eagle, still-bothering-to-be-alive days. This would be another of those 'business transaction' things he used to allude to but never tell her about.

Arms outstretched, Cathy Harper pitter-pattered on the keys of her laptop with her fingertips as she decided what to do. She'd comment. Write, 'I have that photo!' But wouldn't that say, 'Wow, my husband might have known him too,' at a time when everyone in the Widows Together group should just be 'liking' the status and saying how sorry they were? Cathy thought better of it. But then, why on earth would her husband, Bob, have that same photo among his things?

Certain that not a soul in the group had liked her sexy vegetables status, Fleur flicked away to the personal profile she'd stalked for what had seemed like an age. They weren't Facebook friends, but every now and again she would go to this place and look at the single photograph she was able to view. It was Mandy's profile picture, and seeing it still unchanged satisfied her that nothing had changed; she hadn't missed anything of significance. Yet.

'There you are, lass,' Fleur said out loud, the way Charlie would speak to their only daughter while he was alive. Or, to be more accurate, *Charlie's* only daughter. As her fingertips touched the blonde, brown-eyed young beauty on the screen, the young woman smiled back at her like Fleur was still needed. A familiar pain filled her heart as she recalled the truth; she wasn't needed, and hadn't been in the four or more years since her Charlie's death. All because of that damn funeral thing people seem to need to do when somebody ups and dies.

'Oh well,' Fleur told Mandy's photo. 'Who's gonna know I'm looking at you but me, eh?'

She flicked back to the Widow's Together group page, with a sigh.

Joanna-Rose leaned back in her chair with a heavy sigh before taking the last mouthful of her third glass of *Chateaux Neuf Du Pape*.

'To you, my wonderful, darling man,' she said to Robert's picture on the screen. A notification pinged to let her know she had a new comment on her post. It was from a woman called Cathy Harper, and a picture was attached.

THINKING OF YOU TODAY, JOANNA-ROSE. BUT, I HAVE TO ASK, DO YOU KNOW THE MAN IN THIS PHOTO, HERE?

Joanna-Rose strained to make out the flame-haired young man in the picture and pulled a face. 'Well, *he* hasn't troubled a hairdresser for a while,' she slurred, before sending her reply:

NO, I'M AFRAID I DO NOT. SHOULD I? she wrote.

I KNOW THIS ONE! WASN'T HE ON AMERICA'S MOST WANTED LAST WEEK?

Fleur grinned at her comment, feeling sure that even on the anniversary of someone's death, Joanna-Rose and this Cathy person could allow themselves a little smile. And Fleur's long gone husband was in the photo too, after all. It could be four years today for all she knew, it's not like she was keeping track.

A simultaneous post from Cathy made her smile fall.

IT'S MY LATE HUSBAND, BOB.

Oops. Fleur opened up her own comment and hovered over the edit button, when another comment tagged to her from Cathy appeared.

HA! IT COULD BE TRUE, FLEUR. HE WAS A CHARACTER ALRIGHT. CERTAINLY STOLE MY HEART XX

Two kisses. Kisses means it's okay, right? Fleur sighed and pressed the escape button. May as well leave it there; she was rumbled. Now she would wade in with her own two pence, even if she didn't want to talk about *him*. There were still no likes on her own introductory comment, so this would have to be the place for infiltrating the group, even if it seemed no one in it had a sense of humour. Then again, the group was all about grief, death and having to put the bin out by yourself. Yes, the only conversation of interest to anyone in here would be her late husband, Charlie. She would tell them now.

Joanna-Rose looked again at the face of Cathy's husband. Another Robert, no doubt. But Bob Harper didn't look at all familiar to her. The picture had marked one of the countless acquisitions Robert had overseen in his role as a solicitor, and she'd never enquired about it while he was alive. But lately it had become one of more interest to her than any other. Everybody would know the man in the centre of the photo was, Derek Montrose. The subject of the transaction was obvious: whisky, as all four men were raising small shot glasses over an oak barrel. Robert had liked his liquor, but this had been just another business deal to him. To her now, it held a weird fascination that had made her study it for half an hour or more before posting it on a public forum for the world to see. She slugged back the last dregs of her wine and typed under Fleur's comment:

I'VE HAD A GOOD THINK ABOUT IT NOW, BUT STILL, I'M CERTAIN I DON'T KNOW HIM. SORRY.

She paused. Was it any good trying to deny herself that sudden, innate need to know more about Derek Montrose? Should she ask Cathy what she knew?

Screw it. There was another bottle in the kitchen screaming to be opened.

Cathy wasn't reading anymore, she was rummaging through Bob's writing desk in the long neglected office. She hadn't been in this room since a month after he'd died, when she'd been forced to disturb things in order to find their mortgage documents. But she remembered the photograph because he'd attached an open invitation for one of Derek Montrose's shows to it, signed by the man himself, and written a message for her on the back:

'Okay, I give in. Let's go see him together. Or, you can meet me on the other side.'

It had been a joke, after his first battle with cancer was won and he'd believed it to be a permanent victory. They'd been daring to make plans for the future.

She caught her breath as she put her hand on the photograph at last, under another pile of unopened letters, and turned it over to see Bob's familiar handwriting and the open ticket again - a gift from the man himself to attend any performance. Just six weeks after he'd written this... no, she couldn't think of that day again.

Pulling the ticket off the paper clip she stroked Bob's words, as though laying a hand on them was to touch his hand again. Closing her eyes, she could see him in her mind's eye, smiling and shaking his head as he wrote, dreading having to accompany his wife to the kind of show she loved but he loathed. 'A sideshow,' was how he'd described Derek Montrose's appearances.

'Sadly, it's a sideshow we have to attend,' Bob had told her. 'Derek was adamant we go sooner rather than later when he gave it to me. I think he's planning to quit it all soon.'

Well, he wouldn't be going with her now, but she knew that if there was a way in this world and the next, Bob would be at that performance, waiting for her. This was all a sign.

And now Joanna-Rose had posted the photo on Facebook, which had to be another one. This was the universe in action, drawing her back home to Bob. Looking again at the ticket before reattaching it to the photo, she walked back into the living room and putting it down beside her laptop, leaned over to type in the conversation thread:

HOW FUNNY. BOB HAD THAT PHOTO TOO.

Chapter Two

'Knock knock!'

Joanna-Rose jumped at the intrusion and looked up to see the shirtless, grey-haired chest of her gardener, who stood smiling at her through the clear glass door to her conservatory.

'Ah, come in, Isaac,' she said, straining in her inebriated state to keep her gaze at eye level to meet his as he strode purposefully in. Although the words on the still blank page of her latest work hadn't been spilling forth today, the long-missing playwright in her head described his eyes as the narrator of some clichéd love scene would: deep, brown, dreamy pools of...

'Come-to-bed.'

'Sorry?'

Jesus, God, she had said it out loud. Or was it the drink talking?

As Isaac's eyes widened, she felt her stomach tighten and glanced at the damningly silent empty bottle.

'Err... bed,' she stammered. 'I need...' She paused, closing her eyes for the briefest of moments, willing her addled brain to catch up with everything she was saying. 'I need to go to bed,' she finished at last, meeting his perplexed stare again.

Isaac smiled, and she cursed the sympathy that was behind it. 'Oh,' he said, sounding, she thought with a tinge of sadness, relieved.

Her gaze fell to his mud-covered boots, embarrassed by what she knew his would be taking in - a dishevelled shell of a woman who was deserving of little more than his pity. She was perhaps five years younger than Isaac, but the way he found her most days, he could be forgiven for thinking she was much older. Even with her mind bathed and soothed in red wine, she still felt shame; shame for her current state and shame that she loved Isaac more than she had ever been able to love herself.

'Are you okay?'

His words poured through the fog and she closed her eyes again, holding them to her. *What did he ask her? What did she have to say back?*

She swallowed, mentally chasing away the delicious, yet annoying image she now had in her mind as she held him there: one of his arms around her. She hadn't felt anybody's arms around her in forever. Or, that other thing couples sometimes do.

'I'm good,' she said at last, opening her eyes again. But she wasn't, she was bad. *Bad, bad Joanna-Rose. She needs a swift, sharp whomp over the bottom with that newspaper you have under your arm...*

She felt her cheeks burn at her runaway thoughts; both sets.

'Drinking already, Mrs Hepple?' Isaac asked with a teasing wink.

She recoiled. Whenever he called her that, she felt ashamed. Even after all the wine, which should remove the staunchest of people's inhibitions, even driving them to mild BDSM fantasies involving someone's copy of *The Independent,* it was still there.

'Well, it is almost one o'clock,' she replied, looking up to point at the clock on the wall. 'That's past opening time.'

Isaac looked at the empty bottle then back at her and frowned. 'Can I help you with anything?' he enquired. 'Other than the garden, I mean?'

On cue, a dozen very helpful sex positions involving them both flicked through her brain like a silent, dirty movie. This, she thought, was *not* her life.

'No, I'm fine,' she said, as the sound of her heart thumped so hard in her ears she feared he might be able to hear it too. Why couldn't he just stop all the rampant sex going on in her frustrated old brain, do the garden and then go away? Nothing made her feel as inept and tongue-tied as any attempt at conversation with him.

Get up!

'Sorry?' she said, assuming the voice in her head had been Isaac's. He didn't reply, simply continued to watch with a concerned expression as she put both arms on the chair to pull herself to standing, missing the right arm and almost toppling over to one side until she caught herself. He moved forwards to help, but she leaned away before he could reach her.

'I'm okay.'

'Are you sure, Mrs Hepple?' He took a step towards the table to straighten her laptop, which was hanging over the edge where she'd knocked it as she rose, but stopped short, as she reached over and slammed it shut, at once regretting how rude and abrupt that would have seemed. Her second regret followed immediately, as it crashed to the ground.

'I... I don't need any help,' she stammered again, watching him bend down to pick it up for her and replace it on the table. 'I'm fine, really.'

'Something important?' he asked, pointing at the laptop.

'It's everything. My life's work,' she explained. 'I get very, oh, what do I mean?' There it was again, that goddam fog that had nothing to do with wine and everything to do with love.

'Protective?'

'Yes,' she had agreed before he finished speaking, feeling foolish again and knowing full well her face was glowing redder by the minute. 'Could you please leave me? I'm working very, very hard right now.'

It was a lie. The truth was her Muse seemed to have died with Robert, her latest play ever open on the laptop as though she was mid-line, alongside a fast emptying bottle of wine and a window to the world of Facebook. Her editor and agent had given up calling months ago. Yet the ideas still flowed when she was hammered, which was the excuse she gave herself for drinking. One day she might even get some of those ideas down in her notebook before passing out.

Taking a noisy deep breath in, Joanna-Rose continued toward the kitchen in slow motion as she fought to stay upright. Before Isaac could offer a hand again she stopped him.

'I'm fine,' she insisted. 'I've just been having some dizzy spells.'

She turned in time to catch his glance at the obvious cause of her dizzy spells - the empty bottle.

'I... I'm not having any more,' she lied. 'I've far too much to do today.'

With a frantic wave of her hands she shooed him out and he frowned.

'Well, if you're sure,' he said, watching her leave. 'I'll be in the garden if you need me, mind, there's a lot of work needing to be done to your bush...'

As she was stopped in her tracks, he added: '...es.'

Embarrassed himself now, he made for the door and stepped quickly outside.

Joanna-Rose tutted. When had she become a cliché, in love with her gardener, of all things? She couldn't write a story because she was busy living one that had already been written – with a modern twist. Lady Bloody Chatterley, the pissed years.

Joanna-Rose reached for the last bottle on the shelf and sighed. Bugger, she'd have to call Isaac back in for another round of unintentional double entendres before he left after all. A trip to the shop would be required and there was no way she was going to make it herself. But then again, she could just take one more glass and save the rest for tomorrow. That left three glasses which would be sufficient to open the gates of her imagination that little bit wider and start her back on the road to finishing – okay starting - her play. Yes, that would do it. No more buying wine today or tomorrow. No more drunkenness in front of Isaac.

There was so much awkwardness around her employment of him, she wondered many times whether to let him go to maintain her dignity and privacy and put an end to her needless longing. She hadn't forgotten the times he'd found her almost unconscious from an afternoon drinking spree; the first after she'd discovered another of Robert's sordid little affairs, not long after Isaac's appointment, and the last after his death. Still, she had remained aloof as she could in the circumstances, telling him nothing of the indiscretions, nothing of her personal misery and her lifelong acceptance of what was a lonely, barren existence. She was sure she had kept their relationship on a professional level. *She had, hadn't she?*

As she stumbled back into the conservatory, laughingly called her 'scriptorium' - laughingly because she'd written almost nothing she could use in here since it was built - she looked back at the closed laptop where her play still waited to be revived. All of this emotion, all of this longing for Isaac. Surely she could spill some of it out onto the page? Closing her eyes she noticed the familiar wave of wretchedness and want in her stomach and at once she needed to soothe it away as she always did. She raised her glass and threw back the entire contents without tasting them at all, before turning back to the kitchen, stopping to steady herself against the doorframe as another wave of dizziness hit. Just one more glass; just one. That left two for tomorrow and a far better, more productive writing day.

Three miles away, Cathy Harper picked up her laptop again to see if a reply had come yet from Joanna-Rose. There was none, but a friend request notification from Fleur Brookes caught her eye, and she accepted right away.

Fleur hoped Cathy wouldn't think her a bit odd when she realised there were no other friends in her list. She was *not* going to cry. Charlie was history; someone whom she had buried a long time ago in more ways than one. Yet – dammit – she'd *had* to go check that photo to be sure. Seeing his face on the screen had been the first time she'd looked at any photograph of him in four years. Her right hand went back to the keyboard to type a private message to Cathy.

HI CATHY...

She paused. Did she want to talk about Charlie? Everything inside her was screaming, 'Don't do it!' But curiosity was getting the better of her. It was a feeling at odds with the detached personality she'd adopted of late.

As Fleur's message appeared, Cathy blinked in disbelief. God bless this Fleur person, she was such a comedian. Although... she wasn't sure she got the joke. Was it a joke? She looked down at the identical photo to the one Joanna-Rose had posted that she now held in her hand before reading Fleur's comment again:

I HAVE THIS PHOTO SOMEWHERE TOO. THE CURLY HAIRED SPECIMEN WITH THE ROUND FACE AND CHEESY GRIN? THAT'S MY HUSBAND, CHARLIE.

Chapter Three

'Who the hell…? Oh!'

Joanna-Rose had stared at the number on her mobile phone screen for a few seconds, trying hard to focus, before taking the call.

'Hello? Is that you, Ms Hepple?'

There was a pause.

'If I don't say anything,' she thought. 'If no actual words are exchanged, then it won't be happening. Please God, let the world stay frozen in yesterday – just for a while longer.'

'Hello? Hello? Ms Hepple?'

'I was coming to see Mum today,' Joanna-Rose said at last. 'But something, er… came up.'

She stared ahead, grimacing at The Something That Had Come Up. It was an almost empty third bottle of wine, which most certainly would come up again, sometime after supper.

'Oh Ms Hepple, I got you at last. You need to come here now. Right away I'm afraid.'

'Oh, that's going to be a little awkward…' Joanna-Rose interrupted her, feeling a familiar, sickly rise of bile in her throat. Her stomach was crashing to her feet. Not today. Please, not today. Not again.

'I understand, Ms Hepple, I do. But you see your mother is very poorly and -.'

'I… I can't deal with this right now.' Joanna-Rose felt the urge to hang up, but was frozen in time, ensconced in her inebriated bubble. She doubted she could stand, let alone make it to the hospice. 'I've been drinking a little bit. And you have called me in before telling me I had to go now. Twice in fact.'

She heard an intake of breath. Joanna-Rose felt a stab of guilt. She was concerned for her mother yet more concerned at the prospect of making a fool of herself. What must this woman think?

'Ms Hepple,' the nurse said, her voice authoritative, yet sympathetic. 'The doctor says your mother won't last the night. I think you should come. Now. Have you any responsible, sober friends who can bring you here tonight? Or perhaps I could get you a taxi? You see, you really must come. I am aware things have been bad before and your mum has come back fighting, and it's been a long, harrowing twelve months, but I'm afraid this time, well, it is crucial that you come here.'

'I'm... spinning around, get out of my way-ay. I know you're feeling me 'cos you like it like this!'

Fleur accentuated the last 'like' and 'this' with a left then right thrust of her hips, as she danced around her living room with headphones on. Around her waist she wore Charlie's sporran: the handiest thing she could find to put her music player in as she danced. This was her daily exercise regime: freestyle bopping in a sporran. Fleur Brookes didn't *do* handbags.

Taking an almighty swing to the right, she collided with a clothes horse full of drying underwear, which collapsed and crashed to the ground. Tutting to herself, she kicked it and its contents under the sofa.

'Now,' she said, taking off the headphones a few minutes later. 'Some serious cleaning is required.'

She looked over the surfaces, untouched with a duster for at least two – no three – months. As she mused about what to tackle first, Phillip strolled in and began rubbing himself against her sweat-covered legs, leaving bits of dampened ginger fur on them.

'Hello, Phillip,' she said, bending down to tickle him under the chin. 'What do you think? Time to wave a duster about? Find the broom and then, who knows, the floor?'

There were newspapers, old clothes, cereal boxes, takeaway tubs and bits of unidentifiable fluff everywhere in the tiny living room. In Fleur's case, living room meant living organism room. She was cultivating at least four billion species of bacteria in her home; and she couldn't care less.

'I like keeping all my old skin though,' she told Phillip, pointing at the dust. 'You never know when I might need to gather it up for a graft. Or if I get a new man in my life, hey, there are bits of me here that are at least five years younger.'

Phillip stretched, emitting a disinterested yawn. He never laughed at her jokes. Why the heck did she have a cat? A pig would be much more useful. And those buggers ate everything.

'They don't laugh at your jokes either though, I don't think,' she told herself out loud. 'Still, imagine how clean the house would be. Not to mention the bodies I could dispose of.'

She laughed, then stopped to wonder if perhaps there *were* any bodies somewhere. Anything was possible. She hadn't tidied up in a while, or seen her neighbour, Mr Francis, for a couple of weeks, now that she thought about it. She eyed Phillip suspiciously. Was he capable of homicide?

The letterbox rattled, causing Phillip to spring away from Fleur's legs and make for the safety of the chair arm, only to miss and find himself dangling from one claw in the upholstery.

Nope. He wasn't.

'I know,' she said, stepping round a giant pile of magazines and making for the front door. 'Nobody visits me. Maybe it's the big cheque we've been waiting for. You know, the one from Prague who wears tight trousers with his zip always falling down.'

Having recovered his composure, Phillip lifted a paw to his face and began washing it with his tongue.

'Don't forget to do behind your ears,' she told him in passing, as he started to do it anyway.

Seeing the name on the front of the solitary letter on the mat, she sighed. It looked like another one from the eye hospital. She always opened the eye hospital letters, knowing it would be about yet another missed appointment. Mandy had never changed her address with these people after all this time and Fleur knew why. She ripped the envelope open and took out the letter.

```
We have now made a new appointment for your
annual eye test for 10th September at 9.30am.
Please let us know whether you can attend on
this date.
```

This couldn't go on unchecked any longer. Cathy would be here in about an hour; plenty of time to make a quick call before she cleaned up - i.e. cleared some space in the centre of the room, wiped over the surfaces with her sleeve and sprayed some air freshener about. Oh and she ought to start taking down last year's Christmas decorations; it was the middle of August after all. She stretched up to pull the holly wreath down from above her mantelpiece with one hand, succeeding merely in knocking it off, and dialled the hospital with the other, with the wreath now on her head.

The first person to answer wasn't a real person, and was swiftly followed by Katy Perry.

'Oh in the name of God,' Fleur spat. 'Bloody call waiting music! I don't want your bloody call waiting music!'

'Dr O'Brien's secretary. How can I help?'

'Wait a moment,' Fleur replied. 'I'd just like to sing you my very special rendition of *Love and Affection*. You'll like this.'

'Excuse me?'

'*I yam not in lurvvvve. But I'm open to persuasion. East or wesssssst. Where's the besssst!*'

The line went dead. Fleur shook the handset before holding it back up to her ear.

'Hello?'

She sighed. Time for two and half more minutes of Katy Perry. Stomping up and down her living room floor, she dialled again.

'Dr O'Brien's secretary. How can I help?'

Thankful that the music had ended at last, Fleur spoke confidently.

'Hello, I am calling about my daughter Mandy. You've sent her latest appointment here. But she doesn't live with me anymore. She hasn't used this address in three and a half years, in fact.'

'Surname?'

The caller didn't want to know her sad stories. Fleur didn't blame her.

'Her name?' she replied. 'Mandy.'

'What's her surname?' the woman repeated.

'I told you,' Fleur snapped. 'Her name is Mandy Brookes and I'm sure she hasn't been going to these appointments.'

'Date of birth?' The woman continued like a recorded message, making Fleur think of the hours of banking call centre fun she'd had in the past. Somehow, she always ended up in a heated argument with those.

'Press one or say one to tell us you want to hear your balance.'

'One.'

'Press two or say two to report a lost or stolen debit card.'

'One!'

'Press three or say three to tell us about a change in your personal circumstances.'

'ONE!'

'Press four or say four if none of these apply and you want to speak with an advisor.'

'ONE! ONE! ONE!'

'I'm sorry, I don't understand that selection. Press one or say one to tell us you want to hear your balance.'

Fleur took a deep breath and prepared for battle with Dr O'Brien's snooty secretary. She twiddled with the wreath on her head with her idle hand, and continued.

'Well, yes. I'm her mum and…'

'Okay, do you know her date of birth?'

A berry popped off the wreath and rolled across the floor.

'I'm not sure, hang on.' Fleur held the phone to her ear with a hunched shoulder and scrunched the letter up next to the receiver, pretending to search through papers for an answer. 'Ah wait, I've got it now. I vaguely recall a pushing down sensation on October 11th 1984.'

There was no reply, only the sound of keys tapping. Despite her annoyance, Fleur grinned at her jibe. The truth was there had been no pushing sensation for Fleur on the day of Mandy's birth. She hadn't been present. Step mothers generally weren't on opening day.

A few seconds passed and then a still indifferent response came back.

'Ah yes, Mandy Brookes. She should have been here three days ago.'

'I know, yes. That is what I've been trying to explain about. She misses all of her appointments, I know she does. And her eyes are so important.'

She paused for a response, but none came.

'Ears are important too,' she wanted to add, but thought better of it.

Fleur pictured the woman putting the phone receiver on top of her computer monitor and filing her nails. This sort of thing had to stop. After all, you don't need alphabetically sorted fingernails. She cleared her throat and spoke again.

'I'm just ringing to let you have her new address.'

She waited. Still no response.

'You see, she no longer speaks to me and, as for taking care of her diabetes, well; she has been appalling at it. We always felt like she had a death wish or some…'

The keyboard tapping stopped.

'So you have her new address,' the woman piped up at last. 'Why don't you give me that now and we will contact her directly?'

Fleur took a step towards Phillip, who was licking the inside of a half-eaten tub of chicken tikka masala, and made a swipe at him with the handset.

And the ground gave way.

Chapter Four

Cathy flicked on the Widows Together Facebook page and scrolled down to her last message. There was still no response from Joanna-Rose even though a week had now passed. Strange. She hoped she was okay but as they weren't direct Facebook friends, she couldn't make contact to ask her. However, she'd been glad to accept an invitation to meet Fleur. Cathy had no friends to speak of and no family left in her life. The one person trying to befriend her right now was Martin, and she couldn't imagine where that would lead at this point in her life.

It was just over a forty minute drive to Fleur's house, which gave Cathy plenty of time for reflection. She called to mind a young man, with masses of wavy, strawberry blonde hair, bright blue eyes and a dimple – yes there had been an amatory, Kirk Douglas-style dimple – in the middle of his chin. His family had taken her to them after the devastating car crash that had killed both of her parents. She had been alone at the tender age of eighteen, but Martin's family seemed to love her as a daughter, even though they were both so young and had only been dating for two years. It wasn't long after the accident that he'd proposed marriage; and eighteen months after was the date of the wedding day. A day she remembered clearly as being the one time in her entire existence when she had considered taking her own life. She'd been left alone again; the wedding cancelled a month earlier, for reasons Martin had never been able to explain in a way that made any sense to her.

'I still love you, Cathy. But it's over. I'm so sorry. Please try to understand.'

But how could anyone be expected to understand after over three years of togetherness, a proposal, an engagement party and all those wedding plans? How could anyone understand, 'I love you, but I don't want you anymore?'

Martin had refused to answer any of her questions, or even discuss the matter. He'd cut her off, explaining that he felt too young for marriage, something Cathy at least knew now he'd been right about. But then, just two years later and before his twenty-first birthday, Martin McGuire had married somebody else.

Cathy recalled lying alone in the flat she'd moved into with a work colleague after the split, staring at an unopened bottle of paracetamol, wondering if Martin would care if she took them all. She hadn't wanted to die, just to do anything that might make him realise he couldn't live without her. As she'd felt she couldn't live without him.

It was such a long time ago now, but she had all of the memories, wrapped in the grey cloud that was the unbearable sadness of her loss at the time. It was her parents and Martin, all together in a horrible and lonely few years. Even though she had met, fallen in love with and married Bob twelve years later, she still recalled that time vividly, some of the darkest days of her life - until now. She held those memories, not for sentimental reasons, but in the way a person clings to past failures and rejections, as if they were a crucial part of what defined her. As if letting them go would mean forgetting something important about Cathy, the woman. Martin finding her on the widow's forum before sending her a private message, hoping to meet up after over twenty-seven years, had brought it all back again. She hadn't answered, supposing that his wife had died and that's why he was in the forum in the first place, and the reason he was now bothering to try to speak to her. Loneliness did strange things to you, she knew that better than anyone, but it was all too much for Cathy. As if Bob's death wasn't sadness enough.

She pulled the car into Fleur's road at last and sighed. If nothing else, getting out and meeting Fleur would be something of an experience. Something new.

Fleur wondered if she was dead. Then she wondered if she'd put the bin out.

'Dammit!'

She hadn't.

And there was pain, somewhere in the region of her left buttock. So she wasn't dead but something might be broken. No, wait! She'd had a tube of Polos in her back pocket.

'Aww, I've crushed my Polos,' she complained, before a more serious matter reached her attention; a warm, wet feeling in her loins. 'Aww,' she groaned again. 'I've wet myself.'

Phillip's face appeared at the opening above her head where a split second earlier she had crashed through her rotten living room floor.

'Phillip,' she said. 'If you have any idea how to do that *Lassie Come Home* thing and go tell someone your owner fell down a well, this would be a good time to practise it. Only be a good boy and drop some clean trousers down here first, would you?'

Phillip retreated. She supposed getting back to that illicit chicken tikka masala was more important than Fleur's life. She looked up, knowing at once that reaching for the edge would be futile, before slumping back. She was going to die here, undiscovered for ages and ages – her body pickled in her own pee so that everyone would know she'd been stress incontinent. If only her corpse could disintegrate fast, hiding the damning evidence. Where was a pig when you needed one?

'PHILLIP!' she shouted up at the cat. 'YOU MIGHT BE AS COLD-HEARTED AND INDIFFERENT AS THAT WITCH OF A CONSULTANT'S SECRETARY, BUT I NEED YOUR HELP!'

'Hello?'

The voice was a quiet, almost imperceptible one.

'Oh hell, it's The Borrowers,' Fleur shrieked, unwilling to move but straining her eyes to search the blackness around her.

'Hello? Are you still there?'

The witch secretary! She was still on the line!

'Where the heck *is* my phone?'

Without moving too much - after all, something might be broken, she felt round about her with her hands, finding nothing but rocks, wood and plaster.

'HELLO!' she shouted at the voice. She guessed the hole would be almost a foot over her head, even from standing. How the heck was she going to get out of this? 'HELLO? I SEEM TO BE STUCK IN A BIT OF A HOLE.'

The only sound was one of rough cat tongue scraping clean a takeaway tub. Brilliant.

'YOU COW! YOU'VE PUT THE PHONE DOWN, HAVEN'T YOU? SOME NHS THIS IS!'

'Hello?'

Fleur blinked and looked again into the near darkness around her before glancing upwards, spying her phone with The Cow still on the line, brightly lit and teetering on the edge of a snapped beam. She felt around for something to bat it with and, finding nothing, felt something on top of her head. The wreath! She tugged at it, but it was stuck fast in her wiry, not washed for days hair. She pulled hard but it wouldn't budge.

'Argh!' She'd tugged a little too hard.

'Hello?' said The Cow.

Fleur reached in front of her to grasp a piece of plywood and threw it at the phone, making a direct hit with Phillip, who had come back to the edge to see what all the shouting was about. He scuttled away, not willing to partake in a game of Fetch, or Pin The Stick On The Moggy.

'HELLO? CAN YOU HEAR ME?'

A Facebook notification buzzed, the vibration knocking the phone to the floor at her feet.

'Aha!' she cried out in triumph, making a fast grab at it and cancelling the call by mistake.

'Nooooooo!'

Before she had a chance to do what her instinct wanted - launch the phone at the cellar wall - it began to ring again. Feeling for that moment like the luckiest woman in the world, she answered it.

'Hello? Hello? I need help. I fell through my living room floor while we were talking and…'

'This is a message for Mrs Fleur Brookes. Your mobile phone bill is now overdue. Please press or say one to make a payment.'

'BASTARDS!' she shouted at it.

'I'm sorry; I do not understand that response. Do you wish to make a payment now?'

'SOD… OFF…'

'Okay. How much would you like to pay today?'

'Look, what number do I press to speak to an advisor? I'm in a HOLE!'

'Did you say, "SEVEN OH OH? That's seven hundred pounds…"'

'NO. I said I'm stuck in a hole!'

'You'd like to pay the whole balance? That's great! Please enter your card details.'

'SOD… OFF!'

'I'm sorry; we don't seem have that card number on our files. Would you like to try again?'

'What the HELL happened to that nice Katy Perry song?' Fleur said into the darkness.

Cathy put her hands up to the filthy window, wiped away some of the dirt to make a small, clear circle on the glass and peered in. She was sure she could hear shouting, but it didn't look like anyone was home. In fact, the lounge looked like a building site. Did she have the right house?

'Hello?' she called out. 'I tried the doorbell, but I don't think it's working?'

'SOD… OFF…!'

Wait. Sod off? She stepped back again and looked up at the second floor windows to see who was watching her. Yep, this was definitely the wrong house.

Fleur clicked off the phone, realising she was getting no closer towards speaking to a real person, no matter how much she insulted and confused the robot one. She clicked open her contacts, just in time to watch them fade out to darkness.

'Bloody flat battery!'

She sat back and sighed. Indeed, circumstances *had* left a huge hole in her life – and not only the one in the floor. She had no friends. Not that she minded; but one or two people who might miss her would be handy right now, she thought. Her little old house in the countryside was far enough from civilisation to never get callers beside the postman, bin men and an occasional Jehovah's Witness, who always made a swift departure after she asked them to explain some information from their pamphlets.

'This thing here, where it says, "The Coming of David, 10.10". Is that ten past ten in the morning or ten past ten at night? Because I want to make sure I'm awake and in my best Sunday frock.'

No-one ever visited Fleur. She was known to her extended family as the grumpy one. The one who hadn't gone to her own husband's funeral. Even their daughter had nothing to do with her now.

Who would miss her now that He Who Had Buggered Off and Died was gone, if she never got out of this hole? Not Phillip. He found her mildly interesting at dinner time and that was that. And there were enough leftovers lying in her lounge to feed him until her body had turned blue, the worms had eaten her and the flies swooped in for seconds.

'God, I'm a miserable sod,' she said, before congratulating herself on a cracking line of poetry worthy of Dr Zeus.

Sitting back in her car, Cathy looked again at the address Fleur had given her on her phone. No, this *was* the right place. She keyed in her phone number but it went straight to Voicemail:

'I'm not ignoring you, unless you work for British Gas. If you do work for British Gas, please leave a very long message after the beep. Call costs will be so high you'll have to hunt your own food, burn furniture to keep warm and after all this will be cut off. Welcome to my world. And now that promised, brief announcement from my car. Beeeep.'

Cathy climbed out of her car. It was time for another, more forceful go at the front door.

'FLEUR! ARE YOU IN?'

Of course, Cathy was coming! She'd forgotten; she had a friend. She was saved!

'CATHY!' she yelled back. 'I'M IN THE FLOOR!'

Now Cathy was *sure* she'd heard shouting. She bent down, lifted the letterbox and called through the musty opening:

'HELLO? FLEUR? IT'S CATHY.'

'HELLO, YES, CATHY! IT'S FLEUR! I'M IN THE FLOOR IN THE LOUNGE!'

Cathy stood up straight, stepped back from the door and looked at the lounge window.

'WHAT?'

'I'VE FALLEN THROUGH THE FLOOR!'

'WHAT? Oh my...' She tried the front door, which was locked, then went back to peer in the window and looked down. Sure enough, she saw a huge hole in the middle of the floor. 'OH NO!' she yelled. 'ARE YOU ALRIGHT?'

'YES, I'M HAVING A FINE TIME!' Fleur shouted back. 'ME, THE SPIDERS, AND...'

She stopped. Sarcasm was all well and good, but she hadn't thought of spiders until that moment. 'I JUST NEED HELP TO GET OUT,' she added, a little more urgently.

Cathy looked up at the second floor for an open window.

'I CAN'T SEE A WAY IN,' she called back. 'IS THERE ANOTHER DOOR OR AN OPENING SOMEWHERE?'

'NO,' Fleur replied. 'ONLY A BLOODY BIG HOLE IN MY FLOOR.'

'Oh,' Cathy said, more to herself. She thought for a second, and then:

'DOES IT HAVE A WAY IN ANYWHERE OUT HERE?'

'Is she serious?' Fleur said to the cellar wall.

'DID YOU BRING YOUR PHONE?' she bellowed back, telling herself that in some way, this *could* be turned into a rescue.

'YES,' Cathy replied. 'BUT YOU WEREN'T ANSWERING.'

Fleur closed her eyes.

'Oh wait... oh, silly me,' Cathy stammered. 'Of course you weren't answering.'

'WHAT?'

'WHAT DO YOU WANT ME TO DO? SHALL I GET HELP?'

'CAN... YOU... USE YOUR PHONE...?' Fleur shouted back.

Cathy stepped back from the window again. 'OF COURSE, OF COURSE! Oh.'

Everything went quiet. For a moment, Fleur wondered if perhaps she'd gone back to her car to fetch it.

'CATHY?'

'YES?'

Fleur sighed. She was still there. But it was to be a long, long day. Cathy hadn't been sent today by the universe to save her bacon in any kind of hurry this morning. Perusing parts of the wreckage that had fallen down beside her and were illuminated from above, including some magazines she hadn't read yet, she considered ways to amuse herself and swat the spiders.

'FLEUR,' she heard Cathy shout again. 'I'M GOING TO USE IT NOW, OKAY?'

There was an almighty smash, and as shards of glass rained down on Fleur, she covered her head until they stopped, before brushing herself off, getting up onto all fours and feeling around in the dark for Cathy's phone. Yes indeed, she would be here a while.

Chapter Five

'Barry? Is that you?'

Joanna-Rose's heart lurched. This was one of the things that made visiting her mother the hardest. In her lost, befuddled brain, she was always going to keep bringing *him* up.

'It's Joanna-Rose, mother.'

She held the old lady's hand and bent to kiss it, but her mother pulled it away.

'I want Barry!' She screwed her eyes tight shut and began to sob.

Joanna-Rose turned to the nurse stood watching them in the doorway and whispered. 'Can you leave us alone for a while please?'

The nurse nodded before stepping outside, noiselessly closing the door behind her.

'Where is he? Where is Barry? I need to see him!'

Joanna-Rose bowed her head and stared at the ground, feeling weak, sad and just plain useless. It was hard to believe the frail, pallid figure in the bed had once been a formidable force in her life. It had been a tiring fortnight since that last call to visit in the night, sleeping in the hospice guest room, waiting for her mother's final day. The doctor had predicted her demise on two previous occasions, yet still, here they were again. As much as she didn't want to find herself alone in the world, watching the old woman grow ever frailer and more confused had been exhausting. She prayed today would be the day. She'd done that every day since her arrival. In truth, she had been doing this for a year, wrestling between a heart-rending need to keep her mum, while wanting this terrible suffering to end for both their sakes. This cruel situation was too undignified, even though the end of life care at the hospice had been superb, her mother's life had been extended both from artificial means and an almost inhuman fight for survival from the old girl herself. Dementia was a cruel, cruel bastard. The lady lying in the bed before her seemed like a small, lost child who had no idea death was anywhere near and Joanna-Rose was now the parent.

Every breath was coming slower now until they stopped, making Joanna-Rose look up again, to find her mother was trying to sit up. 'I can't go until I see him.'

'Go where?'

'To school! My mum is getting angry.'

The old lady's eyes were already losing their light, yet darted from corner to corner of the ceiling as if scanning a crowd of people up there, seeking familiar faces.

'Okay, shhh, shhh,' Joanna-Rose soothed, guiding her back down on to the pillow and rubbing her arm. 'You will. I'm going to get him for you.'

The old woman's face turned to see her again now, watching with the hopeful, excitable expression of a little girl before a tree full of presents on Christmas morning. It made Joanna-Rose's heart ache so hard she thought the pain might crush it to dust.

'When?'

'Now.'

As she drove home that evening, feeling dazed and broken, Joanna-Rose was thankful. At least the old girl wasn't suffering anymore. And if this thing called 'the afterlife' was to be believed, maybe now at last her mother could find peace, not least in some way, with her father.

In the weeks that led up to her death, her mother had at last shared the details of her real father and it had shaken Joanna-Rose, until she had to ask herself whether the revelation was in fact a product of her mother's delirium. It was enough to try to believe her father was an old friend and client of Robert's, but that he was none other than the world famous, celebrity psychic, Derek Montrose, was mind-blowing. Kathleen Barton had been way too bitter and for far too long at the loss of her long-term lover, which had happened when she was two months pregnant, to ever want to talk of him again. He'd 'decided to give his marriage another go and wanted nothing more to do with them', she'd said, before warning her never to go looking for him. 'It would just be a disappointment. He didn't want you or the embarrassment of a scandal,' was the last she had said on the matter. Cold, emotionless and direct; but the dementia had stolen away compassion and reason. There was nobody now; Joanna-

Rose was alone in the world. Yet, curiosity about a man she'd never known remained. Like a piece of the puzzle that was her was missing.

'Can I get you anything? Cup of tea? Some toast?' Cathy asked.

She regarded the older and very tired woman who sat on her sofa with a thick blanket around her shoulders and a plastic wreath on her head. She rarely ran her heating since she'd been living alone. It wasn't worth it for the cost, she felt. But Fleur had done nothing but complain of being cold since she had brought her back there, a few hours earlier.

'You may as well know now,' came the grumbling reply. 'As well as being incontinent, I think I might be gluten intolerant.'

'Oh dear,' replied Cathy, eyeing the piece of toast she had in her hand and feeling put off from eating it. 'You know, it's quite a common occurrence in women of our age and it *is* treatable.'

'What is?'

'The... err...' She pointed with her toast to Fleur's trousers, drying on the clothes horse beside the fire.

'It was just the shock of the fall, that's all,' snapped Fleur.

'But it was you that used the word incontinent,' Cathy reminded her. 'And there's help for that, that's all I'm saying. You don't need to suffer in silence nowadays, it can be dealt with.'

'I was joking,' Fleur retorted with a sniff. 'But, just out of interest, how would you deal with it?'

'I'd tell my GP for a start off.'

'Easy as that, eh?' Fleur's raised voice boomed. 'Excuse me, Dr Just-Out-Of-School. You know that cough and drop thing? Well, I can do it too.'

'Shhh!' Cathy said, putting a finger to her lips.

'And I don't need reminding with sound effects!'

'No, I mean keep your voice down. The walls here are very thin and I don't want you upsetting the neighbours. This is – was – a calm, quiet household.'

'Well, excuse me for falling down a hole in my floor and wetting my pants because of the shock. Hand them over, give me that toast and I'll go somewhere I can be angry without upsetting anyone else.'

Cathy whipped the toast away, thwarting Fleur's attempt to snatch it.

'I thought you said you can't eat toast?'

'I've decided to commit suicide.'

Cathy brow furrowed in thought. 'You can die from toast consumption?'

Fleur laughed. 'I'm sure I've seen that on a politician's obituary at some point in time. Oh no wait, it might have been "toes consumption".' She shuddered, before adding, 'The dirty buggers.'

'What does gluten intolerance do to you anyway?' Cathy asked, with a puzzled look.

'It gives me magic powers.'

'Like what?'

'Let me eat that toast,' said Fleur. 'And I will show you my Poo Through the Eye of a Needle trick.'

'In the name of... oh, what have I let myself in for with you?'

'I don't know I'm intolerant for sure, I just think that I might be. I've had a dicky tummy lately, that's all,' Fleur explained. 'So,' she said, her face brightening again. 'Can I stay?'

'As long as you promise not to eat any toast,' Cathy replied with a scowl. 'Look,' she went on. 'It's okay, you can stay here for a while. I have the space and, well, now that Phillip is sorted out for a while...'

'Sorted out?' Fleur cut in. 'You sent him to the cattery!'

'Well, I'm sorry but I told you, I'm allergic.'

'How do you know that?' came the retort. 'Have you ever had a cat?'

'Fleur, I'm just trying to help you. Your house is in an awful state and it's going to take a lot of work to put it right,' Cathy said. 'You must have caused quite a crash, judging by the way all the dust and papers got out into the hallway, the kitchen *and* up the stairs.'

'What?' Fleur replied, looking perplexed. 'There was no new mess in the hallway.'

'There wasn't?'

'No! Well, nothing out of the ordinary anyway.'

'It was always like that?'

Fleur nodded.

'You're a bit of a hoarder then?'

'Cathy,' Fleur replied. 'I haven't had a man since Charlie died. The sexy vegetables thing on Facebook was a clue.'

'Oh, er, well...' Cathy stammered, her cheeks flushing pink again. 'There's still a lot to fix before you can go home. But I meant what I said, you can stay here, at least for the time being. That is, as long as you at least try to cheer up.'

She smiled feebly, but the older woman screwed up her face and pulled the blanket tighter around herself.

'There is a hole in my living room floor, they've condemned my house and someone I just met had to take me back to their house in wet pants and trousers. You can bet your still-in-the-box Rampant Rabbit it'll take a day or two to cheer me up.'

Cathy felt her face flush redder. 'Tell me you haven't been going through my underwear drawer?' she whispered.

Fleur nodded, with a solemn, thoughtful expression. 'I was just looking for a flannel for my...' She pointed to her nether regions. 'Places, you know?'

Cathy clasped her hands over her mouth.

'Oh, don't get all icky about it. I only used it once,' Fleur added quickly. 'And I put it back so you'd never know.'

'Are you... are you serious?'

'I mean the *flannel*,' Fleur proclaimed, before standing up and edging towards the fireplace for a heat. 'I didn't see any Rampant Rabbit, by the way. I was joking.'

'Oh yes, as was I,' Cathy added quickly.

'It's bloody freezing in here,' Fleur went on, stretching her arms out towards the flames. 'How do you even live like thi...?'

She felt herself being pulled backwards, the blanket ripped from her shoulders. The clothes horse with her trousers on tumbled to the ground, upended in the tussle. 'Look, I said I was sorry about the bloody flannel,' she protested, trying to steal herself away from Cathy's grasp as she stood exposed in a purple, silk bra and matching thong knickers; both of which were way too small.

'You're on fire!' Cathy shouted, throwing the blanket down and stamping the flames out.

Fleur peered at the scorched edge of Cathy's luxuriously soft, plump blanket before pulling the corner she was still holding up to her chest in an attempt to cover herself.

'What on earth?' Cathy cried, noticing the bright, silken underwear for the first time. 'Those are mine!'

In the briefest of moments, Joanna-Rose thought she saw a child of about seven years of age, sat on the doorstep, crying bitterly. The oversized and battered old army coat around the boy's shoulders looked familiar to her. Yet before she reached her door, he was gone, and in his place she noticed what was real - a new plant pot containing the most beautiful, miniature purple roses. Sticking out of the letterbox was a card with no envelope, which she tugged out and opened to read the inscription:

To Joanna-Rose, so sorry for your loss.

All that is left is to go on being her great legacy.

Isaac.

She couldn't catch her breath, overwhelmed by his incredible kindness. Stooping to breathe in the heady perfume of the flowers, she caught sight of a cardboard label stuck in the soil beside the plant. It read:

The Joanna Rose.

'Mrs Hepple?'

Still stooped over, she turned around to find her nearest neighbour peering over the gate.

'Hello,' Joanna-Rose replied, brushing away a tear before straightening up.

'Hi. I just wanted to say how very sorry I was to hear about your mother.'

Joanna-Rose was taken aback. She hadn't been expecting anyone but Isaac to know the news.

'Oh, I hope you don't mind,' the woman continued. 'It's just that we hadn't seen you around for a few days and so I asked your very handsome gardener if anything had happened.'

Joanna-Rose felt the purposeful emphasis on the words 'very handsome gardener' but ignored it, remaining composed.

'He told me your mum had passed away,' the other woman went on. 'Such a shame. And so soon after losing your poor, dear husband.'

Joanna-Rose and Robert hadn't been married and thanks to her notoriety in the local papers as a playwright, she knew her neighbour would be aware of this.

'Yes, well, thank you,' she said, wondering if the old busybody had been to the doorstep earlier and read the card on the flowers in her relentless search for village gossip. 'But it's been two years now.'

The other woman looked astonished. 'Really? It doesn't seem that long. My, how time flies…'

She stopped, looking at the pot of roses and Joanna-Rose felt sure she had been going to add, 'when you're having fun,' but instead, she stared blankly at her for a few seconds, with a fixed grin. Joanna-Rose smiled back before lifting the plant up to read the card again. At forty-eight years of age, she no longer cared what the local people thought of her, her relationship with Robert, or Isaac for that matter.

'Well, I've been away for two weeks so I'd better get on with brushing away the cobwebs,' she said. 'Thank you for your concern… Mrs Green, isn't it?'

The woman nodded.

'Okay,' Joanna-Rose finished, putting her key in the door. 'Goodbye, Mrs Green.'

The living room smelled musty and old. Perhaps it always had but could be noticed more after she had been away a while. Taking a box of matches from a drawer in the sideboard she lit two fragranced candles before throwing herself on to her favourite reading chair.

A light on her laptop caught her attention. Damn! She'd left it on for two whole weeks! Thanks to a long, prosperous life as a playwright, Joanna-Rose never had to worry about money, but if there was one thing she abhorred, it was waste. Why on earth hadn't she unplugged it? And then she remembered; she'd been drunk when she left. A vague memory of tipping the taxi driver a very generous fifty pound note also came back to her. More waste.

She stood up, walked over to the desk where the laptop lay and flipped it open. It took a few moments to wake from sleep mode, which annoyed her, as all she wanted to do right now was shut it down and go get herself a glass of wine.

After a time, the screen lit up, revealing the Widows Together Facebook page and her last post – the picture of Robert. Of course! She'd forgotten about the chat she had been having with Cathy Harper before the call from the hospice.

Seeing a friend request and more posts from someone called Fleur Brookes underneath, she picked up the laptop and carried it back to her chair to read the rest of the thread. When she'd finished, she accepted Fleur's friend request and began replying to her and Cathy's private message.

Chapter Six

'What do you suppose happened to Joanna-Rose?'

'Same thing that has happened to you, is my guess,' Fleur replied. 'Can't get over the dead.'

'I do have feelings you know,' Cathy snapped back.

'I know, but listen, Cathy. I might be a lapsed Catholic but masturbation is a sin. I'm not even sure I should even be listening to your stories about it.' Fleur was bent over her feet, preparing to cut her toenails. Despite having had a wash and a change, she was still wearing the plastic wreath that had become tangled in her hair in the fall. Cathy grabbed a magazine from the paper rack, opened it out and slotted it under Fleur's bare feet, just in time to receive a toenail bullet to the eye.

'Oops, sorry about that,' Fleur said. 'They're like little moon-shaped Tiddly Winks, aren't they?'

Cathy wiped her eye and shuddered, fighting back her retching reflex. Her thoughts flashed from toenails, to masturbation, and unwittingly on to sexy vegetables. This new lodger was messing with her mind in weird, unprecedented ways.

'I have very clean feet, you know,' Fleur told her, without looking up. 'I'll bet I have the cleanest feet in this entire village.'

'How do you know that?'

'Because I never go out. Never. These two little feet never go anywhere to get dirty.'

Cathy thought of the sight of Fleur's living room earlier that day. Even with a great, big hole in the middle of it, the place had been filthy and she now knew it wasn't all dust from the crash. The other very noticeable thing had been all the half-full takeaway trays and newspapers. Cathy shuddered again. How anyone could live like that was beyond her.

'Are you ever going to take that wreath off your head?' she asked.

'Do you want to wear it, is that it?' Fleur asked. 'Jealous, are you?' She tugged hard at the wreath until it came free at last, marched toward Cathy and placing it on her head, took out her phone. 'Smile for the camera.'

'Don't!' Cathy said, removing the wreath seconds after the camera phone shutter snapped, and throwing it in the floor.

Fleur smiled, before stooping to pick up the wreath. 'You know, Cathy, I reckon I've been sent here to cheer you up a bit.'

'Sent? By who?'

Fleur pointed at the ceiling. 'Him.'

'Fleur, there's no one up there. I told you, I live alone.'

'Not him, Him. The other bloke upstairs. The one you looked like when you were wearing your wreath.'

Cathy leaned across to snatch the Christmas wreath back from Fleur as she was making to replace it on her own head. 'I thought you said you were a lapsed Catholic,' she said, sulkily.

'Well, I thought perhaps you were not.' Fleur said, pointing to a painting of Jesus on the Cross on the wall above the television set.

'I'm not a Catholic.' Cathy sniffed.

'It isn't yours?'

Cathy looked at the painting and sighed. 'Bob was Catholic.'

'And you don't mind keeping the pictures up?'

'No. You?'

It was Fleur's turn to sigh. 'I'm not so much friends with the Catholic Church anymore, if I'm honest. Why you would keep a picture like that on your wall when you aren't obliged to as a member of the guilty crowd is beyond me.'

Cathy pulled her crisp, white robe around her a little tighter, picking the lapel up to her face and sniffing its delicate, white-linen fabric softener scent, willing away the idea of how Fleur's toenail might have smelled as it hit her face. As she breathed in the smell of 'clean', she counted to five in her mind, hoping it might help to relax her. She was aware of the television blaring– at a level that was way too loud for her liking, particularly as the walls between her and next door were very thin. She had lived alone for such a long time, she - and her neighbours no doubt - had become accustomed to the quiet.

'Well?' Fleur asked.

'I don't want to take it down, to be honest,' Cathy replied. 'It was Bob's and it gave him great comfort.'

'And does it do the same for you now?'

Cathy nodded. 'It gives me great comfort to have all of his things just as they were when he was... he was...' She stopped.

'Alive?'

'Yes, when he was alive.'

Fleur looked thoughtful, feeling more understanding for Cathy's position than the other woman could ever know.

'I have a good few pictures just like it packed away in a box somewhere' she admitted with a kind smile, surprising Cathy with her sudden change of tone. 'Charlie and I were raised looking at those things, feeling guilty for all our misdemeanours and praying to statues and the like.'

'Really?' Cathy said.

Fleur stared at the television with a blank expression. 'Really,' she replied. 'Because it's all wrong, all of it.'

'Wrong?'

'Yes, wrong. The whole Catholic faith. Did you know, for example, that there's a missing commandment?'

Cathy blinked. 'There is?'

'Yes. It's the one about the prohibition of idols. "You shall not make yourself a carved image". Okay, they didn't remove it I suppose, just changed it to a more convenient shorthand version. Then they could keep on selling religious statues for all us followers of the faith to feel guilty in front of. Admitting that God said we shouldn't do it would cost the Catholic church a fortune.'

Cathy thought for a moment. 'Don't you think you might just be angry at God because Charlie died?' she asked.

Fleur didn't reply.

'That's it, isn't it?' Cathy uttered, horrified at herself for hitting a raw spot. 'I'm sorry, I was just...'

'I've lost more than Charlie,' Fleur cut in, dismissing the comment. 'But no, I'm not angry at God. I just hate those bloody pictures and all that they stand for. They're so depressing. But it's your house of course. I'm not asking you to take it down. I'm just wondering if it's healthy to keep everything exactly as it was when Bob was alive. Like everything in your life is a shrine to him.'

'I just haven't been able to bring myself to remove any of his things.'

'You know,' Fleur said, still looking at the ground. 'I'm willing to bet you hate that picture.'

'No, I don't,' Cathy shot back. 'It represents so much.'

'You're right. As I said, it represents Catholic guilt.'

'No, that's not it,' Cathy replied, beginning to feel agitated. 'I mean, it represents… me.'

'That's you in the picture?' Fleur asked, looking up to study the picture again. 'Well, you've changed. You're shorter for one, and I hope you've shaved your armpits.'

'No, I meant hope, really, not me. All the pain. The suffering Jesus went through. I know it sounds silly, but, at this point in my life, that painting gives me hope. Because, I feel I've lost everything, as he must have done right there on the cross. I may not be of the Catholic faith or even know the stories from the bible all that well, but I am a believer. And doesn't the bible say that Jesus rose again?'

Fleur nodded. 'That's right,' she said. 'On a Friday.'

'Good Friday?'

'Yes, which is why we get to have all that Easter fun every year.'

Smiling, Cathy said, 'I know this is a terrible thing to admit, but I never really understood the religious significance of Easter. It's been all about eggs, hot cross buns and chocolate for me.'

'Well, I think a lot of people don't remember the story,' Fleur conceded. 'If it helps, I will explain. You see, Jesus died on Good Friday, as I said. Then, when the people went to collect his body two days later, they found he wasn't there.'

'Hence the bit about him having risen again?' said Cathy.

'Indeed.'

'And this is why we have Easter Sunday?'

'Exactly.'

'Hmm,' Cathy said, pausing to glance thoughtfully at the painting. 'So,' she said after a moment. 'What's Easter Monday?'

'A bank holiday.'

Cathy rolled her eyes and shook her head. 'You can take the picture down if you want to,' she said at last. 'I don't mind. I think I can do it.'

Fleur looked back up at the portrait. 'I can't,' she admitted with a shrug, pulling Cathy's scorched blanket tighter around her shoulders.

'Why not?'

'Same reason you can't. We're scared God will smite us.'

'I don't even know what that means,' Cathy admitted.

'Strike with a firm blow,' came the reply.

'You mean he'll hit us?'

'A good, long, ecclesiastical whack to the head,' Fleur confirmed. 'Sort of like sitting through midnight Mass while the rest of the country is celebrating Christmas.'

Before Cathy had time to ponder this further, Fleur had placed the toenail clippers on the coffee table. Cathy scooped them up and put them in her dressing gown pocket, making a mental note to rub them and the table with an antiseptic wipe later.

'I can't imagine what has happened to Joanna-Rose,' she said, trying hard to keep her mind off all the chaos Fleur seemed to be bringing to her previously well-ordered home. 'I hope I haven't spooked her in some way.'

'Spooked her?' Fleur laughed. 'I'm spooked.' She pointed at the TV. 'It's the bloke from the photo!'

'Yes it is,' Cathy said. 'That's him. Derek Montrose.'

Fleur flicked her spectacles from her head to over her eyes and squinted at the television screen. 'So it is, and I was joking,' she admitted. 'What do you suppose that photo was all about then?'

'Whisky,' Cathy replied, without the slightest hesitation.

Fleur looked at her. 'Whisky?'

'Bob loved his whisky. It was the industry he worked in. His job was conducting tours around the Islay and Speyside distilleries, and he was always on about starting a collection of the stuff, although we never had the kind of money you need for that kind of caper. I can more or less guarantee that was what was in the barrel, though. But who knows what particular event brought them all together in the photo?'

'Load of old twaddle,' Fleur interrupted, just as Derek on the screen had called out for anyone with a deceased relative known as Jim, James or Geoffrey.

Cathy watched her, disappointed that her interest in the subject of the photo had appeared to dissipate.

'Oh, it's John,' Fleur went on. 'Come on. Who doesn't know a John?'

'Don't you know him then?' Cathy asked, pointing to Derek. 'I mean, Charlie must have done. Didn't he mention him?'

''Course he knew him,' Fleur admitted. 'He is famous after all. We all know Derek Montrose, let's be honest. Even if we'd rather not. Although he's more famous these days for being a pathetic drunk.'

'Yes, I know,' Cathy agreed. 'Did Charlie ever say anything to you about him?'

Fleur looked pensive, still frowning at the screen. 'Charlie was a solicitor,' she said at last. 'He oversaw a lot of business agreements and transactions, but it was often confidential, of course, and he didn't tell me about many of them. He never even mentioned Derek Montrose to me, if I'm honest, although I had seen the photo. I never asked him about any of it. I've never been interested in celebrities, especially those that lie to the bereaved for a living.'

Cathy raised her eyebrows. 'You think he lies?' she asked.

'Of course he lies,' Fleur replied, turning to face her. 'Don't you know it's all a lot of fakery?'

'I don't think so,' Cathy said. 'He's helped so many people.'

'He's helped himself.'

Cathy frowned, realising she was fighting a losing battle trying to convince Fleur of Derek's genius. 'Do you have a copy of the photo at all?' she asked.

Fleur nodded. 'It's not a photo I have, it's a newspaper cutting, I'm sure of it. It's somewhere in the house.'

Cathy sighed, at once aware of the enormity of the search ahead should they decide to dig it out.

'Whatever it was they were doing happened a very long time ago, before I was with him, I think, and we didn't discuss it,' Fleur went on. 'It's kind of odd that there are more copies floating around. It must have been something significant, eh?'

'Most definitely if it made the papers,' Cathy agreed. 'I can't believe Bob never told me about that.'

'Perhaps he didn't think it important. Were you married when this was taken?'

'We've been together since we were twenty-three,' Cathy replied. 'I mean...' she corrected herself. 'We *were* together.'

'I was never that interested in my old man's line of work, if I'm honest,' Fleur said. 'All that legal-eagle stuff bored me to tears.'

'Why did you ask me to come and meet you then?'

'I was curious, I suppose. Who wouldn't be?' said Fleur. 'I mean, it's interesting that our husbands are in a photo that Joanna-Rose happened to choose to post on the anniversary of her husband's death. It's fateful intervention, that's what this is.'

'Or a message from the other side,' Cathy added.

'Pah! That's Mr Whisky Galore's job, there. And if you ask me, the only message he gets from the other side is the "please drink responsibly" label on the back of bottles.'

'He's fallen on hard times with that awful wife of his though. You can't blame an old man like that for being in a bit of a state,' Cathy replied.

'He feeds the bereaved lies and gives them false hope,' Fleur snapped.

'So you wouldn't come with me to see him, if I asked you to?'

'Nope.'

'If you think it's a load of old twaddle, why are you watching him?' Cathy asked.

'Like I said, it's your house, your remote control. Catch!' And with that, Fleur picked the remote up and threw it across to Cathy, who failed to hold her hands out in time and it hit her chest with a thump.

'Oops, sorry,' Fleur said.

Collecting the remote control from the floor and pointing it at the TV, Cathy said, 'Let's see what's on the other side.'

'A boob without a bruise, I should hope. Ooh, what a great name for a film. A bit like *"Rebel Without a Cause",*' Fleur replied, laughing so hard, she farted. It was a long, loud, drawn-out thunderclap of a fart; the kind that you couldn't follow with, 'Oh, was that me?'

Cathy rubbed her aching chest, closed her eyes and groaned as a foul stench not unlike stale Brussels Sprouts hit her.

'You are so gross, Fleur,' she called out, hoping to let the neighbours at the other side of the very thin walls know she wasn't the culprit.

Chapter Seven

At 2am, Joanna-Rose would normally be sleeping – perhaps even snoring. Life was not so complicated that she had to sit awake at night worrying about things. Robert was long gone and now, so was her mother. That would have been harder to digest had she not felt a sense of relief too.

They had always been close, yet Kathleen Barton had some difficulty expressing her love. Perhaps because her own mother had died before her twelfth birthday, so that any chance she had to learn to *be* a mum had been stolen from her. The relationship Joanna-Rose remembered with her had been less like parent and child, and more like they were friends. Yet for the very first time, near to the day of her death, Kathleen had finally uttered the words a mother should be able to say to her child. 'I love you, Joanna-Rose.' She was grateful for the memory of that day at least, now her mother was gone, even though in truth she would never be sure if the dementia had made her do it. Regardless, it brought her peace on some level; the kind that helped her sleep at night.

So why was she awake?

She turned to look again at the time illuminated on the alarm clock in the huge, dark bedroom and felt small. This was the reason. She was alone, *all* alone. There was nobody left in the world who cared. There was nobody left who knew the real her and loved her anyway. There was elation and sadness at the same time. To be free of the past she had to be alone in the world. How ironic. How very dark.

She reached over the side of her bed to find her discarded dressing gown on the floor, sat up and draped it around her shoulders. Times when she felt the darkest had been, in the past, the best times to create. Be it 2am or 2pm. She should try to write. Or drink. It had been two weeks since her last one, thanks to a long stay at her mother's bedside in the hospice. Perhaps just one drink.

The thudding was getting louder. Cathy pulled the pillow around her ears and turned over.

'Cathy, it's me!'

Not the Wuthering Heights dream again. She hugged the pillow tighter.

'CATHY!'

'Heathcliff?' Cathy turned over and yawned, and then sat bolt upright. 'Fleur?'

'Can I come in or not?'

It was Fleur, and – she pressed the button on her phone to light it up – it was 2am!

'What on earth's the matter?'

'Can I come in?' Fleur insisted.

'Okay, but let me just -'

Before she could say another word, the door burst open. As she'd been sleeping in the nude, Cathy pulled the cover up to her neck.

'There you are,' Fleur said, throwing herself on top of the bed, almost tearing the duvet edge from Cathy's hands as she shielded her modesty.

Cathy scowled at her. 'What do you want?' she said, squinting at the light from the hallway that had also poured in uninvited.

'There's a private message. On Facebook…'

Cathy frowned. 'If it's from Martin…'

'Martin who?' Fleur said, looking puzzled. 'It's the middle of the night. Why would someone called Martin message you in the middle of the night? Anyway, I'm talking about my Facebook.' She sat bolt upright and scratched her head. 'Do you think I'd be sneaking around in your Facebook account?'

Cathy rubbed her eyes and yawned, before laying back down and covering her head with the duvet.

'Oh, I'm half asleep for pity's sake. It's two am,' she moaned. 'That's two o'clock in the morning. Have you lost your mind? What's so important at this hour that you had to wake me up?'

'Joanna-Rose is coming over,' Fleur replied, bouncing on the bed so hard, Cathy almost rolled out on her side.

'Well, that's great,' Cathy replied. 'But why couldn't you wait until morning to tell me?'

'Ooh,' Fleur said, standing back up. 'There's a little spider here on your quilt...'

With a scream, Cathy threw back the quilt and leapt out of bed, standing starkers in front of Fleur.

'Get it off! Get it off!' she yelled, stamping her feet, turning around to check her back and flicking her hair wildly to shake off any eight-legged predators.

'Atta girl,' Fleur said with a smug grin. 'Rise and shine. Joanna-Rose is on her way here.'

'She's not actually coming now is she?' Cathy asked, as she entered the living room in her dressing gown moments later.

'Yes, she is!' Fleur said. 'We were chatting online, as it turns out she doesn't sleep either. So, I was just telling her how we were awake too, and why don't we all get together for a nice cup of hot cocoa? At first she was a bit unsure, but I talked her into it.'

'What? Why? Ohhhh!' Cathy was hardly able to believe her ears. 'Fleur, *we* weren't awake, I *was* asleep. What on earth...? Is she genuinely coming round now or is this another one of your daft jokes?'

'Of course it isn't a joke,' replied Fleur. 'I wouldn't have gone to all the trouble of waking you up if she wasn't on her way over.'

Cathy opened her mouth to speak before closing it again, sighing, and falling into her fireside chair.

'This is great. I love late night cocoa and sneaking out. It's like being fourteen again,' Fleur was saying. 'Throw your Jesus-creeper slippers on. That kitchen floor gets cold at night.'

'What? Cocoa? Now?' And then a thought struck Cathy. She gave her guest a grave look. 'Fleur,' she said. 'What on earth did you say to Joanna-Rose to make her come out here, to a virtual stranger's house, in the dead of night?'

'You know, you used to be more fun,' Fleur grumbled.

'What are you on about? You met me yesterday!'

'I know,' came the quick reply. 'Where's that adventurous, daredevil-you that plucked me out of a hole in my floor?'

'Yes, I brought you in to my house. That's *my* house, remember?' Cathy came back. 'What are you doing inviting people here at two thirty in the bloody morning, one night into your stay? And what did you say to her?'

Fleur blinked. 'Ooh, I made you swear. That's new.'

'For fu-'

'Let's not overdo it now, it's early for you and Jesus is listening.' She nodded to the painting.

'What did you say to her?'

'Okay, so I told her you'd fallen down a hole in the floor,' Fleur replied. 'Now, I'll go put the kettle on, shall I?'

And with that she fled the room, taking her whirlwind of Fleury madness with her.

Cathy sat back in her chair and stared at the ceiling. So, Joanna-Rose was rushing out in the middle of the night to save her. That was nice.

No, that was weird.

'Why would she come all this way out to save *me*?' she yelled to Fleur. 'Why not tell you to call the fire brigade or something?' When no reply came, she realised she was talking to herself, but continued anyway. 'That's what I would have done.'

There was no reply, just the sound of cupboards opening in her kitchen. Cathy picked up her cushion and held it to her face, blowing a silent scream into it. It was then that she heard the sirens, far away at first, but getting closer, much closer.

'Is it true, you have good whisky?'

Cathy and Fleur stared at the dishevelled, staggering mess that pushed past the departing fireman on the garden path. She looked nothing like the elegant, perfectly coiffured and immaculately dressed lady in Joanna-Rose's Facebook profile picture.

'Joanna-Rose, is that you?' Cathy said, catching the other woman's arm as she started to tumble backwards.

One of the firemen turned around, looking concerned. Fleur stepped in at once to help Cathy with her.

'It's okay, officer,' Fleur told him. 'We've got her now. I'm so sorry for all your trouble coming out here in the middle of the night.' Her voice fell to a whisper as she pointed at Joanna-Rose. 'It was her that called you, you see.'

The fireman shook his head and turned back up the path to join the rest of the crew.

'It's okay, I can walk by myself,' Joanna-Rose replied as she allowed the women to guide her inside. 'Glad I got here in time to see you saved,' she went on, stumbling on the doorstep. 'My, there are a lot of steps here. Have you conshittered getting a ramp?'

Fleur pushed the door shut behind them as they led her by the arms through to the hallway. She grinned at Cathy. 'She's right you know. You should conshitter a ramp.'

Behind Joanna-Rose's back, Cathy scowled at her.

'Can I just say, Joanna-Rose, that I'm so sorry that Fleur dragged you out into the night under false pretences,' she said.

Joanna-Rose stopped walking and straightened up to peer at her. 'Eh? Weren't you in the floor?'

'Well, Cathy?' Fleur grinned.

'That's what I mean. Fleur wants to apologise about that, now that she's finished apologising to the fire and ambulance crews.'

Joanna-Rose shuffled further inside, then caught her heel on the edge on a hallway rug and stumbled. The two women held on fast, preventing a fall.

'I've had a little, bittle drink,' she said. 'My mum died, you see. She hated me. Wheresssh the whishhky?'

'Oh dear, you poor thing. How could we have been so thoughtless? You've had such a tough time, what with the anniversary of Robert's death and now your mother. How awful,' Cathy soothed, as she pointed to the kitchen doorway to indicate to Fleur that that was where they were taking her. 'No wonder you've had an, ahem, *little* drink.'

'Yes, and a little bittle drink at that,' Fleur said. 'It's those that catch you out when you're not looking.'

Joanna-Rose stopped, seeming to consider this. 'How did you know about my mother?' she asked Cathy, with a puzzled look.

'You were telling me on Facebook Messenger,' Fleur replied for her. 'Don't you remember?'

'I was?'

Cathy threw Fleur a quizzical look, but she shrugged her shoulders.

'Let's get you sat down,' she said to Joanna-Rose.

The women led her to a chair at the kitchen table, before taking seats on either side of her.

Immediately, she began to cry. 'She hated me!'

'Now, I'm sure that isn't true,' Cathy said, rubbing her back.

'It is!' Joanna-Rose wailed, so piercingly the two other women were startled. 'She said I was an abonimon... an admoniball... an abnominal...'

'An abominable snowman?' Fleur asked, earning a glare from Cathy.

'An abomination,' Joanna-Rose wailed, before hunching forwards and burying her face in her arms.

'Cathy?' Fleur whispered over her wails. 'How do you think she got here?'

'I was BORN!' Joanna-Rose shouted without raising her head, startling them both a second time.

Cathy patted the distraught woman's hair. 'No, no, no. Fleur means how did you get *here*, to my house?'

'You didn't drive like this, did you?' Fleur asked.

The response was merely more loud sobbing.

Cathy shook her head. 'No, she couldn't have,' she said to Fleur. 'Look at the state of her.'

'My mother hated me, she hated me,' wailed Joanna-Rose. 'She just wanted Barry. It was always, "I need Barry", "Get Barry". Even at the end.'

'Perhaps she came in a taxi?' Fleur said.

'Yes, I had a taxi,' Joanna-Rose cried. 'It was a hundred pounds! Where is the whisky?' You told me there was whisky.'

'A hundred pounds?' Cathy whispered to Fleur, looking horrified. 'I think someone has taken advantage of her.'

'No! Nobody has touched me in years!' Joanna-Rose hollered, making Cathy jump. 'Not even a fumble!' She stopped and turned to Fleur, whose face was turning purple from stifled laughter. 'You know,' she spat. 'I think I've healed up again down there.'

'Again?' Fleur repeated, with a look of confusion. As Cathy shook her head, with a silent, 'don't go there,' Fleur said, 'I think I'll go get the whisky.'

'Don't!' Cathy cried, with a warning look. 'That's Bob's collection.'

'He isn't going to need it now, is he?' Fleur asked.

Cathy sighed and shrugged. 'I guess not,' she relented, feeling heart sorry for Joanna-Rose.

'I was never enough for anybody!' Joanna-Rose continued, looking up at her. 'And Robert, *my* Robert,' she said. 'I loved him so, so much,' she cried.

'I know you did,' Cathy soothed, patting her hair again and nodding an 'okay' to Fleur, who left the room in search of the whisky. 'You did your best, I'm sure.'

In a moment, Fleur was back with a bottle of Bowmore whisky. 'Got it!'

'Oh no, not that one Fleur! It's an old one-'

As Cathy spoke, Fleur broke the seal, pulled out the cork and was already reaching in the cabinet for some glasses. 'It doesn't look like an old one,' she said.

'Fleur!' Cathy cried, starting to stand.

Joanna-Rose caught her arm. 'He didn't want me,' she said, her cheeks lined and wet with thick, black mascara. 'He never wanted me. It was all a lie.'

'Bob told me that it's a thousand pounds a bottle.' Cathy's voice trailed off as the whisky was poured into three tumblers.

Fleur turned the bottle round in her hand to examine the label. 'It says it's a fifteen year old,' she said, taking a gulp from her glass. 'Doesn't look like an expensive one to me.'

'But all he wanted washhh Charlie. Bloody Charlie,' Joanna-Rose mumbled on, before thrusting a hand into her pocket with a snivel, taking out a photograph and slapping it on the table.

Fleur sniffed the whisky glass and gave an appreciative nod as she made her way over to the table. She spied the now familiar picture of three smiling men, glasses raised over a barrel.

Cathy was looking at the photo too. 'You don't mean *that* Charlie?' she said, pointing to the photo.

Joanna-Rose looked from Cathy to Fleur and, nodding, held her hand out for the whisky. 'First Charlie, then came the others,' she wept. 'So many others.'

Fleur felt as though her knees were about to buckle. She grasped Joanna-Rose's chair to steady herself, before tipping back her head and draining the entire glass of whisky in a single swig.

Chapter Eight

The following morning Cathy stepped into the cold kitchen, flipped open the cover to the combi boiler controls on the wall and clicked the button off then on again. There was nothing. No whoosh of ignition and no burrr of inner workings. No heat and no hot water on the way. She frowned. This day had been coming for a while; if only it didn't have to be right now.

She stole a glance around the room, at the empty glasses - one tipped over on the kitchen table with some of the contents spilled - and the crisp packets, chocolate biscuit wrappers and greasy plates. A reminder of the munchies that had hit all three of them last night after they'd emptied the one thousand pound bottle of Bowmore. Ah, the Bowmore! She looked at the empty bottle on the worktop and felt a stab of guilt. Bob's collectable bottle, or so he'd told her. It was the one he'd forbade her to touch. The one that would have paid at least some of her gas bill had she chosen to sell it rather than drink it. Not to mention the mortgage arrears, letters about which she had been ignoring for a while now. And the pile of unopened ones from a solicitor's office she'd never heard of, which she knew would be about more debt. What had she been thinking?

Her gaze rested on the photograph, somehow unsoiled amidst the unprecedented chaos around it. Ignoring the vast array of solicitor's letters and unpaid bills was one thing, but Cathy had never seen her kitchen so untidy, not even when she and Bob had held dinner parties in the house. She had always been one step ahead of everyone, with a black bin bag and a dustpan and brush to hand. And she had never been as wasted as she'd allowed herself to get last night.

Her head throbbed and her throat felt dry. She opened the fridge and a plastic bottle of orange juice fell out, bouncing on the floor.

'Awww!' she grumbled, kneeling to pick it up again. As she stood to replace the bottle she stopped in her tracks and stared, open mouthed, at the middle shelf in the fridge, where the juice had tumbled from. On it was an oversized carpet bag.

'What in God's name?'

She pulled the bag from the fridge by the handles and held it up in front of her face, staring in disbelief as it swung to and fro. It wasn't hers, that was for sure. Dropping the ice-cold bag on the table, she made her way through to the lounge.

'Joanna-Ro...'

The scene that met her eyes was not unlike the one in the kitchen, with food wrappers and empty glasses everywhere, except this room had sleeping bodies in it as well. Two, to be exact. Fleur was lying, fully-clothed, mouth open and snoring on the first couch, and Joanna-Rose was sprawled on her back, legs akimbo on the second couch, both hands grasping a glass with a single measure of whisky in it, rested on her stomach.

'Is anybody alive?' Cathy boomed.

Fleur snorted but Joanna-Rose didn't stir.

'Wakey, wakey!' she shouted.

'Steam engines,' Fleur mumbled, turning over onto her other side.

Cathy shook her.

'Wha, what?'

'Time to wake up, it's quarter past eight,' Cathy said.

The snoring continued. Cathy sighed. The previous night's events perhaps called for a little extra rest for both of the women.

'Well, I have to go to work,' she said, aware it was herself she was telling. 'I'll see you both later.'

The village post office looked as though it had been around for a century, and probably had. Cathy had memories of calling in with her mother after school and not being able to see above the counter when asked which sweeties she would like in her ten pence mix bag. Although the ability to see the selection was never necessary, because she would call out her favourites: Sherbert Pips, Popping Candy and Flying Saucers. A brief recollection of the soft, slow-dissolving sugary sensation as she munched and sucked on those fizzy delights made her ache for her mother. Even as her twilight years approached, she felt the loss as though it were yesterday. She could understand, though did not agree with, the reason Joanna-Rose had turned to drink last night.

The very old, brass bell over the door announced her arrival as she stepped in to the shop. An unfamiliar face greeted her at the counter.

'Oh,' Cathy said, taken aback. 'I'm the assistant here, erm, usually. Is Joan in today?'

'Yes, hello! I'm Joan's niece, Jodi Henderson.' She stretched out a hand in greeting, which Cathy accepted. 'I've just started here. It's so nice to meet you at last.'

The young woman looked all of eighteen years of age; four foot eleven with long, brown hair that in itself was about three foot eleven. She reeked of *Jean Paul Gautier* perfume and oranges.

A portly old lady waited at the counter, her gaze focussed on the door to the office. Cathy followed the direction of her gaze to see Joan, who was stood making a phone call inside, holding a package in one hand and the handset in the other. The lady huffed.

'Parcel to go, she's put on it,' Joan was grumbling down the line. 'To go indeed! What am I supposed to be, psychic? I knew right away it looked suspicious.'

'I've tried to explain to her,' the old lady told Cathy.

There was a pause and Joan sniffed the parcel loudly, as if to assure the unseeing person on the other end of the line that that it was a suspicious whiff. Seeing Cathy, she waved, then shook her head before cupping her hand over the receiver.

The old lady in the shop sighed louder. 'I keep telling her,' she said to Cathy. 'It's Togo… you know? In West Africa?'

Cathy turned back to Jodi, who had taken a mirror from her pocket and was brushing her eyebrows with her forefinger.

'What's the problem?' Cathy asked.

Jodi looked over the mirror at her with a disinterested expression and shrugged. The old lady tutted.

'Look,' Jodi said to her. 'I haven't had the training for this. I'm very sorry for your *wait*.'

Cathy heard the accentuation on the word 'wait', and the disdainful up-and-down look the girl gave the old woman, which suggested 'Sorry for your weight,' was what she actually meant.

The old lady looked embarrassed but said nothing.

'Can I help?' Cathy asked Jodi, feeling sorry for the poor woman.

'Well,' she sniffed, looking to her aunt who was still busy on the telephone. 'I'm not sure. You are on leave officially, aren't you?'

'No, I'm not,' Cathy replied. 'I'm due back today, as I was about to say.'

'No, it's okay,' Jodi said, raising a hand to silence her. 'Best to let my aunt check it out with the powers that be.'

'But what is she checking out precisely?' Cathy asked.

The waiting customer huffed again. 'She says I haven't addressed the parcel correctly and I told her I have,' she explained, indicating to Joan, who was still talking on the phone. 'She refused to take it, telling me I can't just put Togo. It's preposterous!'

Cathy sighed, leaning on the counter and smiling sympathetically at her, before feeling something sticky on her arm and lifting it to find a swirl of orange peel on her elbow. Detaching it, she spied several more pieces dotted all over the counter; remnants of Jodi's snack. Cathy never ate at the front counter. Joan had forbidden it.

'Not in front of the customers,' she would say. 'No one wants to see staff chewing away like cows with their cud while they're collecting their pension.'

'I mean,' Joan went on into the receiver. 'She said it was for her granddaughter who is volunteering abroad. Staying in one of those Menstrual Camps. Menstrual *Camps*, I ask you!' She shook the package, which rattled like a bottle of pills.

'I told you, it's tablets for menstrual cramps,' the woman corrected her crossly. 'Although, I have no idea why I had to tell her that,' she said, addressing Cathy. 'It's none of her bloody business what I'm sending, is it?'

'We do need to ask what is in a parcel,' Cathy replied. 'Although, you don't need be specific. Tablets would do; herbal medicine even.'

'Which, let's be honest, is often a hidden term for drugs,' Jodi butted in, with an air of indifference that made Cathy feel embarrassed and uncomfortable on the old lady's behalf.

'Menstrual camps,' Joan went on, not paying the slightest heed to the woman's protests. 'Who'd have thought there was such a thing?' She turned away to whisper the next part, but could still be heard clearly. 'I think it's drugs.'

The woman gasped.

'Oh really?' Joan looked at the old lady still waiting at the counter and retreated back inside the office, closing the door. Within a few moments, she was back out, thrusting the parcel on the counter in front of her.

'The silly old bats around here think I was born yesterday,' she snapped, referring to the poor woman who was now pink with embarrassment. 'At least I check everything!' she grumbled, before smiling sweetly at her. 'That'll be eleven pounds forty five, my love.'

The woman tutted, grabbed her parcel and stormed out without a word.

'Well,' said Joan, looking shocked. 'That just proves I had her number, doesn't it? Perhaps we should call the police as a civic duty. Always check these things out,' she directed to Jodi. 'It's a clear warning sign when they do a runner after you question them.'

'She said she was sending it to Togo,' Cathy said. 'And Togo is in Africa.'

'Well, how was I supposed to know it was to go to Africa? Why didn't she *write* Africa?' Joan protested.

'Oh dear!' Cathy said, starting to take off her coat. 'Thank heavens I'm back today to help out again. You got my three voicemails last week, I trust?'

She noticed a brief look pass between the two other women before Joan stepped in to put an arm around her shoulders, lifting her coat back on to them at the same time.

'Yes, I got those,' she said. 'Why don't you come in the parcel room for a little chat? Jodi can hold the fort for a second, can't you, love?'

'Well, I don't think she can, by the look of things,' Cathy began, pulling away from her.

'Ah, well now, Cathy,' Joan said. 'It's been a little while since Bob's death and, you know, I didn't want you to feel you had to hurry back.'

'I told you I was coming in today. When you didn't reply, I just assumed it was all okay.'

'Well, I have Jodi to help now. The franchisee, Mr Rahmid, said it was all fine. I've squared it all with him. I took the liberty of telling him you needed a little more time, because you do really, don't you?'

'Without speaking to me?' Cathy felt an odd mixture of fury and anguish rise in her throat. 'But I am ready to come back today.' She caught Joan's arm. 'Joan,' she said, pleadingly. 'You don't understand. I need to come back today.'

'Now don't you worry about anything, Cathy,' the other woman went on. 'It's all sorted out for you. I just forgot to call you about it, that's all. It's been a bit crazy already this morning. You know what that early morning rush is like.'

Cathy looked round at the empty shop and scrunched up her nose in puzzlement as she allowed herself to be led towards the door.

'Jodi and I have everything covered so you can just go on back home for now. We can hold the fort here, and when Jodi has her six weeks' worth of training under her belt, we can all work together. One big, happy family.'

'But there's hardly enough work in this small village store for just the two of us,' Cathy protested, turning to Jodi, who shrugged and gazed back at her with expressionless eyes.

'You just need to get your rest. We will run everything,' Joan assured her.

Cathy thought of home, the house that once was hers and Bob's, but which she was, for the time being, now sharing with Fleur. The very cold house, which could be repossessed soon. How would she cope for another six weeks?

'But...' she tried to protest again.

However, Joan was already opening the shop door. 'Just go home,' she crowed, pushing her out on the pavement. 'Everything will be just fine. We'll see you in six weeks. I'll call you.'

Chapter Nine

'In all honesty, I just can't fathom it out,' Cathy said.

The women were in her lounge, wrapped in blankets and huddled around the coal fire – now the only source of heat in the entire house. Fleur hugged a more reasonably priced bottle of Bowmore whisky, which was now almost half empty, most of it consumed by Joanna-Rose, who was now legless enough to have conceded that all there was to do was stay another night.

'Fathom what out, Cathy?' Joanna-Rose asked.

Cathy was holding her drink in front of her face, peering at the liquid as she rolled it around inside the glass.

'How my Bob came to be in that photo with Derek Montrose,' she mused. 'It doesn't make sense.'

'Wait,' Fleur cut in. 'I thought you had an open ticket for his show?'

Cathy nodded. 'I do.'

'And it was attached to the photo.'

'No,' Cathy replied. 'It was me that attached it to the photo when I first came across it, which was ages ago now. I suppose I must have been subconsciously putting the two things together. It wasn't until Joanna-Rose posted it on Facebook that I started to think about it again though.'

'Makes sense,' Joanna-Rose said. 'A photo of Derek and having an open ticket to his show does suggest a connection. They clearly knew each other.'

'Then why didn't Bob tell me that?'

Joanna-Rose leaned forward in her chair and held her glass out to Fleur for another dram.

'Wow,' Fleur laughed. 'You like a touch of the hard stuff, don't you?'

'It takes one to know two,' Joanna-Rose replied, her eyes glazed and wet from tiredness. 'It's either going to help me think or make me sleep. Either way, I don't think my legs will work just now. You don't mind if I sleep right here in this chair do you, Cathy?'

Cathy shook her head, still focussed on her glass. The room was beginning to spin around her, but the glass had become her centre of normality; the single thing that looked the way it should, and it felt nice. She loved the numbness of this alcohol-fuelled haze; it felt like nothing or no-one could touch her. Even the pain of bereavement seemed far, far away. She had no idea what she would do; her job was unavailable for the time being, although she had lied to her companions - saying she had the return date wrong - rather than admit she'd allowed herself to be cajoled into giving her job to Jodi for a few weeks. The gas had been cut off and the electricity was due to follow, but she hadn't admitted this to the other women either. She would tell Fleur the truth once Joanna-Rose had gone home, but for now, the others believed they were waiting for a part for the boiler, after Cathy had faked a phone call to a gas engineer.

It was all such a mess, but the whisky took her problems farther away in her mixed-up head. Whenever she closed her eyes, she felt like she was floating on the ceiling, smiling as though everything below belonged to tomorrow. For the time being at least, it all did. This was nice. She had missed the company of wine, whisky and friends.

'I think Bob wants me to speak to Derek, that's what I think,' she mused. 'It's all connected, I know it is.'

'Itssh a sign,' slurred Fleur, stabbing the air with her glass as if to punctuate the point.

'Mmm, a sign,' Joanna-Rose agreed, rubbing her itchy cheek, which was still blackened by yesterday's tear stains. She knew she must look even more dishevelled than the previous evening, having slept in all clothes and makeup for the best part of the day before waking up to begin again. Cathy's home was smaller, simpler and downright colder than hers. But the whisky; oh, the whisky was good. She hadn't tasted such a good single malt in a long, long time. Neither had she ever enjoyed a drink in the company of others. It was strange to know that all of them were connected by the man she now knew she had to find.

'I fear I spilled more beans last night than I meant to,' she announced at last.

Without missing a beat, Fleur nodded to Cathy. 'Don't you worry,' she said. 'Julie Andrews here will have cleaned them up fashter than you can shay "Red lolly, yellollolly".'

She sat up, looking puzzled. 'Ooh,' she added. 'I can't even say it.'

All three women burst out laughing.

'Okay, okay,' Fleur said in the midst of all the hilarity. 'I may be shlightly abbreviated.'

'You mean inebriated,' Joanna-Rose corrected her.

'Yes, that too,' Fleur said with an over-exaggerated nod. 'And I think I have a right, given that your hushband fancied mine.'

'He wasn't my husband. And I don't like to be the bear of bad news or anything, but…'

Cathy and Fleur erupted with maniacal laughter, leaving her puzzled.

'The bear of bad news!' Cathy screeched, spitting out whisky and almost choking.

Fleur held up two fists, imitating huge bear paws, and said, 'I'm very shorry to have to tell you this, but Winnie the Pooh died.'

'Bahahahaaaa!' Cathy laughed aloud, to a stern, still-puzzled look from Joanna-Rose.

'Oh, stop,' Fleur sniggered. 'I think I'm going to pee myself!'

'So juvenile,' snorted Joanna-Rose, catching up at last. 'You know what I meant.'

Fleur crossed her legs. 'I am honestly going to have an accident if someone doesn't change the subject,' she cried.

'Oh God, my sofa,' Cathy cackled, only half-joking.

'Now, come on. What were we talking about?' asked Fleur.

'My "not" husband,' said Joanna-Rose.

'Ah yesh,' Fleur replied, pointing a finger at her. 'Your whatever he wazsh.' She raised her glass to look in it, finding she couldn't focus. 'This shtuff really goes for your speech… and your eyes, doeshn't it?'

'Only if you drink too much of it,' said Cathy.

Fleur sat up in her chair and peered at her. 'I don't think I have,' she said, huffily. 'It's not my fault I've been upset by the Bear of Bad News over there.' She pointed to Joanna-Rose, who raised her eyes to the ceiling and tutted.

Cathy snorted, choking on her drink so hard that Fleur had to lean in and pat her on the back.

'What was the bad news, anyway?' Fleur asked.

'I meant the fact that I had to tell you that about Robert and Charlie. I haven't anything else to tell you,' Joanna-Rose said.

'Yes, Robert was at university with Charlie and yes, he had a crush on him. Well, more than a crush. But your husband never knew about it, as far as I know. And as for that picture, all I know is that Robert treasured it. It was the reason that we met.'

'So, you knew all along that he was gay and perhaps in love with another man?' Cathy asked.

'He was in love with Charlie?' said Fleur.

Joanna-Rose pushed back her chair, stood up and staggered to the window to look outside. 'When we met, yes, it was true. They were friends, but he confided in me, telling me he could never tell Charlie how he felt because, as you know, he was straight. I'd just found someone I could share my life with, who made me happy when neither of us could find real, true love. We were friends at first, roommates, sharing our woes. It was... complicated. He was desperately in love with someone who didn't love him.'

'Your Charlie,' Cathy cut in unnecessarily, making Fleur grimace.

'...and I think we both just filled a space in each other's lives. It was companionship. But the truth was, while he was keeping me at arm's length, I was falling in love too. Ironically, with someone who didn't love me. He had countless affairs with men for many years. Well, I say "affairs" but the truth is, we weren't married. We weren't even a couple as far as he was concerned. He took care of me. We shared a life, and to the whole world, we were together.'

'How did you meet Robert?' Cathy asked.

Joanna-Rose felt a familiar heaviness in her heart. 'My mother introduced us,' she replied.

'This is all so sad,' Cathy lamented.

'So, you knew my Charlie,' said Fleur.

Joanna-Rose shook her head. 'No, I never met him,' she admitted.

'How did you come to take Robert's name?' asked Cathy

'I changed mine,' she replied. 'I changed my entire life for him. But in the end, he was just... just...' She bowed her head. 'He was never mine, that's all. He was the best I could hope for, in the circumstances.'

'What a bastard.' Fleur said.

Joanna-Rose turned back round to face them both, her expression sad. 'No, he wasn't a bastard, he was my best friend. And I...' She stopped, taking a moment to compose herself. 'Well, let's just say I knew what I was letting myself in for.'

'A marriage of convenience,' Fleur said matter-of-factly. 'Only without the marriage part.'

'Where did you find that photo then?' Cathy asked. 'Did he have it in a frame?'

'No,' Joanna-Rose replied flatly. 'I found it in the sideboard after he died. It just seemed like the right photo to remember him by. Maybe I was torturing myself by focusing on the man who was to be the cause of my loveless relationship.' She glanced at Fleur, before adding, 'Not that Charlie knew, of course. I don't blame him. Just looking at the picture was like... like...'

'Peeling off a scab?' Fleur offered.

Joanna-Rose nodded. 'I guess I do like to torture myself somewhat,' she admitted. 'It's been a lifelong trait of mine.'

'Maybe Derek Montrose will be able to tell us something more, after all,' Fleur said to Cathy.

Joanna-Rose turned to face them both, looking astonished. 'What?'

'Oh, she's talking rubbish...' Cathy began.

'The psychic guy from the telly,' Fleur explained. 'The famous man in the photo? That's what we were saying earlier, Cathy has tickets to his last show.'

Joanna-Rose's face darkened and she made her way back to her seat to sit down. 'Ah, yes, Derek Montrose,' she replied, nodding at the television after the briefest of moments. 'When is he on?'

'Not at all, for much longer,' Cathy replied, looking up at them both. 'I mean, there will be repeats of his show, of course, but he's retiring.'

'He is?'

'The tickets are open for any show, she just has to call when she wants to use them. We thought we'd try and catch his final public appearance,' Fleur told Joanna-Rose. 'We could go there and find out the answer, what with him being able to channel dead people and all.'

69

'How can you be so sure we'd even have a chance to ask?' Cathy said. 'There will be loads of people there. Plus there might not be enough seats left.'

'He'll speak to me, that's for sure,' Joanna-Rose remarked.

'He will?'

Cathy and Fleur had both spoken at once. Joanna-Rose shook her head, cursing the whisky. This was the reason she drank alone. Privacy mattered so much to her, yet the tongue would slip whenever the liquor flowed. She was sure she appeared lucid, but couldn't think straight.

'I think so, yes. Robert and he were friends,' she admitted. 'I mean, I don't know that man at all, but we have another thing in common too.'

'Which is?' said Fleur.

'We have the same agent.'

Fleur screwed up her nose. 'Don't tell me you're a psychic too?' she said.

'Not quite, but I do get inside people's minds – all fictional, of course. I'm a writer, you see.'

'What do you write?' Cathy asked, her interest further piqued by this new revelation.

Joanna-Rose tried to sit up, before noticing the room was beginning to spin and falling back again. 'Oh, let me try and think,' she said, screwing her eyes tight shut as she searched through a twenty year back catalogue in her inebriated mind for something the other women might recognise. '*Where Friendships Are Forged*,' she announced at last.

'...whisky disappears,' Fleur added.

'Is it a book? I've never heard of it.' Cathy sniffed.

'*I'll See You in Hell*,' Joanna-Rose went on.

'Rude,' said Fleur.

'It's a play!'

Both women stared blankly back at her.

Joanna-Rose sighed. 'Well, I suppose they might not be two of the better known ones. Perhaps my name will be familiar?'

'Joanna-Rose Hepple,' Cathy said, tapping her temple. 'Er... let me see...'

'Joanna-Rose Hipple,' Fleur said, scratching her head. 'Do you make gin?'

'What about Saorla Nardone?'

'Oh him,' Cathy gushed. 'Yes! Didn't he write *May Brings Us Love*?'

Joanna-Rose nodded. 'Well, *her*,' she said.

'Oh yes, Bob took me to see that,' Cathy exclaimed. 'That was you?'

'Yesssh, I am she.'

'I wonder if that's why Bob had Robert's picture? Because he was a fan of Joanna ... I mean... Saorla Nardone's?'

Joanna-Rose shook her head. 'Out of the quesshtion,' she said. 'Not many people know who I am. I've never given an interview in my life. No-one would link Robert to me. Unless...'

She stopped short and looked across at the wedding photo on the wall. 'Unless they knew us very well.' She pointed up to the picture. 'Can I see that photograph of you and Bob up close please, Cathy? Just to see how he looked as an older man?'

Cathy nodded and stood up to take it from the wall before passing it to her. 'Here you go,' she said.

Joanna-Rose studied the picture with a solemn expression, before shaking her head. 'No,' she said at last. 'I definitely haven't seen Bob before. Do you have any other photos? Perhaps, more recent?'

'Yes,' Cathy said, standing up cautiously as the room began to spin again. 'The albums are in the bedroom,' she told them, steadying herself on the back of the chair. 'I'll go get them. Hang on.'

As soon as she had left, Fleur moved from her chair to sit beside Joanna-Rose on the sofa. She leaned in conspiringly.

'Joanna-Rose,' she asked her. 'You don't think that Cathy's husband and Robert might have been lovers?'

Before Joanna-Rose could reply, Cathy was breezing back in the room.

'Here you go,' she said, handing a photo of Bob to Joanna-Rose and waving the show tickets in her other hand. Both of the women were staring at her guiltily, open mouthed.

'What?' she said.

'Oh, nothing,' Fleur replied, giving Joanna-Rose a nudge in the ribs to make her close her mouth. The other woman looked down and began studying the photo she'd been given.

"Okay, well,' Cathy went on. 'As I said, I have two open tickets we can use for Derek Montrose's final show. There was a letter in the envelope with the tickets giving a number to call, I think it might be his agent or promotor, and I've simply to tell them who I am and when I want to go. His last public appearance is next week, so this will be my only chance. So, I've been thinking. Would you like to come, Joanna-Rose?'

'I thought you wanted me to go?'

'I thought you didn't want to?' Cathy told Fleur.

Joanna-Rose was still staring hard at the photo of Bob; a prematurely-grey, kind-eyed man with perfect teeth. Much younger than Robert, as she'd known he would be. Fleur was looking at the photo now too, quietly seeking evidence of homosexuality in his facial expression - as though that were possible.

'No, I've never seen him before. I'm sure of it now,' Joanna-Rose said.

'Well, maybe the answer will come to us at Derek's show?' Cathy suggested.

Joanna-Rose breathed out a loud sigh, much louder than she'd meant to. Her mind turned to her mother, just laid to rest. A familiar pain filled her heart. A public show was not the time for her to go and see Derek Montrose, even though she knew she would have to face him – and soon. She shook her head.

'I don't know if I'm ready to go to one of these kinds of shows so soon after mum's death,' she replied. 'It's still raw.' She paused, her mind turning to thoughts of the last year of her mother's life. 'People are polite when someone close to you is ill for a long time,' she continued. 'They send their well wishes in an email or a quick, perfunctory phone call. They might even send flowers. Then they start to cross the road when they see you coming.'

'Or close the door when they notice you stepping out at the same time as them,' Cathy added. 'That happens after they die suddenly too.'

'Bob stepped outside after he died?' Fleur asked, with a look of genuine astonishment that, despite the pain of her moment of sad reflection, made Cathy smile.

'And they make decisions without consulting you,' she went on. 'That they say are the best thing for you.' Cathy sighed, feeling as though the weight of the world was kneeling on her heart again. She was returning from her woozy place in mid-air, reminded of the laughing man in *Mary Poppins* who began sinking from his tea party on the ceiling, after he allowed sad tales to bring him down. 'Best for who?' she continued with a new wave of anger. 'How do you know how I'm feeling? Did you ask *me* what I needed?'

'Was it a long illness Robert had?' Fleur addressed the question to Joanna-Rose, seeming not to notice Cathy's sudden, rising anger.

'Oh, err, no.' She shuffled uncomfortably in her seat. 'It wasn't... that.'

Fleur threw Cathy a sly glance, holding in the urge to press her further, at least for the moment.

'It was sexual misadventure,' Joanna-Rose announced, to the surprise of the other two women.

'Wow!' Fleur blurted out, as Cathy gave her a cross look.

Joanna-Rose picked up her whisky glass and threw back the contents in one slug. It dulled her pain, the alcohol. It made her remember things as if from within a protective bubble. She could stand by and watch the most agonising events play out in her mind, like she had been outside of them all along.

'He was a huge drinker. We both were,' she admitted.

'Were?' Fleur said, receiving another glare from Cathy.

Joanna-Rose went on, seeming oblivious to the dig. 'For me, it was anaesthesia for the heart. But for Robert it was recreational. He would drink then wander out into the night, and I knew he was out to look for sex.' She swallowed hard and looked searchingly along the mantelpiece. 'Is there any more of that whisky left?'

Fleur stood and reached for the bottle, before pouring her another.

'Go easy with that,' said Cathy, forgetting her sympathetic self. 'It's an eighteen-year-old. You don't just throw eighteen-year-old whisky down your neck in seconds, so Bob told me. You're supposed to -'

'Go on, Joanna-Rose,' Fleur said, steering the conversation back to its original course. 'Tell us what happened. How did he die?'

'Oh it's too... awful... too... Oh, how can I put it?'

'Just spit it out. I always find that's best,' Cathy coaxed her.

'Rip that scab off,' said Fleur.

'He choked to death. You couldn't write it. *I* couldn't write it.'

Cathy flinched. 'Ooh, I didn't...' she began.

Fleur had to ask. 'On what?'

'A black leather, strap-on mouth gag dildo.'

The room fell silent, for all of five seconds.

'Ouch,' said Fleur, screwing up her nose. 'That particular scab could've come off a bit more gradually, if I'm honest.'

There was another brief silence.

'What on *earth* is a mouth gag dildo?'

Fleur gave Cathy a look of disbelief.

'There was no foul play involved,' Joanna-Rose continued, sounding solemn and more sober now. 'It was just an unfortunate accident.' She took another long drink.

'I'm so glad they left the chickens out of it,' Fleur said under her breath, before changing tack as she saw Joanna-Rose look her way. 'A mouth gag dildo, eh? You're right, you couldn't write it.'

'I suppose Stephen King could,' she replied, without a hint of irony.

'Unfortunate is an accurate description, I think,' said Cathy, struggling for anything more constructive to say.

Fleur, however, always had something to say; and hang its constructiveness. 'But how did he choke on that?' she asked. 'Isn't the – ahem – appendage, worn outside the mouth?'

Joanna-Rose sighed, then swallowed more whisky before throwing her head back to stare up at the ceiling and deliver the ending. 'They think someone very heavy had been sitting on it.'

Cathy looked at Fleur, who now held a hand over her mouth, stifling a fit of the giggles. She shushed her, feeling sick with embarrassment, yet all the while overcome with a desperate need to have an outburst of laughter as well.

For a moment they sat in silence, each unaware they were all mentally picturing the same, somewhat surreal scene. Joanna-Rose continued to stare at the ceiling, whirling the whisky round and round in her glass.

It was Fleur who cracked first. She couldn't contain herself. In fact, the words, 'Fleur' and 'contain herself' had never belonged together in the same sentence for her entire adult life.

'BAHAHAHAHAHAHA!'

Cathy crossed her legs, her mouth clasped as tightly closed as she could keep it. Yet, as Joanna-Rose turned to look at her, revealing giveaway tears of suppressed laughter in her own eyes, both women found they could hold back no more.

It was Cathy who ended up peeing on the couch.

Chapter Ten

Cathy drove into the car park in front of Fermory Hall and pulled into a space, before turning off the engine. Although the night was dark and damp, the hall was cheerfully illuminated by what looked like a thousand pale-blue fairy lights, hanging from the gutters and all over the trees on the front lawn.

'You'd think it was Christmas already,' Fleur grumbled. 'Look at it! And it's only the first week in October.'

'Well,' Cathy replied. 'It's for him, isn't it?'

'I don't think Jesus would mind if there were no lights in October,' said Fleur. 'After all, it isn't His birthday for another twelve weeks or so.'

'Not Jesus, *him*.' Cathy pointed to the sign over the doorway to the hall.

Fleur leaned forward in her seat and squinted to read it. 'Oh, you mean Derek. The Corpse Whisperer,' she remarked.

Cathy flinched at the word 'corpse'. Sometimes she wished Fleur could be a little more compassionate. But then, she'd been living with her for a few weeks now. She was beginning to become accustomed to it.

'I do so wish Joanna-Rose could have been persuaded to come with me,' she sighed. 'It would be nice to go with someone who was genuinely interested.'

'Didn't you get the feeling she wanted to?' Fleur asked.

Cathy nodded. 'Do you know, I did!' she agreed. 'Odd, isn't it?'

They stepped from the car out into the cold, and followed a small crowd of people to the entrance.

'I am interested, you know,' said Fleur. 'I like to believe there's an afterlife, of course I do. There have been many convincing stories about reincarnation that have had me questioning a few of my own beliefs about things; I'm very open to persuasion. But Derek-Slimeball-Montrose won't be the one to do it. The man is a fake and that's a fact.'

'Well, I think you might be are surprised this evening,' Cathy snapped, so uncharacteristically that it made Fleur look round at her in surprise. 'Lock the door when you get out,' she finished.

And with that she threw open her car door, got out and closed it with a bang, leaving Fleur to watch open-mouthed as she stormed off to join the queue at the entrance without her.

Fleur took a slow, despondent breath inward before opening her door and getting out of the car. She began following Cathy to the entrance before stopping abruptly in her tracks. 'I'll tell you what, Charlie. We'll make a pact,' she said, looking up to the sky before almost colliding with two giggling, attractive young women who were tottering past in high heels and a cloud of Jimmy Choo perfume. Apologising, she waited for them to be out of earshot before finishing, 'If Derek Montrose mentions my falling into our lounge floor, not only will I take back everything I've ever said about him, but I'll run down on to that stage, kiss his baldy, little head and show him my tits.'

'Two please,' Fleur said to the young girl on the door as she caught up with Cathy, who was the last in the queue. She handed the tickets over as her friend was frantically searching her own pockets. 'You gave them to me, remember?'

Cathy sighed. 'Oh, thank goodness for that,' she said, snapping her bag shut. 'I thought we would be going home disappointed.'

'Are you hoping for a message from someone special?' the girl asked them, in an over-cheerful, sing-song voice Fleur supposed she only adopted at the end of her shift.

'Oh, yes,' Cathy said. 'We wouldn't be here otherwise.'

The young girl's cheery smile faded and she cocked her head to one side. 'Aww,' she said, her voice lower and more solemn than before. 'Who from?'

'Derek Montrose,' Cathy replied, without a hint of irony.

Fleur bowed her head and put her chin on her chest, trying not to laugh.

The girl smiled awkwardly, then brushed her bright, cherry red fringe from her eyes and said, 'No, I mean -'

'FIVE MINUTES TO SHOW TIME!'

The call, which came from a portly, suited gentleman just inside the door, seemed to startle the people that were loitering in the foyer, and begin flocking to the theatre entrance behind him. The girl handed the women two stubs from their tickets and, letting them through, pointed to a table with some paper and pens on it. 'If you have any specific questions for Derek, we're asking people to write them down,' she told them. 'You should just have enough time.'

The women headed gratefully inside from the bitter cold and towards the table.

'Can you... channel... Winnie the Pooh?' Fleur read out as she scribbled on a piece of paper, before looking up, winking at Cathy and passing the pen back to the grey-haired, smartly-dressed gent who stood guarding the table. 'Haven't you heard?' she told the unsmiling man. 'He died recently.'

Cathy scowled at her, and pulled her away from the table. 'Can't you grow up?' she said. 'You're sixty-eight, for heaven's sake.'

Fleur put both hands on her friend's shoulders, her expression cheery and blithesome. 'Dare to never lose the silly side of yourself, Cathy,' she told her. 'Did you ever read an article called, "Top Five Regrets of The Dying"?'

Cathy shook her head.

'Well, I did,' Fleur said seriously. '"It was written by a woman who counselled the dying in their last days. And what do you think was one of the most common regrets people have at the end of their lives?'

Groaning, Cathy looked down at her piece of paper and began scratching the side of her face, considering the question she had to write down. 'I have absolutely no idea,' she replied, without looking up, fully expecting a daft answer.

'TWO MINUTES!'

The shout sounded out suddenly, making both women jump.

Fleur spun round to see the portly gent from earlier standing right behind them. 'For God's sake, man!' she shouted at him. 'I have stress incontinence, you know!'

'Fleur,' Cathy whispered, pulling her away from earshot of the man, 'It shouldn't make you wee when someone shouts. You really should -'

'Oh, not that again,' Fleur moaned.

'Please put your questions in the big goldfish bowl there,' the man at the table instructed them coolly, nodding towards an oversized, clear glass container on a sideboard next to the performance hall entrance. As the pair looked round at it, they realised that besides the two men, they were the only ones left in the foyer.

'Come on, we'd better get inside the theatre,' Fleur said, grabbing Cathy's arm and rushing her toward the entrance.

'Okay,' Cathy said, following her while scribbling her question down. 'But what was it?'

'What was what?'

'The most common regret thingy!'

'Oh, that. It was, err -'

'If you can just put your questions in the bowl,' the man at the table said again as they reached him.

'WE KNOW!' Fleur shouted at the man, who looked visibly taken aback.

'Well?' Cathy said, throwing her question into the bowl and chasing after Fleur as she strode off purposefully into the theatre.

'WELL WHAT?' Fleur snapped, without turning round.

'What was the final regret of the dying?'

'I wish I had let myself be happier,' she huffed.

Chapter Eleven

The show was only ten minutes in, when, after a short series of misses, Derek hit a target. 'I'm getting a jolly, robust man with a really powerful, almost booming voice,' he announced. 'Is there a Margery, Marge or Margaret here?'

'Here!'

Fleur twisted around in her seat to look in the direction of the woman's voice. She spied a very old lady getting slowly to her feet. She was across on the opposite aisle, a few rows behind them to the left.

'Ah,' Derek replied. 'Is it Margery?'

'Margaret,' she said.

'Margaret, yes that's it,' he said, nodding as though he'd known this all along. 'Was this robust, very loud person your husband?'

'Yes!' she shouted. Her teary face broke into a huge grin as some members of the audience let out a collective gasp. 'That's my Orson.'

Fleur studied the woman some more, deciding she looked at least ninety. Perhaps not old enough to be who Fleur thought she might be.

Derek nodded. 'It is,' he agreed. 'And he's showing me his ear. Do you know why that is?'

'Was it Orson Wells that cut off his own ear?' Fleur asked Cathy quietly.

'Don't be silly,' Cathy whispered back. 'He's not talking to Orson Wells.'

'Did he pass from some sort of brain injury?' Derek continued.

Fleur and Cathy watched the puzzled woman turn to the younger lady beside her, who shrugged.

'No, it wasn't that. I…'

'He's showing me that it's something to do with the head,' Derek said, looking puzzled. 'Or perhaps he had problems with dizzy spells? You know, these often stem from problems with the inner ear?'

'Ears are in your head, he's right there,' whispered Fleur.

The woman raised her hands to her cheeks, her brow furrowed as she struggled to think of a connection.

'Oh wait, now he's saying something about September,' Derek said.

Fleur threw her hands up in glee and gasped, to several annoyed looks and shushes from people around her. 'That's it!' she declared. 'I bet Orson had ears in September!'

Cathy shot her an aggrieved look. 'Shush!' she said.

'Oh now wait,' the old lady cried out. 'My birthday's in September.'

Derek smiled, looking pleased with himself. It was an act Fleur thought worthy of an Oscar. 'Did he ever buy you earrings?' he asked.

'Maybe,' the lady replied. 'I suppose so. Sometimes.'

'Good, well it's definitely him then and he says to send you all of his love, my darling,' Derek replied. 'Now, I have another name coming across at me. Oh, this person is very insistent.'

'Is that it? All this way to be told her husband bought her some earrings once?' Fleur said, looking at Cathy, hoping to see some level of disbelief on her face, but finding none. The other woman was captivated.

Derek addressed the entire audience again. 'I'm looking for someone who has a husband whose name is Robert. Or, it could be that she calls him Bob. Yes, I'm quite sure that's it. It's Bob.'

'Oh!'

Cathy felt her face burn all the way to her ears as Fleur jumped up from her seat. The chair she'd been sitting on rocked backwards, toppling to the floor with a clatter.

'HOUSE!' Fleur called. 'I mean, err, BINGO!' She beamed an enormous grin at Cathy and tried to drag her up by the arm. The two pretty young girls from earlier - who were sitting on the other side of Cathy - watched the commotion with their mouths agog.

'You've won, Cathy,' Fleur went on, before adopting the deep-toned voice of the National Lottery voice-over man, pointing at her with her thumb and forefinger extended. 'It's you!'

There were some bemused chuckles from the crowd around them.

'Get off,' Cathy hissed, looking about to see if anyone else had stood up. Nobody had. She could hear her heart thudding in her ears, as though the starter credits for *Casualty* had begun playing somewhere. Other sounds around her dulled as she turned around to pick Fleur's chair back up, and heard a familiar voice.

'Stand, Cathy. Stand.'

It was Bob, she was sure. It was so real she began looking around, expecting to see him smiling back at her from a nearby seat. The voice had been loud and succinct - but as she searched the unfamiliar faces around her, she thought perhaps it had come from the deep recesses of her own mind. Such was her longing for Bob, they had tricked her before. Her eyes had already begun welling up with tears, as she turned her attention back at the short, slight, bald man on the stage, who was smiling and signalling to her to get up.

'Stand up, dear. Don't be shy.'

'Go on,' Fleur said, sitting herself back down.

Noticing all eyes in the room were on her, Cathy got shakily to her feet. There was no backing out now.

'Yes,' she said. 'I...' She looked back down at Fleur, who mouthed, 'It's you' again, and flinched. 'I have... erm, *had*... a Bob,' she called out, turning back to Derek.

'She just keeps it shoulder length and gets a demi-wave now,' Fleur began explaining to the two young girls, who nodded in understanding.

'That's right,' Derek went on from his place in the spotlight. 'And you lost Bob, didn't you? Was it cancer, my love?'

Cathy nodded.

Derek had closed his eyes and was nodding now too. He scratched his head and held a finger to his lips, as if he was listening to someone who had continued to speak after Cathy. 'Bob's telling me you have your friend beside you, just like he does.' He paused, cocked his ear and then let out a small laugh before opening his eyes to look at Cathy again. 'He says - and forgive me, this sounds quite random and I'm not sure what it could mean – that his friend, Charlie, I think it is, wants to say that your friend fell in the -' he stopped, just as Fleur strained her neck to look right at him and their eyes locked for the briefest of seconds. Her mouth fell open as he finished. '- in the... in the floor,' he stammered. His face had turned from smiling to horror-struck, as though he wanted to wind his words back in.

Fleur froze. 'That's me,' she said, pointing to herself. She turned to the young women and Cathy, telling them, 'It was me! I fell in the floor!'

'No, I... I think actually it might have been one of the young ladies to your right...' Derek began, his complexion turning from a pleasant, healthy pink to pale grey. He pulled a hanky from his breast pocket and began dabbing his now sweaty head with it.

Fleur's chair clattered to the floor a second time, as she stood up and fought her way along the line of seated people between her and the aisle leading down to the stage. As she reached it, she held out her arms to Derek and shouted:

'I'M COMING FOR YOU CHARLIE!'

'No, wait!' Derek cried, holding out his hands to protect himself. But resistance was futile.

Chapter Twelve

AT EIGHTY-TWO YEARS OF AGE, BRITAIN'S MOST FAMOUS PSYCHIC, DEREK MONTROSE, MARKED THE END OF HIS LIVE PERFORMANCE CAREER WITH A SMALL SHOW IN HIS HOME TOWN WHICH ENDED ABRUPTLY AFTER HE WAS SEEN TO FALL ILL ON STAGE.

Cathy read the morning's newspaper report aloud to Fleur at the breakfast table.

'Psychic. Pah! They forgot to mention "freakishly short". Did you see him? And what a way to end a final show,' Fleur said, shaking her head. 'Carried off stage by a couple of minders.'

Cathy put down the paper and rolled her eyes in disbelief. 'Perhaps they wouldn't have had to carry you off if you hadn't just sexually harassed the man.'

'That's just hearsay, if anyone asks,' Fleur told her flatly.

'There was a hall full of witnesses!'

Fleur sniffed and examined her fingernails. 'I would have got off with a caution if he'd decided to press charges, I'm sure of it.'

Cathy picked up her mug and blew into it to cool her tea down. 'I'm never going to get my message from Bob now,' she complained. 'Never.'

'Cathy, the man's a crook,' said Fleur.

'Still?' Cathy replied, her voice raised in irritation. 'Still after everything he said? Everything he knew about us?'

Fleur glanced over at the ticket stubs from Derek Montrose's show that Cathy had discarded on the shelf, under which now sat the painting of Jesus. Anger at God had now overtaken her former, placid friend, as though she was channelling Fleur.

Cathy sighed, following Fleur's eyes to look at the tickets and the painting too. Bob's hands touched these things once, when he was alive. When she could still touch him. How she ached to hold him now, even if just for one minute more. She was glad to have at last found the strength to take that stupid painting down.

'God, if you're real then you're a thief,' she told Him in her mind. *'Give me my husband back.'*

The autumnal weather was taking a turn for the better. As Isaac pulled his car into Joanna-Rose's drive and blinked under the sun visor at what looked like a lit candle in the bay window, he sighed. She'd passed out drunk in there again, he knew it. A lit candle at 8.30am was all the confirmation he needed; he'd seen it all before.

Letting himself in the back door with his spare key, he was met with the sombre, familiar face of Robert Hepple; a photo that loomed large in a walnut frame on the hallway wall. To Isaac, it served as a reminder – a warning – about a promise he had made long ago. He needed Joanna-Rose to be happy; she *had* to be. If he could just work out how to stop her drinking herself into an early grave.

'Mrs Hepple?' he called out, not expecting a reply. He pressed ahead, on through the entrance hall to the kitchen, spying two empty wine bottles and a broken glass on the work surface. There was no evidence of any attempts of cooking or crumb-filled plates. He knew Joanna-Rose often skipped meals, heading straight to the dessert wine. He carried on to the lounge, breathing in air that was pungent with the aroma of eight hours' worth of lemon and lavender scented candle burning.

'Mrs Hepple?'

As he had anticipated, she was on the couch with one arm outstretched over the edge, a dropped wine glass lying below her on the floor. She would be sad about this when he woke her. It was the second of the set of five vintage glasses her mother had left her; the first being the one he'd just seen, smashed, in the kitchen. Only yesterday, she had been showing them to him; telling him stories of how Robert had ruined the set by breaking one of them in anger, during a fight. Joanna-Rose barely spoke to Isaac about her relationship with Robert, except when she'd been drinking. And she had already started before he'd left the previous day.

He paused to stand over her as she slept and sighed. What could he – the gardener – do to stop her binge drinking? In time he would make her see who he was. But not now; not yet.

'Mrs Hepple?'

He touched her cheek and stood back as her eyes flickered open, then closed again.

'Hmm?' she murmured.

'Mrs Hepple,' Isaac said again. 'It's eight thirty. Shouldn't you be starting to write, or something?'

Joanna-Rose rubbed her nose hard, which made a noisy 'schlip' sound. 'Huh?' she said, opening her eyes again and beginning to come to her senses at last. 'It's half past... what?'

'Eight,' Isaac replied. 'It's half past *eight*. Shall I get you some coffee?'

'Isaac,' Joanna-Rose replied, sitting bolt upright and pushing her hair behind her ears. Too late for recovery, she realised, catching a dribble that was now running from her cheek to her chin with the back of her hand. 'For a moment there, I thought you were...'

She stopped herself.

'Robert?' he finished for her, stooping to pick up the pieces of the broken wine glass. 'See what you did?' he asked, showing them to her.

Her heart sunk. 'Oh no, not another one.'

He reached over to the box of tissues on the coffee table at her side and offered them to her. She smelled deodorant mixed with his familiar bodily scent as his arm reached out to her and was drunk again for a brief, delicious moment. She took a tissue and held it to her damp, throbbing head. Drunkenness wasn't at all pleasant. But love? Love was the pain of a thousand morning afters.

'Here,' he said, handing her another tissue. 'You have panda eyes.'

'Panderize? What on earth does that mean?'

He smiled kindly, and said, 'Do you have a mirror in your purse?'

She nodded, reaching down beside the couch to find her handbag. He covered her hand with his to grasp the mirror too as she pulled it out, regretting his action at once as she withdrew from him.

'Sorry, you do it,' he offered, handing the mirror back to her.

Taking it once more, she held it up to her face to find thick, black smudges of leaked mascara under each eye.

Joanna-Rose was mortified; and not just because she was about to vomit in Isaac's lap. 'I need to get to the bathroom,' she announced, pushing him back and getting to her feet.

Back in her kitchen later that evening, Cathy pulled her housecoat tighter round her neck, stirred the tea and carried the mugs through the hall to the lounge, pulling back out of view as she spied Fleur studying the old photo of Robert and Charlie. She noticed a downcast, almost desolate look on Fleur's face, which took her by surprise. After observing her for a time, she continued on into the room, humming a cheery tune to make her presence known.

Fleur threw the picture back at the sideboard, and leaned in to the fireplace for a heat. 'It's bloody freezing in this house,' she grumbled. 'When are the contractors going to get their fingers out about that boiler part?

'So, are you willing to go with me to find him?' Cathy said, pretending not to have noticed the other woman throw the photo back.

'I don't think it's a good idea stirring all this stuff up with Joanna-Rose, you know,' Fleur said. 'All over some bogus old bloke who claims to speak to the dead? It's not right.'

'That bogus old bloke, as you call him, has commanded crowds of thousands, at theatres across the country,' Cathy said.

'Yeah, he *commands* them all right,' Fleur snapped. 'He commands them to get sucked in to his bull crap and pay him bucketloads of money for the privilege.'

'Do you know how many famous people have had a reading from Derek Montrose?'

'Cathy,' Fleur said. 'Famous people aren't always famous because they're smart.'

'I just can't help thinking there must be more,' Cathy replied. 'Okay, he came out with things I might have put on my piece of paper in the goldfish bowl, but I didn't say anything about you or Charlie. Did you?'

Fleur scratched her chin, looking deep in thought. 'You know I didn't,' she said. 'I asked him about the Bear of Bad News. But then, there's always bin rifling. Do you think anyone's been through your rubbish lately?'

'Apart from you? No,' Cathy replied. 'Anyway, you've changed your tune somewhat, don't you think? I thought you wanted to find out about the photo connection? It was *you* who asked me to meet you. It was *you* who dragged Joanna-Rose in to it all – in the middle of the night too. I'm merely suggesting we go see her again and invite her to come on a trip with us, and at a more reasonable hour, I might add.'

'She didn't mind me calling her at night,' Fleur huffed. 'She got to quaff down about half a bottle of Bob's expensive whisky for her trouble too. But asking her to help her with this because she and Derek have the same agent is taking a bit of a liberty, don't you think?'

'It's borderline cheeky, yes,' Cathy agreed. 'But she owes us. She did stay here for two nights afterwards.'

Fleur looked doubtful. 'Are you suggesting we're all best mates now?' she asked.

Cathy changed tact. 'Okay, not owes us,' she said. 'We could just casually suggest that Derek Montrose might have some useful information for her. After all, Robert's in the photo too. It could be a bit of an adventure. And let's face it, all three of us could do with one of those.'

She was desperate now, and Fleur knew it. It was something she felt sure a lot of Derek Montrose's bereaved audience members experienced after the enticing snippets of useless information he drip fed them in his shows, purporting to be from their lost loved ones. 'But Cathy,' she said. 'It might not be kind for us to drag Joanna-Rose into this.'

Cathy stopped to consider this for a moment.

'What about all that, "he's the best I could expect to get", stuff, eh? The self-loathing?'

'You noticed that too?'

'You couldn't fail to notice it. Let's face it, you and I have bereavement issues of our own enough to be able to see it in another person.'

'I'm okay,' Fleur snapped back. 'There's nothing wrong with me.'

'Fleur, you have lost your faith as well as all the floors in your house,' Cathy retorted.

'It's just the living room floor,' the other woman replied, adding an indignant huff. 'And I've given you some rent money, at least.'

'There is not one single floor that can be found in that clutter-dungeon of a house of yours,' Cathy reminded her. 'Hoarding is a sickness too, you know.' She grinned, only half-joking.

Fleur sucked in her cheeks, taking a deep, slow breath in and holding it, counting to five in her head before releasing it out again. It wasn't annoyance or anger she was suppressing, it was something else; something much, much deeper. Something that she liked to deny even had any place in her life.

'Between us,' Cathy rambled on, as Fleur recovered her composure. 'I think Joanna-Rose might be hitting the bottle hard. I mean, who turns up drunk at a stranger's house in the middle of the night, stays over, and then necks more booze again all the second day? How bad a state do you have to be in to behave like that?' She paused, waiting for some sarcastic comment or disagreement from Fleur, who only shrugged her shoulders.

'I don't know her at all, but I do feel sad for her,' Cathy continued. 'I can't describe it but I feel we can help her, that's all. Maybe a trip away with some friends is just the escape from loneliness she needs. Maybe it's what we all need.'

'And taking her psychic medium-chasing will help her, will it? Like it's not going to help you?' Fleur said.

Cathy sighed. 'I feel I want to give her something to do, don't you see?'

Fleur nodded, because in reality, she did. Joanna-Rose seemed like a sadder case than any of them, but it was hard to put a finger on why.

'With the photo connection, she's involved,' Cathy continued. 'Whatever either of you might think about Derek Montrose – or indeed psychics in general – you have to admit, this is tantalisingly interesting and I don't know about you, but I don't have much better to do right now. The least we can do is ask her to get his address and invite her along to meet him with us.'

'Along where?' Fleur asked. 'You don't even know how far away he lives. This could turn out to be an expensive trip you know. Shouldn't you be paying that mortgage of yours?'

Cathy gasped, as the realisation that Fleur had seen some of her letters hit home.

'It's pretty hard to miss it all, Cathy,' Fleur added more gently. 'Everything in this house is pristine, except for all the red letters tumbling out of Bob's old writing desk. There are a pile of solicitor's letters there you haven't even opened. You're not facing things, are you?'

After a pause, Cathy shook off her embarrassment, deciding to ignore the subject of Fleur's prying for the time being. Getting the rest of her message from Bob was far more important than anything else right now. All of it could wait – the mortgage, the energy bills, the blasted solicitor – all of it. 'It might not be that far away and none of us are doing anything else right now,' she said finally. 'And you're right, I need to start addressing things and I will...' She paused, heaving a sigh. 'Soon. Right now though, I'm going to give Joanna-Rose a call.'

Chapter Thirteen

'What's in the box?' Isaac asked, with what sounded to Joanna-Rose like a casual air of indifference, because of course, her personal life wasn't of particular interest to him.

'Oh this,' she sighed, the unexpected weight of sorrow battling for space with the air in her lungs. 'Just a few of my mother's effects from the hospice. Thank you for carrying it in for me. It's time I sorted it all out.'

She thought she might ask him to leave, but then, she needed a friend right now. If anything was to be too much for Joanna-Rose, he had always been there to catch her.

Plunging the tip of a biro into the parcel tape that was holding the box lid down, and dragging it along to tear it open, she peered inside. This was everything. All that remained of an eighty-two-year long life, packed into a single cardboard box; a fact that in itself was heart-breaking. There would be women walking about town in her mother's clothes, which had all been sent to the local charity shop, but the rest was here in the box. And on the table next to the window, inside a bright, purple gift bag that looked like a forgotten birthday present, sat the woman herself, encased in a large, generic plastic bottle labelled: KATHLEEN BARTON. She had yet to scatter her ashes, not really knowing where would be the most appropriate place for it. Her mother's wishes had been few; all of them asking that Barry be taken care of. Even the box in front of her now had been addressed to him, passed to Joanna-Rose by an understanding and sympathetic nurse who knew all about Barry Barton.

'Robert Hepple is a decent man,' she heard her mother telling her, an echo from years before. 'You'd do well to hold on to him. It's so good of him to take you in like that. You treat that man well.'

The old lady never knew anything of her and Robert's real life together. As Joanna-Rose pulled back the cardboard flaps, a sigh escaped her and she stopped to hold herself, not sure she could bear to look now the moment was here. A hand on her shoulder brought her back to the moment.

'Are you okay?' Isaac asked.

'Fine,' she said, glad to have him near to her. She had never felt so alone in the world. Even though, in many ways, she had been. For a long, long time.

'I'll stay, shall I?' he asked, uncertainly.

She nodded. 'Yes, please do that.'

Dipping her hand into the box, she pulled out the scrunched up brown paper pressed in to cushion the contents and held her breath, not knowing what to expect. What would she learn of her mother from this simple box of effects? Of course, there would be photos of her darling little boy, the ones that had adorned the locker beside her hospice bed. Tears welled up in her eyes and she blinked them back, aware of Isaac watching her.

'You know, perhaps I should do this alone,' she said, drawing her hand back from the box again, a familiar fear engulfing her. 'This is a little bit emotional for me. Would you mind leaving?'

Without a word, he did as she asked and she felt a familiar sinking sensation. It was the sense of desolation she felt almost every time he left a room and she hadn't said the words that remained stuck in her throat. 'Isaac, I'm in love with you. Please stay.' Only, this time the pain was two-fold; one for the inability to give Isaac her truth and another for the absolute certain knowledge that she would be a noticeable absence in her mother's box of memories. The love for Barry had never left her mother, and Joanna-Rose had become a poor second best; of little comfort to the old woman who had begun grieving for her loss again as though it had been yesterday, all because of the dementia.

She peered into the box at last and, sure enough, Barry's boyish face looked out from under glass and tracing paper in its pinewood frame. She picked up the cherished photo that had taken pride of place on the bedroom wall in the nursing home that her mother had lived in for eleven years, with flowers all around it, giving it the odd, almost misplaced appearance of a shrine. As she stared at Barry's smiling face, the events from an afternoon long, long ago played out in her mind. It was all just the way she had pieced it together some time later, and still painful enough to make her grateful for the passage of time.

'I've got you now, freak!'

Yvonne Murphy was blocking the alleyway that led home. He turned to look back up the hill he'd scrambled down seconds earlier in an attempt for a shortcut, through prickly bushes and knee high nettles that had stabbed through his grey socks, leaving smatterings of hot, itchy bumps. He spied William Shacklefield and William Fienes running down, blocking any hope of an escape route back up it. How had they discovered his short cut? Every night, Barry bolted out of school before any of them could get a chance to see which way he went.

On that afternoon they'd managed to follow him; the long promised beating ready to be delivered at last. All he could do was sink to the ground, cover his head with his arms and taste his own blood and tears as the three bullies rained blows all over his arms, chest and body. Yvonne's sharp nails cut into the back of his hands, ripping huge, bloody, red grooves into his skin as she tried to stop him protecting his face. Then came a sharp, hard kick to his back, before William's boot sunk into his belly with a sickening thwomp.

'Kick the creepy fucker in the head!' He heard Yvonne shout.

The boy had never known pain like it. He closed his eyes, just as darkness arrived anyway.

A *brinnnggg* from the mobile phone in her handbag made her jump, and she dropped the photo back inside the box, as though recoiling from an electric shock.

Composing herself once more, she reached down into her bag. Cathy's name flashed out in neon white on the screen and she picked up the call.

'Hi Joanna-Rose, it's Cathy. How are you?'

Joanna-Rose swallowed, staring hard at the box of her mother's things. 'Fine,' she replied. 'How are you?'

'I'm good,' Cathy said. 'I've got some interesting stuff to tell you about the thing with Derek Montrose though, if you're not busy?'

Joanna-Rose recoiled inwardly at the mention of that name. 'Ah, yes, how was that show?' she asked.

'Interesting. Very interesting, in fact. I wonder; do you fancy grabbing a coffee with us?'

There was a pause, as Joanna-Rose began thinking of her so far private world, the one she had opened wide - quite spectacularly - in two drunken evenings at Cathy's house over bottles of delicious and expensive scotch. Following that, she had supposed neither of the women would contact her again.

'I don't know,' she replied. 'I have some things to sort out here of my mother's. Can't you tell me over the phone?'

'Of course.' Cathy took a deep breath, before telling Joanna-Rose about the events on the night of the show. When she had finished, she waited for the other woman to speak, but there was silence on the end of the line. 'Are you still there?' Cathy asked.

Joanna-Rose coughed. 'Yes, I'm still here,' she replied, sounding distracted. 'Cathy, can you give me a moment? My gardener, Isaac, is waiting at the door to be paid. I won't keep you long.'

Realising she had been rambling, Cathy wished she had let Fleur make the call. One thing she knew for sure was that Fleur would have gone straight to the point. 'Can you get us Derek Montrose's address, please?' Simple as that. No faffing, no long tales, no feeling she had to spend time justifying herself, no nonsense. Cathy swallowed, feeling a tightening in her chest. She had never been brave enough to ask anyone for anything, and she knew this was at the root of so many of her current problems. It was behind the house repossession that now loomed over her, her failure to take her job back, and the reason for her freezing cold home. Cathy couldn't ask for help. When Bob had been alive, he had done all of the asking that was needed for both of them, and everything else he took care of himself.

Joanna-Rose returned to the phone. 'Hello, are you still there?'

Cathy breathed in new air and puffed out old anguish through pursed lips. 'Just ask her,' she told herself.

'It's just that, while Derek was delivering my message, he mentioned Charlie. Neither of us had written anything on our bits of paper about him. It was incredible. Right then, I knew Bob was there with him.'

'Well, that is interesting,' Joanna-Rose said.

'That's what I thought,' Cathy replied. 'How could he have known to blurt out that name? I was stunned, but then, he collapsed. Right there on the stage. Well, Fleur did play a part in that bit but they had to cut the show short and rush him off to emergency.'

Joanna-Rose froze, feeling a tightening in her belly not unlike anguish that she didn't understand. 'Emergency?'

'Yes, Accident and Emergency… and -' Cathy stopped. 'You mean, you haven't read the news?'

'Is he alright?'

'Who?'

'Derek!'

'Oh, yes,' Cathy replied, feeling annoyed at herself for forgetting the importance of this particular part of the tale. 'At first they thought it was his heart, but the paper said it was a panic attack. Look, Joanna-Rose, I need to ask you something.'

'Yes?'

This was it, the can-you-help-me part. Bob wasn't there for her anymore, but for the sake of finding him again, for one last chance to hear from him, she had to do this. 'I wanted to ask for your help with contacting Derek again,' Cathy said. 'That's if you are willing? I know it's a bit presumptuous and forward of me, but I have to get to Bob again, I have to.'

'How do you suppose I can help?' Joanna-Rose replied.

'Well, you have the same agent,' said Cathy. 'I thought you might know where we can find him. Fleur says he is bound to be doing some private consultations.'

'I'm not sure I can –,' Joanna-Rose began.

'If you'd just come and speak to me,' Cathy cut in, beginning to feel more desperate by the second. 'I'd be so grateful. Just let me explain everything. I know I can do this better in person. Please.'

Joanna-Rose heard Cathy's pain and understood it. She was lost alone. Joanna-Rose was lost alone too. She looked over at the purple gift bag and a feeling of overwhelming isolation engulfed her. 'I can be there at four-thirty this afternoon,' she replied. 'Assuming it's your place again.'

Cathy breathed a sigh of relief. 'Yes,' she replied. 'See you at my house at four-thirty then. Thank you so much, Joanna-Rose. You won't regret it.'

Chapter Fourteen

That afternoon, as she put on her coat and prepared to drive to Cathy's house, Joanna-Rose found herself talking to a purple gift bag, with a plastic bottle full of ashes inside it.

'I want to take you somewhere, mum. Somewhere special; somewhere - perhaps - where everything began for you. I believe every person returns to the place where it all began in the end. But I don't know anything of your life before I was born. Why didn't you tell me anything? How can I know so little about my own mum?'

Kathleen Barton had grown up in a children's home before being discovered by a photographer when she was just fifteen. He had introduced her to the agency that brought her fashion modelling work for the next twenty years of her life. Later, she had become a photographer herself, until giving up that world to be a full-time mum. She'd never married and never brought any men home that Joanna-Rose could recall. It had seemed such a lonely, reclusive existence, she thought sadly. How alike their lives had been.

But where did her family originate from? Her mum hadn't known her own parents; therefore Joanna-Rose had no idea where she was from. They say many stories of your distant past are lost forever when a parent dies. Kathleen Barton had none of these for her daughter to lose. She had no idea what or where would become her mother's final resting place. She just knew she didn't want it to be in a memorial garden full of strangers. It had to be a place of some significance, because this was the last thing to do for her.

'I love you, mum,' she told the purple gift bag, before turning to leave her.

Grateful to have remembered the way to the house, Joanna-Rose stepped out of her car and walked up the short path to Cathy's front door. Within minutes, she had been welcomed as a friend and was huddled around a coal fire drinking tea. But for the meagre fire, the house was cold, yet Joanna-Rose felt warmer than she had in a long while.

'So, Derek Montrose, the psychic, is your father?'

As Fleur spoke, she was nursing a cup of peppermint tea she hadn't wanted in the first place, which was all part of Cathy's plan to help her digestion. She was scrutinising Joanna-Rose's features, looking for a likeness, and decided there wasn't one.

'If the testimony of a very confused old lady is to be believed then yes. But I really don't know,' Joanna-Rose replied.

'Are you sure?' Fleur asked. 'I mean, Derek is about five foot in a pair of heels if he's lucky. You look a good bit taller.'

'My mother was a fashion model in her younger years. It would have been around the time she and Derek met - if, indeed, they did meet. She was five foot eleven. I am two inches shorter.'

'What a bizarre pairing,' Fleur said, scratched her chins as she considered this.

'Look at his current wife, Libby, though,' Cathy said. 'She was a model too. He definitely likes taller women.'

'Did your mother say whether Derek even knew about you?' Fleur asked Joanna-Rose.

Joanna-Rose shook her head. 'She seemed very angry about it all. But, quite honestly, she was angry and confused about a lot of things in the end,' she explained, omitting the final part of the problem, which was that Kathleen had told her that Derek would be ashamed to know her.

'Well, this makes the reason we brought you here all the more relevant now,' Fleur said at last.

Cathy's face brightened. 'Oh yes!' Yes it does!' she said.

Joanna-Rose lowered her chin to peer at them both over the rim of her glasses. 'And that is because you want me to ask my agent where Derek is,' she said.

'No,' Fleur replied quickly. 'I think now we'd like to ask you to come with us to find him.'

'Why would you want to find him? There are more psychic mediums in the world than Derek Montrose,' Joanna-Rose said.

Fleur looked at Cathy, who swallowed. 'Well,' Cathy said. 'I just want the rest of my message from Bob. He had him there, I know he did.'

'Yes, but others will claim to be able to do that for you,' Joanna-Rose told her kindly.

'It's a feeling she has,' Fleur explained. 'About the photo and the reason we three have been brought together. Cathy thinks these coincidences are signs that the universe is devising a plan to teach us all something important.'

'Cathy thinks she would like to get the rest of the message Derek had for her, actually,' Cathy said, feeling annoyed. 'The one I would've got if you hadn't... hadn't -'

'Flashed him,' Fleur finished for her.

Joanna-Rose's serious face broke into a huge grin. 'You flashed him?' she said, peering at Fleur over her glasses again with wide eyes.

'Well, I made a promise to Charlie -' Fleur began in earnest. But before she could finish, Joanna-Rose was laughing so hard, her glasses popped off her nose and the top set of her false teeth almost spilled out. She had to push them back in twice, making her roar even more.

Fleur gave a puzzled look to Cathy, but seeing her friend's indignant expression, coupled with the false teeth moment which she had tried hard to ignore, she could hold back no more - and burst into a fit of the giggles herself.

'I fail to see how all this is funny,' Cathy said, looking annoyed at them both. 'This is serious. We have to find Derek so I can talk to my husband. Do you know, as they were trying to carry him off stage for treatment, he was shouting out, "But I have to speak to that woman! I have to!" He had a message for me.'

'I'm sorry to break this to you, Cathy, but I think he just wanted a little bit more of the Fleur sunshine,' Fleur told her, readjusting her breasts inside her bra proudly.

'He had a message for me, from Bob. I know it,' Cathy insisted, before turning to Joanna-Rose to ask, 'Do you know where he lives?'

'Yes, I think I do,' she said, wiping tears of laughter from her eyes and gathering her composure again. 'He has a house in Islay, everybody knows that.'

Cathy blinked. '*I* didn't. Wow, I've been there a couple of times with Bob.'

'Derek lives on the Isle of Islay?' Fleur said, still choking back dry laughter. 'I always imagined it would be a big city dwelling.' She lifted an arm and wiped both eyes on her sleeve.

'No, he has a house there,' Joanna-Rose corrected her. 'Don't any of you read the tabloids?' She bent down, reached into her oversized carpet bag and pulled out her copy of the day's news, before opening it out on to the coffee table in front of them.

RECENTLY RETIRED PYSCHIC STAR FLEES TO WESTERN ISLES RETREAT AFTER THIRD WIFE DUMPS HIM.

'Yesterday's news, his last show is cancelled,' Joanna-Rose said. 'Today, let's pick apart his scandalous, wreck of a marriage.'

'How insensitive,' remarked Cathy, pulling the newspaper toward her for a closer look.

'How convenient,' Fleur added, grabbing Cathy's face away from the paper and rubbing her cheeks. 'We're going on a road trip!'

'Who isth Derek'sth wife anyway?' Cathy asked, with Fleur's hands still squashing her face, leaving her little room to move her lips properly. She pulled away from her.

'Libby Colquhoun,' Fleur said, reading the name from the newspaper report and tapping the picture of Derek and his wife together in happier times, that accompanied the article. 'Model and gold digger. She could wait for him to die of course, but then, she needs to get all the cash now he's stepped out of the limelight. Oh!' Her eyebrows furrowed as she noticed another snippet of information further down the page. 'It says here that there are unconfirmed reports that the Inland Revenue have begun investigating his business affairs, too.'

'Oh dear,' said Joanna-Rose. 'It seems Derek Montrose's retirement might not be so restful after all.'

It was Cathy's turn to look surprised. 'Really?' she said, looking at the newspaper story again.

'It's all going tits up for our tiny, psychic friend, by the looks of it,' Fleur said to Cathy. 'Perhaps you should think about consulting another one?'

'No, he started to tell me something,' Cathy said, without looking up. 'He mentioned Charlie. Then there's the photograph and meeting you both before discovering he might be Joanna-Rose's father. This all has meaning, I know it. We all have to go find him.'

'I think so too,' Joanna-Rose agreed with a nod. They both turned to look at Fleur, who took a long sip from her tea before pulling a face.

'Yeuk,' she said. 'Can I have something stronger now, as we're celebrating?'

'Celebrating what?' Cathy asked.

'Three widows on tour,' said Fleur, standing up and pouring her peppermint tea into a plant pot on the windowsill, much to Cathy's disgust. 'When do we fly?'

'Drive,' Cathy corrected her. 'I'm afraid of flying.'

'Drive then,' she replied. 'A road trip! I'll drink to that.'

Cathy shook her head, her eyes darting towards Joanna-Rose, who was looking at Fleur.

'Are we all free to go tomorrow?' Cathy said, quickly changing the subject.

'That soon?' Fleur asked, before she and Cathy turned to look at Joanna-Rose together.

The other woman thought of home, a cellar full of wine, of Isaac and lastly, the purple gift bag.

'Why not,' she said finally. 'The sooner the better.'

Chapter Fifteen

As Cathy drove with Fleur to pick up Joanna-Rose the following morning, a thought occurred to her.

'I'm going to take a little detour,' she said. 'Pop in to work to make sure they're not going to need me.'

'Is this the same place that told you to get lost last time you went in reporting for duty?' Fleur sniffed.

'They didn't tell me to get lost,' Cathy said. 'Merely that I should take a break while everything with Bob is still so raw.'

'He died over a year ago. I think that's long enough to allow yourself re-entry to the land of the living, don't you? Want me to come in with you and tell them where to shove their unrequested extended leave?'

'No, no,' Cathy shot back, alarmed at the prospect. She hated confrontation of any sort. 'I'll just park up outside and pop my head in. Tell them I'm going away, that's all. Then I'll tell *them* when I'm going back to work. I won't be long.'

Cathy pushed against the front door at Manlington Post Office and bounced back. It was locked. She looked down to find the 'closed' sign in place before checking her watch. Odd. It was eleven thirty. Lunch wasn't for another hour and a half.

She cupped her hands round her eyes and pressed against the door to peer inside. The shop was empty; no one was stocktaking. There wasn't a soul stood at the counter. It was through the door in the office beyond the desk that her eyes rested upon a topless, horizontal Jodi, laying on the parcel counter. Furious, she thumped on the door.

'Bloody hell, Cathy, can't you read? It says closed.'

The voice behind had made her jump and she turned around to see Fleur's bemused face.

'I... I...' she stammered, feeling embarrassed and not knowing why. 'I told you to wait in the car.'

'What's going on?' Fleur asked, pushing her aside to peer in the door too. 'It's empty, isn't it? They must have go...' She stopped, and Cathy knew Fleur was seeing what she had been watching. 'Oh right,' Fleur said.

'Why on earth is that girl lying on the counter in full view of everyone?' Cathy said, looking incredulous. 'The blind isn't even down! And what is that person doing under the counter?'

'What? Oh yes, I see now,' said Fleur. 'There is someone's head between her –. ' She stopped, deciding to leave it there.

'It isn't even closing time,' Cathy continued, looking up at the list of shop opening times on the wall.

'It's definitely opening time in there,' Fleur said.

'I'm going to have words,' Cathy said, thumping harder on the door 'Jodi!' she shouted. 'I see you in there, let me in!'

As Fleur and Cathy both pressed their hands to the door to peer inside now, there were sounds of commotion as Jodi and the other person scrambled to their feet.

'That other person with Jodi,' Fleur said, still looking inside the shop. 'Isn't that -'

'The cheek of it!' Cathy snapped, standing back from the door again. 'If she thinks she's getting away with this... this... whatever it is, she has another thing coming.'

Fleur stood back and looked at her. 'She has *another* thing cumming?'

'I'll call her aunt right now and tell her what she's up to,' Cathy went on, taking her phone from her handbag and dialling the number for Joan.

Hearing a mobile phone ring inside the store, they both pressed their faces against the glass door again, to see the shop now looked empty and the door to the office had been closed. A phone was lit up and vibrating around on the post office counter.

Cathy sighed, pulling back and snapping her own phone shut. 'She left her phone in the shop.'

'Yeah,' Fleur agreed, straining her eyes to examine the packet on the counter. 'Right next to that opened parcel.'

'Huh?' Cathy leaned against the door once more for another look and sure enough, there was an opened parcel on the counter. She stood up straight and reached in to her handbag again. 'I have a key you know,' she said to Fleur, who grinned conspiringly.

'Well, what are you waiting for?' Fleur said. 'Let's go investigate. You be Cagney, I'll be Lacey.'

'Investigate is right,' Cathy replied, as she rattled the key in the door. 'All these parcel opening shenanigans. Hey.'

She stopped and turned to Fleur. 'Was that what Jodi was lying on the counter for? Trying on someone's new tights or something?'

Fleur gave her a coy smile, deciding whether to enlighten Cathy as to the full extent of what she was about to find, or enjoy watching her work it out for herself.

'Cathy,' she declared after a moment's thought. 'Someone is definitely trying something on.'

'Now listen,' Cathy replied. 'Whatever is going on in here, I don't want you to interfere, okay?'

Fleur nodded.

'Good,' she went on. 'Just let me deal with this myself, *my* way.'

She turned the key in the lock and they both walked inside.

'It's okay,' a voice called out from within. 'I'm just coming.'

'Thanks for being so quiet about it,' Fleur said as she followed Cathy to the counter.

The office door was flung open and Joan appeared, catching Cathy by surprise.

'Joan, I…' she began, feeling embarrassed without knowing why.

'Sorry, Cathy,' Joan said breathily. 'We were just doing some stock taking.'

Cathy and Fleur stared past her, as a flustered looking Jodi appeared. Her blouse was buttoned up incorrectly, revealing a bright pink bra.

Fleur glanced at the parcel on the counter, which was emblazoned with an Ann Summers stamp. She idled over behind Cathy's back to peer at the packaging inside, before looking at Jodi, who looked mortified.

'I don't know where you were, Joan,' Cathy went on. 'But we could see her.' She pointed at Jodi. 'Outside, through the door. We could see her.'

'On the counter,' Fleur added, not taking her eyes off Jodi.

Joan looked puzzled. 'Where?'

'On the counter,' Cathy said. 'We could see her in a state of undress, I might add, trying on this, what is it?' She pointed to the parcel, before leaning in for a closer inspection. 'Trousers? A skir...' She stopped.

Cathy's eyes moved from the box inside the parcel to the younger woman, who shuffled from foot to foot uncomfortably but said nothing.

'Undressed? Where?' Joan asked again, pushing the parcel back behind another away from Cathy's view.

'The office,' Fleur and Cathy said together this time. Cathy shot Fleur a quick look to remind her of her promise to keep out of it.

'She's right,' Jodi cut in. 'I was just changing my top.'

'This change of clothing seemed to involve some quirminging about from what I could see,' Fleur said throwing her a sharp look, making the girl blush. 'And as for the contents of that parcel there...'

Joan thrust the package behind her back.

'Cathy,' she said, beckoning her to join them behind the counter, before leading her and Jodi back inside the office. 'It was just a bit of stock taking, as I said. I must have forgotten to put the sign up.'

Cathy turned back to Fleur, who stared wide-eyed back at her, trying to nod to the parcel behind Joan's back. Cathy shrugged, looking baffled.

Unable to contain herself a moment longer, Fleur pointed accusingly at Joan. 'Always open people's mail do you?'

'It's addressed to me,' she bit back. 'What does your friend take me for,' she said, turning to Cathy. 'Some kind of criminal?'

'No, no,' Cathy replied, throwing Fleur a disdainful glance. 'Please, Fleur let me deal with this, would you? I'm quite capable.' She looked back at Joan. 'Of course we don't think anything is amiss here, Joan.' Fleur interjected with a loud sigh. 'It's just that, well, we - *I* – thought -'

'Oh dear, dear,' Joan said, putting an arm around Cathy's shoulder and continuing to lead her to the door. 'I don't know what you thought, Cathy, but you should be at home. You're clearly still very unstable, which is understandable in the circumstances. I know it's been such a tough year for you and, as I keep telling you, we can cope here.'

'But you were closed.' Cathy tried to protest.

'You're quite right,' interrupted Joan. 'I should have reopened by now. Silly me. My bad, as kids today would say. But this time on a Tuesday is always quiet. It hasn't hurt. Look.' She pointed outside. 'No one is waiting. No harm done.'

And with that she eased Cathy out of the door, signalling Fleur to follow, which she reluctantly did.

'Now, you go ahead and get your feet up and don't worry about a single thing here,' Joan continued. 'My niece and I have it all under control.'

At this, Fleur coughed to cover a laugh, making Cathy look at her. 'You were going to tell them both about your return to work, remember?' she told her.

Cathy stood still and thought for a moment. 'Just ask,' she told herself inside her head. She breathed in new air, and then anxiety out. 'Look,' she said at last. 'I'm going away on a trip for a few days. But when I get back, I am coming to work.'

'Don't be so hasty, Cathy,' Joan reasoned.

Cathy looked at Fleur again, who raised her eyebrows but remained silent. She took a cleansing breath again. 'No, Joan, I mean it this time. I want to come back to work. Truth be told, I need to.'.'

'Now Cathy, there's no need for all that,' Joan replied, now with a more serious expression. 'If you feel so strongly about it, I'll sort something out for you to return gradually.' Fleur saw the woman's eyes dart back to Jodi who was still stood motionless beside the office doorway. 'I tell you what,' Joan continued, turning back to Cathy. 'You go and have your break, then see how you feel. Why don't you give me a call on Monday and then we'll *discuss* your return. How does that sound?'

Cathy considered this.

'Just to see how you feel?' Joan said again, sounding a lot kinder than Fleur thought she was.

Cathy nodded, to another loud sigh from Fleur.

'Okay then, we'll do that,' Cathy agreed. 'But you mind, I'll be in touch first thing on Monday, okay?'

'Is Joan married?' Fleur asked Cathy when they were back in the car and on their way to collect Joanna-Rose.

'Yes, why do you ask?'

The older woman sighed noisily. 'Well, let's just think about things for a moment,' she offered. 'Like how it seems apparent to me that she wants you out of the way for a start.'

'Oh no, she doesn't,' Cathy replied. 'She's just concerned for me, that's all. I was in a pretty bad way when Bob first died, you know. You didn't know me then. You didn't see what I was like. I was a mess.'

'Okay, well,' Fleur went on. 'It seems very obvious to me – an outsider looking in - that in spite of everything you've just told me, Joan is very much interested in keeping you out of the way. She wants to keep working with Jodi, is my guess.'

'Why do you say that?'

'For heaven's sake, Cathy,' Fleur replied. 'Don't you *know* what we just interrupted back there?'

'No?' Cathy replied blankly.

'Did you see what was in the parcel Joan was hiding?' Fleur asked.

Cathy almost careened into the barrier at the side of the road as she remembered.

'What has that got to do with anything?' she asked, pulling the car back under control.

'If Jodi's her niece,' Fleur replied in a sardonic tone, 'I'm Derek Montrose's mother.'

'You are?'

Fleur raised her eyebrows in disbelief. 'Consider the evidence, Cathy,' she said. 'A locked shop, a young woman, partially undressed and horizontal on the desk in the office, and an empty strap-on dildo box torn open on the counter. You don't see a connection here?'

'I don't see where you're going with this, really, I…'

Fleur raised her eyebrows, waiting for the other woman to catch up.

It took about thirty seconds in all, and almost the front left wing of the vehicle, as they careened towards the barrier for a second time.

Chapter Sixteen

While the women stood on the top deck of the ferry, watching tiny diamonds of sunlight dance on the tips of a million waves, Fleur remembered Charlie telling her how terrible weather was a favourite complaint of those who talked about, but never visited, the velvety green, rolling hills and glens of the Scottish highlands and islands. 'It's true, Scotland has two seasons,' he told her with a wry smile. 'They are winter and a summer's day. And the summer's day might be on a weekend or bank holiday; you never know your luck, Flurry.'

Yet here the three women were on *The Queen of the Hebrides* in October, approaching the tiny, picturesque harbour of Port Askaig on the Isle of Islay under clear, blue skies and with the sun on their faces. The same sun Charlie would refer to as: 'look, UFO', should it make an appearance whenever they visited his beloved home country. Yet, as Fleur knew, visiting Scotland had a magical way of making visitors forget the weather, as well as themselves, as they left smoke-choked, overpopulated cities behind to become encapsulated in a wilder, greener world. Once Scotland had them in her resplendent, fertile bosom, they were content to marvel in the discovery of a land Mother Nature must have called her finest hour, forever.

'Scotland needs no Queen,' Charlie would say, on any of the occasions he would turn the car into a parking place, roll down the windows and invite Fleur to feast her ears, nose and eyes on the rugged, green and blue wilderness. 'This is her majesty,' he would say.

As the ferry slowed, a selection of elderly, multi-coloured buildings sitting idly by on the water's edge came into view, making Fleur think Port Askaig could pass for a place in Italy. This was not at all what she had been expecting.

'This is her majesty, indeed,' Fleur said aloud, just as the ship's captain instructed all non-foot passengers to go back to their vehicles.

Joanna-Rose sighed, as she and Fleur turned to make their way down the staircase to the car. 'What a shame,' she said. 'I could have stayed on this ferry for another hour or more, this was such a beautiful journey.'

Cathy stood for a while longer taking in the view. She crossed her arms, hugging herself as she called to mind the way Bob had held her on the same ship during their last visit to the island, which seemed like more years ago than it was. She took a deep breath in, certain she could smell his aftershave. Then she felt him again, close behind, wrapping his heavy duffle coat around them against the wind. It was the way he had always been: her shelter.

Bob had adored Islay. A deep, long-overlooked love for the island washed over her like warm rain on an ice cold day – how could she have forgotten it? 'I need to go now,' she told him in her mind, tearing herself away from his invisible embrace before following the line of people that were heading down to the car deck.

Bowmore House Hotel stood across the road from Loch Indaal, which glistened in the late afternoon sunlight. As Cathy switched off the ignition and they each stepped out of the car, everyone stopped to drink in the splendid view. Aside from a single car that passed them as they stood, the road was silent but for the sound of gentle waves licking at the shore.

'Glorious,' Fleur said.

There was no reply, which she knew was as good as an agreement. The view of Loch Indaal from Bowmore town was a little piece of heaven that needed no words. Its quiet, understated prettiness, she decided, was more deserving of attentive silence than anywhere she had ever been before.

'I could stay here all evening,' Joanna-Rose said finally. 'But I must have something to eat.'

The women crossed the road and climbed the steps to the door of the hotel, but the gentle, lapping sound from the loch's waters seemed to say, 'Look back. I am here, waiting for you.'

'You could never grow tired of that view,' Joanna-Rose said, as she stopped to press the bell, before turning to admire it again. The other two followed suit, before a tall, slim bespectacled gentleman answered the door.

'Hello,' he said to their backs, with a wide smile. 'I'm Andrew. Are we expecting you?'

'I sincerely hope so,' Joanna-Rose replied, turning to offer him her hand in greeting. 'You should have three rooms booked, in the name of Hepple.'

Andrew held the door open wider and beckoned them in. 'I do,' he said. 'Well, two rooms actually, but let's get you and your bags inside, then we'll sort it all out.'

'I don't know why she's complaining,' Cathy whispered to Fleur, as they watched Joanna-Rose express her displeasure to Andrew about the mix up with their rooms. 'She has a double room with a beautiful view of the loch. You and I have bunk beds. Bunk beds, I ask you.'

'Oh, the joys of being on a sleepover again,' Fleur said. 'Can I go on top? And I mean that in a non Joan and Jodi kind of way.'

Cathy shuddered, then cut in to Joanna-Rose and Andrew's conversation, with, 'You know, Fleur and I really don't mind sharing a room.'

'Good,' said Andrew. 'So, that's settled then. Breakfast will be between eight and nine. It'll be a good Scottish fry up with square sausage, tattie scones and maybe a little haggis, if I can catch one.' He chuckled.

'Which reminds me,' Joanna-Rose agreed. 'Will you be serving any food this evening?'

'I'm afraid we won't,' Andrew replied. But you can get a meal at the Lochside Hotel, which is just down the road from here, if you're quick.

'I'm famished,' Fleur said. 'Let's be super quick.'

'Okay,' Andrew said, looking round as a pretty, young blonde lady with a perfect English Rose complexion came out of the kitchen wiping her hands on her apron. 'Perhaps my wife, Alison, can show you your rooms now?' he offered, just before disappearing into the kitchen behind her.

Alison smiled, taking two sets of keys from her pocket and waving them at the women. 'Follow me,' she said.

'The double room is our penthouse suite,' Alison said, offering the first set of keys to Joanna-Rose. 'That's up in the attic. And the bunk room is in The Fisherman's House across the driveway out there, which I'll show you two ladies first,' she said to Cathy and Fleur, pointing through the open back door to a white building next door.

'Wonderful,' said Cathy. 'Let's go and get settled in, shall we?'

As the women made their way towards the back door, Andrew reappeared, carrying an enormous, and very much alive, pink crab.

'We don't often serve food here except breakfast,' he said. 'But on occasion I order in some fresh crab, like this chappy here,' he waved the beast at them. 'And I have some extra lobster arriving in the morning that I'll be cooking for a group of guests for tomorrow night. You can join us then if you like? There's plenty.'

'That would be magnificent,' Joanna-Rose began, admiring the crab. 'He looks a nice, fresh one.'

'Yes, just caught this morning,' Andrew confirmed.

'Is it dead?' Fleur asked, looking horrified.

'Oh yes,' Andrew told her. 'Don't worry, his nipping days are over.'

'How fresh is the lobster?' Cathy asked. 'Because you cook those live, don't you?'

Still looking at the crab, Fleur shuddered.

'For sure,' Andrew replied, nodding. 'It's the safest way to ensure they don't poison you.'

'Horrible,' Fleur said, with another shudder.

Andrew and Alison glanced unsurely at each other.

'Sounds good, but I think we'd better pass,' Cathy said, sensing the discomfort in the room.

'I think it's cruel,' said Fleur.

'Come on, Fleur,' Joanna-Rose reasoned. 'Lobsters don't feel pain the way we do. It's not so bad and as Andrew has said, they can be poisonous if you don't cook them live. It's the way of the kitchen.'

'Not in my kitchen, it isn't,' Fleur huffed. 'I'm not a vegetarian, but I just don't like the idea of it. Boiling something while it's alive, that's not at all agreeable to me. Poor things.'

Alison touched her arm, smiling kind-heartedly. 'I understand,' she said. 'I don't like it either if I'm honest. I don't go in there when Andrew's cooking the lobster. I hope we haven't offended you.'

'Oh, I'm not offended. I can't speak for the lobster in this scenario though.'

'So, this Lochside Hotel is the only place we can go to eat?' Cathy asked.

'If you're quick,' Andrew replied. 'One thing before you go though,' he placed the crab down onto a teacloth on the table, and said, 'You can't come to the whisky isle without having a welcome dram. And, as you're in Bowmore.' He opened a cabinet in a huge sideboard, pulled out a bottle before pouring some of its honey coloured contents into five small glasses and offering the women one each.

'Slàinte mhath!' he said, holding up his glass in a toast before taking a drink.

Everyone did the same, relishing the delicious taste of Islay malt.

'One more?' Fleur said.

'Yes sir,' Joanna-Rose said, holding out her glass for a top-up too. 'I think I'm going to enjoy our little break here, Andrew.'

'It's not meant to be a holiday,' Fleur reminded her, whispering low as Andrew and Alison walked away after sploshing another dram into their glasses. 'We have to go find Derek's house. Where is it, anyway? Did your agent tell you?' she asked.

'Not far from here, I don't think,' came the reply.

'You mean he didn't tell you?'

'No, *she* didn't, exactly,' Joanna-Rose replied with a wry smile, adding, 'Client confidentiality and all.'

Cathy looked horrified. 'Then we came all this way to find someone whose house we may never find?' she cried out, making Alison stop and turn round, as Andrew disappeared back into the kitchen.

'You know, this is quite a small island,' Alison she said. 'Nothing is that far from anything. Who are you looking for? I may know where he or she is.'

'Oh, its -' Cathy began.

113

'Just an old friend,' Joanna-Rose cut in. 'It's okay, I do have an idea where the house is and we'll go hunt him out in the morning. We all need to eat and get a good night's rest first.'

'To finding old friends, and something to eat in this place,' Fleur said, clinking glasses with Cathy, who managed a stiff, forced smile.

Chapter Seventeen

The view from the front door of Bowmore House the next morning was just as spectacular as the previous evening. In spite of the chill, the early autumn sun made the surface of the loch look like a sheet of glass. It was mesmerising. Cathy stood on the top step looking down at the sparkling view and found that it hurt her to breathe. Last time she had woken up with to a glorious view of Loch Indaal, she had been with Bob.

'Close your eyes, Cathy,' he'd said, leading her to through the bar of the Lochside Hotel and out towards the conservatory at the back.

'Why? What for?' she'd protested, closing them anyway, as instructed.

'Because I want you to see something so spectacular, you will think I've taken you straight from a whisky bar to heaven.'

'Aren't they the same thing?' she'd said. Her love of Islay malts had grown over time with his. With the commanding, white distillery firmly in the bosom of Bowmore itself, she had imagined the very air would taste of peat and barley and she'd been right.

'Now,' he'd told her. 'Open your eyes!'

The glassy loch was a mirror, reflecting twelve or more barnacle geese that swooped low over its surface. She'd shielded her eyes as the huge ball of golden sun sank down below the horizon, passing the evening watch over Bowmore to the moon. Cathy thought it was the most beautiful view she had ever seen.

Until now.

Cathy closed her eyes as she stood on the step and listened to the air. It was filled with nothing but chirring birds and the small, almost indistinct lapping of gentle waves lapping on the shoreline across the road. Islay was such a jewel. She knew why Bob had loved it so much and why he let showing it off to tourists from all over the world take him away for days on end.

Joanna-Rose stepped outside behind her, jolting Cathy back to the present. The older woman slipped on an over-large pair of sunglasses, pulled her wrap more tightly around herself and started down the steps.

'Oh Joanna-Rose,' Cathy gushed, holding her back before pointing to the water. 'Just look at it. I'm so glad we came here. I'd forgotten its beauty.'

'You could have remembered its climate though,' said Fleur, appearing at the doorway with a thin, navy blue parka jacket on. 'It might be sunny, but it must be all of two degrees!'

'Here, take my scarf,' Cathy said, unravelling it from her neck.

'No, no, you keep it. I'll be fine,' Fleur said, through chattering teeth. Looking about for Cathy's car she remembered that it was much farther up the road, in the one parking space they'd been able to find the previous evening. She shivered. 'Can't you bring the car up to the hotel? I'm freezing!'

'Yes, what a pity the hotel has no car park,' Joanna-Rose agreed.

Just as she said this, a white van passed by and slowed to turn onto the drive of the B&B.

'Aww, shite,' Fleur grumbled.

'Oh stop complaining, there's room in front of the hotel this morning,' Cathy said. 'Wait there. I'll go get the car.'

'I'll come too,' Joanna-Rose said, grabbing her arm and shaking her head in disbelief at Fleur. 'I don't mind, it's just a short walk.'

As Fleur watched them go, she heard Andrew shout from the door at the side of the house.

'Hullo Brian!'

She watched as a young red-headed man in white overalls jumped out of his van and slid open the side door.

'How's it going?' the young man replied to Andrew.

'Not too bad, sir. Have you got me some live ones?'

Nodding, Brian produced what looked like two rolled-up newspapers from his van. 'Yep,' he said, handing one of the newspapers to Andrew before following him through the door to the kitchen. 'These are fresh from the sea.'

'Oh, dammit,' Fleur said to herself, watching as Cathy manoeuvred the car into a space over the road.

'Can you wait there a minute?' Fleur shouted out. 'I've gone and left my bag.'

Cathy rolled down the window and cupped a hand to her ear. 'What did you say?'

As Fleur disappeared through the side door of the house behind the two men, she called, 'I'll be back in a minute! I've forgotten my bag.'

'But your room's over there.' Cathy pointed to the fishermen's cottage on the right of them, and frowned as Fleur disappeared inside the main building.

'What on earth is she doing?' Joanna-Rose asked, lifting her bag on to her lap and taking a notebook and pencil from it.

'She says she's forgotten her bag. But knowing Fleur, she's off to chat up the guy with the van. What are you doing?' Cathy asked, eyeing the notebook with suspicion.

The skin around Joanna-Rose's eyes crinkled as she gave her a huge smile, the likes of which Cathy hadn't seen on her face before.

'Do you know, Cathy,' she replied. 'Ever since we got here, I've begun to feel inspired. It must be the sea air.'

Cathy thought of the state Joanna-Rose had been in the first night she'd arrived at her house, the state she'd stayed in until leaving two days later, and how she looked this morning after having had just two small drams the previous evening. She looked refreshed, invigorated and more alive than before. Sea air or coming up for air? she wondered.

As Joanna-Rose scribbled notes, Cathy turned her attention back to the door of the B&B, rapped impatiently on the steering wheel and sighed. 'What is she up to?'

After a few moments more, the fishmonger re-emerged, got into his van and drove away. Cathy straightened, expecting to see Fleur behind him and, when she didn't, sighed and switched on the radio. Just as she found a channel she liked, there was an almighty jolt as the car boot was opened and then slammed shut again, so hard that the car rocked. She switched the radio off again.

'What on earth? Close the boot, Fleur.' she said.

'Sorry!' shouted Fleur, opening the back door and climbing into the seat. 'I've got it now. We can go.'

Cathy turned back to glare at her. 'What an earth took so long?' she demanded.

Fleur shrugged. 'I went and left my bag in the breakfast room, didn't I?' she replied, looking flustered. 'Then I got held up chatting to Andrew.'

'Oh that's nice,' Cathy snapped. 'Because we weren't waiting for you or anything.'

'He was telling me about the best beaches to visit,' Fleur explained. 'He said Currie Sands is a little hidden gem, but the best beach by far is Saligo Bay.'

'I thought it was Machir Bay,' Cathy said, starting up the car again. 'And anyway,' she added, with a shake of her head, 'we're not here to look at the beaches, remember?'

'Oh, wait one more moment,' Joanna-Rose pleaded as the car began to move. 'I need to finish off this paragraph.'

Fleur sat up straight in her seat to look over Joanna-Rose's shoulder, before stealing a glance back at the door of the B&B. 'What are you writing?' she asked. 'And can it be quick?'

'Things I should have been writing all last year,' the other woman said, shielding it from her.

'Like what?' Fleur peered anxiously back at the door of the B&B again.

'Like my play.'

Fleur's eyes widened as she turned back to look again over Joanna-Rose's shoulder. 'You're writing a play, right now? Here, in the car?'

'I didn't know you were writing a play,' Cathy added, pulling on the handbrake as she brought the car to a proper halt.

Fleur was beginning to look more agitated. 'Can we move on further down the road? You can write it all there.' She prodded Cathy in the ribs to give her a start. Cathy resisted, keeping the brake on.

Without looking up and still scribbling away, Joanna-Rose spoke. 'I've been writing this play for an absolute age. Well, to be more precise – I've been stuck for the last year to write any kind of anything, but as far as my agent is concerned, I've been working on a play in all this time.'

'And now you feel like writing again?' asked Cathy. 'That's great.'

'Bloody great,' Fleur added. 'Does this mean we're in it?' She waved a finger between herself and Cathy, who looked startled at the thought.

Ignoring the question, Joanna-Rose got to the end of her sentence and snapped the notebook shut. 'All done,' she beamed. '*Now* we can go.'

'Good! Go!' Fleur said to Cathy, who looked over at Joanna-Rose with a startled expression.

'You've finished the play?'

Before Joanna-Rose could answer, Fleur patted Cathy on the back. 'Yeah, it's all done,' she said. 'Don't you know all great plays take approximately three minutes to write?'

Cathy grumbled under her breath as she started the car again. Before she took off the handbrake, she felt something familiar and prickly land on her head with a whomp and she looked in the rear view mirror to see Fleur grinning at her, empty carrier bag in hand.

'I brought it from the house,' Fleur said, still grinning at the plastic wreath that adorned Cathy's head once more. 'Now lead on, Jesus.'

Chapter Eighteen

'Libby, you can't leave me like this. I'm not at all well and I need you.'

Hugging the phone to his ear, Derek rocked back and forth in his favourite armchair and eyed the sea of turquoise outside his window.

The house had two, wide floor-to-ceiling windows in the centre of the living room where he sat, which presented the Singing Sands before him like an imposing and resplendent painting. Were it not for his failed marriage to the once young and ambitious fashion model, Libby Colquhoun, whose body he craved from morning 'til dusk, this would be his oasis of calm as it had always been before. Today, this particular view merely held pain. Right there on the beach, amongst dunes and jagged rocks, they had made naked, passionate love just three months earlier; although Libby had called it 'raw, monkey sex'. At eighty-two years of age, he'd felt more alive, and more cold, than he'd ever been in his life. He still had the scars on his backside. And it would have been a wonderful moment he held in his memory, had she not begged him for more an hour later. He was an old man who could no longer satisfy his wife's insatiable sexual appetite, which had increased, in her case, with age.

'Derek, I have company!' Libby held her phone in one hand while examining her glitter festooned nails on the other. 'I've asked you over and again to stop calling me.' She held her free hand over the receiver and winked at the bronzed hunk who lay on the bed next to her. He raised his eyebrows and pointed to his groin.

'I'll get it in a minute,' she whispered.

'Libby, please,' Derek pleaded. 'Just come over here. I can have you flown in from Glasgow airport in next to no time. I can't live another day without you, I mean it. I can't breathe.'

'He can't breathe,' Libby mouthed to the young stud, shaking her head and laughing.

'Good news,' the man replied, before shouting, 'Put the bloody phone down and come and get some more of this, Libby!'

'Don't!' She laughed into the phone.

'Libby,' Derek said, his voice changed from pathetic and pleading, to urgent and probing. 'Who is there with you? Who is it?'

The young man sat up and prised the phone from Libby's hand. 'Now listen here, Derek,' he sneered into the handset. 'Can you hear this sound?' He picked a piece of paper up from the bedside table and scrunched it up in front of the receiver. 'Did you hear that?' He flung it the air before kicking it to the floor. 'That is the sound of your divorce papers, the ones you both signed, which are underneath me and your ex-wife now. We were shagging on top of them while drinking champagne. Something we'll be doing a lot more of after her divorce settlement. Sorry about that, old chap.'

And with that, he switched off the phone.

Derek stood on the shore and stripped down to his vest and pants. It was a chilly, autumn day, but it wasn't this alone that made him shiver and shake; it was the journey ahead. Even though he had planned it all meticulously well, he was very afraid. Folding his trousers and jumper, he placed them on a rock before adding his shoes and socks to the pile and slipping the gold watch from his wrist. He paused, turning it over to read the inscription for the hundredth time.

To my husband,
Eternally yours,
Libby.

This was how they would identify him, he thought, placing it on top of the pile of clothes. Taking off his wedding ring, he took a step back, lobbed it into the air and watched it plop into the Irish Sea.

'This is it,' Joanna-Rose said. 'This is the house.'

Cathy pulled the car in to a passing place and the three women stared over the hedge at the impressive view before their eyes.

A large, whitewashed house, just visible over the hedge. More imposing was the deep green-blue Irish Sea beyond it, stretching out for miles to the horizon with a smattering of tiny islets scattered between. Without a word, all three women climbed out of the car and stood with the ice-cold breeze in their hair, taking in the magnificent scenery.

'So *this* is God's country,' Joanna-Rose gasped.

'How do you know this is the place?' Cathy asked her.

'Because it looks like a rich bastard lives here,' said Fleur.

Joanna-Rose grinned and turned to Cathy. 'My agent couldn't tell me Derek's address,' she told her. 'But describing the house and the area on a little island? Well, it was nice of her to inform me of this very pretty spot, don't you think?'

'Very nice of her,' Fleur agreed. 'And a bit dodgy. What kind of agent does that?'

'The kind that has also been a dear friend for over twenty years,' Joanna-Rose replied solemnly.

They got back into the car and Cathy drove them round the narrow, winding lane until they came to the driveway to the house.

'It's beginning to occur to me how crazy this is,' she said, turning the wheel to take them on to the drive before bringing the car to a slow crawl toward the front door. 'I mean, we've stalked a television star, haven't we? But you know what, I have to see him. I have to.'

'I guess we have stalked him,' Joanna-Rose admitted.

'But he *is* your dad,' Fleur reminded her. 'Come on,' she said to Cathy. 'We're going to knock on the door, claiming to be tourists that just happened to be passing, and ask about that last performance. I mean, we had tickets for a full show and we didn't get the whole experience. We got half a reading. Surely he won't mind if we just ask for the rest or our – I mean *your* - money back?'

'For a free ticket?'

'Cathy, he isn't going to know that,' Fleur replied.

'Just happened to be passing?' said Joanna-Rose, with a smirk.

'You heard what Alison at the B&B said,' Fleur said. 'Everyone knows everyone here. And I'm willing to bet all the locals know this is Derek Montrose's house.'

Cathy looked doubtful, turning to meet Joanna-Rose's gaze, who smiled and nodded back. 'I do think Fleur's right, you know,' the other woman assured her.

Cathy started the engine. 'Well, in any case, I don't think you should go to the door,' she told Fleur. 'There is no way he's not going to remember you.'

As they neared the end of the driveway and found it continued to the rear of the house, Cathy said, 'Should I pull up at the front here, or carry on round?' Desperate as she was to speak to Derek, her nerves were beginning to get the better of her.

'I bet it has a private beach at the back,' Fleur said.

'It does, that's what my agent said,' Joanna-Rose told them. 'Let's just go right on through. There's no gate, after all.'

Cathy drove round to the rear of the house, which revealed a huge parking area, a short lawn and steps that appeared to lead down the rock face to the sea below. She stopped the car and turned off the engine, feeling exhilarated and apprehensive all at once.

'Will he speak to us?' she asked Joanna-Rose, the uncertainty in her voice obvious.

Joanna-Rose stared up at the house, which, up close, was almost mansion-like. Two enormous windows revealed a vast, open plan living space. She shrugged, unable to stop herself comparing it to the tiny, damp and cold council house where she had lived with her mother.

'I don't know,' she admitted.

'Well, no one has come to the windows yet to see who's here,' Fleur said. 'Looks like the game's a bogey. What now?'

'Oh please, can we just try the door?' Cathy said.

The three women paused, regarding the house and its vast expanse of grounds again, each with their own thoughts and reservations at where they had found themselves at the end of their trip.

'Such a huge place for one, lonely old man,' Fleur commented, breaking the silence. 'Toot the horn first, Cathy, see if the old scammer's here.'

'No, don't,' Joanna-Rose protested, the urgency in her voice betraying her edginess.

'Yeah, on second thoughts, don't,' Fleur agreed. 'Let's sneak up and check if he's expecting us. He is psychic, after all.'

Joanna-Rose dipped her head to look across to the door. 'No one's coming out, are they?' she said.

Fleur shook her head. 'Doesn't look like it.'

'I can't back out now,' Cathy mused, feeling the familiar squeeze of pain as she imagined how close she might be to her husband at this moment, fewer than a few meters from the man who could speak to him. 'Laugh if you like, but I happen to think there are no coincidences in life and the reason we all met was to bring us here today. I think Bob brought us here today. The least we should do is knock on the door.'

'On you go then,' Fleur prompted her.

Despite her brave speech, however, Cathy knew she couldn't be the one to do it. She looked beseechingly at Joanna-Rose.

'Well, we haven't come all this way for nothing,' Joanna-Rose said. 'Let's do as Cathy says and at least try the door. He's an old man, after all. He might be taking a nap.'

'Or having a walk on his beach, as I imagine you would do when you have one to yourself,' Fleur said, before adding, 'ooh, I hope he doesn't come walking by in his Speedos.'

'I tell you what, you go knock on the door,' Cathy said to Joanna-Rose, trepidation rise in her throat. 'And I'll take a walk down the steps to see if he's having a walk on the beach or something. I've got to see him. He's got to talk to me. He will talk to me, won't he?'

Joanna-Rose nodded. 'I expect so,' she said, trying to sound reassuring. Cathy's desperation had taken on a new urgency that now troubled her.

'I'll go with Joanna-Rose then, shall I?' Fleur asked.

'Noooo,' Cathy said, with a look of horror. 'Remember what happened last time you met? He'll never answer the door.'

'He'll probably phone the police,' Joanna-Rose added.

'Look, the man's never going to remember my face,' Fleur said with a huff. She pointed to her breasts. 'Have you seen these puppies? These are what the man's going to remember, and they're fast asleep in my cardigan today. I'm going to go knock on the door too and that's that. He'll have to see me at some point if we're going to do this thing.'

Cathy looked uncertain. 'I just don't want you to scare the man from the off,' she said.

'Just you take the wreath off your head before getting out of the car or you'll scare the old git to death,' Fleur replied. 'He'll be waiting for the reaper at his age.' She looked at Joanna-Rose. 'Sorry, I was forgetting he's your dad and all.'

'Possibly,' she reminded her.

'Okay, possibly,' said Fleur. 'So let's go and find out.'

Joanna-Rose followed Fleur to the back door of the house as Cathy walked down the steps to the beach. Joanna-Rose first rang the bell then knocked. They waited for a minute.

'I don't think he's here,' Joanna-Rose said.

She started towards the living room windows and peered in. Fleur followed suit.

'Let's try the front door,' Fleur suggested after a moment. 'It's an enormous house. Maybe he's upstairs or something.'

Joanna-Rose leaned in closer to the window and strained to focus through the tinted glass before taking a sharp in breath. She spied a wooden rocking chair, with papers strewn all over it and on the floor around it. On one wall was a dark, wet streak with a broken glass on the ground, as though someone had thrown a drink at it. As her eyes searched over to the right of the room, she noticed a broken mirror on the wall and splinters of glass and chunks of pottery littering the floor. In the fireplace, the flames of a roaring fire were licking round a wooden statue that had been cast into it.

'Oh, this is not good,' she said, as the other woman leaned in to take a closer look herself.

'Let's try round the front,' Fleur said again.

After several minutes of knocking and ringing the bell, the two women decided to give up.

'He isn't here anyway by the looks of it,' Fleur said. 'And it's not like there are any signs of a break in.'

'I don't know,' Joanna-Rose said, rubbing her chin with a thoughtful expression. 'Something just doesn't feel right. Do you get that sense?'

'I get the sense he got drunk and started trashing the place,' Fleur said with a sniff.

'Fleur, I need to tell you now I get a feeling for things, and this doesn't feel right,' Joanna-Rose explained. 'I can tell when something is bad and this is bad. Something's wrong here.'

Fleur laughed. 'Inherited the psychic gene, eh?'

'That's not what I meant,' Joanna-Rose said. 'I mean I kind of sense things. Emotions, unrest, bad vibes…'

'Arguments between spirits?'

'No, no,' Joanna-Rose replied. 'I'm not psychic, for pity's sake. I'm saying I feel this is bad. Someone here is in trouble.'

'Yeah, with the taxman.'

'What if it's a robbery or break-in of some kind?,' Joanna-Rose said.

Fleur tried the front door, which didn't budge. 'Okay, well the door's locked and there are no smashed windows. But let's say it does look like someone has had something of a breakdown,' Fleur said. 'What can we do if he won't come to the door? It's a bit massive for us to break down, and what if your feelings are wrong?'

'I think we should call somebody.'

'The police?'

'Yes. Just as a precaution. We don't have to wait around, I'll tell them what we've found and let them deal with it.' Joanna-Rose opened the zip of her handbag and searched inside for her phone.

'Better hurry,' Fleur told her. 'I need to get back in the car. It's getting cold standing here and two things Derek might recognise, should he appear, are beginning to stick out.'

Chapter Nineteen

As Cathy drove them out of the drive and back on to the open road, Fleur said, 'You think you've ended up somewhere to be saved. Then it turns out, you're the one doing the saving.'

'Oh, don't say that,' Joanna-Rose replied. 'Now I feel terrible and I don't profess to like the man very much. Do you think we should have stayed and waited for the authorities to arrive?'

'The what?' Cathy said, sitting bolt upright to stare at Fleur in the rear view mirror. 'Did you call someone?'

'Yes, the police,' Joanna-Rose replied. 'And if Derek Montrose was there at home, they're the ones best placed to sort him out.'

Cathy's face drained of colour. 'What? Why did you do that?' she asked. 'I mean, he isn't even there!'

'We thought it best in the circumstances,' Fleur replied, watching Cathy's reflection in the rear view mirror and feeling puzzled. 'Why are you so worried?'

'Well, did you see anything that made you think he might have hurt himself or something?'

'Not exactly, no,' Fleur admitted. 'But Joanna-Rose said she had a feeling.'

'That the man was in a bit of a bad mood and smashed a few things about his own house? How is that a matter for the police?'

'Cathy, something didn't smell right,' Joanna-Rose said. 'And it's not like you to be so dismissive of things like that,' she added.

'Okay, well, maybe they'll come and check things out, see everything is fine and go away again, don't you think?' Cathy asked.

'If there's nothing to find, sure,' Fleur replied, noting Cathy's immediate relief at her reply.

'Let's go and check out the beach at Currie Sands,' Cathy said. 'It's literally a stone's throw from here. Very small and quite remote, and I know you're going to love it.'

At the end of a narrow, winding lane, Joanna-Rose and Fleur gasped as the car pulled in to a car park in front of a small house, that stood alone facing the tiny, twinkly-blue bay of Currie Sands. All around were high, green cliffs, and the steep climb down to the pretty, little beach was via a small gate. Behind them, to the right stood a bigger, white-washed house on a cliff, commanding incredible views of the entire bay. Cathy remembered this particular house well. She and Bob had talked many times of buying it.

'Gorgeous!' exclaimed Joanna-Rose.

'Isn't this someone's drive?' asked Fleur, eyeing the house for signs of someone watching them through the curtains.

'No, it's okay to park here,' Cathy said, bowing her head under the visor to look in the windows. 'It all looks very quiet anyway, thankfully.'

'What was that?' Fleur asked.

'What?' Cathy and Joanna-Rose said together.

'That knocking sound. Didn't you hear it?'

THUMP. THUMP.

'There it is again. Did you hear it?'

'No' said Cathy.

'Yes,' said Joanna-Rose, at the same time.

'Hell, I hope your exhaust hasn't come loose or something,' Fleur said to Cathy. 'That's all we need.'

'I didn't hear anything,' she replied. 'Let's get out and have a walk down to the water. It's a beautiful day and it's such a pretty, quiet spot. Bob used to bring me here.' As she spoke, a couple with two children appeared at the top of a grassy hill in front of them, heading down in the direction of the beach.

'Oh, perhaps not,' Cathy said suddenly, starting up the car again.

'What's the matter?' said Fleur. 'I thought we were going for a walk?'

'Change of plan,' Cathy replied sharply, before softening her tone. 'I mean, it looks like that family are heading down there and it is far better when you have the beach to yourself.' She put the car into gear, turned it around and began driving back the way they had come.

'That doesn't matter to me -' Joanna-Rose started to say.

Then they all heard another thud. Fleur felt this one too.

'Ooh, that doesn't sound good,' Joanna-Rose said. 'How far are we from the B&B?'

'Oh, not far,' Cathy said, slowing the car to a halt at a passing place to let another vehicle by and looking around. 'Gosh, it is busy here today,' she mumbled to herself, before adding more loudly, 'fifteen to twenty minutes maybe. But I was thinking perhaps we could take another detour first.'

'Another detour?' Fleur said, looking incredulous.

A further thud from somewhere behind made them all jump.

'What on earth?'

Fleur turned about to examine the back of her seat.

'Something is wrong with the car, Cathy,' Joanna-Rose said. 'Perhaps we'd better stop and have a look.'

'Don't worry,' Cathy said quickly. 'We'll be far enough away – I mean, at the B&B – soon. I'll get out and check then.'

'Later?' Fleur jumped, as another thud rang out behind her head. 'Stop the car, Cathy. Just stop.'

Suspicious of her sudden evasiveness, Fleur noticed a bright, red rash creeping up the back of Cathy's neck. 'No, I think we'd better keep going,' she said.

'Cathy, stop the car. Now,' Fleur demanded.

They turned in to a small, unsurfaced lane lined with hedgerows, which looked more like a wide footpath.

'We'll just head up here, away from prying eyes,' said Cathy, as the car bumped and skidded over loose stones, mud and gravel.

'Prying eyes?' Fleur retorted. 'It's October in Islay. We've passed all of five people, and two of those were Highland cows.'

'Since when were cows people?' Joanna-Rose asked dryly.

'Evomootion,' said Fleur, opening her door as the car came to a standstill in the middle of the lane. She climbed out and walked around to the back, a jittery Cathy following her every move, before stooping to looking under the wheel arch.

'See,' Cathy said. 'Nothing wrong, is there?'

The knocking happened again – three times this time.

'What is that?' Joanna-Rose asked, twisting to look in the back seat.

'Go switch off the ignition,' Fleur said to Cathy.

Knock. Knock. Knock.

Fleur went back and leaned in the open door of the car. She patted the back of the seat, her brow furrowed in confusion.

Knock. Knock. Knock.

Joanna-Rose opened her door and got out of the car, noticing as she did a look of sheer panic on Cathy's face. She eyed her up and down, puzzling at what was unnerving her so much. 'Cathy?' she said after a moment's thought. 'What happened to your coat?'

'What?' she replied, looking down at herself.

'Your coat,' Joanne-Rose insisted. 'When you left the car earlier you had on a raincoat, now you don't. Where is it?'

'I… err…'

'Give me your keys,' Fleur told her.

'It's okay, I'll open it,' Cathy said, moving sheepishly back towards the car boot.

'No,' said Fleur, beginning to look shifty now herself. 'I'll look.'

'Oh for heaven's sake,' said Joanna-Rose, opening her door and striding up to take the keys from Cathy. 'I'll do it.'

'Wait…!' Cathy and Fleur cried together.

There was a click and the car tilted a little before the boot sprang open.

'Oh… my… No!' Joanna-Rose exclaimed.

'I can explain!' Fleur cried, running up behind her to where Cathy stood looking in the boot too now, with a hand over her mouth, looking pale.

'Oh my goodness, what have you *done*?'

'I… I just didn't want them to be cooked alive,' Fleur said, sounding flustered.

Joanna-Rose was astonished. 'What?' she said, looking from her to Cathy. 'I don't mean the bloody lobsters!'

Chapter Twenty

THUMP. THUMP. THUMP.

'There's a man... in the boot...'

Cathy's hands shook as she grasped the driver's wheel, feeling the enormity of Joanna-Rose's words hanging in the air around her. Beads of sweat trickled from her forehead, stinging her eyes. She had driven them back out onto the open road before pulling into a passing place, not really knowing where to go next. Everyone was in shock.

'Stop that thumping, we're trying to think here!' Fleur shouted into the back of her seat, making both her companions jump. Joanna-Rose turned, open-mouthed, to stare at her.

'Well,' Fleur sniffed a retort. 'It was you that shut the boot on him again.'

'As opposed to doing what?'

'I don't know,' Fleur replied. 'Letting him out?'

'We're all criminals,' Joanna-Rose cried. 'All of us.'

'Oh no we're not,' said Fleur, folding her arms and shaking her head. 'It's just Cathy.'

THUMP. THUMP. THUMP.

Joanna-Rose faced front again as an articulated lorry whooshed past the layby where they sat, rattling the car and all occupants in its wake. 'I don't know... what to... think... do...' she said.

'I just wanted him to finish the message, that's all,' Cathy explained. 'I didn't mean it! I told him I needed to know what it was Bob had to tell me. Just five minutes of his time! But he kept bawling and swearing at me. He wouldn't let me explain. He wouldn't listen.'

'So you chucked him in the boot of your car?' Fleur gasped.

'He's eighty-two-years-old!' Joanna-Rose could hardly believe her ears.

'Yes, but he kept shouting...'

'We saw smashed glasses and upturned tables in that house. He could be having a mental breakdown,' Joanna-Rose continued. 'I... well... I hardly think tying him up with elastic bands and bundling him in to a car boot could be good for someone in that state.'

Fleur caught Cathy's eye in the rear view mirror and stared in disbelief at her.

'You tied him up with rubber bands?'

'He's absolutely plastered and... and... I just wanted him to speak to me,' she explained. 'I opened the boot to get out a pen and a piece of paper to give him my number, beg him to call me when he'd sobered up and calmed down. But then, I opened a packet in the boot, saw the lobsters and that made me jump and scream.'

'What did you go and do that for?' Fleur said. 'You must have scared them to death!'

'The next thing I know, Derek was waving one of them at me. He threatened me with a lobster. Put its claws right up to my face! I panicked!'

Fleur's look was incredulous. 'He held you up with a lobster?'

She nodded. 'He said, 'Your husband is glad to be free of you' He called me a lunatic!'

'He has a point,' Fleur remarked.

'*Me*,' Cathy raved on. 'And then, I started to feel angry. So I began to fight back and somehow managed to grab the lobster off him -'

'So, now he's disarmed,' said Fleur.

'- But he was so drunk, he was all over the place. And the next thing he was swatting me with his hands so I snapped an elastic band off the lobster's claws, grabbed both his hands and wrapped it round his wrists. I was just trying to stop him from attacking me.'

'Then you pushed him in the boot?' asked Joanna-Rose.

'Then I pushed him, and the lobster, in the boot.'

At once, Fleur sat up straight in her seat, looking horrified. 'Oh my God!' she exclaimed.

'I know,' Cathy said. 'I did a terrible thing. He's an old man.'

'Not him,' Fleur snapped. 'The other lobster! You must have squashed it!' She turned around, put her face against the back seat and shouted, 'Derek! Are the lobsters alright?'

The other women watched her, open-mouthed.

'I don't think I did,' Cathy said at last. 'I don't recall hearing any kind of…' She hesitated, as Fleur swung back round to look at her, her face filled with panic and concern. 'Crunch.' She finished, reluctantly.

'I need to look!' Fleur said.

'No!' Cathy's voice was panicked. 'Please don't open the boot again. Not now. I need to decide what to do.'

'You need to start the car,' Fleur told her. 'Then we're going to a beach so I can let those poor lobsters go. It's cruel keeping them cooped up in… in…' She stopped as Joanna Rose swung round in her chair to glare at her in disbelief. 'Well, they need water that's all,' she finished, looking sheepish but deciding at last to close her mouth. 'And one of them might be a bit shell-shocked.'

The thumping was now accompanied by muffled, angry shouts.

'There is a man… in the boot…' Joanna-Rose said again, shaking her head as she felt anger rise in her throat. 'A frail, ill, very elderly man! And you're worried about a couple of lobsters.'

THUMP. THUMP. THUMP.

Cathy nodded.

THUMP. THUMP. THUMP.

'I feel like I'm in a weird and terrible dream,' Cathy admitted. She started the car, before adding, 'Do you suppose he's okay?'

'He's alright,' Fleur went on. 'It's not as if the old bugger can't breathe or anything. There's bags of air. But no water.'

Joanna-Rose threw her a warning look.

'I'm just saying…'

'She's right though, there is air in there at least,' Cathy said, flashing a hopeful look at Joanna-Rose, who frowned back.

THUMP. THUMP. THUMP.

'Clearly,' Fleur commented. 'Perhaps we should take a bit of it out?'

THUMP. THUMP. THUMP.

'What am I going to do?' Cathy cried, as the car started on up the road again.

'You mean you didn't have a plan for after you kidnapped the world's most famous psychic medium?' Fleur asked.

'Oh, and here comes the local policeman. Because *we* called him.' Joanna-Rose sounded in an almost dreamlike state now, the sudden fear of discovery sending her sense of reality spiralling away.

THUMP. THUMP. THUMP.

All three women watched as the sergeant's car approached in the lane in front of them. Moving in a way that he couldn't see what she was doing, Cathy stretched out a shaky hand to turn the radio on, twisting the volume to loud.

THUMP. THUMP. THUMP.

As she pulled into a passing place and the car went by, *The Beatles* sang '*Help!*' at full volume.

THUMP. THUMP. THUMP. THUMP. THUMP. THUMP.

The policeman smiled and waved at the women. Instinctively, all three waved back, each with a blank expression.

For a few moments, none of them spoke and the briefest of silences fell as the song came to an end.

THUMP. THUMP. THUMP. THUMP. THUMP.

'*...And that was Help by Liverpool rock legends, The Beatles, a great driving track for anyone stuck in a car today...*'

'There's...'

'I know, Joanna-Rose, I know,' Fleur said. 'There's a man in the boot. And we need to decide what the hell we're going to do about it. But first, can we please free the Lobster Two?'

Chapter Twenty-One

Cathy turned the key in the ignition again, after stalling the car in her panic, and pulled out of the passing place.

'Where are we going to go?' Joanna-Rose asked.

'Back to the B&B, I suppose,' said Cathy.

Joanna-Rose stared at her in disbelief. 'Are you serious?' she asked.

Cathy kept her eyes on the road ahead, the continual thumping from Derek making her head throb.

'I know this isn't the popular priority here, but please, can we at least find a quiet beach of the road somewhere and let the lobsters go free?' Fleur asked. 'Please?'

'Oh, I can't handle anymore carnage than I've already created today,' Cathy said at last, turning the car into another unsurfaced lane. 'Let's do it and get it over with.'

Above the dunes, the women could see the turquoise waters of Lossit Bay, which rolled over and over before spilling on to the bleached-sand shoreline with a pleasing, rhythmic lush. The sun was still shining, although as each of them stepped out of the car, they could feel that the air was cooler than the confines of the hot, closed car had made it seem.

'Help me, both of you,' Joanna-Rose said.

Together, they lifted Derek Montrose from the boot and up on to his feet. He was wearing nothing but his vest and pants and had a blue raincoat tied around his mouth. His eyes looked tired and beaten.

Joanna-Rose and Fleur both turned to Cathy.

'I had to shut him him up,' she said weakly. 'I told you, he was screaming at me.'

A closer look about his person revealed another startling addition: a lobster firmly clamped to his vest over each nipple.

'Well, they'll have found him nice and wet and they're dry,' remarked Fleur. 'And did you strip him for any kinky reasons?'

Derek's eyes rolled up to his forehead. 'No, I did not!' Cathy snapped. 'That's how I found him.'

'Why is he wet?' Joanna-Rose began, gingerly tugging at the lobsters to try and remove them but finding them stuck stubbornly to the vest.

'I don't know,' Cathy said. 'I think he'd been swimming or something.'

Derek shook his head and mumbled angrily.

'Oh, come on,' Fleur said to him, unclamping the lobster from his person. 'Some far more distinguished people than you would pay good money for this kind of experience, but I'm going to let you have this one on us. Well, maybe a discount. Say, fifty quid?'

Cathy began to feel faint and she swayed, leaning against the car to keep herself upright. 'I cannot... believe I... did this,' she stammered. 'What have I become?'

Joanna-Rose made to untie Derek's mouth, but Fleur put out a hand to stop her.

'Don't!' she said. 'We're all in it up to our necks now. If you untie him he'll scream blue murder, won't you, Derek?'

To the other women's astonishment, Derek shrugged his shoulders and nodded.

'We can't possibly leave him like this,' Joanna-Rose said, reaching in to the back shelf to get the picnic blanket and wrap it around his shoulders.

'I'm so sorry, Derek,' Cathy said, her eyes pleading and desperate. 'I didn't know what else to do. I panicked.'

'What about the lobsters?' said Fleur.

'Oh heavens,' Cathy said, looking at Joanna-Rose for inspiration.

'Let's take the vest off him,' Fleur suggested, taking the blanket away, pulling the elastic band off Derek's wrists and tugging the vest over his head. He gave a muffled groan as she did so, but he seemed placated as Joanna-Rose wrapped him in the blanket again.

'Now,' Fleur told him. 'I'm happy to leave the bands off your wrists, if you promise to be a good boy.'

Derek stared back at her, his eyes bloodshot from booze and despondent. He swayed, telling all three of them he was still drunk.

Joanna-Rose picked up Fleur's bag from the boot, and placed the vest – complete with lobsters – in it, before handing it to her.

'It's cold out here,' she told her. 'We'll wait here in the car while you do what you need to do. But hurry up about it.'

'What are you going to do with him?' Fleur asked, zipping up her bag of lobsters and indicating Derek.

The two women looked wordlessly at her, before looking at each other and climbing back in the car.

'Back in he goes then,' said Fleur.

Joanna-Rose and Cathy waited, listening to sounds of more muffled, angry protestations from Derek, before feeling the boot slam and watched Fleur stride past them holding her bag out at arm's length.

'I didn't say I liked them,' she shouted back. 'I just don't like to see them suffer.'

As Fleur walked up the sand dunes and over the other side, she noticed a two-man tent on the beach below. In front of it sat two young men wrapped warmly in waterproofs, hats and scarves, cooking on a disposable barbeque. She took a deep breath and continued past, nodding to them as she went.

'Just dropping off some friends,' she said, before adding, 'I don't mean I'm going to the toilet or anything.'

One of the men answered in cheerful, broken English. 'Yah, good day today!'

Back at the car, as the women waited for Fleur's return, Cathy glanced in the rear view mirror and her eyes met with darkness.

'Oh my God,' she shrieked. 'She didn't close the boot properly!'

As an old man in his underwear ran up and over the dunes behind them with a bright, blue raincoat tied around his mouth, the two young Swedes continued to watch Fleur with interest.

'Lovely day for a barbeque,' Fleur called out, opening her bag at arm's length and tipping the contents out. Both lobsters hit the white sand with a thud, landing just short of the water. Now she would have to touch them. Or perhaps… She turned around to smile sweetly at the men. 'Could you... ooh!' The smile faded at once.

As the happy campers grinned back at her, Fleur's eyes followed Derek, with Joanna-Rose and Cathy in hot pursuit, charging across the dunes in the background. Quick as a flash, she beckoned them both to her.

'Could you help me get them into the water?' she asked, trying hard to keep a calm air about her.

The two men began walking towards her, chuckling and chatting to each other in a language Fleur didn't recognise. The lobsters were already crawling towards the surf and freedom, just as the men caught up and gave them a gentle tap of encouragement with their feet. Finally, the lobsters reached the waves and were dragged out with the water.

'So,' she said, throwing an arm around each of their shoulders and turning them farther away from the action to concentrate on the barbeque. 'What's for lunch?'

As she flopped down on the ground beside them, out from the corner of her eye, she noticed Cathy and Joanna-Rose catch up with Derek and all three fell down into the long grass, just as the young men turned around to see what she was looking at... and found nothing but acres of seemingly empty sand dunes.

One of them looked back at Fleur with a shake of his head that said, 'Crazy lady,' and pointed to the busy barbeque. 'You want lobster?' he asked.

Fleur caught her breath, putting a hand over her hammering heart and somehow, someway, found it within herself to keep smiling.

'You know what?' she answered. 'I've never tried it before. 'Why not?'

Chapter Twenty-Two

Joanna-Rose looked down at the notepad she had dropped at her feet. This was not the ending she had planned. Neither was it the way she had intended to confront her father after all these years. How could she tell him now?

'He'll think you're a disease.'

She flinched as she recalled the last conversation she had had with her mother on this very subject. Joanna-Rose had to keep reminding herself that the old lady had lost her mind in those last, painfully drawn out months. She hadn't meant it, had she? But then, could a person's true thoughts, held to themselves for many, many years come out in an involuntary, uncensored way when you no longer had the good sense to keep bad ones buried? She shook her head. No, this was not the mother she knew and loved. Her story of an affair with Derek Montrose felt fantastical too. She could have known him in some capacity for sure; he was Robert's friend at one time and her mother had introduced them, so they had a mutual acquaintance for sure. But *was* he her dad? When in the world would her life become simpler?

Her mind turned to thoughts of Isaac back home, dutifully caring for her garden as always, unaware that she had suffered the pain and guilt of loving him for over ten years. Not as a married woman of course, but as one with a partnership she had committed to, even though her significant other had not. Robert had preferred men and she had known this long before they'd moved in together. But he had been all she deserved, hadn't he? Not Isaac. She could never be with Isaac.

And now this. Complications didn't come much more testing than the one Cathy had, albeit unwittingly, presented to her. She was an accessory. Maybe they'd call her a kidnapper too. After all, she hadn't done anything to prevent the whole thing once she'd realised what had happened. *She'd shoved him in the boot too*.

For reasons she couldn't quite put her finger on, she didn't want to call the police and hand her two, brand new friends in. Why *was* that?

Maybe it was the photo; the one, sure and extraordinary thing that had found and connected them.

None of the other women realised it, but Cathy was driving them round in circles. Islay was a small island, full of hidden corners and long, quiet lanes, particularly at this time of year, but where oh where could she take them? And what on Earth was she going to do about Derek Montrose? He was an old, slight and frail man. This wasn't right. But what could she do?

Why didn't she just drive to the police station, jump out and tell them what she'd done? They'd believe a plea of temporary insanity, which must be what it was! Why would she, a sane, normal person most of the time, do such a thing? Because it had been a moment of madness, a mistake which was in no way the calculated act of a real criminal.

But, wait. She had also run after Derek at the beach a few minutes earlier, before helping the other two women bundle him back in the boot! Apologising to him all the way of course, but nevertheless. Oh, this was bad. What on *Earth* was she doing? The mere thought of it made her feel sick. Whichever way she thought about it, revealing that Joanna-Rose might be Derek's daughter wasn't going to get them out of this.

Cathy thought she'd had an instinct for working out personalities, often weighing people up in the first few seconds of meeting them. When Joan had come to work at the Post Office, taking the senior position Cathy had applied for herself, Cathy had her marked out right away as someone that couldn't be trusted. But the franchisee had chosen Joan for the job. If she'd expressed any concerns, they would just think it was sour grapes. Cathy knew Joan, although she'd missed the relationship with young Jodi that Fleur had spotted right away - and the reason for their wanting her out of the way. That had come as more than a bit of a surprise. And Fleur had helped her see this.

Was that the reason she wasn't on the way to the police station right now? Because handing herself in would drag Fleur and poor Joanna-Rose in to her mess too.

She glanced in the rear view mirror to watch Fleur, who was staring out of her window. Yes, she was a little loop the loop. And deep down, Cathy knew Fleur was lonely and delaying the repair on her home so that she could stay with her. She was kind, but not altogether stupid. She let Fleur stay because she sensed her need for company, but there was something more. And then it hit her, like that ridiculous, not-in-the-least-bit-funny holly wreath the older woman kept planting on her. Cathy was enjoying the company too.

Nobody had spoken for over fifteen minutes. Even Derek hadn't thumped or called out from the boot, which had worried Fleur until she decided it would be best to remove the back shelf so that she could check on him. When she did, she found him back in a drink-induced sleep. There was a strange silence as they all racked their brains trying to work out what the next move could be. She supposed each of the women was hoping one of the others would come up with an answer.

That's how it had always been with Charlie.

She would point out the problem, and he would charge her with solving it. Every time, and over every matter.

'We never talk anymore, Charlie.'

'Well, what should I do?'

'You're never home. Mandy doesn't even recognise you some of the time.'

'What's the answer then, Fleur?'

'Mandy's not going to her diabetes clinic appointments.'

'She's twenty-three for God's sake, what do you want me to do? Can't *you* talk to her?'

Their twenty-year marriage had been held together by her. So much so, that a part of her had – rather guiltily – felt some relief at his passing. At least now she could make all the decisions without feeling let down by the other person in the relationship. Being a widow wasn't such a challenge for Fleur; she'd been alone for over twenty years. Except for tiny, motherless Mandy, whom she had loved as her own from the very first moment she laid eyes on her. How any parent could walk out on their beautiful and perfect baby, she had never understood. She supposed Claire had had her reasons for needing to be free, but none of them could ever be properly explained, since she had perished in a forest fire whilst travelling the world five years later.

It would be her decision what the women would do next, Cathy decided at last. Bundling Derek in the car boot had been the only thing to do in the circumstances. The other women couldn't understand that of course, but she did. And so did Derek Montrose.

She broke the silence at last. 'I still think we should take him to the B&B.'

'Are you nuts? How can we take him there? It's buzzing with people,' Fleur said.

'Whose dinner Fleur just released back to the sea too, remember,' Joanna-Rose added.

'It's almost laughable when you think about it,' Fleur said. 'We're all accessories to kidnapping - a fraudster, I might add - and lobster liberation, all in the same day. You'd think the good deed would cancel out the bad.'

'He's not a fraud.'

Cathy swallowed hard, but kept her eyes on the road as a mental picture of Bob filled her mind. She was driving the car, as he sang, 'It's a Long Way to Tipperary!' at the top of his voice. It had been their last trip to Islay, when they had no idea he had only weeks to live. They had thought he was cured, free of that terrible disease. The fight was over; they were leaving it all behind. This wasn't only a day for singing. It was for being grateful for the very air in your lungs.

'I'll always be here, you know,' he told her, stroking her arm after the singing had stopped. 'Always. Whereever I'm bound for. If there's more pain to come...' She'd flinched at the thought, but he'd held her face up to his and smiled. 'I'll always find a way to you. If there is one, I'll find it. You'll never be alone, Cathy. Not really.'

Cathy believed him and she believed in Derek's gift. Bob would be around her and it was no coincidence he'd left her the tickets for that show. There were no coincidences. Fleur was wrong; she had to be.

'Look,' Joanna-Rose said. 'We can argue about this life after death thing until the cows come home, but we still have to decide where to go now. Whatever Derek has or hasn't done, we have to take him somewhere and let him out.'

'Maybe we could take him back home and ... say sorry?' Cathy asked.

'The police sergeant will be at the house now,' Joanna-Rose replied. 'And with no one there, he isn't going to simply give up and go home, much as we might like him to.'

Fleur bit her lip and turned back to looking out the window.

'But maybe the policeman has gone for now, after finding nothing but some smashed stuff and no evidence of a break in,' Cathy went on.

'It's not like they have that much crime to deal with on this island, though,' Joanna-Rose said. 'Even if he has gone, the chances are he'll keep going back.'

'Well, where can we go then? Even if it's just to let him out and try to reason with him?' Cathy turned again to look at Fleur. 'It has to be the B&B,' she suggested again. 'Fleur and I are in the house across the driveway, remember? At least it's separate.'

'Cathy,' Joanna-Rose replied. 'How the hell are we going to get a little old man – and not just any little old man but the world famous psychic, Derek Montrose, tied up and gagged and in nothing but his underwear, from the car to your room without anyone noticing?'

Fleur sniffed and scratched her chin thoughtfully. 'She's right,' she said. 'We'll wait it out and do it at night. Then, if anyone does see us, they'll just assume it's a weird sex game and be too embarrassed to question us.'

Cathy looked horrified.

'Have you got a better idea?'

'I have as it happens,' Cathy replied. 'My idea would be for stupid, desperate, unthinking me to not kidnap the poor man in the first place.'

'So your bright suggestion is time travel then?' Fleur said. 'Some Messiah you turned out to be.'

Cathy tutted, her sullen face looking like that of a petulant teenager. 'For the love of God,' she grumbled.

There was a pause.

'God!' she added, straightening up and looked excited. 'That's it! I've just thought of where we can go.'

'Huh?' the other women said together.

Fleur's eyes widened. 'You're not going to kill him?' she said.

In the boot, Derek had stirred again.

THUMP. THUMP. THUMP.

Cathy shook her head. 'But first,' she said, looking in the rear view mirror again as if expecting to see Derek sitting up in the back seat. 'We're going to have to dress him.'

They pulled in across from the almost deserted car park at Caol Ila distillery, facing the sound of Jura. Cathy got out. Fleur followed suit.

'You're in charge,' Cathy told her. 'Stay with the car.'

'Joanna-Rose can do that, can't you?' Fleur said, looking to Joanna-Rose in the passenger seat, who waved them away.

'Well,' Cathy hesitated. 'Okay then, but hurry. We need to be quick.'

Where are we going?' Fleur asked, as they hurried across to the distillery entrance.

'Jura Parish Church,' Cathy replied.

'Over on Jura?'

'The very same,' Cathy said.

'Why?'

'*I want to write another book, which is impossible unless I can get six months' quiet; somewhere where I cannot be telephoned to.*'

'What? You want to write a book? Now?'

'No. That's what George Orwell said,' Cathy explained. 'Before retreating to Barnhill on Jura to write *1984*.'

Fleur looked surprised by this new information.

'He did?' She turned back to look across the water to the island opposite, which was entrenched in a misty, blue hue. 'It looks deserted,' she said.

'Exactly.'

'And I'm buying whisky because…?'

'There's just one way to get over there,' Cathy replied. 'Passenger ferry.'

'So… What? We're going to bribe the boat people to keep quiet?'

'No,' came the swift reply. 'We are going to give Derek a little top up, the afternoon of his life...'

'What can be more fun than a dungeon and nipple clamps?' Fleur cut in with a smirk.

'...and, hopefully,' Cathy continued, 'keep him subdued so he can sit beside you, Fleur, for the trip.'

Fleur grimaced as she held open the door to the distillery shop. 'Can you get me a bottle of this whisky too?'

'You're a genius at this kidnapping game,' Joanna-Rose said sardonically, after listening to Cathy's plan twenty minutes later when the women had returned to the car. They were pulled over through an open gate in a quiet lane, and now faced a field. 'One more question, though,' she went on.

'Yes?' said Cathy, offering Derek more whisky. He grimaced, but after a sharp look from Fleur, whom he was now sat beside in the back seat, took the drink without argument.

'Why are we taking him to church, of all places?'

'Because they are always unlocked,' Cathy replied. 'And on a tiny island of only two hundred people - and six thousand deer, incidentally - I'm guessing there's one service a week. Maybe the minister is elsewhere every day but Sunday.'

Joanna-Rose clapped her hands on both knees and loudly cleared her throat.

'This all sounds like a wonderful plan,' she said. 'But there's one issue you haven't considered.'

'What if the deer grass on us?'

Cathy frowned at Fleur.

'They're expecting us back at the B&B,' Joanna-Rose went on. 'All our things are there. Won't someone raise the alarm if we seem to just disappear?'

'Good point,' Cathy said, looking at Fleur, who only shrugged. 'In that case,' she continued. 'We'll have to catch the next ferry across. And make a quick detour.'

'He also needs some dry clothes,' Fleur commented, nodding at Derek, whose face now lit up with a sheepish, drunken smile. 'Where on earth will we get some of those?'

'God only knows,' said Joanna-Rose.

'Are we going to my housssse now?' Derek slurred, spitting in Fleur's face on the 's'.

She wiped her face with her sleeve and glared back at him. 'No we are not,' she snapped. 'You just drink your whisky and be quiet or it's back in the boot for you.'

'Your husband just shhpoke to me,' Derek spluttered. 'He'sssh telling me about your love life.'

Fleur turned away to look out of the window. 'Oh yeah?' she said. 'What did he say?'

But Derek was already snoring loudly.

'Well,' she said, with a sniff of indifference. 'I must say, that's about the worst review I've ever had.'

Chapter Twenty-Three

'We can't find the lobsters,' Alison said, looking perplexed. 'One minute they were wrapped in newspaper in the fridge, the next, they were gone.'

Cathy had been staring at her car outside from the dining room window as Alison spoke, watching for signs of life in the back seat, where Derek was now sleeping soundly again. He hadn't needed much. From the moment the raincoat was removed from his mouth and they'd placed him in the back seat, it became clear he was capable of little except drunken raging and rambling. He was a mess.

She turned back to Alison and threw Fleur a guilty look, heat rising in her cheeks.

'Maybe they escaped? Cut their way out?' Fleur asked, making pincer grip motions with her fingers. Cathy grimaced and went back to watching the car.

Alison scratched her chin and frowned. 'Hmm,' she said. 'I don't *think* so.'

Joanna-Rose's eyes met the younger woman's as she placed a sympathetic hand on her shoulder. 'I'm sure there's some sensible explanation,' she said, with such a convincing show of knowing nothing about it that Fleur began to find a new respect for her. 'Perhaps, an opportunist thief got in through the side door?'

Alison nodded. 'I suppose that has to be it, although it is a bit unusual for Islay. We have very little crime in our community.'

'Ah well, there's no stopping them in that case,' said Fleur. 'They must have slipped in under the door.'

Cathy chewed on her fingernails, wishing they could get far away – and now.

'Ahem,' Joanna-Rose said, offering a confused-looking Alison her hand in farewell at last. 'Thank you to you and Andrew for looking after us so well. I'm very sorry we have to leave early. I am of course willing to pay for any losses.'

'Oh no, that's okay,' she replied. 'We've let the rooms already.'

'Well, here's a little something for the staff, on account of the extra bed changing,' Joanna-Rose said, passing her a twenty pound note, which Alison waved away.

'It's not a problem. Between us, the house cleaning staff wouldn't know what to do with all that money.' She nodded towards two pretty, smiling faces that were watching them all from the kitchen.

'Your children?' Fleur asked.

Alison nodded. 'The staff,' she said, with a wink to her daughters and a proud, beaming smile. 'And besides, there won't be as much cooking for Andrew and me to do tonight now, given that the main event is missing.'

Fleur gave Cathy a satisfied smirk, feeling exonerated.

'And please,' Joanna-Rose said. 'Don't think our leaving so early is any reflection on Bowmore House or your hospitality. It's been excellent. You have a beautiful, warm and cosy place here and in such a magnificent spot. I've never seen such an incredible sunset from my window as I saw last night.'

'Yes, it's been lovely,' Cathy agreed, turning away from the window to shake Alison's hand too. 'We just need a bit more private space for, er...'

'Our work,' Fleur finished, scowling at Cathy, before changing her expression to a beaming smile as Alison turned to face her.

'Oh?' said Alison. 'This isn't a break for you all then?'

Joanna-Rose and Cathy exchanged awkward glances behind her back.

'More of a pilgrimage,' Fleur informed her with a serious look.

'A pilgrimage?'

Cathy's gaze fell to the floor. She hated lying. 'I guess it is, of sorts,' she agreed. 'A spiritual journey, if you like.'

It wasn't altogether a lie.

'Well, there's no better place for one of those than Islay, in my opinion,' Alison told them with a laugh, as she led them to the door. 'I wish you every success.'

'Speaking of spiritual journeys...' Fleur began, as the door closed behind them and they stood at the top of the steps, taking in the late afternoon view of a glimmering Loch Indaal in the autumn sunshine... and Derek.

'Oh, my God,' Cathy gasped.

Joanna-Rose turned to Fleur. 'Whose idea was it to get him even more drunk again?' she demanded.

Fleur pointed to Cathy, who was still staring open-mouthed at the old man across the road, in his underwear, heading for the loch in a series of exaggerated zigzags.

'Derek! Stop!' Fleur called out, as he stumbled towards the water, slipping and landing with a smack onto his backside.

They looked at each other, before dropping their bags and racing across the road.

'Ply him with drink, you said,' Fleur grumbled, as she stooped to retrieve Derek, who was now lying on his front trying to swim away in water that was up to their ankles. 'It'll make him sleepy, *you* said!'

'Leave me!' Derek protested. 'Leave me to die. I just want to die! Why won't you all just let me die?'

'Oh for God's sake,' Fleur said, pulling him back up by one arm as he tried even harder to swim away using the other, flicking water up over her as he did. 'He's all skin and bones and light as a twelve-year-old boy. Never mind killing himself, he's going to catch pneumonia anyway.'

'Here, let me,' said Cathy, taking over to gather him up, flick him over and pick him up like a baby before he had the chance to offer any more protests. 'You don't want to die, Derek. Remember?' She stole a glance at Joanna-Rose, who was watching her wide-eyed with surprise.

'Can you grab the picnic blanket from the car to wrap him in?' she asked.

The other two women watched speechlessly as she carried a now sobbing Derek away.

'Now we know how she got him in that boot on her own,' Fleur observed.

They followed Cathy back to the car, spying Alison watching the commotion from the window. Spotting them looking at her, she waved and opened the window a fraction to shout to them.

'Is everything alright?'

Joanna-Rose took a loud and exaggerated deep breath in. There was no answer at this point, or so she thought.

'It's okay,' Fleur called back. 'Just another whisky lover who's had the extended tour of Bowmore, I expect. We'll take him home, don't worry.'

'I see,' Alison replied with a knowing laugh. 'Well, if you're sure you can cope. I can telephone someone if you like?'

'It's fine,' Joanna-Rose smiled back, trying to look calmer than she felt. She opened the car to retrieve the blanket for Derek as Cathy laid him on the back seat. 'There's three of us, and you have your hands full this afternoon, as you said. We'll manage. He says he's staying not far from here.'

'I just want to die,' Derek moaned softly to Cathy.

'Shhh now,' she said, wrapping the blanket around him and closing the door. She walked around to the driver's side and got in the car, unable to look Alison in the eye.

'Oh?' Alison asked, laughing. 'Whereabouts?'

'You know, I forgot where he said now,' said Fleur, opening the door on her side and signalling to Joanna-Rose to hurry up. 'But Cathy knows it. We'll sort it out!'

Joanna-Rose jumped into the passenger seat, mouthing 'just drive!' to Cathy as Fleur's door slammed shut.

Satisfied, Alison retreated back and closed the window, leaving Cathy to start breathing again.

'I thought that was it, game over,' she breathed, starting the engine. 'I was sure she would recognise him! What the hell am I getting myself into? This is utter madness!'

'What are you getting yourself into?' Fleur asked, her eyes wide in disbelief. 'What have *you* got *us* into?' She prodded Derek, who was sitting up now, still mumbling something about wishing he was dead. 'If you don't be quiet,' she told him. 'I'll give you your wish.'

'Please,' he whimpered, throwing his arms around her and covering her in wet sea slime. 'Please help me die. Ohhh…'

'Maybe we should tie him back up again?' she suggested.

But Derek was already asleep on her.

'Let's get that ferry, fast,' Cathy said, grimacing at Fleur's disgusted face in the rear view mirror. 'I'm not sure how much longer he's going to stay asleep for. And there's no whisky left.'

She moved the car into first gear and drove out onto the road again.

'Four adults,' Cathy told the man at the ferry port. He looked at Derek, still wrapped in a picnic blanket in the back seat and smirked.

'Had a wee skelp, has he?' he laughed.

All three women in the car nodded in unison.

'It's no called the whisky isle fir nothin',' the man went on with a wink to Fleur in the back, who patted her hair down and offered him a flirty smile. 'But some people just cannae hack it.'

He waved them onwards, and Cathy started the engine again to board the ferry.

'This will be the longest, short ferry crossing ever. Do you think they'll think us weird if we just stay in the car?'

Fleur's eyes were following the ferryman as the car rolled on by, who watched her back with amused interest.

'It's a five minute trip,' Joanna-Rose said. 'They'll think you're strange if you get out.'

'Well, I wouldn't mind getting out for a wander,' said Fleur, making to push Derek off her.

'NO!' Joanna-Rose and Cathy shouted together.

'Don't move him,' said Cathy. 'You mustn't wake him up.'

Fleur looked back at the new object of her desire, who was now walking around the cars collecting tickets, being careful to keep catching her eye from time to time.

'Just when it was looking hopeful I might be able to give up the carrots,' she said with a sigh.

None of the women spoke, just stared ahead as they sat, the silence broken by Derek's rasping snores. The Paps of Jura loomed in mysterious hues of slate-blue and gold, although Fleur was staring with regret at her grey-haired new admirer, wide-shouldered and resplendent in a hard hat and hi-vis jacket. As he peered down at Derek from time to time, she tried to think of ways to say, 'He's not my husband,' without the other two women noticing.

Cathy remembered Bob again now, silver-haired and with clear blue, smiling eyes that saw every inch of her soul. He had brought her here many times out of season for short breaks. Or at least, that's what they were *supposed* to be. He would always leave her alone, often for hours, as he visited various attractions and distilleries, talking to managers and planning new tours. There had been much to do while they should have been spending time together, but he had loved his work so much, Cathy had never minded. She loved the island's remoteness and its long, sandy, almost empty beaches even more than Bob did. It was a part of Scotland which was often warmer than the rest of the country, thanks to its proximity to the Gulf Stream. And boy, when the sun shone the way it was today, there wasn't a more beautiful place in the world.

Whilst she had wandered up and down lanes picking wild blackberries or ambled through sandy dunes alone on most of the days, they had spent countless happy evenings in a holiday cottage, with him seated on the floor watching the crackling, open fire as she massaged his neck and ran her fingers through his hair, talking of her love for the island and how she'd wished they could buy a place there. She'd forgotten - or at least tried to – until now. The truth that she had been trying to keep from the others was that it was painful to come back. It was like losing Bob all over again, coming here without him. This was their place; their somewhere.

Fleur prodded Derek to see if he was still alive.

'Dammit,' she sighed, looking up at her ferryman and shrugging her shoulders as the old man mumbled a protest. The ferryman seemed to understand the joke, throwing his head back in exaggerated laughter.

'What are you doing?' Cathy asked, looking over her shoulder.

'Nothing.'

'We're here now, thank goodness,' said Joanna-Rose, looking hesitantly around her at the other cars, all packed in together with little space between them. 'I was so sure someone would recognise him.'

'There's no saying they don't,' Cathy replied. 'I think the people on these islands must be used to celebrities, royalty, politicians and the like. Out here in the wilds. It's a great place to escape to and I bet no one bats an eye. That's the beauty of the Scottish Isles, so far away from it all and peaceful. The queen herself visited the Islay Woollen Mill unannounced one day, just to get tweed.'

'I didn't know she smoked grass,' said Fleur.

At that moment, as Cathy moved the car off the ferry with a bump, Derek stirred. 'Mahumphtamumph,' he grumbled, before heading back to the land of pink elephants.

'Don't you wonder what it's like?' Cathy asked.

'Weed?' Fleur asked, eyeing her ferryman with regret as he waved a farewell to her. She took Derek's arm and had him unwittingly blow the man a kiss.

'Yes,' Cathy responded, to Fleur's surprise as she hadn't been serious. 'I know it's wrong, but I've always wanted to try a little, just so I know.'

'That's what losing someone close and before their time is supposed to do to you,' said Joanna-Rose. 'It should make you want to experience more things, pack more stuff into your life, shouldn't it?'

'Well, you've certainly achieved that with that mahoosive carpet bag you're lugging everywhere with you,' Fleur said. 'Is there some in there?' She leaned forward, making a mock snatch for the bag.

'NO!' Joanna-Rose shouted out, the outburst making Cathy lean away from her in astonishment. She pulled the bag tighter to her chest, and pursed her lips.

'I'm sorry,' Fleur said, feeling foolish. 'I was just playing around, you know me.'

'No, I'm sorry,' Joanna-Rose said, her voice a low murmur. 'I don't know what that was about, forgive me. I'm a little tense today.'

As an awkward silence fell over everything, Cathy began to hum and stared out of her side window at the sea.

'Go on then,' Fleur said at last. 'How many ounces are you carrying?'

To everyone's relief, Joanna-Rose let out a peel of laughter, although it wasn't the kind to show in her eyes. Loosening her grip on the bag, she opened it and took out a small, silver flask, before twisting the top off and taking a swig. As the liquid spilled down her throat, making its way to the tense, gnawing, empty ache that was living somewhere in the pit of her stomach, she was restored.

Cathy cast a worried glance at Fleur in the rear-view mirror.

'Ooh, what have you got? More whisky?' asked Fleur, leaning forward to receive the flask, which Joanna-Rose offered.

Fleur took a long drink from the flask with one eye on Cathy's face in the mirror. Cathy frowned knowingly back at her, just as the cars they'd been waiting behind moved at last. Releasing the handbrake and easing her foot off the clutch, she stepped on the accelerator and the engine died with a jolt. 'What is wrong with this thing?' she said, smacking the steering wheel with both hands in frustration.

The driver in the 4X4 waiting behind beeped her horn. Cathy started the car again, waving her past. She revved her engine and made a move, shaking her head at her as she went.

'Can't you see we're drinking in here?' Fleur shouted, waving the flask at her. 'Flick her the V's,' she said, using Derek's hand to do exactly that as they passed her.

'Don't say that, she'll think I'm a drink driver,' Cathy said, looking worried.

'And kidnapping is such a fluffy, non-offence,' Fleur retorted, before leaning over to hand Joanna-Rose her flask back.

To everyone's relief, the traffic began to move at last.

'Look,' Cathy said, changing the subject as she changed up a gear. 'I admit I haven't thought any of this out, but the people on here will no doubt know Derek has a house on Islay, so he will be someone they're used to seeing about. This whole thing is going to be tricky, but I do think it's a good shout bringing him over here. It's a much smaller community and very remote. It's not an ideal plan, but we might at least have an isolated space to try and talk to him. I just want one shot at it. One last goodbye with my Bob. Please, just help me to do that. I promise I'll hold my hand up to everything if after all of this he refuses and decides to have us charged, which I know is highly likely.'

The other women stared at her, astounded.

'What?'

'I'm willing to take that chance,' she finished. 'What do I have to live for anyway?'

'Everything!' said Fleur, aghast.

'Well, anyway, there's been nothing on the radio about any kind of man hunt or missing person's report,' Joanna-Rose cut in. 'Maybe none of us will have to hold our hands up to anything once we've had a chance to reason with him.'

'Reason with him is right,' said Fleur. 'It takes a lot to explain to an eighty-two-year-old man why we plied him with copious amounts of whisky, bundled him into a car boot and took him off to Jura. I can't wait to hear Cathy's explanation on our reason for that.'

'I wonder if anyone's noticed he's gone,' Joanna-Rose said. 'I'd be willing to put money on him not having had any company for a while.'

'It's a bit sad to think no one is missing him though,' Cathy added, taking another sympathetic look at Derek's sleeping face in the mirror. 'He's an international superstar. It's very, very sad.'

'No one will be. He's got nobody,' said Joanna-Rose.

'How come you're so sure?' Fleur asked.

'I just know,' Joanna-Rose replied. 'And we all know that his dear, young wife is hardly ever with him these days.'

Fleur's sceptical look turned to one of surprise. 'I thought you weren't that interested? You seem to know enough about his life.'

'I do read the papers *sometimes*,' Joanna-Rose admitted. 'Thanks to them, the whole world knows the gruesome and intimate details of the split with Libby and his alcoholism.' She paused, before adding, 'And all this at an age when anyone else would be anticipating a nice, peaceful retirement.'

'Which he hasn't got, has he?' Fleur said, making Cathy feel fuller of remorse than ever.

'It wasn't just his career he was planning to abandon,' Cathy added thoughtfully.

'Why do you say he abandoned his career?' Fleur asked. 'He retired. That's not at all unusual at his time of life.'

'I think he could have gone on for a while yet,' Joanna-Rose said. She opened her bag again, took out the flask and lifted it to her mouth for another sip.

'You think?'

Cathy looked at the old man in her rear-view mirror. He was so slight and fragile. It was hard to believe, looking at him in his current state, that he had commanded audiences of thousands all over the world. Over the years, Derek Montrose had been consulted by royalty, as well as some of the biggest celebrities of the time. How his illustrious career had ended with a show in a tiny town hall was incredible to her. But like a lot of famous people, his game of celebrity had turned to one with more snakes than ladders, thanks to the demon drink.

'He's a broken man,' Joanna-Rose added, as if reading Cathy's thoughts.

'You got that right,' said Fleur. 'He's still a feisty old stick though. Don't you be fooled in to thinking he's all frail and helpless. He might seem it now, but that's because...'

'I tied him up and shoved him in a car boot,' Cathy finished for her. 'So sad that he just wants to die, though.'

'He doesn't want to die,' said Joanna-Rose. 'That's the whisky talking.'

Cathy bit her lip, her mind far away for the moment.

'It's one way to be sure he can contact your husband, letting him die,' Fleur said, before addressing Joanna-Rose. 'So, what are we to do now? Do you want to give him your news or are we going to get him to speak to Bob first?'

Cathy looked at Joanna-Rose, who merely shrugged, not wanting to say any more with Derek – albeit fast asleep – sat behind her.

'We take him to the church and I ask – no *beg* – him to finish my reading,' Cathy said.

'After he's sobered up,' Joanna-Rose added.

Chapter Twenty-Four

Cathy pulled the car into a small parking bay next to the island's only hotel, overlooking the beach. All three women sat awestruck by the enduring, noiseless air of Jura, its sense of peace and isolation - there for the drinking in by work-tired, sea-air-thirsty lungs in this tiny, barely accessible corner of God's earth. It was almost four o'clock, yet, despite autumn's chill, sunbeams danced on gentle, lapping waves over the Sound of Islay, making its silvery surface appear like the soft, crinkled foil inside a candy wrapper. It was enough to make them forget the unfortunate event which had brought them there.

'What an extraordinary view,' sighed Joanna-Rose, feeling a long-forgotten, yet still familiar, itch to reach for a notepad and pencil. 'I just want to write this, all of it. I'm so glad we came. I would never have thought of coming here by myself. Look what I would have missed.'

'That's why George Orwell came here,' Cathy replied. 'It inspired him.'

'And now it's inspiring you,' Fleur added. 'Which is pretty, damn cool by all accounts.'

'Thank you,' Joanna-Rose said, feeling an enormous sense of relief. Her muse had arrived on the island with her; she could almost sense the waif-like, smiling nymph, waving from the water's edge. 'My mother would have loved this place.' She picked up her bag, placed it on her lap and patted it. 'Mum loved nothing more than to splash through water in bare feet, it's one of my many, joyful memories of her.'

'I feel you,' Cathy said, placing a hand on her arm. 'I lost my mother when I was fifteen and nothing prepares you for the sense of loss on that scale. She was everything to me. There's nothing to compare with the bond between a mother and daughter, I don't care who you are or what kind of relationship you had. No connection in life affects you so profoundly.'

Joanna-Rose nodded. 'I know,' she said softly, with a heavy sigh. 'I never saw a sunrise before she was here. Now, it hurts to look. Your mother gave the world and all its beauty to you, and when she leaves, a little piece of it leaves too. Nothing can ever be the same again.'

'I never knew my mum,' Fleur said. 'We were raised by my grannie, and what a tough old boot she was. She collapsed and died from a heart attack at the age of eighty-two, while knocking in fence posts with a sledge hammer. She left a hole in my heart… and the fence.'

The three women chuckled.

'Thank you for bringing me here,' Joanna-Rose said after a moment, placing her hand over Cathy's. 'I didn't know it was going to be just what I needed.'

Derek mumbled and turned away from Fleur to lean his head against the window. Joanna-Rose's face fell again, as his presence reminded her of the real reason for the trip.

'Don't mention it,' Fleur said, wiping alcohol-laced mucus off her blouse with her hand. 'Next time we bring one of Cathy's hostages here, consider yourself invited.'

Cathy sighed and reached up under the sun-visor for her map.

'Are those palm trees?' Joanna-Rose pointed to what indeed appeared to be palm trees at the entrance to the hotel lawn across the road.

Cathy nodded, without looking up.

'Extraordinary,' Joanna-Rose said again.

'Now all I need to do is find the church and get us inside,' Cathy told them, studying the map.

'And what if someone sees us go in?' asked Fleur.

'They won't,' replied Cathy. 'Ahh!' She straightened up and tapped the map. 'Here it is. It's just a half a mile from here.'

'Half a mile? From here?' said Joanna-Rose. 'But I thought you said it was an isolated place?'

Cathy put down the map and stared ahead at the ocean, her brow furrowed in thought. 'The whole island is pretty isolated,' she said.

'But there are houses here,' said Fleur. 'What if one of the villagers sees us go in?'

'Then we pass ourselves off as devout, religious visitors to the church on a deep, private and supremely spiritual journey.'

A loud, sharp knock on the driver's side window made all three of them jump.

'JESUS CHRIST!' Cathy had gasped audibly, the realisation that a woman with a microphone was staring in at them hitting her like a slap from a wet fish. Behind the woman was a cameraman, wearing a jacket emblazoned with *'Channel Nine News.'*

'Hello?' the reporter called out, rapping again on the window with the microphone, leaning in closer. She had a beaming, white smile and perfectly coiffured, auburn hair with one strand waving in the wind, having escaped the freeze of half a can of hairspray.

'It's Murran Douglas!' Cathy said behind the clenched teeth of her forced smile, experiencing a weird mix of alarm and excitement at seeing the famous news presenter. She waved, not sure what to do next.

'Don't open it!' Fleur hissed, as Cathy's hand moved to the button to open the window. She froze. 'I gon't know what to goo,' she said to Fleur through her teeth.

'Hello,' Murran said again, still smiling at them all. The cameraman walked in front of the bonnet, filming their faces. 'Can we please have a moment of your time?' the presenter persisted.

'Is that him? Is it Derek Montrose?' they heard the cameraman ask. 'That tip-off was right!'

'Go,' Joanna-Rose instructed, taking the map and lifting it up to put a curtain between the cameraman and the drunken man on the back seat. 'Go!' she said again.

Cathy felt panic rise in her throat. 'What?'

'She said go!' Fleur was shouting in her ear. 'Put the car in reverse,' she cried. 'Go!'

Cathy threw the car into reverse gear, released the handbrake and put her foot down. The vehicle jerked backwards, sending the microphone which had been leant against the window catapulting out of Murran's hand.

'I'm sorry,' Cathy called out to the startled presenter whose face had gone from jolly, to puzzled, to terrified in the space of three seconds. She selected first gear, turned the wheel and put her foot down again to take them back out onto the road.

'They were filming,' Cathy cried. 'Filming! Oh my God. I am going to prison!'

The car raced on through the tiny village of Craighouse, narrowly missing parked cars, a woman on a bicycle and a man walking his dogs, who threw up his arms and shouted expletives as they passed.

'Don't be ridiculous,' Fleur assured Cathy, patting her on the shoulder and urging her to slow down. 'They didn't get anything, just some footage of us taking off because we didn't want to be filmed. But if you kill someone now -'

She was thrown back in her seat again as Cathy took another bend in the road at high speed.

'Not everyone wants to be filmed you know!' Fleur shouted, exhaling in relief as the car was steered back again safe on the straight road and, frightened by her own lack of control, Cathy did indeed begin to slow down. 'I bet they get that all the time.'

'But... but... they knew him!' Cathy cried. 'And... and... there's nowhere to go to get away. We're on this tiny island with one road!'

'There are side roads,' Fleur said, as they whizzed past one.

'You didn't do anything wrong,' Joanna-Rose assured her.

'Except the whole part about kidnapping him,' Fleur added, lifting Derek's head off her shoulder where he had flopped at the last bend and edging his body back towards the other side of the seat. He muttered to himself, then continued to dream.

'Are you sure?' asked Cathy, drawing back her foot from the accelerator so that the car finally slowed again.

Fleur rolled her eyes. 'So, we're on the quietest bloody island in the Inner Hebrides and we run into a film crew, it was bound to happen. Stop panicking.'

'Right, well it's okay because I think we lost them,' Cathy said, nodding at the rear view mirror.

Fleur turned to look behind them. 'Lost who?' she said. 'Nobody was chasing us.'

'*Them*,' Cathy said. 'The film crew!'

Fleur sighed. 'Cathy,' she told her. 'The people have gone. Murran has gone. The camera has gone. We're fine. No one is following us.'

Feeling the enormity of everything at once, Cathy began to cry. 'This is my fault,' she sobbed. 'What was I thinking? I've never been in trouble in my entire life. My *entire* life! Not one misdemeanour. I've never so much as popped a sweet from the pick & mix counter in my mouth without paying.'

'You've thought about it though, haven't you?' Fleur teased. 'Otherwise, why would you choose that as an example?'

'Thinking about it is not the same as doing it.'

Fleur blew air into her cheeks. 'Wow, I was kidding. You really are a serial offender. How long have you been having these occasional thoughts of a criminal nature?'

'I can't see,' Cathy sobbed. 'I can't see to drive.'

'I don't think she's ever thought about kidnapping anyone,' Joanna-Rose remarked, offering her a sympathetic pat on the knee as Cathy sniffed and wiped her eyes with her sleeve.

Fleur regarded the sleeping, slobbering man beside her. 'Tell the truth, Cathy. Even while watching him on the TV, you never once thought, "Ooh, I'd love to just shove that Derek Montrose in my car boot"?'

'Please, don't put me back in the boot,' mumbled Derek.

Joanna-Rose glanced over, looking alarmed. 'Is he coming round?'

Fleur shook him. 'Derek? Are you awake?'

'Libby?'

'He's just dreaming,' she concluded. 'I think, to be honest, he's sure to need a night to sleep it off before we can have any kind of sensible conversation with him.'

'We didn't give him that much whisky, did we?' said Joanna-Rose.

'He was already seriously drunk when Cathy found him,' Fleur told her. 'I don't think we made that much difference to his state to be fair. He's probably out for the night, which is just as well for us.'

'Oh, I do hope so. I think I need a night to sleep things off myself,' Cathy said. 'Maybe I'll get lucky and wake up tomorrow morning to find this whole, bizarre day was just an incredible dream.'

'Me too,' Fleur agreed. 'Although incredible is pushing it. I'd rather be in that one where I'm smothered from neck to crotch in fresh cream, with some hungry, dairy-loving, young Spaniard lying at my feet, to be honest.'

'God,' said Cathy. 'I think I'm going to be sick.'

Fleur leaned over to tap her on the shoulder. 'Talking of God,' she said. 'Did you know you drove past the church about a mile back?'

'Oh, crap!'

As Cathy pulled over to make a U-turn in the road, Fleur made a final observation.

'And just one other, teeny, tiny detail we should be perhaps be thinking about before we get there,' she said. 'Did anyone else notice that film crew seemed to be expecting to see Derek here today?'

Cathy and Joanna-Rose's widened, shock-filled eyes met briefly, before they spun around to gape at their sleeping captive.

'Oh... crap!'

Chapter Twenty-Five

'What are the chances?'

The three women stared at the makeshift sign on the lawn which Cathy had pulled up beside before voicing her thoughts. JURA CHURCH FÊTE HERE TOMORROW. The wording was scrawled as though a child had painted it, and was festooned with pretty pink, purple and blue flowers.

'You have got to be kidding me!' Fleur's hands went to her forehead and she rubbed her temples, before glowering out of the window and up towards the sky. 'Seriously?' she asked Him.

'And it's right next to a playground! Perhaps the only one on the island too!' exclaimed Joanna-Rose.

Sure enough, Jura Parish Church had turned out to be yards away from a row of houses and a mere stone's throw from a small playpark, where two women were sitting watching a toddler play on the slide. The only saving grace was a row of very tall trees shielding the right side of the church from the first house and there were no more properties in immediate view beyond it.

Cathy turned round in her seat to Fleur, who asked, 'What now, Einstein?'

'We do as planned. Go in pretending we are here for spiritual direction.'

Derek sat forward and turned towards Fleur. 'I think I'm going to be si -'

As Fleur leaned in, wondering what he was trying to say, she received a projectile stream of diced, grey stew that smelled not unlike whisky into her lap. Then she knew the answer.

'Awww,' she said, pushing Derek's forehead back away from her with the palm of her hand, before opening her car door and bursting out, shaking her trouser legs with her hands and shouting, 'JESUS, GOD IN HEAVEN!'

The women in the park stopped chatting and stared at her.

Fleur stopped, turned towards the church and clasped her hands to her mouth as if in prayer. *'Oh Jesus, God in Heaven, you are the almighty!'* she sang out, to the tune of *Match of the Day*, offering a sly wink to Joanna-Rose and Cathy, who were watching – horrified – from the car, until a sound of shuffling from the back seat made them both dive out too.

'Get off me! Get bloody off me!' Derek yelled, as they made a dive to stop him spilling out onto the road. Pushing the women's hands away, he crawled out of the vehicle on his forearms, before following first with one leg, then the other, eventually pulling himself to standing in all his damp, sick-covered vest and pants glory.

'What are you effing looking at?' Derek yelled at the women in the park, who had been staring in astonishment at him.

The women stood up, and one reached a hand out for the little boy, who ran eagerly to her side. They scuttled out of the park and began hurrying away up the road.

'Now, now, Father Abraham,' Cathy said loud enough for them to hear her, putting an arm around Derek's shoulder to turn him away from the direction of the playground. 'I know it's been a long, laborious journey.'

Fleur covered her mouth with her hands and coughed, 'Bollocks!'

Cathy looked at her. 'What?'

'Hairy brain! Hairy brain!' Fleur covered her eyes with one hand and pointed down towards Derek's very loose, baggy pants. Cathy and Joanna-Rose stared where she was pointing before letting out simultaneous gasps of horror.

Fleur started to heave. 'We have an escapee in the centre midfield,' she said between exaggerated retches, before adding quietly to Joanna-Rose, 'Do you think that's the one *you* came from?'

'Oh Lord,' Cathy announced, feeling a little sick herself. She pushed Derek up the path towards the door of the church with a scowl. 'We have to get him inside, now.'

Jura Parish Church looked smaller inside than out, with only twenty pews. Joanna-Rose sat at the front, staring up at a large, pine cross on the white-washed wall. The only sound to interrupt the solitude of her thoughts for the last ten minutes had been Derek's rasping snores and the occasional grunt, as he lay sleeping two rows behind her, now sporting a clergyman's gown and covered with the picnic blanket.

That was, until Fleur came crashing back in from the toilet where she had gone to change her clothes. 'Thank feck he's asleep again,' she said, before pouring herself into the pew beside her, sitting so close that the other woman had to shuffle away a little for comfort.

'Have you ever thought about proxemics?' Joanna-Rose said with a sigh.

'No,' came the flat reply. 'I think my boobs are big enough as they are, thank you for asking. Where's Cathy with the food? I'm starving.'

'Maybe she's having trouble finding anything. It is almost five o'clock.'

Joanna-Rose had been thinking there was nowhere on Earth she wouldn't rather be than here now. Strange. She had wanted to come, but now she was so close to facing Derek with her story, knowing there was every chance it may turn out to be complete nonsense, it didn't seem so easy. The cold light of day was indeed as sobering as it sounded. 'This place will be swarming with people tomorrow morning,' she said.

'I wouldn't say "swarming",' Fleur replied. She was looking at the cross on the wall too now. In a past life she bowed at the altar of her church. 'There are only two hundred people on the entire island. How many of those will be church-goers?'

'You never know in a small community like this.'

'Then we'll just have to make sure we wake up early, that's all,' sniffed Fleur.

There was a thump and a retching sound from behind, which made them both turn around - to find Derek, red-faced and drooling, with a bible open in front of him, leaning forwards and wiping his mouth on the pages.

'God, give me strength,' said Joanna-Rose.

Fleur put her hands on her hips, stood up and exhaled slowly. 'Or at least some toilet paper. I'll go get some.'

'It's okay, Derek,' said Joanna-Rose, rising to help as he fought with the blanket on his legs to try and stand up. 'We've got you.'

Tearing himself free of the blanket, Derek stopped to look down at the cler'yman's gown he was wearing, before gazing back up at the pair. He blinked. 'Am I dead?'

'Yes, you're dead and now you're doing your own funeral,' Fleur replied dryly.

Before he had time to consider this further, the women were hauling him to his feet.

'I'm... I'm dead?' He staggered, forcing the women to dance in a zigzagging motion with him up the aisle towards the bathroom.

Fleur huffed with the effort of keeping up with him, before stopping him short. 'Derek,' she sighed. 'Can you hear yourself?'

'Yes,' he replied.

'Then you're right. You're dead. And the great news is it looks like you're the world's only genuine medium too. Congratulations.'

'Come on,' Joanna-Rose coaxed, attempting to guide the old man onwards, but finding herself forced to stop as he tripped and fell into her.

'Don't make us carry you,' Fleur told him. 'I'm still tired from chasing you on that beach and pushing you in the boot.'

He grimaced and stood tall, pushing their arms away. 'I can do it,' he wheezed, before taking a spectacular sideways dive into the opposite pew.

Chapter Twenty-Six

'It's all a bit... fuzzy,' Derek said, rubbing his bald head with a scowl. 'Oh and my head, it feels like I've been booted in the temples.'

'I never touched his temples,' Fleur said, looking at the other two women and raising a hand in denial.

'Oh no,' Cathy added. 'Nobody kicked you. I can assure you of that Mr Montrose. We just have some things we want to ask you. Very simple things. Nothing too detailed.'

'I already know you don't want to hurt me,' Derek said, chewing hungrily on one of the steak sandwiches Cathy had managed to bring them. She hoped the food might make help him sober up a little, but he was still bleary-eyed and slobbering. 'You saved my life,' he finished, wiping his mouth on the sleeve of the gown.

Fleur met Joanna-Rose's equally astonished look.

'Saved his life?' Fleur mouthed to her.

Focussed on tucking into her own sandwich, Cathy said, 'It's a long story,' without looking up.

'This steak is delicious,' Derek cut in. 'Did you get it from The Antlers?'

'Cow's backside is my guess,' said Fleur, examining the remaining piece of her own dinner.

'No, The Antlers. We're on Jura, aren't we? The Antlers is a little café across from the shop,' Derek said.

'What shop?' Fleur asked, feeling irritated that he knew so much more about where they had brought him than they did.

'The shop,' he said. 'There's only one of them.'

'Closed,' Cathy said. 'But I managed to get a takeout from the hotel. They were very accommodating.'

He nodded. 'Yes, they are that.'

Joanna-Rose finished her sandwich, took a bottle of water out of the carrier bag Cathy had brought everything in and threw the paper packet from her dinner into it, with a sigh. No wine. It had been several hours since her last drink. With a thoughtful expression she turned back to address Derek. 'How exactly did Cathy save your life?'

'So what is it you all want?' Derek went on, ignoring the question. 'Ransom money? Because I'm sorry to inform you that not a single person is going to miss me enough to pay up. Not one.'

'We could figure that out for ourselves,' Fleur replied wryly. 'And speaking of which, you should already know what we want you for, with you being psychic and all.'

'I ssshpeak to the dead,' Derek spat, peppering the bench in front of him with little bits of half-chewed sandwich. 'At least, I used to. What I don't do is predict the future. Which is why I'm wondering what the hell I'm doing in this church!'

'Used to? I hope you're not about to tell us the voices have stopped because that - and nothing more - is what we have brought you here for. We don't want your or anyone else's money,' Fleur snapped back.

'You bundled me into the boot of a car and dragged me all the way over to Jura for a bloody reading? Are you three out of your actual minds? I'm not doing it, I tell you! I'm a professional, and professional people need the right surroundings, and the right set of circumstances for my gifts to manifest. I need to feel I'm in a circle full of love and compassion. And you might be interested to know that I have retired from public life. You raving lunatic women belong in jail!' He tugged at the neck of the clerical gown he was wearing, as if trying to remove it, before giving up and shaking it at them. 'And why the hell am I being held captive in a church?'

'I'm a sixty-eight-year-old Catholic,' Fleur said. 'I've been to more Sunday Masses and drunk more Aldi's vinegar of Christ, than you've had ride refusals at Disneyland for being too short. Don't talk to me about being held captive in a church.'

'You're here because we're going to sacrifice you at the altar if you don't agree to the reading,' Joanna-Rose cut in impatiently, without a hint of a smile.

'Don't you know someone is going to come in here and find us?' Derek raged on. 'It's outrageous, it really is -' He stopped and stared at Joanna-Rose. 'What did you just say?'

As Derek's pale grey eyes widened in shock, Joanna-Rose could see that they were bloodshot, the product of a long day's drinking, she surmised. She knew that particular side effect, as she'd seen it many times before in her own reflection.

'You're joking, right?' he said, before appealing to Fleur. 'Tell me she's joking.'

Fleur made a slicing action across her neck, which had Derek whimpering like a baby.

'You can't. I... I'm a very famous man.'

'Where's that spirit guide fella that takes over your body when you visit spooky castles? What's his name? Jean Claude Van Damme?'

'It's just Jean Claude,' Cathy corrected.

'That's it,' Fleur replied. 'Can you get him to take over for a while we gut you like a fish?'

Derek turned ashen, but for the first time that day, Joanna-Rose felt herself wanting to chuckle. Although she would never admit it to the other two women, in the twelve months since her mother had dropped the daddy bombshell to her, Joanna-Rose had watched Derek on television, read about him in the papers and studied his life and background. It had become a morbid fascination. Maybe she had been looking for similarities: qualities they shared, features that were the same. But in all that time she had found nothing to convince her that she and the great, all-knowing, all-achieving celebrity that was Derek Montrose were alike in any way at all. He had seemed so confident and aloof on the television, even though she knew his personal life had been falling apart and his alcoholism made the headlines enough times for her to recognise he had a problem not a million miles away from her own. That, at least, was an attribute they appeared to share, but she had never noticed until today how sad, pathetic and ludicrous he was. Yet, something about that made her feel even more bereft than the loss of Robert and her mother. But why? She hadn't come to find a father, had she?

'You can't do this to me,' Derek said. 'I'm not someone you can just command a performance from. People pay me a lot of money to -'

'Fool the vulnerable for private gain,' Fleur finished for him.

'How dare you!'

Derek's face had gone from ashen and terrified to purple with rage in the space of a minute. He stood up. 'If I only had a pound for every loser that chased me for a private reading after a show. For more information. Always more! I don't have it, you know. I only have what the spirits are willing to gift me.' He tried to fold his arms, but missed, falling back in to his seat. 'You ordinary people just don't get it, do you?' he went on, with indignation. 'I'm a spirit medium. I was chosen to do great work.'

'Well now you've been chosen again, as a sacrifice,' Fleur declared angrily. 'Cathy, did we pack my dagger and black candles?'

'Noooo!'

'I was joking,' Joanna-Rose admitted at last. It was clear to her that he believed the women were not only insane – and she couldn't blame him for that in the circumstances - but also capable of doing him some serious harm. Despite everything, she didn't feel good about frightening a very old man. 'We just want a reading,' she said more softly. 'Well, not even all of us. Just one.'

A wicked, inebriated smirk spread across Derek's face. 'Someone's husband die, did he?' he spat. 'Is that what you saved me for? To trouble a poor man who's probably grateful to be allowed to rest at last?'

'You're the psychic medium,' said Fleur. 'You tell us.'

'It was me. I just wanted you to finish what you started to tell me,' Cathy pleaded. 'At your last show.'

Derek rocked back and forth in his seat now, roaring with mocking, inebriated laughter. 'At my last show? Bloody marvellous.'

'Yes, your last show,' Fleur said, before standing up, turning towards him and lifting up her t-shirt. 'Remember these puppies?'

He stopped.

'We came to your last show and you started to tell me something, just as it all came to a sudden, erm, end,' said Cathy. 'Don't you remember?'

Derek's mouth fell open and he turned to Cathy with a new recognition. She thought her heart might burst from excitement. He remembered!

'It was you?' he said. 'And you,' he looked again at Fleur, who was pulling her t-shirt back over her braless chest. 'At the show?' He went on, clasping his hands together, before holding them up to his face as if in prayer. 'I do remember,' he said. 'Oh yes I do. You're Cathy Harper!'

'Yes,' she replied, even more excited now. 'Yes, that's me, Derek. What were you going to tell me? Please, I have to know.'

'After my whisky, are you?' he spat.

'What? I think you've had enough,' said Cathy.

He stopped wriggling and looked at her, his expression thoughtful. 'You don't want any of the whisky?' he asked.

'No I do not,' she said. 'I don't want to have a drink with you, I simply want to know what message my husband has for me, that's all.'

He grinned. 'Seriously?' he said, looking as though he could hardly believe his ears. 'That's it?'

She nodded. 'That's it. I loved him so much, Derek. He was a wonderful, kind and caring man -'

His grin disappeared almost as soon as it had arrived. 'Wonderful, caring man?' he barked, his eyes flashing with renewed anger. 'Bob, wasn't it? Yes, I remember it all now. He had a message for you, alright. And I had one for him. I was going to tell that husband of yours I'm glad he's dead, because at least now he can keep his filthy, smarmy, tour-guiding hands off my wife!'

'His... his what?' Cathy stammered.

'That's right,' Derek shot back, his eyes wide with genuine anger. 'They were at it for a year, maybe more. And in my bed! That's your message, you can have that one on me!'

The women all gasped at once, and Cathy felt her knees begin to give as though she might fall over. She heard a voice say, 'Are you okay?' before her world turned black.

Chapter Twenty-Seven

There was never a more beautiful place to stand and cry. Jura church looked out over the glassy strait to Islay, which from where Cathy stood looked like a painting in hues of blue and grey. It was a still evening, and light was fading fast. She watched tiny, rippling waves deliver seaweed and foam to Jura's shores, listening to the song of it all – lip, lap, lush. Cathy loved the sound of water; it calmed her, while serving as a reminder that the earth was as alive as she. All her happiest memories came from water: to splashing through puddles in purple, flower covered wellingtons as a child. Beach holidays she'd never wanted to end; early swimming lessons, when her father had walked beside her as she took her first few, front crawl-attempting strokes in the local pool, shouting, 'Kick those legs!' to her. Then there was Bob's work in Islay. And that's when the tears came again, the latest of so many. Tears of joy the moment she said, 'I do,' to tears of sadness and crippling, agonising fear when Bob died. Tears here on this pivotal evening, for a life with Bob that she now knew had been full of deceit.

'You know, our friend, George Orwell, almost lost his life out there, many moons ago.'

The voice belonged to Joanna-Rose, who unbeknownst to Cathy, had followed her outside and was standing a few feet behind.

She wiped her eyes with her sleeve and turned back to the other woman. 'He did?'

Joanna-Rose nodded and smiled. 'Yes,' she replied. 'You don't know that story? He was attempting to sail past the Corryvrecken and was almost sucked under. Want a crisp?' She held out a bag, but Cathy shook her head, turning to face the sea again.

'Isn't that a kind of mythical creature?'

Joanna-Rose hugged the bag of crisps and smiled. 'No,' she said. 'He was a real person.'

'I meant the Corryvrecken. Not that I could know myth from reality,' Cathy admitted, wiping her eyes and nose on her sleeve. 'In fact, I'm beginning to think I don't know anything anymore.'

Joanna-Rose's brow furrowed. 'Don't think that. It isn't your fault.'

Cathy felt the tears well up again. 'Everything that I thought was real in my life, as it turns out, wasn't. At least, that's what it feels like. It must be my fault. How could I have been so blind?'

Despite Cathy's obvious misery, Joanna-Rose found she couldn't help but ponder the mythical sea creature comment for a few seconds, before her face brightened. 'Did you think I meant the Kraken?'

'I know you didn't come out here to tell me tales of the sea,' Cathy went on, oblivious to her blunder. 'So let's cut to the chase. I just found out that the man I love was in fact a love cheat and you came to ask me if I'm going to be okay about that.' She bit her lip, before bending down to pick up a stone and tossing it into the water.

Joanna-Rose sighed. 'Horrible business,' she said. 'I... I...' She patted Cathy's shoulder and stared out to sea with her, feeling useless. After a while, she said, 'I'm not good at being sympathetic, I fear. All I can say is don't make us have to drag *you* out of the sea today. Do you want a ride home in your own car boot?'

Despite everything, Cathy managed a smile.

'Jokes,' Joanna-Rose continued, feeling stupid as well as useless now. 'I do jokes when there's nothing else I can think to say. I'm sorry.'

'Don't be,' Cathy said, rubbing her eyes again. 'It's strangely comforting to have you be normal. Don't you find that with grief in general? It's nice for someone to treat me like I'm not made of glass for once. Even after I just found out the man I paused my life for was, in fact, a lying, shagging bastard.'

Taken aback by Cathy's uncharacteristic outburst, Joanna-Rose stared at the sea in silence for a while, not knowing what else to say.

'Can you believe it?' Cathy said after a moment. 'I thought he was agreeing to bring me here with him because he wanted us to spend more time together, as I did. My entire life was about him.

I took weeks and weeks off work to be with him here. And all the while, I was just getting in the way of his plans.'

'Look,' Joanna-Rose said. 'All I know for sure is you can't live all your days like you're in someone else's play. Be the writer of your life, not the actor. I should have told myself that one a long time ago too. This is terrible, shocking news. But that miserable excuse for a human in there has just given you a reason to stop dwelling on a lost past and move on. I mean, I know you need to cry and get it all out of your system, Cathy, but it's been a good while now, don't you think you've grieved enough?'

'What do I do now?' Cathy whispered, more to herself. 'What can I do? I want to ask him why and tell him how he's hurt me, but I can't. I want to scream at him, but he isn't here to scream at. I've loved him for fifteen years. Who knows for how many of those years he wasn't loving me back?'

Joanna-Rose frowned. 'You don't believe that, do you?' she asked.

'Who knows?' replied Cathy. 'I thought we were happy, but it's clear I had it all wrong. Oh how stupid I've been. A first class fool.'

'Were there any signs? I mean, Robert was always off with some person or other. I always knew.'

'Oh, Joanna-Rose, I'm sorry,' Cathy said, turning to offer her a hug. 'What am I saying? You know exactly what all this is like.'

Accepting the hug awkwardly, her carpet bag bouncing off Cathy's back as she returned it, Joanna-Rose said, 'I didn't have to ask what Robert was doing, I just knew when he was with someone else. My situation was not like yours. I settled for a certain kind of life that I thought was the best someone like me could get.'

'Someone like you?' Cathy said, pulling back to look into Joanna-Rose's sad eyes. 'Why would you say it like that? You're lovely, and you deserve love.'

'Maybe Derek is lying?' Joanna-Rose said, uncomfortable at the switch to discussing this particular part of her life. She wasn't ready for that, not yet.

Cathy shook her head and closed her eyes, feeling fat tears squeeze through her lashes, the pain in her heart almost choking her. 'Do you suppose Bob loved her?' she asked after a moment. 'I mean, he only had the time and opportunities to see her in the summer months. Perhaps it wasn't that serious? Maybe he was just using her for... for...'

'For sex?' the other woman finished for her.

Cathy felt a sudden, all-encompassing wave of nausea and she felt panic rise in her throat as she feared she might faint again. She wanted to speak, but couldn't. The pain was too intense. Bob, *her* Bob, had been seeing someone else. It didn't feel real, yet she knew it was.

'Don't you still have questions for Derek?' Joanna-Rose asked, putting a hand on her shoulder again.

'I don't want to speak to Bob *now*, do I?' Cathy replied. 'What's the point?'

'I didn't mean for Bob's message, I meant to ask him more about the affair,' Joanna-Rose explained. 'You will have questions, of course. How long had it been going on? Were they in love? Was Bob leaving you for... her?' As she spoke, the look on Cathy's face made her wish she could reel the words back in. The horror of her last question hit Cathy like a train.

'Leaving me for her? How could he? Was he?'

'No, no, of course he wasn't. I'm sorry Cathy. I don't know why I said that. I told you I'm not good at this. Look, let's go back inside, it's getting dark.'

'He wouldn't,' Cathy went on, walking further out towards the shore with her shoulders hunched as though the world and all its woes rested firmly between them.

Joanna-Rose watched her go. She had never been very good at being anyone's friend, she knew that. But now she wanted to be. She wanted to help Cathy, and the right words just weren't coming. But she knew all too well the terrible, empty feeling of grief; the awareness that a person in your company doesn't know what to say when they see you're in pain. She recognised this, because she had experienced it too; as the receiver of life-changing, earth-shattering news. She loathed that thing she called the, 'How are you?' syndrome. *How am I? My life partner died, my mother is dead. Two people that have filled almost every memory I have of my life up until now. I'm all alone in the world. How do you think I am?'* Joanna-Rose could see this internal, angry dialogue lived in Cathy too, because she knew how it was to be in that place, yet she didn't know what to say now *she* was the outsider looking in.

'Look, please come back in,' she begged.

'I can't,' said Cathy, 'I can't bear that rat-faced little weasel's face.'

Joanna-Rose was surprised. 'I thought you liked him?'

'I do... well, I did,' Cathy replied. 'But that's before he dragged me all the way out to his show to rub my nose in Libby and Bob's affair. What a shit! As if I didn't have enough grief in my life to contend with.'

Joanna-Rose looked puzzled. 'How did he know though?' she asked.

'What do you mean?'

'How did he know who you were?'

Cathy sighed. 'I had to call first in order to use my ticket, remember? Derek Montrose is no more a psychic medium than Bob was a doting husband. I'm so bloody stupid, I trust everyone. Everyone!'

Starting to turn and walk away, Joanna-Rose paused and looked back. 'Do you want to know something, Cathy?' she said. 'No one was more mortified than me when I turned up at your house, drunk as a skunk, and proceeded to spill out my and Robert's sordid life story to you and Fleur – a couple of virtual strangers. In the sober light of day I wanted to sneak off back home and avoid you for the rest of my days. I don't speak to anyone, would you if you were me? Bloody death by sexual misadventure. Thank you, my dearest Robert.' She shook her fist in the air, as though he were in the sky above her. 'Nobody knows anything about me,' she went on. 'Talking to someone would make me open and vulnerable, and if there's one thing I hate it's being open and vulnerable.'

Cathy turned back and nodded her understanding.

'I haven't been anywhere, I haven't seen anyone. The only time I ventured outside was to visit my mother and now she's gone too,' Joanna-Rose went on, hugging her enormous bag to her chest as though it were a comfort blanket. 'I started to write my play two years ago, but all of a sudden I'm stuck; frozen in time. I haven't been able to write, or think, or even function. All I can concentrate on these days is pretend relationships in online forums, while consuming copious amounts of wine. It's like it was me that died. I'm beginning to see that for the first time in myself now, because I can see the same thing in you. Do you understand?'

'Yes, I think I do,' Cathy replied truthfully.

'And the hardest thing about it all is that, in all honesty, I did. I died.' She hung her head, looking so defeated and sad that Cathy began making her way back to comfort her, which she had to do over the huge bag that Joanna-Rose was hugging tightly. 'I'm dead,' she went on. 'And I'm just going to come right out and say this. If there's one thing I know about this horrible, desolate, godforsaken place I find myself at, it's that I don't care to watch another person die while they're still alive too.'

'Bob said, "See you on the other side",' Cathy said. 'He wrote it on a note with the tickets to Derek's show. I thought he wanted me to speak to him, to make contact through Derek. He always said, when he thought he was dying, that he would try to find me again if he did. Why would he have done that if he didn't love me?'

'But he was sleeping with Derek's wife!' Joanna-Rose reminded her. 'Don't you think there is an element of sickness in his sending you there? Perhaps Derek was hell bent on getting revenge at the show.'

'You think that was what he was going to do?'

'Not in the way you might think,' said Joanna-Rose. 'He's a slippery little weasel. Derek knew more about Bob than he could ever hope to find on anyone else's dead relative at that show. He could have gone out on the highest point of his career with a series of amazing and very accurate hits. He must have been rubbing his hands with glee when he learned you were going to be at his last show. And then Fleur ruined it all by nearly killing him with her tits.'

Despite the melancholy of the moment, the women burst out laughing.

'What an absolute snake,' Cathy said. 'And to think I saved his miserable, sneaky little life.' She turned away and started back across the road towards the church. 'I'm going to throw that little shit back in the sea myself!'

Watching her go, Joanna-Rose blinked and looked at the ground, thinking over everything Cathy had just said. After a moment, she smiled and headed after her. 'Atta girl,' she said.

'He said he needed to go to the little boy's room,' Fleur told Cathy, after she had come bursting back in to the church. 'I've been watching the doorway from here, so he couldn't run out the other way. It's fine. He's still in there.'

'He called it "the little boy's room"?' Joanna-Rose chuckled, as she ambled in behind Cathy.

'Where?' Cathy insisted. 'Where is the toilet? How could you let him go alone?'

'What did you want me to do, go with him? It's just there, opposite the door you came in,' Fleur said.

'Yes, yes I did want you to go with him!' Cathy replied. 'What if he's making his escape, right now?'

'To go where?' Fleur replied huffily. 'We're on an island, for heaven's sake. And the last boat off it left already.'

'Oh, I don't know,' Cathy shot back. 'To tell some local residents that we kidnapped him?'

'He's half drunk, no one will believe him.'

'He's fully drunk, if you ask me,' Joanna-Rose said.

'Are you serious? How long has he been gone?' Cathy turned to Joanna-Rose. 'We need to go check he's still there, and quick!'

'Look, I walked with him to the door and saw him go in,' Fleur told them. 'But he said it would be a big job, you know? I wasn't going to wait outside the door of the toilet. These things linger, you know.'

Cathy and Fleur looked at each other and screwed up their faces.

'So, I left him there and came back in here. And I've been watching from a nice, safe distance. He was fine! I saw him go in the lavvy and I haven't seen him come out yet. *And* he said he's happy to do you a proper reading,' Fleur said to Cathy, with a sympathetic smile. 'Ecstatic, once I told him I'd buy him some more grog. He'll do it, Cathy. That *is* still what you want after all this, isn't it?'

As she finished, a long, anxious wail came from behind, making each of them look round.

'Fox?' suggested Joanna-Rose.

'Werewolf?' said Fleur.

There was a second, weaker cry, coming from the direction of the toilet.

'Ooh,' said Fleur, screwing up her nose. 'It was a big job, I told you.'

'HOAH... ELP... ELP... ELP!'

'Hoahelp?' Cathy repeated, looking with a puzzled expression at the other two.

Okay,' Fleur said. 'It's a Gaelic werewolf.'

'That doesn't sound right,' Joanna-Rose said, turning towards the door and beckoning for them to follow her.

The woman raced to the toilet door, just as another loud, wall-shattering howl erupted from inside. Cathy put a hand on the door.

'Wait!' said Fleur, stopping them. She ran back in to the church hall, picked up a bible and, hugging it to her chest, ran to join them again. 'Okay, now go!'

Chapter Twenty-Eight

'If someone could just tell me how the hell…'

'Ooh, you can't say "hell" in here.'

Cathy was not amused by Fleur's joke; not remotely.

'If someone could just tell me how we are going to get the world's most famous medium out of this window frame, I would be very pleased right now,' she said sternly.

'Medium?' scoffed Fleur. 'I'd say from this angle he looks more of a large. Who knew such a little man could have such a sizeable backside?'

Joanna-Rose was staring open-mouthed at the old man's rear end, underpants exposed, as his legs waved madly in mid-air and he continued to howl in pain. Derek was not a large man; but the tiny, stained glass window he'd smashed before trying to squeeze out of it wasn't either.

'Should we grab his legs, perhaps?' she suggested at last.

'It's sticking in me! It's sticking in me!' Derek wailed.

'Maybe we should leave him there,' Fleur said. 'Let him have his fun.'

'The frame!' Derek cried again, louder this time. 'The frame is sticking in me. Is there blood? Am I bleeding?'

Cathy and Joanna-Rose took a leg each and began trying to tug him free.

'Oooh wahhhhhhh!' He screamed, his short, bare legs flailing so wildly that Fleur couldn't stop herself from chuckling – much to the annoyance of Cathy, who glared at her. After a minute of heaving and puffing, the old man was still stuck fast.

'It's no good,' said Cathy. 'He's not budging.'

'Try pushing instead of pulling,' Fleur suggested.

'Wahhh oohhhhh owwwwww!'

'Stop, stop. We're hurting him!' Cathy said, forgetting her earlier wish to kill him herself.

'Oh move over,' said Fleur, pushing the women aside and taking both of Derek's legs. 'Now, as I push, you breathe in, Derek,' she said. 'And if I can't get you out, you at least make a terrific, ornamental wheelbarrow.'

'Please, get me out,' pleaded Derek. 'I… I feel faint.'

'Breathe in,' Fleur repeated. 'I'm pushing now!'

'Arggghhhh ahhhhhh owwwww!'

'No, no! It's hurting him!' Cathy shouted, trying to stop her.

'Maybe he does have a little something stuck in him,' Joanna-Rose suggested. 'Perhaps we'd better not push him anymore.'

Cathy nodded. 'She's right. Let's have a good look all round where he's wedged in and see, shall we?'

The three women leaned in for a closer inspection of the frame around Derek's backside.

'Can't see any blood,' said Fleur.

'Nothing this side either,' Joanna-Rose confirmed.

'Let's all just lean against his butt and push!'

'Arrrrghhh nooooooooo, please stop! Please don't let her push me!' Derek screamed.

'No, Fleur, stop!' Cathy pulled her backwards. 'Go outside,' she ordered.

'Why?' Fleur said, looking irritated.

'To see if you can push him in from there.'

'No,' said Joanna-Rose. 'Let's you and I go outside and see if we can push him in. I think Derek's had quite enough of Fleur's freakish, ox-like strength for one day.'

'Freakish?' Fleur retorted. 'Thank you very much!'

Cathy nodded. 'You're right, we should look at the problem from outside. Stay here, Fleur, and if we pull as you push, we might get somewhere. But wait until I say it's okay, okay?'

'Okay,' Fleur agreed.

In a few moments Joanna-Rose and Cathy were behind the church, looking at a very red-faced and distressed Derek.

'Can you hear me?' Fleur heard Cathy call.

'Yes!'

'We can't see any injury out here either,' Cathy told her. 'He's just stuck fast.'

'I... I think I can feel something in the top of my thigh.' Derek snivelled.

'You're in shock, that's all,' Fleur heard Cathy tell him. 'We're going to get you out. Hold on.' 'Fleur!' she shouted again. 'We're going to pull his arms this side and I want you to push his behind at the same time.'

Fleur's eyes dropped unwillingly to Derek's backside. 'Can't I just push his legs?' she called back.

'Whatever!' Cathy said under her breath, before calling out, 'We're going after three. Are you ready?'

Fleur stood behind Derek and took the weight of his legs again. 'Ready!' she shouted.

'One... two....' said Cathy.

'Three!' Fleur cried out, pushing with all her might.

'Arghhhhh ahhhh ohhh woahhhhhhhhhhhh!'

'Stop, stop!' Fleur heard Joanna-Rose and Cathy shout at the same time. 'We weren't ready!' Cathy added.

'Ah, err... sorry!'

'Calm down, Derek. I told you, we're going to get you out,' Fleur heard Cathy say amongst a torrent of pathetic groans and whimpers from the old man.

'You have to get somebody,' Derek cried at last. 'Please, just get somebody.'

'Just one more push,' Cathy told him. 'One more. That's all.'

'Then you'll get somebody?'

'Okay... yes, we'll get somebody,' Cathy replied. 'Are you ready, Fleur?' she shouted out. 'This time, wait till *I* say three!'

'Okay. Ready!'

After fifteen minutes of fruitless efforts, the women sat on the grass verge outside the toilet window, each deep in thought.

'We can't leave him dangling like that. Won't the blood rush... I don't know; somewhere?' Cathy asked.

Fleur shuddered. 'I dread to think,' she said quietly to herself.

'Please get help. Please!'

Fleur leaned forward to give Derek's bald head a reassuring pat. 'Don't you worry, old fella. I'm thinking.'

'You know, we can't get anyone,' Joanna-Rose said to the other two women. 'He'll have us arrested.'

Derek raised his eyes to her and shook his head. 'I won't tell anyone anything, I swear!' he said. 'Just please get me out. I feel dizzy and my legs hurt.'

Fleur thought about Derek's legs, still dangling mid-air inside the church, his feet not quite touching the floor. 'I'll go find a couple of chairs and put them under him,' she said at last.

She stood up and ran up the stairs into the Laird's Loft above the church, before returning moments later with a wooden, hard-backed chair.

'I found one,' she told the women. 'Are you coming back inside?'

Cathy and Joanna-Rose followed Fleur back in to the toilet and watched her place the chair with its back under Derek's legs for support. 'How's that? Better?'

'Well, it's a little bit hard,' Derek whimpered. 'Have you got any cushions?'

Fleur looked to Cathy, who shrugged.

'There might be some on the congregation benches,' Joanna-Rose suggested.

Fleur left the room again, returning moments later carrying a giant bible.

'There were no cushions?' Joanna-Rose asked her.

'Yes, there were cushions,' Fleur said, between huffs and puffs from the strain of the book's weight. 'But I found this.'

'What use is that?' Cathy asked, looking perplexed. 'Are we going to pray for him?'

'I thought we could hit him with it,' Fleur replied seriously. 'You know, knock him out.'

Cathy was horror struck. 'That's ridiculous! Isn't it?' she asked, looking to Joanna-Rose for affirmation, but finding none.

'Might work,' she agreed, to Cathy's astonishment.

'What's that you're all talking about?' Derek cried, panic rising in his voice again. 'Did I hear the word "hit"? Are you going to hit me with something? What is it? Don't you ridiculous, ill-informed people have any brains? Typical women. Bloody typical.'

Fleur kicked away the chair, squared up level with Derek's backside, and raised the bible for a strike.

'No, no!' Cathy cried out, making a grab for the book to try and stop her. 'You can't -'

'Owwwwwww! My teethsth! My teethsth are on the grassth!'

Chapter Twenty-Nine

'Try not to bite my finger this time,' said Fleur, screwing up her face as she made a second attempt to help Derek push his dentures back in. This time, they slotted in with a 'schlup'.

The three women sat on the grass bank, eating crisps and all looking perplexed.

'Want a crisp, Derek?' asked Fleur, standing to force one in his mouth anyway.

'So, while we're all here with nowhere to go, Derek,' Joanna-Rose said at last. 'Tell us more about Libby and Bob.'

'Hmph frumph shog,' he replied.

'I'm sorry? I don't speak Flemish,' Fleur said, shoving another crisp into his mouth while he was still chomping on the first three.

'Stop that, Fleur,' Cathy snapped. 'Can't you see he's got a mouthful already?'

'Well, he said he was still hungry,' she retorted. 'I'm just taking care of him, like the good, little, ill-informed and senseless woman I am.'

Derek spat the crisps out on to the grass. 'You,' he raged. 'Are the three dumbest, craziest, most silly creatures I have ever laid eyes on. And you?' He looked at Cathy. 'No wonder your husband was cheating!'

'Not sobered up yet, I see?' Fleur said, as Cathy's bottom lip began to tremble again.

'And to think I was feeling sorry for you when I found you trying to drown yourself,' Cathy said quietly. 'Well, not anymore. You can stay there all night.'

'So that's what happened,' said Fleur, sitting down on the grass bank beside the other two women. 'And there was me thinking you'd been out jogging in your underpants.'

'Hah, jogging.' Derek sneered. 'Well, you can leave me here if you like, but I may as well tell you now I'm expected at the Prime Minister's house tomorrow to do a private reading for his wife.'

'So *that's* what that cameraman meant,' Cathy said. 'The press were expecting you.'

Not for the first time since he had been stuck, the blood drained from Derek's face. 'The press were waiting for me?' he said, looking astonished.

'Wait a minute,' Fleur cut in. 'This morning you were trying to kill yourself, yet now you're anxious to attend an appointment you made for tomorrow?'

'I didn't say I was anxious, I just meant I'll be missed if I don't turn up.'

'And, while we're on the subject, why do you suddenly care about being stuck if you were so keen to die eight hours ago?'

'Well... it's uncomfortable,' Derek stammered, slapping the wall with both hands as he tried to wriggle himself free again.

'So is drowning, I should imagine.'

'If only I didn't have this damn dress on,' he complained, glaring at Cathy. 'While you were saving me from drowning, you could have picked up my bloody suitcase!' He stopped wriggling.

Fleur's mouth fell open. 'Suitcase?' she said, looking at Cathy.

'Yes, I remember,' Cathy replied with a smile. 'How could I forget? There was a leopard print suitcase, right beside his discarded clothes, which I couldn't carry as well as him. I wasn't planning to take him away with us, was I?'

'A suitcase, eh?' said Joanna-Rose, her eyes fixed on Derek. 'Interesting item to take along to your suicide.'

'It wasn't mine,' Derek said quickly. 'It was Libby's. I left her some things - mementos.'

'And how about now, Derek,' Fleur asked him. 'Still want to die, do you?'

He breathed heavily, in then out, wincing in pain as his girth expanded. 'Let's just say I've, well, seen the light,' he said at last, looking at Cathy.

'That's what happens when you stick your head out of a window,' Fleur quipped.

To everyone's astonishment and amusement, Derek blew a long, loud raspberry at her.

'Need the toilet, Derek?' she asked, without smiling.

'I think it's time we all tried to get some sleep,' Cathy said. 'We have to be up very, very early tomorrow.'

'You're not going to leave me here like this are you?' Derek pleaded, his tone turning from anger to pathetic. 'What if I do need the toilet?' he sobbed. 'What then?'

'Well, your bottom half *is* in the right room at least,' said Fleur.

Cathy looked uncertainly from Fleur to Joanna-Rose. Neither spoke. 'I don't think we have any choice but to leave you,' she said finally. 'At least for tonight. There isn't anything else we can do.'

'Unless you want some more salt and vinegar?' Fleur asked, holding her crisp packet out to him.

'No, please don't leave me here,' Derek pleaded again.

Fleur shrugged and stuck her hand in the crisp packet to grab some, as the three women turned and began walking away.

'My stomach hurts, my legs hurt and I'm certain there is something cutting into my groin,' Derek barked after them, changing tone again faster than a nudist doing cartwheels on the pitch at a World Cup final. 'Now you can add assault and battery to your already extensive list of police charges.'

Fleur turned on her heels and strode back up to Derek. Leaning in, she rubbed his bald head with her salt-covered hand, the way you might ruffle a cheeky schoolboy's hair, and gave him a falsely sympathetic smile. 'Now, Derek,' she said. 'It was *you* that went and got yourself stuck in that window, so you will have to deal with it. I bid you, Goodnight.'

'*Man, I Feel Like a Woman*!'

Fleur snorted and began rummaging urgently through her jacket pocket for her phone to switch off the alarm. Finding it, she swiped a finger across the screen to silence Shania Twain's voice, which echoed around the church walls for what seemed like an age afterwards. She raised her head and shone the light from her phone over to find Cathy and Joanna-Rose still sound asleep in opposite pews.

Squinting to look at the time, which said 6am, she noticed a text notification on the bottom of the screen and sat up.

'Who the he -' she began, before remembering where she was. She gave a respectful nod to the cross on the wall and said, 'Sorry,' before looking back at the phone. She pulled it closer to her face, not quite believing the name next to the text notification. It was from Mandy. Pushing her blanket off her legs, she stood up and raced outside.

Chapter Thirty

Joanna-Rose had stopped travelling after Robert died, and even when they had ventured away, it was never anywhere further than the southern coasts of England. She had been abroad with her mother once; a modelling assignment she had the rare joy of being allowed to accompany her to in Madrid, but she had little memory of the experience. The rest of the world remained an enigma, full of places she would visit in books and on television, then attempt to write about them as though she was a native. In truth, she hadn't even been to Scotland before now. And this, she thought, as she stood outside Jura Parish Church witnessing the first hint of fierce, eye-blinding gold tease itself out over the horizon to become the most incredible sunrise she'd ever seen, this was a view to awaken the story-teller within.

She noticed a stag watching her from the water's edge, further down the beach and stayed still, not wishing to startle it. Yet after only regarding her for a moment, it bowed its head and continued sniffing the ground, disinterested. Amazed, she continued to watch him, forgetting the rest of the world as though she and the stag were the only living creatures in it.

Joanna-Rose knew beyond a shadow of a doubt she could write now. Not begin again or carry on from where she left off; *really* write. For the first time in her entire adult life she was struck by a new knowledge: she had never been able to do it before. All the plays, even the notoriety one or two had brought her, it was all nothing compared to what she had been capable of. Her written words had been shallow up till now, her work riddled with false representation. She hadn't seen enough sunrises, or smelled enough fresh, sea air to write about any of it. She hadn't trodden on distant soil, learned new languages and dined with strangers. Or kidnapped a psychic medium...

'Have you checked on Derek?' Cathy asked, appearing from the church doorway. 'Wow,' she exclaimed, as she reached her side. 'Look at that sunrise!'

'You didn't pop your head in the loo on the way out?' Joanna-Rose asked.

'No. You?'

'No. I thought perhaps Fleur was with him.'

The pair turned away ruefully, both knowing that watching the sunrise over the Sound of Islay was far preferable to what sights might be awaiting them inside.

'He was very drunk last night,' Cathy said as she opened the toilet door and peered inside.

'Help me,' Derek was saying weakly. His legs were kicking wildly about, almost knocking over the chair.

Joanna-Rose looked at Cathy. 'Perhaps we better go and look outside,' she said.

'God, I hope he hasn't been sick after all that booze,' said Cathy.

As the women rounded the corner, a deer bounded past, startling them.

'It's licking my head,' Derek sobbed, his eyes screwed shut.

Cathy stared, open-mouthed at him, before turning to look for the deer, which had gone.

'You mean -' Joanna-Rose began.

'The deer!' Derek sniffed, looking exhausted and pale, but sober. 'It's licking my head,' he repeated.

'Derek, there's nothing there. It's gone,' Cathy told him.

'Oh.' He stopped, opening his eyes to look about him. 'It was the salt on my head, from the crisps. I've been tickled to death! She did it on purpose, her!'

'What's he on about?' Fleur said, appearing from behind as Derek nodded in her direction.

'I started to cry,' Derek went on. The woman all turned back to him, looking astonished. 'Well,' he said with an indignant tone. 'I thought the thing was going to eat me or something. Then it started licking my face! I've been a deer's breakfast all morning! Please, please, you've got to get me out of here. I have someone expecting me.'

'Now I'm intrigued,' Fleur said. 'Go on, tell us. Who is it?'

'I'm not at liberty to sa -'

Fleur walked up to him and began lifting her top. 'Tell us, or I'm going to give you another coronary,' she said.

'The Prime Minister,' he barked. 'It's the Prime Minister!'

'Ooh, that could well be right,' Cathy said. 'Bob once told me the Prime Minister's wife has family with an estate over here.' As she spoke, her face darkened. She turned to the other two women. 'We've kidnapped a world famous psychic medium, who is expected today by the Prime Minister!'

'You couldn't write it,' Fleur said.

'I could,' said Joanna-Rose, without a hint of irony.

'Okay, this fête thing begins at midday,' Cathy reminded them, clapping her hands. 'And people are going to be on their way here to set everything up. We have to think. How are we going to get Derek out of that window?'

'I've already thought of that,' Fleur said, standing up straight and producing a saw from behind her back. 'I've been on a scavenger hunt,' she told the other two, startled women. 'We can cut away the frame.'

'He's pretty wedged in there,' Joanna-Rose said. 'I think perhaps we might be in danger of doing more harm than good.'

Fleur produced a sledgehammer from her coat pocket. 'Chip away at the wall then?' she suggested.

'Have you seen how thick these walls are?' replied Cathy. 'And solid concrete too. We couldn't do it. And there's no time for all of this. No, I think it's time to make a run for it.'

Derek gasped. 'No,' he pleaded. 'I don't want you to leave me, Cathy. There is something I have to tell you. Bob does have a message for you. He came to me last night –'

'Stop it,' Joanna-Rose snapped at him. 'We all know what a fraud you are now.'

Derek continued to stare at Cathy with pleading eyes. 'We were both wronged,' he told her, sounding much more reasonable than before. 'I'm not a fraud, I swear it. Please give me a chance to make it up to you. I have a message for you. That's why you came to find me, right?'

Cathy hesitated.

'He loved you, Cathy,' Derek went on. 'Only you. Bob has told me himself.'

'We'll call someone, I promise,' Fleur said quickly. She turned to the other women. 'We have to go, now.'

'But, we can't give up now we've come so far,' said Cathy, looking defeated and sad. 'I may as well know. Perhaps he does have a message from Bob.'

'But you have to get me out of this window, before I do any reading,' Derek said. 'Or, sure as I'm wearing a minister's robe, you'll all be arrested when the real minister arrives.'

'Well, if you're sure, Cathy, I do have a third idea,' Fleur said, producing a carrier bag out of her other jacket pocket.

'What?' Joanna-Rose and Cathy replied together.

'Butter,' she said, taking two packs out of the bag.

The women and Derek stared at her. There was a brief silence.

'We cut off his dress, and cover him in butter,' she explained.

'Don't be -' Cathy began.

The three women looked at Derek, all with thoughtful expressions.

'Oh no, please,' Derek begged. 'Do you have to? Look, I have to be where I'm expected or your cat is well and truly out of the bag. I'm supposed to be at Viscount Fraser's estate for an audience with the PM's wife. They'll be looking for me!'

'Can we come?' asked Fleur, without a hint of irony.

'You know, I'm not a swearing man,' came the quick, sharp reply. 'But you lunatic women can fu -'

'Okay, okay,' Cathy exclaimed. 'Let's cut the dress off.'

Chapter Thirty-One

Minister MacFarlane watched his wife place four glasses from the sink on to the draining board, one after another. Breakfast was over; it was time to face a new day – and not just a run-of-the-mill day at that.

'Do you suppose I've remembered everything, Jeanie?' he asked, the concern on his lined face, evidence of years of worry and self-imposed perfectionism, apparent.

Jeanie grabbed a tea towel, dried her hands and picked up the clipboard that lay on top of their glossy, American-style fridge.

'Aha,' she said, nodding as she read the detailed reference points her husband had written down. 'Aha. Done that, did that. Yes, aha. Yep,' she concluded, getting to the last point in the list. 'I think we covered it all. It'll be fine, Douglas, don't fret.'

The back door opened and a large, bearded man entered the kitchen, bringing with him the fresh scent of horse manure.

'Have you heard of knocking, Michael?' Minister MacFarlane said, looking both disgusted and unamused.

The young man beamed a near toothless smile, but looked very embarrassed. 'I... err... sorry, Minister.' He nodded to Jeanie. 'So sorry, Mrs MacFarlane. I just came tae... err... tell ye that the ferry's in.'

'Ah good,' the Minister replied, folding his newspaper before getting to his feet. 'I take it you're all loaded up with the tables?'

Michael nodded, shuffling awkwardly from one foot to the other. 'Aye.'

'Okay, well, we'll get going down to the church then, Jeanie, to start setting up. I trust you'll join us when you can?'

There was an almighty thud, followed by the clattering of busy footsteps and some excited screams from upstairs, making them all look up at the ceiling.

'Are the bairns no in school the day?' Michael said to Jeanie.

'Nobody's in today, Michael,' Jeanie reminded him. 'It's for wee Skye, so all her friends from the school have been given a day off.'

'Oh, isn't that kind of Mrs Henry?' Michael replied, referring to the headmistress of the school. 'Skye's mum will be pleased.'

'Yes, indeed she will,' Jeanie said, nodding and smiling at him, before turning back to her husband. 'I'll get the twins into their Sunday best, call Mrs Nesbit and the others and we'll follow you over with the cakes and sandwiches. Give us half an hour or so, okay?'

'It's a fine day for it today, Michael,' Minister MacFarlane said as they drove the van the short distance from the harbour to the church.

Eyes fixed ahead on the road, Michael replied, 'It is that.'

'The whole community will be turning out,' the Minister went on. 'Even Viscount Fraser and, you never know, his very famous son-in-law might make a little unannounced, hush-hush appearance too, but you can never be sure, of course. Everyone wants to offer their support. I think we will be sending wee Skye to Disneyland.'

'Have you asked her what other things she wants most in the world?'

'While Skye was ill in hospital, her mum couldn't work. And with her man passing away the summer before…' Minister MacFarlane paused. 'Well, things were tight. Then, the week of wee Skye's leukaemia diagnosis, a man came to take their TV away.'

Michael's chest expanded as he took a deep and deliberate breath in. 'They repossessed her TV? That's terrible.'

'Yes, it is.'

Michael sighed. 'So she asked for a new TV?'

No,' the Minister replied. 'She's a sunny, funny little angel is our Skye, in spite of everything she's been through. None of her requests were material. Even the Disney trip was her mum's idea.'

'So what was it she wanted?'

'She wants to have the man that took their telly put into stocks so she, her friends and her mum can throw tomatoes at him. Can you believe it?' He shook his head and chuckled. 'I had to confess I couldn't arrange that one.'

Michael grinned. 'Is that all she wanted?'

The Minister nodded. 'That's all. And Michael, I'll let you into a wee secret. Jeanie and I gave her mum a new TV ourselves.'

'Oh that's good. And very kind of you and Mrs MacFarlane.'

'It was the very least we could do. Turning up with such a simple thing as a new TV was what young people of today would call, a "no brainer".'

As the van pulled up outside the church, Minister MacFarlane turned to Michael and, placing a hand on his arm, said, 'This afternoon will be a celebration as well as a fundraiser; to thank God for little Skye's recovery.'

'Aye,' said Michael, patting the Minister's arm in a friendly return. 'This will be the best fête yet, whether any VIP's make an appearance or not.'

'Have you got anything for chafing?'

The woman leaned on the counter, observing Cathy through concerned, brown eyes while tapping her bright, red lipstick-covered lips with her forefinger in contemplation. The badge on her very ample chest read, 'Helen Rooney, Pharmacist'.

'Hmmm,' she said. 'What kind of chafing?'

'How many kinds of chafing are there?' Cathy asked.

The pharmacist cocked her head to the side and grinned, revealing lipstick-stained teeth. 'You can tell me anything you know,' she said, her voice lowered and husky. 'I've heard it all in this place.'

Cathy glanced around the empty store and blinked in disbelief. 'Really?' she said.

Helen nodded. 'I only come get to come across in my wee van once a week, but that's all I need to get the good stuff, if you know what I mean. People know they won't be walking by me on here all week, so they tell me all their secrets. Just give me a minute though,' she said, reaching under the counter and coming back up with a mobile phone which she placed on the counter between them. 'I like to record things,' she explained, before biting her lower lip and giving her a wink. 'For research, you know?'

'Well... I...'

The woman let out a loud, melodious giggle. 'Ahm pulling your leg,' she laughed, nudging Cathy's shoulder very hard. She turned to grab some ointment from the shelf and handed it to her, before leaning in to speak more softly. 'But seriously, the chafing thing? It's always best to get something for – ahem – before the horse has bolted too, you know.'

'No,' Cathy said, shaking her head. 'I think this will do.'

The pharmacist turned to a shelf behind her and pointed to the lubricants. Thinking of Derek's current predicament, Cathy nodded. 'Yes, that's it!' she said, her face brightening. 'That's what we need! I'll take some of that too!'

Helen looked eager. 'We?'

'Yes, I'll take four bottles,' Cathy replied, before realising how all this was sounding. 'It's not what you think,' she added. 'It's for me and my two women friends. We need to help a very old man... and I thought we were going to have to get firemen...' She trailed off, noticing the pharmacist's eyes were widening.

'Wow,' said Helen. 'And I thought all those spandex wearing men in the fell race brought all the best action to Jura. How long are you here for?'

Chapter Thirty-Two

'Somebody will be here at any moment, you know. We have got to make a decision and we've got to make it now.'

Joanna-Rose was looking at Derek's limp, naked legs as they rested on some cushions on the chair. Outside, his sleeping head was resting on a chair with cushions also. In the history of catastrophes in her life, this was one of the greats. Yet, despite foreboding in her stomach, her fingers itched to grab her notebook. Maybe it was the fresh, sea air, maybe the company of people other than Isaac for the first time in years, but she felt the need to write. How ironic that it was the one thing she didn't have time for at this point.

They had a problem: trying to work out what kind of stretch they would each get for kidnapping.

'We could leave him here and scarper,' Fleur suggested, with a grim look that told Joanna-Rose she was serious.

'And then what? Go into hiding?'

Fleur thought for a second, before piping up, 'There's a hole in the floor at my house. We could live there?'

'I thought you were having that fixed?'

'Ooh yes, you're probably right,' replied Fleur.

'Probably?' Joanna-Rose asked, looking stunned. 'How long does it take to fix a floor?'

Fleur shifted in her seat, looking uncomfortable. 'There was all kinds of structural damage to attend to. It's a very old house.'

'Anyway,' Joanna-Rose continued, her eyes fixed on Derek's legs. 'Going on the run is not an option. They'd find us eventually.'

'Maybe we could explain that we just wanted to get the end of our reading? Cathy's tickets were worth two hundred pounds to paying guests after all. We just won't tell them she didn't buy them. They're bound to take pity on her situation. She's flat broke'

Joanna-Rose raised her eyebrows. 'She is?'

'Yes,' Fleur told her earnestly. 'It's lucky I moved in to help her pay the mortgage. They're threatening to repossess her house and you should see the size of her gas and electricity bills, not to mention the pile of solicitor's letters she has and won't open. I don't think she's paid anything in months.'

'How do you know all this?' asked Joanna-Rose. 'Do you read her mail or something?'

Fleur shrugged and gave Joanna-Rose a coy look. 'Yes,' she said at last.

'I have no idea how or why she puts up with you.'

'I told you,' Fleur said. 'I help her pay the bills.'

Derek grunted and both women turned to look at his legs again. Most of the minister's gown he'd been wearing lay in shreds on the floor, with some remnants still around his middle.

'I think he's waking up. Run away now?' said Fleur.

Joanna-Rose stood up and walked to the window. 'Hello, Derek, can you hear me?'

She was rewarded with a feeble, 'Yes.'

'He's exhausted,' Joanna-Rose whispered to Fleur. 'I think it's time to try pulling him out again. I don't know where Cathy's gone with the ointment, but time is running out and both of us know it won't help him that much anyway. We're just going to have to hurt him a bit.'

Fleur nodded. 'Cathy means well,' she said. 'But you're right. The ointment will only help after we've dragged his skinny backside out.' She shouted to Derek, 'We're going to have another go at pulling you out, okay? Perhaps you've lost some water weight since last night!'

As Derek let out a feeble okay, Joanna-Rose cast her an 'Are you kidding me?' look. Fleur shrugged. 'It's worth a try,' she said. 'I always wake up with a flatter belly in the morning, don't you?'

The two women grasped his legs again and pulled with all their might. Derek let out another wail.

'Let's go out and try the other side,' suggested Fleur.

As the women disappeared behind the church, Michael's van pulled up at the front door of the church.

'We've got three hours before everyone starts arriving,' Minister MacFarlane said, as Michael pulled on the handbrake and turned off the ignition.

'Okay,' he replied. 'We'll just unload these tables and chairs the now, and I can go back for the rest.'

'Perhaps just put all of it over by the playground on the grass,' he said, pointing to the far right of the building. 'Everything's very light. I can arrange it all while you go back for the rest.'

With the van unloaded and Michael off up the road again to the harbour for the supplies, Minister MacFarlane stood with his hands on his hips, looking at the swings and slides where little Skye had often played, before raising his eyes to the sunlit sky. 'Well, you gifted us a beautiful day for it, thank you Lord,' he said.

He paused. Was that a squeal coming from the church? He turned around. There it was again. Walking back towards the door he shouted out, 'Hello? Is somebody there?'

Silence.

He continued to the door and went inside.

'Look, we've got to get you out and now! People will be coming,' Fleur snapped.

'But it hurts and I'm so, so tired,' Derek complained. 'Please, get help. I think they're going to have to cut me out of here.'

'No, you've definitely moved a bit,' said Joanna-Rose. 'Fleur's right. A couple more pulls and I think we're going to have you out. Look, I can see another line on the pattern of your vest and I definitely couldn't before we started. You're coming free.'

'Let's take it off him,' said Fleur.

'NOOOOO!' Derek's extra loud protest startled them both.

'I mean, you're not taking any more of my clothes off,' he said more calmly.

Joanna-Rose bent down to look beneath him and tugged at the vest.

'You know, it's almost out,' she said. 'Perhaps if we just pull the hem out of the...?' She stopped and examined it more carefully. 'What is that?'

'What?' said Fleur and Derek together.

Joanna-Rose felt the vest and smock material around Derek's middle and gave him a sharp look. 'What on earth?'

'It... it's okay,' Derek stammered. 'Just leave me here. I'll be fine. You get away while you can. I... I won't tell a soul what happened.'

Joanna-Rose gave a second, firmer tug on the material and as it broke free, she felt underneath.

'There's something hard. Leather-like,' she said.

'Oh God, don't touch that thing,' said Fleur, looking repulsed.

'No, Fleur, look under here. Help me pull it out.'

'Are you ill?' Fleur asked her.

'Just LOOK!' Joanna-Rose shouted. 'There's something under him.'

'I think I hear someone coming,' Derek said, desperate to distract them.

Fleur leaned in to where Joanna-Rose was feeling for a closer inspection.

'It's a bloody book,' she cried out. 'No wonder you're stuck. There's a ruddy great book wedging you in!'

They both began to try pulling it out from under him.

'It's no use,' said Joanna-Rose at last. 'It's stuck fast.'

Fleur sat back on her calves and eyed Derek. 'What were you trying to nick?' she demanded.

'I... I wasn't...' he began.

'Don't give me anymore of your bull shit,' she snapped. 'What were you taking from the church?'

'Nothing.'

'TELL ME!'

'It's my diary!' he yelled.

'Cathy pulled you from the sea yesterday, and there was no diary in amongst your things! What have you got under you?'

The old man gave a whimper, but didn't reply.

'Derek,' Fleur said, leaning in so that they were nose to nose. 'Tell me what you were thieving from these people. And it better not be any of the historic albums from the Laird's Loft. What were you planning to do, sell them to pay your tax bill?'

Joanna-Rose gave a gasp. 'Oh no, that's terrible!'

'It's not the photographs!' cried Derek. 'It's the... it's the... oh, heavens...'

'Spit it out,' Fleur insisted.

'It's the book of condolences,' he spat at last, looking for all the world like he might burst into tears.

'The book of... Why would you take that?' Fleur asked him, disappointed to learn it was something less serious than the theft of Jura's historic photos.

'Oh, wait a minute. This is good, this is *very* good,' Joanna-Rose said, straightening up.

Fleur let go of the book and stood up too. 'It is?'

'Yes it is,' Joanna-Rose replied, turning to give the old man a satisfied grin. 'Isn't it, Derek?' She opened her bag, took out her mobile phone and pointed it at Derek. 'Smile for the camera!'

'My grandmother died here,' he replied, as she filmed his pathetic excuses. 'It's an old one I just wanted as a keepsake. They aren't using it anymore and I don't have any memories.'

'Don't even try to explain this one away,' Joanna-Rose said.

'Some of my family signed this book,' he continued to explain.

Fleur put both hands on her hips and glared at him. 'So you thought you'd just take it?' she said. 'You really are a rotten, selfish git, aren't you?'

'No, no, Fleur,' said Joanna-Rose. 'That's not what this is about.'

'...and other people on Jura will have long passed family in there too. Didn't you think how they might feel about losing the book?' Fleur continued.

'Catch up, Fleur!' Joanna-Rose snapped, stopping her in her tracks. 'He doesn't have any grandmother in that book.'

'He doesn't?'

'Think about it, Fleur,' said Joanna-Rose. 'What would a so-called psychic medium want with a book of condolences?'

A door slammed somewhere inside the church, making all three of them fall silent. Fleur looked at Joanna-Rose, with panic in her eyes.

'Cathy?' she whispered.

Minister MacFarlane stared open-mouthed at the pair of naked-except-for-socks, elderly legs dangling from the bathroom window.

'What in the name of…?'

Chapter Thirty-Three

'I've got lubricants!' Cathy called triumphantly as she burst into the toilet, to find a startled Minister MacFarlane gazing at her in disbelief. She hid the bottles behind her back in shame.

'On this... of all days,' he stammered. 'Am I being robbed?'

Cathy blushed, looking from him to Derek, whose legs were kicking away in mid-air as the chair had been pulled to the side. She knew she needed that thing – oh what was it? – words. But she couldn't find any.

'Well? Am I?' the minister asked again.

'No. I mean... no,' Cathy replied, shaking her head and trying to think whether robbery or kidnapping carried the longest jail sentence. 'No,' she said again, her choice made.

'Then would you care to tell me what is going on?' the minister asked, before pointing to Derek's flailing legs. 'And who this man is?'

'That man?' Cathy answered, pointing to Derek's legs herself as if she had just noticed them. 'That is, erm, Derek.' She was thinking hard, trying to fast track her brain to her next sentence – the vital explanation for everything. 'Derek Montrose,' she finished.

'Who?'

'Derek Montrose,' she repeated, feeling her cheeks glow poker hot.

'*The* Derek Montrose?' he asked, looking back at the naked legs, uncertainly.

Cathy nodded.

'Well, should we pull him out?'

'We can't,' she admitted. 'He's stuck. All three of us have tried.'

Minister MacFarlane took a step back and looked unsure. 'There are three of you?' he said, craning his neck to see over her head to the doorway beyond.

'Yes,' she said. 'But we're not robbers, I promise you. We're just three... well... women.'

Minister MacFarlane blinked, looked at Cathy, then Derek's legs, then the floor. 'I... I don't understand,' was all he could say.

'There's a perfectly reasonable explanation for all of this, I assure you,' Cathy continued, still unsure of what that explanation would be. She needed Fleur. If there was one thing she had gathered about Fleur in the short time they'd known each other was that she could talk her way out of anything. Even a famous-man-stuck-in-a-church-toilet-window situation.

Minister MacFarlane blew out his cheeks and shook his head in disbelief. 'Good,' he said, finally. 'Because I can't wait to hear it.'

'I can hear two voices. One is Cathy's for certain.'

Fleur had her ear pressed up against the tiniest of gaps under Derek's right arm and was straining to hear through the window as she continued to edge the book out from under his jumper, pulling first on one side and then the other.

'Get away from me,' he hissed.

'Shhhh!' she said, trying to lean in closer. 'Yes, there is another voice. A man's.'

'It must be the minister,' said Joanna-Rose. 'Is that thing coming out, Fleur?'

'Yes, we'll get him out eventually,' she replied.

'I meant the book.'

Fleur tugged harder at the leather-bound journal. 'Almost there,' she said.

Joanna-Rose reached in to help and together they eased the book out, corner by corner, until finally it slipped out on to the grass. Derek let out an enormous sigh of relief.

'I can breathe,' he said. 'At last, I can breathe! And...' He pressed on the wall under him with his hands and jiggled his body. 'I think I can get out.'

'Stay right there,' Joanna-Rose barked.

Derek stopped stock still.

'Okay,' she said. 'It's time for us to get a very quick story sorted out.' She reached down to pick up the book and waved it before Derek's face. 'Now,' she told him. 'You are going to listen to me and do exactly as I tell you.'

'Why?' Fleur asked. 'What is it with the book?'

Joanna-Rose turned to her and smiled. 'What is in the book, Fleur?'

Fleur looked blank. 'Condolences?' she said.

'Names and dates,' Joanna-Rose told her. 'Details of a whole lot of people on this island that have passed away, not to mention those they have left behind, *and* some of their memories.'

'So?'

'What do you suppose a fake psychic medium looking to earn a few quid from the gentry over here would do with all that information?'

Fleur's eyes widened. 'Like, the Prime Minister?' she said.

'Now you're on the right track,' Joanna-Rose told her with a nod.

Fleur clapped her hands with glee. 'You slippery, old sod!' she told Derek, slapping him on the head. 'Just think,' she went on, with a wide, triumphant grin. 'If you weren't such an underhand, sneaky so-and-so who'd rather shove a book up your shirt than throw it out a window before you, you'd be home and free by now. That is priceless!' She looked at Joanna-Rose, who was smiling too, and said, 'Do you think that journalist is still on the island?'

'You see, the thing is, Minister,' Cathy said, nervous tension making her fiddle with the bottles still hidden behind her back. 'We kind of *took* Mr Montrose. Not on purpose, you understand. Well, I did it to be honest, and my friends were just accidentally pulled along, you see?'

Minister MacFarlane didn't see.

'Can you hear me in there?' Derek called out through the window frame. 'Hello?'

The minister's eyes darted up at the ceiling.

'I think Derek's shouting to us,' Cathy said, pointing to the old man's legs, as the minister looked at her again. She wanted to add, 'in case you thought it was God,' but thought better of it.

'Hello?' They heard Derek shout again, clearer this time.

Minister MacFarlane walked towards the window.

'Can you please pull me back in?' Derek shouted out.

As the minister grabbed his legs, Cathy dropped the bottles of lubricant on the ground behind the open door, hoping God would forgive her, before racing to help. Although she had expected the struggle to get them nowhere, she gasped in surprise as Derek tumbled to the floor, free after a single effort from them both. She stared at the minister, her face agog.

'Divine intervention,' she blurted out, feeling foolish as soon as she'd said it.

Derek picked himself up and stood before them, pulling his vest down to cover his modesty. He held a hand out for the minister to shake it, which, despite his obvious confusion, he did.

'You... *are*... Derek Montrose,' Minister MacFarlane stammered.

'We've been waiting for you, Minister,' Derek breezed, as though he wasn't standing there in his vest, pants and socks.

'You have?' said the minister.

'You have?' added Cathy, looking as surprised as the minister.

'Ahh, there you are Minister,' Fleur said, poking her head through the space where the window had once been. 'I'm so sorry about the glass, but Derek here has promised to replace it.'

'I have?' he said. Fleur shot him a sharp look. 'I... have,' he agreed with a nod.

'Well, that is fine, thank you very much,' the minister replied. 'But if someone could be kind enough to tell me what on earth happened here, I'd be most grateful.'

'Oh, it's a fine story,' Fleur replied. 'Just give me and Derek's biographer Joanna-Rose out here a minute to come round there and we'll explain everything.'

Chapter Thirty-Four

'I can't believe you've come,' Minister MacFarlane gushed, shaking Derek's hand for the third time. 'Karen will be delighted!'

'Karen?' said Joanna-Rose.

'Skye's mum,' the minister explained. He turned back to Derek. 'This is so very, very kind of you. I mean, we asked your people, but they said you weren't available. Of course, I did hear on the news that you'd retired.'

'Ahh, yes,' Derek replied. 'My people being my assistant, Fleur here.' He indicated to her as she stood behind the minister. She glowered back at him. 'She can be a little, shall we say, remiss, at times.'

'Well, he didn't have a window until now,' she commented, making Derek's smile fall.

'Of course,' Derek went on. 'When it comes to anything charity-related, I'm always eager to do all I can.'

'I'm just so sorry you got caught up in our window, Mr Montrose,' the minister said, looking very guilty.

'Derek,' the old man told him. 'No need for formalities here.'

'Derek,' said the minister. 'What I don't understand is what happened to that lock. It's always seemed fine to me.'

He walked over to the door and clicked the lock back and forth, open and closed.

'It is a very old lock,' he admitted with a frown. 'Imagine if it had been me right before a service!'

'Yes, that would be a bit awkward,' Fleur agreed.

'It's not like I could shout through and ask the congregation to start without me,' Minister MacFarlane said, making everyone smile.

'We arrived on the boat this morning,' Joanna-Rose said. 'To find poor Derek stuck.'

'You can't imagine the struggle we've had,' added Cathy, feeling confused but happy to go along with the story. 'Including cutting off all his clothes.'

'He was here all night too, peering out the window in the dark,' Fleur added. 'Lucky the wolves weren't hungry.'

'The deer were though,' said Joanna-Rose. 'Unfortunately,' she added, noticing the minister's concerned face. 'He just had a moment there where he became a deer's breakfast, thanks to his sweaty head,' she explained to him.

Fleur folded her arms, covering her mouth with her upper hand as she did, thinking she might burst out laughing at any moment. Derek scowled at her.

'Oh dear, a rather unfortunate situation,' Minister MacFarlane said to Derek, placing a sympathetic arm around his shoulder 'Thank heavens we don't have wolves on Jura, just deer. Lots of deer.'

'Oh don't you worry, Minister. Derek has the most wonderful sense of humour. We were just saying outside, if only he'd become stuck climbing *in* the window,' Fleur said. 'He'd have made the most excellent hunting trophy in that frame, don't you think?'

'And what if he'd had a sweaty backside?' Joanna-Rose added.

Minister MacFarlane chuckled, while Derek glared at the now gleeful women.

'Why didn't you call to tell me you'd arrived last night?' the minister went on. 'Jeanie and I would have been delighted to offer you a room in our house. The island does get rather booked up during the half term break.'

'No harm done,' said Derek, beginning to shiver. 'It was my own fault. I arrived late, foolishly thinking I could get in at a hotel or B&B. With hindsight, I should have come across this morning with the ladies. I'm becoming a worry in my old age.'

'Oh but having to spend a night here in the church,' the minister said. 'How dreadful. I'm mortified.'

'He's fine,' Joanna-Rose said. 'All good, humorous fodder for the biography.'

'Yes, but let me at least get you something to wear,' the minister said to Derek. I am sure there are some robes I can get you. Come with me, please.'

As the two men left the room, Cathy looked at the other two women. 'Why is Derek helping us?' she said.

'Did you get the cream?' Fleur asked.

'What? Oh...' She felt inside her pocket and produced the tube of ointment the pharmacist had sold her. 'Yes, here it is. But Fleur...'

'Give it to the old bugger for his sores and we'll explain everything later. There's no time now, you're just going to have to trust us. Derek is not going to tell a soul, ever, that we kidnapped him. You can stop worrying now. We all can.' Fleur slapped her on the back, before she and Joanna-Rose started outside.

Cathy stood for a moment in shock. Could this be true? Was she saved from a prison sentence? Starting to close the door, she spotted the bottles of lubricant on the floor. 'Fleur!' Cathy piped up, racing out to pull her back inside again. 'What shall I do with these?' she said, showing her the bottles behind the door.

Fleur looked horror-struck. 'What are those for?'

'I thought we could cover his sides in it to get him out,' Cathy explained. 'Now, what am I going to do with it? I can't leave it here in a house of God.'

'I'm sure it's not the first time there's been any of that lying around a church,' Fleur replied, earning a slap on the back from Cathy.

Fleur held out her hands to take the bottles, before shoving them in her jacket pocket. 'Leave them with me,' she said.

As the pair entered the church, they saw Derek standing in a shirt, trouser and tie. The trousers were too long and rolled up at the bottom, which made Cathy giggle.

Fleur looked at her. 'Where did they come from?' she asked.

'I've given him mine. I can go home in my robes, it won't matter,' Minister MacFarlane told her.

'As I was just saying to the minister,' Joanna-Rose said. 'Now that we are here so early, we can all help with the setting up of the fête.'

'Marvellous idea,' Fleur said. 'Where do you want us?'

As the group headed outside, Cathy tapped Derek on the back. 'I got this for your chafing, as you asked,' she whispered, handing him the ointment.

He snatched it from her, offering nothing but a scowl.

Cathy caught up with Fleur. 'What have you done to him?' she whispered, as Derek stormed ahead.

Fleur grinned. 'Our Derek's a reformed character,' she replied with a wink. 'Everything has fallen nicely into place.'

'Is he going to give me my reading?'

Fleur gave her a pat on the back. 'I think perhaps the goal posts have changed too,' she said. 'But I'll explain all later.'

The afternoon was as sunny as the last, and as children ran and played along the beach and in the playground, their parents perused cake, book and bric-a-brac stalls on the church lawn. The place was alive with chatter; a contrast to the quiet, serene island the women had found when they arrived. If Jura had a community of two hundred, Joanna-Rose thought at least that many had turned out in support and celebration of a local six-year-old who was in remission from leukaemia after a long, arduous battle back to health. It was a wonderful thing to see. There may well have been more Islay inhabitants too, having come over on the ferry that morning. She wondered if any of them would be friends of Derek's. As she turned her attention to looking out over the breath-taking Sound of Islay, she saw Michael approached Derek, who stood a few yards in front of her with Cathy and Fleur.

'It's awfy nice of you to come, Mr Montrose,' he said, shaking Derek's hand so hard he thought his arm might break.

'I just wanted to make the little girl's dream come true. That is what this day is for,' Derek replied, pulling his hand back and rubbing it for comfort. He signalled to the women. 'I told my associates here to follow me over here quick smart as soon as I learned about it all.'

'You're here to make her dream come true?' Michael said, his eyes brightening. 'Are you planning to stand in, like?'

'Of course he is,' Cathy said. 'Like Derek says, as soon as he heard about little Skye's dream, and the fête you've all arranged to raise funds for her and her mum, he insisted on dropping everything to come and do his bit.'

'Well, that's just brilliant, sir. Brilliant!' Michael beamed. 'None of us thought of getting a stand in. Great idea! I must tell Minister MacFarlane.'

And with that Michael was off on his heels, weaving through the handful of stalls and people to hunt down the minister.

'A stand in?' said Derek, his brow furrowing. 'I'm not sure what he means.'

Fleur shrugged, just as Joanna-Rose stepped forward to join them. 'Well, this is lovely,' she said, putting an arm on his shoulder.

'Isn't it?' Derek said, smiling at people through gritted teeth as they eyed him in passing, many seeming to recognise him but being reluctant to say more than a passing, 'Hullo'.

'Yes, it is,' Cathy agreed. 'I'm so happy we've turned this all around into something positive.'

'Are you?' he spat, through his still smiling teeth.

'You will do some readings for people, of course?' Joanna-Rose said.

Derek glowered at her.

'Well,' she continued. 'What else do you think they're going to imagine you're here for? They want to make some money.'

'Yeah,' Fleur agreed. 'Like you said to Michael, you're here to make little Skye's dream come true. And my guess is these dream's cost money. You'll have to do some freebies.' She leaned in to whisper in his ear, 'Without any book to help you.'

'Did you put it back?' Derek asked quickly, flushing crimson, just as a grinning Minister MacFarlane rushed towards him, Michael at his heels.

'Derek, what a brilliant idea and so decent of you too!' the minister gushed. 'Little Skye won't know who you are like we do, will she? If we adults keep your identity hush-hush, of course, which will be easy if I just put the word around. Although, that means no readings. Oh dear...' He trailed off.

'No readings? Well that's just fine, Minister,' Derek piped up, the look of relief on his face obvious. 'I am retired, after all. Anytime you need a stand in, I'm most definitely your man.'

'Derek will be able to make a donation too, of course,' Fleur chipped in.

'Yes, yes,' Derek agreed. 'Whatever it is, I'm your man.' He paused, looking to Michael. 'Can you remind me again,' he asked. 'What is it I'm to do?'

Chapter Thirty-Five

'You've gotta love that kids show, *Horrible Histories*,' Fleur said.

'I've never heard of it,' said Joanna-Rose.

'I've seen one or two episodes in passing, but never saw the funny side of it. Until now,' said Minister MacFarlane, with a chuckle.

Cathy watched, open-mouthed, as twenty or more giggling children, led by little Skye Law, rained fresh tomatoes on Derek's face, head and arms.

'You did a grand job at such short notice,' Minister MacFarlane said to Michael, who stood watching the spectacle with them.

'Ach, it was just a couple o' bits o' timber and some old rope,' Michael replied. 'Not as strong as proper stocks, but it's done the job.'

'You can say that again,' Fleur laughed, as a beef tomato splodged off Derek's right cheek. 'Look how much fun they're all having!'

'And at twenty pence a throw,' Joanna-Rose reminded her.

Fleur leaned in to whisper in her ear, 'I'd pay ten times that for a shot myself.' She shouted out to the laughing children, 'Boo to the smelly telly thief!' To her absolute delight, the crowds of children and parents copied her.

'BOO TO THE SMELLY TELLY THIEF!'

'Now, that one (pah) hurt a little (pah) bit,' Derek said, in-between spitting out bits of tomato skin and juice.

'Okay, okay!' Minister MacFarlane called out. 'I think, Mr… er… Brock here has had enough punishment for one day.'

Scores of 'Awww's' rang out across the car park, as children began lowering the tomatoes and leaving the queue for the 'Sock Mr Brock' game.

'Such a terrible waste of food anyway,' Minister MacFarlane whispered.

'Oh not at all, Minister,' Michael replied aloud. 'They're smelly, out-of-date ones from the community store.'

Fleur looked at Joanna-Rose and Cathy. 'Marvellous!' she said, clapping her hands in glee. 'I don't think I've had this much fun in ages.'

Joanna-Rose couldn't resist a small chuckle, but Cathy was horrified. She pulled the other two women aside.

'How awful,' she said. 'Don't you think that poor man has suffered enough?'

'He volunteered to do it!' Fleur told her.

Joanna-Rose nodded. 'Fleur's right, he did,' she said. 'We all heard him.'

'He didn't know this was what he was letting himself in for,' said Cathy. 'Poor Derek. I'm going to help get him out of there.'

As she walked towards a wretched and tired-looking Derek, who had just been released from his shackles by Michael, she saw Skye and her mum heading their way.

'Mr Brock,' Karen said, making him look up.

'Ah yes, Mrs Law,' Derek replied, his mouth curving into a smile that didn't go all the way to his eyes. 'I have something I should say.'

Cathy bit her lip, knowing this was where Derek was supposed to tell her he had brought with him a shiny, new TV, whereby Minister MacFarlane and Michael would produce the new one. She wasn't altogether sure, by the irate look in his eyes, that this was in fact what he was about to say.

'I'd like tae say something first,' said Karen.

She knelt down, still holding on to her daughter's hand and spoke softly to her.

'You've had a lot of fun with poor Mr Brock today and he's been very good to let you. But he isnae a criminal or a bad man, Skye. People that have to come and take people's tellys back are just doing their jobs. Yer mammie got a telly on tick and ah couldnae afford tae pay for it any mair. That's no this man's fault.'

She grinned at Derek, who managed a grin back.

'Now say thank you tae Mr Brock.'

As Skye turned to speak to Derek, a voice boomed out from behind them, making everyone in the group turn round to see a tall, grey-haired gentleman in a long, brown, sheepskin coat with a silken red cravat at his throat.

'My goodness, if it isn't Derek Montrose! And doing his bit fir the community for once.'

'Well hello, Viscount Fraser,' the minister said, stepping toward him to shake his hand. 'I'm so pleased you could make it.'

'His name's Mr Montrose?' The question came from Skye, who was eyeing Derek with suspicion.

'Why yes, little lady,' Viscount Fraser replied. 'And you must be Skye Law. I've seen your photo in the Jura Jottings.' He put out his hand to shake hers, and she pulled back shyly, hiding her face in her mother's skirts.

'Oh dear,' the minister said to Karen. 'I fear we need to tell Skye about our wee, white lie.'

A small crowd began to gather round the group and a freckled face, auburn haired boy shouted out, 'Hey, I seen that guy on the telly!'

His mum, who stood at his side shushed him. 'You mean you saw him *with* the telly, Alistair,' she said.

'No, he's the guy that speaks tae deed folk,' the boy insisted. His mum shook his arm and shushed him again.

Before anyone could say anything more, Skye trudged to where Derek stood and tugged on his shirt. 'Do you talk to deed folk, Mr Montrose?' she asked. 'Is that true?'

Derek looked from Minister MacFarlane to Karen and shrugged, not knowing what to say.

'It's okay,' the minister said. 'Wee Skye's had her fun, haven't you, sweetheart?' He looked at the little girl's face, still flushed from all the excitement of earlier, noticing that now, she looked uncertain.

'This is Derek Montrose, Skye,' her mum cut in to explain. 'He's a very kind man who agreed to act as the person that took our TV because he wanted – as we all did – to make your dream come true.'

'I thought he looked different,' Skye said, making everyone except Derek laugh. 'I thought maybe when I was sick, I was remembering things all wrong.'

'Maybe it's time to say thank you to Mr Montrose for all the fun you've had throwing smelly tomatoes at him now?' said Karen.

Skye giggled, then stepped away from her mum to put her hand in his. 'Thank you, Mr Montrose,' she said.

Fleur observed Derek's face as he looked down at the little girl and thought she saw something different there – something softer in his gaze. He sighed. 'That's okay,' he affirmed with the briefest of kind smiles.

'Mr Montrose just wanted to make your dream come true,' said Cathy, with a guilty lump in her throat.

The little girl looked from Cathy to her mum before signalling for Derek to bend down to her so she could speak quietly to him. 'How do you speak to deed people,' Mr Montrose?' she asked.

Derek's eyes met Fleur's and he swallowed. 'Well, I erm…' he floundered.

'I expect that's a bit of a secret, Skye,' her mum interrupted with a kind smile.

'Well, that's okay, I think,' Skye continued, before looking at the minister. 'Minister MacFarlane?' she said. 'Would it be okay if I ask for just one more dream come true today?'

'Of course it is,' Minister Macfarlane said at once. 'Anything you want. It is your day, after all.'

Skye turned to Derek again, who leant over to hear her request as she signalled down to her height.

'Mr Montrose,' she asked, her big, brown eyes full of hope. 'Can you talk to my daddy?'

Chapter Thirty-Six

'What was I supposed to say?'

'No. You were supposed to say no. She's a little girl, for heaven's sake. Is there no limit to the levels you will sink in your fake career?'

'We don't know he's not a fake!' Cathy had been witnessing the exchange between Derek and Fleur as they stood at the sea's edge, across the road from where the fête had been. As a few stragglers were just leaving, her yell made them look over. Derek, Fleur and Joanna-Rose turned round as she approached them.

'We don't know he's a fake,' she said again, more quietly this time. 'How could he have known the things he did when we were at the show. How could he have named Charlie?'

'Because I wrote his name on my piece of paper,' Fleur replied. 'And he knew all about you, remember? You called to book your seats and Bob was having an affair with Derek's wife. He knew all about you before you arrived.'

'But how could he have known who you were?'

'Ah well, I have given that a lot of thought since, to be honest. And it didn't take an awful long time for me to make a good guess,' replied Fleur. 'It'll be thanks to his people hanging about outside, whose job it is to listen to conversations and tell him things they see and hear. Things like you have a friend with you, and maybe pointing out where we are, thanks to the seating number we were given. This is how these people work,' Fleur said. 'The thing is, I spoke to Charlie on the way in.'

Cathy raised her eyebrows. 'You did?'

'Yes,' Fleur admitted. 'You see, I talk to Charlie a lot when I think no one is listening. And the thing is, that day I was telling him I'd flash my tits at Derek if he mentioned the hole in our floor thing. It was meant to be a little deal between us, I never thought it would happen. Only, as I was speaking, I bashed right into a couple of sexy, young girls. Still makes me chuckle, that one.'

'Why?' Cathy asked.

Fleur turned to Derek with a triumphant grin. 'Imagine my surprise when we ended up sat beside those young things in the performance hall. Your little spies pointed out the wrong woman, didn't they, Derek? Wanted to give you a retirement to remember, did they?'

Derek flinched at the memory.

'I think you achieved that alright,' Joanna-Rose remarked with a laugh.

Cathy hung her head, looking desperately sad. It was a look that made Fleur's heart hurt. 'He's a conman, Cathy,' she told her gently. 'Truth be told I wasn't sure myself until we got to see some more of his antics. All of this – our trip to see his last show, the gifted tickets and now this journey to find him - it was all a waste of time. He's a big phoney.'

Cathy looked from her to Derek, desperation in her eyes. 'You're not, are you?' she said to him. 'Tell her. Give her some information you couldn't possibly know.'

He didn't answer.

'Just prove yourself!' she insisted. 'You've helped thousands of people. All those shows, the TV programmes. You're one of the great successes.'

'Who is also flat broke,' Joanna-Rose commented.

Cathy's mouth fell open. She looked at Fleur.

'It's true,' Fleur told her. 'He's lost it all. The house, the flash car, the lifestyle, the money, Cathy. He's not a success story at all. He's a fraudster.'

'I am not a fraudster,' Derek replied at last.

'Give it a rest, Derek,' Fleur snapped. 'We caught you, red handed.'

'I already explained about the book.'

'What book?' said Cathy.

'The reason he was stuck so fast in that bathroom window was because he was stealing a book from the church, or at least, attempting to,' Joanna-Rose explained.

'What book?' Cathy repeated.

Joanna-Rose reached across to put a comforting hand on Cathy's shoulder. 'The book of condolences,' she told her.

'So?' Cathy said, looking perplexed.

'I already told you, there are messages for my grandmother in there,' Derek insisted. 'It was just a keepsake for myself.'

'Bit of a selfish one, don't you think?' said Fleur. 'You're so full of shi -'

'You know, I'd like to see that myself,' Joanna-Rose said thoughtfully. 'It hadn't occurred to me, but...' She stopped.

Everyone was watching her.

'But what?' Fleur asked.

'Oh, nothing,' she said, seeming to correct herself. Cathy's eyes began to brim with tears. 'So this is what you do?' she said to Derek. 'You lie, cheat and misinform. You take people who have lost someone dear – widows like me - even a little girl who almost lost her own fight for life, and you make sure we can never move on.'

'What do you mean by that?' asked Derek.

'You make us think there's a chance for one more day, one more window to look into and speak to the person we've lost. I wasn't moving on, I was in limbo, waiting. Waiting for you to let me have one last conversation with my husband. Do you know what I witnessed, Derek? Do you know how my husband died?'

He stared blankly at her.

'He choked to death on his own blood, in our kitchen! It happened, right in front of me and there was nothing I could do,' Cathy wailed. 'I'll never forget that day, never! We thought he was in remission.' Her voice trailed away, as the two women rushed forward to comfort her. 'It was all I had,' she went on after a pause. 'My last, awful memory of Bob. I didn't want it to be like that, I couldn't bear it! I needed him to tell me he was at peace.'

'He is at peace, Cathy,' said Joanna-Rose.

'How do you know that?' Cathy asked, her eyes pleading. 'I wanted to have one last moment with him and I thought Derek was the answer. Why do you think I pushed him in the boot when he went mad at me? I was desperate! But my moment was already gone, wasn't it Derek?' she turned to stare at him but he was looking at his feet. 'I've already had it,' she went on. 'And I could have made some headway to accepting that months ago, instead of dragging it all with me, waiting for a fraudster to take the pain away for me.'

'I'm not a fraud -' Derek began.

'Really?' Cathy shouted. 'Really? After everything we've found out about you? What about the suitcase on the beach when you were faking your suicide? The book of condolences? The free ticket for me to go along to your last show and have you call out information you already knew about my husband because he had been sleeping with your wife? Have you no shame?'

From the corner of her eye, Joanna-Rose spotted Viscount Fraser making his way across the road to them.

'Change the subject,' she snapped.

'What? Why?' said Cathy, before looking in the direction of her gaze and getting her answer. She wiped her eyes with her sleeve and put on a fake smile.

Fleur turned and spotted him too. 'So, all in all, I don't think it's a great idea to be giving readings to a little girl, Derek,' she declared. 'Are we all agreed?'

'Yes,' said Cathy, nodding. 'Not a good idea at all.'

'Derek,' the Viscount said as he reached the old man's side, patting him on the back. 'I just wanted to have a quick catch up before tonight. You're still okay for that private reading we arranged, aren't you?'

Derek cast a hasty look at Fleur, who nodded.

'Yes, of course,' he replied.

'Good, good,' Viscount Fraser went on. 'Because I've given Minister MacFarlane my donation and I'm heading back to the estate now. You'll stay the night, of course?'

'As always,' Derek nodded, before catching a scowl from Fleur. 'Err, Findlay, my friend. Do you think it would be alright to have my three associates here stay too?'

Viscount Fraser regarded the three women and smiled. 'Yes,' he said. 'Of course. Any friend or associate of yours is welcome. I'll have the extra rooms made up. See you all at six then?'

'Wonderful, thank you,' Derek replied.

Viscount Fraser made his way to his car, pausing to shake hands and say farewell to the minister.

Joanna-Rose turned to Derek. 'So,' she said. 'I was right about the little cash-in-hand private readings with the gentry, then? Quite the professional tax dodger, aren't we?'

'I don't plan to do them for long,' he replied curtly. 'I have plans.'

'Can't we just get away from this horrible man, now?' said Cathy, with a sniff.

'Actually, this was Derek's suggestion,' Fleur replied. 'And I thought a little tour of the Viscount's estate might be nice end to our trip,' she went on. 'The floor show should be spectacular, given that we haven't given Derek here much time to do his homework.'

'Of course,' exclaimed Cathy, her face brightening in realisation. 'That's why you were stealing the book! Viscount Fraser's family have been here on Jura for centuries.' She cast Derek another disappointed look, before reaching in to her pocket and taking out the photograph. 'This is what brought us here to you, Derek. This!' She slapped the picture into his hands. 'I just can't believe it's true. I thought we were all in some way cosmically connected and your reading seemed to confirm it. So my husband stole away your wife? Well, I've been duped – by you *and* him. I have to wonder how you both have been getting away with it for all these years!'

As Cathy stormed away, Derek stared down at the picture and at once became more animated.

'I'm not a liar, or a fake,' he announced, putting the picture in to his trouser pocket with a grin. 'And tonight I'll prove it to you all. So, okay, I may have some "issues" with the tax office. But that is all to be resolved very soon. Admittedly, there have been huge misunderstandings. But a fraud, I am not. Derek Montrose isn't finished yet!'

He strode away towards the crowd at the fête, shouting, 'Minister MacFarlane? A word in your ear, if I may?'

Chapter Thirty-Seven

'What's she doing?'

Minister MacFarlane scratched his chin, looking deep in thought, before shaking his head. 'I have no idea, Michael,' he replied. 'I don't think I've ever seen anything quite like that before.'

As they continued to stand, staring and open-mouthed, Cathy walked over with a stack of chairs she'd collected. 'Shall I just load these straight into the van, Minister?'

'What? Oh,' he replied. He tapped Michael's shoulder. 'Could you help Cathy load those chairs?'

'Is it some ancient Celtic dance?' Michael asked, still staring across the road.

Cathy turned to the direction of their gaze, to find the subject of their interest, silhouetted against an early evening summer sky. Fleur was at the seashore, earphones in, hopping rhythmically from one leg to the other and swinging her hips. Cathy could make out the tassel from Charlie's sporran flicking out to the side with every move of her waist.

And there was singing: '*Got my man… got my hips… got his freaky finger tips…*'

'Oh no,' Cathy said, putting the chairs down as Fleur, with her back to them, thrust out her chest, bent over and shook a tail feather for all she was worth.

'*Shake my style… show my class… I got rhythm in that ass!*'

'It doesn't *sound* Celtic,' Minister MacFarlane observed.

'Ray Charles?' Michael suggested.

Cathy shot across the road and tapped her on the back. 'Fleur!'

'*Ahm a freaky… little…* arghhhhh!'

Startled, Fleur swung round and pulled off her headphones to find Cathy glowering at her.

'What'd you do that for?' she complained. 'I almost had a heart attack!'

'You're supposed to be helping us clear up,' Cathy said. 'Even Derek's doing his bit.' She pointed to where he was stood, struggling to pick up a small table. 'And here you are swanning off to have a party for one on the beach.'

'It's my daily work out,' the older woman said. 'And I imagine you don't want me doing a shimmy in Viscount Fraser's gaffe, do you?'

'You didn't do one yesterday.'

'Oh yes I did.'

'Where? When?'

'When you were asleep.'

Cathy's eyes widened. 'You mean when you were supposed to be outside keeping an eye on Derek's upper half?'

'Yes, but I didn't leave him,' Fleur explained. 'I just had a kind of... well... captive audience.'

Cathy raised her eyes to the heavens. 'Oh good grief,' she said. 'I do wish you'd stop giving me reasons to feel sorry for that awful man.'

'Hey, some old men would have to pay good money to see me shake this booty in their face,' Fleur said.

'You didn't?' Cathy gasped.

Fleur nodded, with a wide, mischievous grin.

'Come and help us clear up,' Cathy said with a sigh. 'The minister's wife, Jeanie, has offered us her bathroom for a clean and tidy up before we head out to the Viscount's estate, so we need to hurry if we're going to have time.'

'What? We have to clean someone's bathroom?' Fleur exclaimed.

Cathy sighed, looking to the heavens in exasperation for a second time.

Joanna-Rose watched the scene from the doorway of Jura Church and smiled to herself. Jura's beauty, the saline and peat scent of the air and Fleur's nonsensical dance routine; everything before her made her fingers itch to write. It was a longing that had been missing for what seemed like a hundred years. And still there was the personal matter of Derek to deal with. Now the kidnapping problem was resolved, there was little time left for her to confront him. Confrontation, she thought, was always simple to imagine and more complex in practice. She bowed her head and, as the rest of the group were busy tidying away the last remnants of the fête, turned to slip inside the deserted church.

Cathy had come for one last conversation with her late husband. Now that she knew this was never going to be, and that both Derek Montrose and her beloved Bob had turned out to be not what they seemed, it was time for her to go home and start to rebuild her life, if indeed, she still could. All that remained for her to do was try to get her job back. At least then she might keep her home. Damn Bob, not only for shagging around, but for failing to make provision for her. She was lost, alone and now she knew she'd been unloved too. The pain of that realisation weighed heavier than the five plastic chairs she was lugging towards Michael's van as she considered her future.

'Thank God that's done,' Fleur said, before nodding an apology to the minister as they sat on the grass bank sipping cold lemonade, watching Michael drive away. 'Sorry, I mean, really, thank God.'

'Are you a religious person, Fleur?' he asked,

She blinked. 'Why'd you ask?'

'We ministers know a thing or two.'

'Amazing,' Cathy said. 'She's a lapsed Catholic.' Fleur scowled at her.

Minister MacFarlane chuckled. 'When we were inside earlier,' he said, holding up his glass to watch tiny bits of lemon swirling around in the sweet liquid, 'I thought I noticed you bow your head at the altar. The things we can't help but do after years of repetition can give you away.' He smiled. Then asked, 'Why lapsed?'

'She's angry with God.'

Fleur's eyes narrowed as she glared at Cathy again 'What?' she said. 'No, I'm not!'

'Then perhaps you no longer believe?' the minister said.

'Oh, I do.'

'Myself, Joanna-Rose and Fleur – we've all lost someone,' Cathy explained. 'Not all at the same time, but, recently.'

'Well, that's a terrible thing,' he said, looking concerned. 'If there is anything I can offer in the way of comfort…'

'There isn't,' Fleur said, before adding, 'in my case, anyway.'

The minister fell silent for a second, regarding Fleur with serious and thoughtful eyes.

'You know, in my position, as you can imagine, I meet all kinds of people,' he said finally, placing a kind hand on her shoulder. 'I've seen a lot of pain and I've witnessed people struggling to survive through the most indescribable circumstances. I've been to the depths of despair with some of my parishioners. I haven't spent my entire life here in Jura. I've been to Africa, to Romania and worked with some of the poorest people on this planet of ours. The things I've seen, well, they could make any person question the existence of God. It's not unusual.'

'Michael will be straight back for us, won't he?' Fleur said, picking up her glass and standing up to leave.

Minister MacFarlane nodded.

'Then I'm going to take a quick walk along the lane, if nobody minds,' she said. 'It's a good eight miles to the village, isn't it? So I have some time?'

'Yes, it is,' the minister agreed.

'Do you want company?' Cathy asked.

'No, thank you.'

Cathy and the minister watched her walk away, each with their own thoughts, neither saying anything.

Chapter Thirty-Eight

'You may or may not welcome me in your house, but here I am, God. And tomorrow, I think I'm going to tell my father who I am.'

Joanna-Rose sat in the galley in the church with her hands clasped around her carpet bag and her eyes closed, talking to God.

'It's out of your hands.'

She raised her head and turned around, to see Derek watching her, having just come from the room where he had spent the previous night.

'What is?' she said, feeling the heat of alarm rise in her throat.

'Whatever becomes of that conversation with your father,' he said. 'You just have to get out there and say your piece. Let it go, out into the universe, as it were. And *que será, será.*'

'That's... actually very good advice, in the circumstances,' she said. 'I suppose I should say thank you.'

'*De nada.* Hey, I must be channelling Spanish people today. Is your dad a Spaniard?'

She shook her head. 'You're in a good mood all of a sudden.'

'What can I say? It's a beautiful day, we're on a beautiful island and I'm a free man.'

Joanna-Rose stood up and faced him.

'Look, Derek, give Cathy a reading would you? Please?'

'I thought you said I was a fraud?'

'I *know* you're a fraud,' she replied. 'Why do you think we stood in the way of you giving that beautiful little girl fake messages from her father?'

'So, you are asking me to lie to your friend, are you?' Derek said.

Joanna-Rose shrugged and bowed her head. 'It's just, I had no idea she had that horrific last memory of Bob. It must be terrible. How does a person get over such horrors?'

'So you agree, what I do can help people?'

'I agree enough people have been fooled by you to find false comfort. Whether that makes you a good or a bad man is for Him to decide,' she replied, raising her eyes to the ceiling.

'So, you are happy for me to lie to your friend? Because that's what you believe I do, right?' he said.

She sighed. 'Living a life full of lies would weigh heavy on a good person. Do you consider yourself a good person?'

He blinked, the nearest creep of a smile starting on his face. 'Listen, I would like to help Cathy,' he said seriously. 'And I fully intend to.' He walked to the first pew opposite her and sat down, bowing his head as if in prayer.

'You do?' she said, taking her seat again. 'Does part of that quest to help Cathy include using everything you know about her husband to give you the most talked-about show of your career?'

He looked up at her. 'Is that what you think?' he said, looking astonished. 'That thought never entered my mind.' He paused to stare down at the floor and Joanna-Rose had a feeling he was wondering why he hadn't thought of it. 'Look,' he went on after a moment. 'I didn't know Bob had died until the night she came to my show without him. He had disappeared without a word. I was glad that -' He stopped, chewed his lip as if wanting to say something else and changing his mind. 'Libby had no idea where he'd gone and neither did I,' he said finally.

'You knew the man that was sleeping with your wife well, then?'

'Of course I did, he's in your photo, isn't he?'

'How did you know him?'

'He was helping me with something -' Derek's voice trailed off. He slid nearer to the end of the pew, looking at her with renewed interest. 'Your mother?' he said, his voice now low and full of concern. 'You lost her?'

Joanna-Rose clutched her bag more tightly, feeling a sudden chill which she shook off immediately. 'Don't do that,' she told him. 'I've no wish to see your show.'

'I'm sorry,' he said, leaning an elbow on the shelf in front to put a hand to his forehead. He looked deep in thought. 'Something very strong is coming through, I just have to go with it. She's making me.'

Joanna-Rose sighed loudly.

'Did you have a nasty fight with someone significant, maybe as a child?' he said.

Joanna-Rose found she couldn't speak, her voice paralysed by a feeling like an electric shock.

'That's it, isn't it?' Derek said, closing his eyes. 'You were bullied in school. Oh, it was terrible. I can feel a searing pain in my... in my hands.' He rubbed the back of his right hand as if nursing an injury.

Joanna-Rose put both hands on the shelf in front of her and stood up, to find herself staring at the three, familiar crescent moon shaped scars on the back of her left one. 'Is this what you do to people?' she asked, showing him her hand as his eyes shot open. 'Cold read them?'

'I don't know what you're talking about,' he snapped. 'But if you don't want the message from your mother, fine. I can't do anything else.'

'Have you ever had children, Derek?' she snapped. 'Do you even know what it is to care for another person more than you care for yourself?' She glared at him: this tiny, phony of a man who could be her dad. As Fleur had done before, she looked for elements of her in his face, a family resemblance of any kind, and saw none. The single trait they shared for sure was alcoholism. Why had Robert been this man's friend?

'If you don't believe I have any psychic ability, why don't you just let me talk about your mother?' he said. 'Then you can decide whether I'm telling the truth or not. After all, I could never have known her or you.'

She stiffened. 'What about my mother?'

He paused, seeming to consider his words before straightening himself to speak again. 'The bond between a same sex parent and child is just about the strongest one there is. And so, she hasn't been able to leave you in the afterlife.'

'Very good,' Joanna-Rose said, wiping away a tear before clapping her hands. 'Now let me read you, Derek. Let me see...' She scratched her chin and cast him a quizzical glance. 'You had an affair in the sixties with a young model called Kathleen, didn't you? And Kathleen went on to have a son.'

Derek's eyes narrowed, but he ignored her to continue his reading. 'Your mother says, oh now wait, what is it?'

'My mother's name was Kathleen Barton,' Joanna-Rose went on. 'She was quite a successful model in the seventies and eighties. You might know her as Kat. Do you remember my mother, Kat Barton? Do you, Derek?'

Derek's expression altered immediately from contemplative to surprise. Slowly, he nodded. 'Yes, I... I do,' he stammered. 'Are you... are you -'

Before he could continue, Joanna-Rose offered him a shaky, outstretched arm in greeting. 'Kat says you should say hello,' she said. 'To the transgender woman who could be your son.'

Chapter Thirty-Nine

Fleur wondered how much further she would need to walk in order to get to Barnhill, the house where George Orwell had hidden away to write most of *Nineteen Eighty Four*. She knew he'd lived a solitary existence there for two years, something that sounded like heaven to her. The only information she had on its location was that it stood alone on the north side of the island, tucked far away from the rest of civilisation, and that you could only reach it by boat, 4x4 or on foot. Could it be reached in an hour? She didn't know, but its situation would suit her enough to live there for the rest of her days. For now, it would be a nice place to spend an evening away from nosey people.

'Fleur!'

She spun round to see Minister MacFarlane jogging towards her, waving his hands.

'Oh, have I been too long? Is Michael back?'

'No, no,' the minister said, catching up with her. 'I just… thought…' he stopped, gasping for air, his face red as a tomato. 'I'm no runner,' he said between breaths, leaning on her shoulder for support. 'I just thought… I could walk along… with you, if you don't mind?'

'You're right,' she said, looking bemused at the state of him. 'You're more like a should-take-it-easy-er.'

Minister MacFarlane looked about him. 'Can we sit down for a moment?' he asked, pointing to some rocks a little further up the path. 'It's not ideal, but it's the best Jura has to offer at this place and time,' he said.

She nodded and followed him to the group of flat, dry rocks. They sat down and looked out over the water together. It was incredible to Fleur how every stopping place on the island demanded careful contemplation of the sea's beauty. It was mind-medicine for humanity.

'This is a great place to come for peace and quiet reflection,' he told her.

'Not surprising,' Fleur said. 'There are more deer than people.'

He laughed. 'This is very true. And for many it's the ideal escape, this island with not too many people on it. The great "get away from life" retreat. It's breath-taking, isn't it?'

She nodded in agreement. 'I should have thought to come here years ago.'

'Ah, but if you live here as I do, this isn't an escape from life. This *is* life. It's boggy, it rains a lot and, even though it's beautiful it still remains largely uninhabited. Whenever I go to the mainland or away for a holiday as Mrs MacFarlane and I do with the children from time to time, I may be escaping from all of this, but the truth is Jura stays with me. It's in my heart.' He patted his chest and smiled at her, his kind eyes twinkling in the afternoon sun.

'It is an enchanting place,' she agreed. 'And trust me, Minister, I don't use the word enchanting often.'

'It is amazing how much a heart can hold,' he said, his gaze turning back out to sea. He scratched his beard, looking thoughtful. 'It's a place we keep things that no one can touch. And yet, like everything, it has its breaking point. If you're not careful, you can carry too much, for too long.'

'Says the man who nearly needed a jumpstart a minute ago.'

He turned back to her. 'I'm in training for the fell race, you know,' he said with a grin.

'Jesus. Do they have anyone else here that can do funerals?'

Minister MacFarlane shook his head and laughed heartily. 'Oh dear, wonderful Fleur,' he said. 'You've an infectious, young humour about you.'

'You mean juvenile?'

He patted her hand, making her turn to look at him. 'There are more than a few people on this earth that would do well to remember what it is to laugh like a child again. As my granny used to say, it's the things you keep inside that can kill ye more than the things ye let oot.'

'She never met a bullfighter then?'

'Clearly not,' he laughed.

Her mood lifting, Fleur exhaled slowly.

Minister MacFarlane scratched his chin and stared out to sea again. 'It's funny,' he said after a moment. 'You can meet all kinds of people from all kinds of places, and you can share stories about the place you come from. The place you hold in your heart. And then, well, it will always be there but it will feel lighter because you shared it.' He stopped, looking puzzled at his own comments.

Fleur's brow furrowed, but she didn't look at him. 'It would be a lot easier if you just came out and said what's actually on your mind, wouldn't it?' she said.

He nodded. 'Faith is a very personal thing. I would never offer any advice about someone's crisis of faith unless they asked me for it and then – and only then – I would tell them to listen to the tiny voice in their head that has never left them. That voice will lead you back to the right path.'

'I don't hear voices.'

'Perhaps that's because your soul is shouting out in pain,' he said. 'But it's there. It's the voice that stopped you from going so far from the church that I might not find you, even though your heart told you that you wanted to escape. It's the warning light that's always there and it's the best and most sensible part of you. The same one that made you seek out a couple of widow's like yourself for friendship and to work with. Keep listening out for it, because it's served you well to this point and, believe it or not, it's always there.'

'Would God forgive someone that didn't go to their husband's funeral?'

The minister straightened. 'You didn't go?'

'No,' she replied. 'His family and his daughter wanted this huge, Catholic funeral and I couldn't bear it. I just... I couldn't go. I was so angry with... with...'

'With God?'

'Yes. When Charlie was in hospital after the first heart attack, he begged God to help him. He was terrified. The next day an even bigger one took him. I lost my husband and my faith all in the same week.'

The minister blinked, idly resting his hands on his chest and intertwining his fingers as he considered Fleur's words. After a while, he cleared his throat, and replied, 'Well, I feel sure God and Charlie understood. But I don't think you ever lose your faith. It can just go underground for a while. And you can trust me on that one, because I know.'

Fleur blinked. 'You?'

He nodded. 'I may be a man of the cloth, but I'm not immune to doubt, you know. I've seen terrible things that have made me question God. You're not on your own.'

'Isn't that just early retirement to you guys?'

Minister MacFarlane smiled, clasped his hands together and looked down at his thumbs, which he rolled idly round and around one another.

'And what did you do?' Fleur asked him after a moment.

'I waited until I was ready for Him to come back to me.'

'That's it?'

'That's it. But He was always there, Fleur. You can't do anything about that.'

'Even when I was taking His pictures down?'

Minister MacFarlane laughed out loud. 'Hah, you make it sound like a divorce.'

'Charlie's daughter hasn't spoken to me since the funeral,' she went on seriously.

The minister stopped laughing. Even in the short time that he'd known her, he recognised a long-locked heart that was opening.

'I was in her life for most of her childhood,' she said. 'And for the two years since his death we haven't seen each other. She was furious with me. She thinks I don't care.'

'And you couldn't just go and explain it to her as you have to me?'

Fleur shook her head. 'How could I explain it to her when I wasn't able to explain it to myself? I didn't cry and I didn't go to my own husband's funeral! But I just couldn't... couldn't...' She stopped, the pain in her heart taking her breath away. Anger rose in her again. She didn't want to feel all of this emotion. She had shut it out. Her former life with Charlie was covered over now, cloaked in papers, rubbish and dust in the home they once shared. She couldn't clear away the debris for fear of seeing the big, empty space left by the people that had lived and loved with her there but were now gone.

'You couldn't grieve,' Minister MacFarlane finished for her. 'So now, in self-imposed punishment, you won't give yourself permission to move on.'

'No, that's not right,' she replied, feeling her anger rise again. 'I've moved on. I enjoy life. I'm not like Cathy, all closed and leaving all my husband's things untouched. I've touched things! Okay, then I just covered them up and learned to live with them.' She stopped, beginning to hear for the first time how much alike she and Cathy were. For a moment she was dumbfounded into silence. Then, she looked up at the minister, her expression confused. 'What did you say?' she asked him.

'Me?' he replied, with a look of genuine surprise. 'Nothing.'

'I thought you said -' she began.

'You heard a voice that wasn't mine? What did it say?'

Fleur shook her head and blew out her cheeks angrily. 'Oh, fiddlesticks!' she said.

'Well,' he replied with a solemn expression. 'It's not new age, but it's a start.'

She glared at him and then, despite every urge she had to scream out in frustration at the world, she slouched down, letting her shoulders relax. 'It's no use,' she said. 'Any of it.'

The minister put his hand over hers and looked into her eyes, seeing tears begin to well up in them. 'Yet, you have all this anger,' he said. 'Fleur, you haven't allowed yourself to grieve and I have to tell you that a funeral is a very important beginning. It's the start of a very natural process for everyone that has lost someone. You don't dwell on their death. But you do honour their life and use that time to remember it. You have to allow yourself time to do all of that. You jumped over that part and now it's shaking your very core. If you don't allow yourself to grieve, it festers and it has to surface sometime. It will come out in other ways. You make peace with that, and, trust me, you'll make your inevitable peace with God.'

'But what if all I want to do is shout at Him? Maybe even swear?'

The minister smiled. 'He's got very broad shoulders, you know. Shout all you have to, but don't be alarmed at the scattering grouse if you do it here and now.' He patted her knee and stood up. 'Now, I'm going back to the church to wait for Michael's return,' He looked at his watch. 'He should be about ten minutes away now. I'll let you have a long, last look at that lovely, Jura view on your own. Because, I've got to tell you, it's so perfect you could scream.' He placed a comforting hand on her shoulder, before taking off back down the road.

Fleur sighed and watched him go, feeling a strange concoction of hurt and gratitude. She looked up the hillside, thinking she might climb a little way up for an even better view. If the minister wanted her to see some things for herself then she'd better do as she was told. Everything always looked better from above anyway, she thought.

Charlie had been a keen hiker when he was alive; a pastime that was somewhat hampered by his terrible chain-smoking in later years. After they were married Fleur had begged him to stop, warning that it would be the death of him. She felt no comfort now in the fact that she had been right.

'Heart disease,' she grumbled under her breath as she began the slow, cautious climb upwards. 'Trust you to leave me over something preventable, you old bastard.'

Having gone a few feet up, she stopped at a flat part and turned around to take in the view. With the minister now out of sight, she was alone in the wilds – and moments like this were always when she talked to Charlie. Her house in the back of beyond also provided ample opportunity for this; perhaps that was why she stayed, even though it was, she had to admit now, a lonely existence. Only Phillip could hear when she spoke to Charlie and she felt sure he already knew she was quite mad. It helped to know that he could neither tell anyone nor understand what she was on about.

'Minister MacFarlane asked if I doubted the existence of God back there, did you hear that?' she said aloud.

Somewhere behind her and to the left, a bird peeped and cawed, before fluttering away.

'I do though,' she continued. 'I believe in God.' She looked up at the sky. 'I believe in you, okay? I just don't know why you had to go to all that trouble to gift me the great love of my life and then take him away.'

Turning back to her husband in her mind, she said, 'Oh yes, okay, I bloody loved you. And I expect God hears these kinds of complaints from plenty of people who are far worse off than me and you, Charlie.' She swallowed hard, Minister MacFarlane's words still fresh in her mind.

'I'm angry. There, I bloody said it,' she told him. 'And I have been for a long, long time now. But once you and I had fun, didn't we? Some good, good times. And we could have had more, you silly, smoking, drinking, bacon-double-cheeseburger-eating bugger. You'd have loved it here in Jura. Look at that view, all the velvety shades of Scotland green. You don't see green like this anywhere else in the world, do you? Although, I expect you've seen it all now from where you are. What do I know? Where are you, Charlie?' Her voice started to break and her mouth trembled as she fought back the first sting of tears. 'You weren't supposed to go and bloody leave me here on my own! And don't you tell me "Mandy". Don't you say that to me! She's not mine to have, she doesn't even want me in her life anymore. She was yours, and you bloody left her too.'

She looked up at the sky and shook her fist. 'We had so much left to do together. I'm only a young thing in my sixties! I wasn't ready to be a widow! How could I go and put on a black trouser suit and listen to them talk about you in the past tense? I still feel you here! I didn't want you to go! I didn't bloody tell you you could! I made your favourite mince and potatoes that night before you sodding decided to keel over and win yourself a free blue and white taxi to A&E!'

Looking round about her, she yelled, 'Where were you, God? Where were you?'

She felt behind her for a dry, flat space and sat down, taking a tissue from her jacket pocket. And there, on a rock on a Scottish hillside, Fleur Brookes cried voluntary tears.

Chapter Forty

'My son? But... I don't have a...' Derek stopped, regarding her with confusion. '...daughter.'

The sound of books crashing to the ground made them both turn to see an astonished Cathy standing in the aisle watching them. 'I... I'm sorry,' she stammered, stooping to begin picking up the books. 'Minister MacFarlane asked me to bring these in here.'

Joanna-Rose raced up to help her, as an ashen-faced Derek watched her go. 'Are you okay?' she asked quietly, kneeling down to pick up a book and hand it to her.

Cathy stared back and bit her lip, her face pink with embarrassment. 'I feel such a fool -' she started to say.

The other woman put a reassuring hand on her shoulder. 'I'm sorry you feel that way,' she said with a sigh. 'I didn't mean to mislead you. Yes, I was born a boy. My name was Barry Barton.'

'What? Oh no, no!' Cathy reached across to clasp Joanna-Rose's hand in her own. 'I meant because I was snooping! I heard you talking about Bob, you see. And... oh, I tried to be quiet, but I couldn't hold on to all these damn books.'

Looking around them at the mess on the floor, the women burst out laughing.

'Are you going to tell me what on earth this is all about?' Derek shouted, making them laugh harder when they turned to see his confused and indignant expression.

'Well, you're the psychic,' Joanna-Rose told him between snorts. She looked back at Cathy. 'Did you see his face? I mean, when I told him?' She stopped laughing, grabbing both of her friend's hands. 'I should have told you earlier, I know -' she said seriously.

'Why?' Cathy replied with a shrug. 'Listen, the worst news of the day here is that that weasel...' she pointed at Derek, '...might be your dad.'

Joanna-Rose let go of Cathy's hands and stepped forward to hug her in a tight embrace. 'Oops, sorry mother,' she said absentmindedly, as her carpet bag bashed off Cathy's shoulder.

'Ha ha,' Cathy laughed. 'I'm not your mother -' her voice trailed away. She pulled back to look at her and blinked. 'Your mother?'

'Ahh,' the other woman replied, clasping the enormous bag to her bosom. 'Another thing I need to explain.'

'Excuse me, is this the Norman Bates Motel or something?' Derek cut in angrily. 'I've been kidnapped by a transsexual, who thinks I'm their dad, and who has his mother in his handbag.'

'Well, I think that's highly offensive -' Cathy began.

Joanna-Rose raised a hand at Cathy to silence her, before turning, arms folded, to face him. 'I came here to find you because, after my mother died, I have felt so completely alone. She was the only person who accepted me, the real me that is, until now.' She looked back at Cathy and reached for her hand. 'Cathy,' she said. 'Robert was my friend, but he couldn't love me. In coming here to find this...' she turned to cast Derek a look of contempt which he returned defiantly, '...this *ignoramus* of a man with you, I've realised something important.'

'What is it?' Cathy asked.

Joanna-Rose took a deep, inward breath and paused, her gaze falling down to the ground. After a moment, she looked up and said, 'I've done it again, the very thing I've been doing all my life.'

'What?' her friend repeated.

'I was here for acceptance when I didn't need it. I've never needed it, have I?'

Cathy smiled and shook her head. 'You don't need to explain yourself,' she said kindly.

'Oh but I do,' said Joanna-Rose. 'I've never needed this hidden existence, buried away behind someone who could look after me. I never even tried to make friends before. I always felt I needed shielding from the outside world. I've led such an insular life up until now.' She regarded Derek again, before walking back towards him and reaching down with her hand outstretched. As she drew nearer, he drew back in surprise but then put his own out to meet hers, unthinkingly, and they shook hands. 'Thank you, Derek,' she said, as he pulled his hand quickly away with a look of disgust. 'Thank you for being so rude, so bigoted and so blind. You can't see the real me standing in front of you, but you could take the time to notice the scars on my hand. You searched for the clues, the things I could give to you, instead of the comfort you could give me, which is the worst, cheapest, and most cruel trick of every fake clairvoyant on the planet.'

'I'm not a fake,' he barked. 'What about your scars, and the fight?'

'My whole life's been a fight,' she told him. 'And my scars were indeed from one of them, Derek. Perhaps from the most honest show of bigotry I've ever had to face before you gifted me some more today. I was beaten to unconsciousness at the age of thirteen,' she held a hand to her heart, tears welling up in her eyes again. 'My crime was to wear high heels to school. I thought it was the worst day of my life and I've been in hiding ever since,' she said. 'Ever since!' She spat the words so mightily, Derek flinched. 'Do you know what it is like to realise that after so much of your life is behind you?'

Derek rolled his eyes and shook his head, not looking in the least bit sorry. 'I know more about it than you think,' he said, still wrapped up in his own self-pity.

'I came here with Cathy and Fleur curious to know something about who I am,' she went on, sitting down beside him as he edged away.

Cathy walked around the other side of the pew and sat down, blocking him in.

'And I thought I might get that from you,' Joanna-Rose continued. 'But as it turns out, I'm finding it all out from them.' She paused to smile, as memories of every wild, emotional and hysterical event of the last twenty-four-hours came to mind. 'I have friends now, for the first time in my entire life.'

'So, why don't you go back to wherever it was you came from and leave me alone?' Derek barked, snapping her back to the present.

'Oh, you horrible, horrible man,' Cathy said, shaking her head. 'How can you claim to be a spiritual person? You have no heart and no soul.'

'You have to feel sorry for him, Cathy,' Joanna-Rose went on. 'Being insincere all your life must be wearing. Walking around being something you never were, so fake -'

Derek let out a guffaw so loud that it bounced off the church walls. 'Look who's talking,' he said. 'Do you actually think you are the person you were born to be? Walking around pretending to be a woman? You're a freak of nature!' He turned away from her and folded his arms.

Joanna-Rose regarded his back with sad eyes. 'Everything around us is a freak of nature,' she said. 'Each thing you see was new once. Never seen before, undiscovered. And then it was.' She tapped him on the back, making him turn around. 'And then, *I* was,' she told him.

'You're no child of mine,' he hissed, turning back, unwilling to meet her gaze. 'It's impossible. We are nothing alike.'

'You could be right,' she agreed. 'When I look at you, all I see is everything I'm not.' She paused, her gaze falling to the bag on her arm, feeling a familiar lump in her throat. When she spoke again, she didn't look up. 'But I think perhaps you are my dad,' she told him, getting to her feet. 'I won't have anyone try to make me believe my mother would have been the type to sleep around, even if you were married when you met. But I've realised now I don't want or need to know either way. Because I'm not on my own anymore,' she sighed, wiped her eyes and looked across at Cathy, who gave her a reassuring smile and stood up too. 'And, as you said,' she told Derek. '*Qué será será.*'

'Oh, I love that movie,' said Minister MacFarlane, as he breezed in the door, his unexpected arrival startling everyone. 'Erm, sorry,' he said, sensing some awkwardness in the room. 'But I came to say that Michael will be a little late back as the ferry he was unloading on to is delayed. He says he'll be another thirty minutes or more.'

'Well, if the worst comes to the worst we'll just have to spend another night in here,' Joanna-Rose said, taking great pleasure from seeing Derek visibly flinch as she spoke.

The minister looked from Joanna-Rose to Derek, his smile faltering. He cleared his throat to speak, and said, 'I'm sure there'll be no need for that.'

'It's not all bad news,' Cathy said, desperate to lighten the atmosphere in the room. 'We're going to meet the Prime Minister tonight!'

'Yes, indeed,' Minister MacFarlane agreed. 'Now, if you'll excuse me, I will just continue on with things outside in the sunshine. It's turning into another glorious evening.'

When he had left the room, Derek turned to the women and said, 'I'm going to ask you one more time, what do you want from me?'

'Nothing,' Joanna-Rose replied. 'I think I'm ready to leave now.'

'Oh, but I was looking forward to meeting the Prime Minister,' Cathy complained.

'It's not a party for anyone and everyone,' Derek said. 'It's a very private and personal event. So please, if you have to come along I must to ask you to keep the details of this evening forever to yourself.' He stood up and cast an accusing eye at Cathy. 'Now, Mrs Hesitation-At-Leaving,' he said. 'Do you want to tell me and your friend what this kidnapping was *really* about?'

Cathy looked surprised. 'What do you mean?'

'I mean, this...' he pointed to Joanna-Rose, '*person* tells me he's my son -'

'Well... that's just... your son?' Cathy replied. She stopped, not sure what to say next.

Joanna-Rose put an arm around her friend, before turning to Derek. 'Yes,' she said. 'I was born a male. But I'm now a woman, in every sense, and I have been for many, many years. Would you like to see some evidence?'

Cathy put her hand over her mouth and chuckled as Derek looked horror-struck.

'Well, I... I...' he stammered. 'I'd sooner see Fleur's breasts again!'

'That can be arranged too,' Joanna-Rose told him dryly.

'So let's say you are my son,' Derek spat, his eyes now full of rage. 'Just tell me what you want from me. Is it my money? Because in case you haven't read the papers recently, I'm facing ruin. The taxman is about to make me bankrupt and if it hadn't been for her sordid little affair, Libby would be about to take the rest. But I'll happily leave you some of my debt.'

'I don't want anything from you,' Joanna-Rose replied. 'And Cathy doesn't want your phoney reading either.'

'No?' Derek asked, his expression darkening. 'Well let me guess for myself, shall I?' He turned accusingly to Cathy. 'Spit it out! It's the cask, isn't it? I had a feeling that was your game as soon as I found you lugging along that photo.'

She stood back and stared at him, her expression horrified. 'What cask?'

'Oh, very good,' he replied. He looked at Joanna-Rose. 'She's very good, I'll give her that.'

'You mean the cask in the photo?' Joanna-Rose asked, looking as confused as Cathy.

'The bottling *has* to be tomorrow, I suppose they must have told you that? Are you going to tell me all of this is a coincidence?'

The two women looked at him, both unsure what to say.

'Well, Cathy, when I tell the police what you did, you'll get none of it,' he said, folding his arms and casting them a satisfied look. 'Perhaps a whiff of the angel's share, if you're lucky. Because now you're a criminal and criminals don't get to keep their gains.'

'The angel's share?' said Joanna-Rose. 'Are you talking about whisky?'

'I… I don't understand,' Cathy stammered, looking at her. 'What is he on about?'

'It's *my* whisky,' Derek told them. 'It was mine from the beginning. Robert and Charlie were only overseeing my acquisition,' he glared over at Joanna-Rose, 'so don't you and that Fleur be thinking from that photo that you have a piece of the action too. You don't.'

'So *that's* what the photo was all about,' Joanna-Rose replied. 'And they're bottling it tomorrow. Hmmmm.' She scratched her chin and thought for a moment.

'Let me guess,' Derek went on, sneering at Cathy. 'Bob passes away and you start getting letters from the distillery, am I correct?'

'I don't know about any letters from a distillery,' Cathy said, before pausing, as a mental picture of a whole pile of unopened correspondence on the writing desk in her home sprang to mind.

'I'm going to fight this all the way, I tell you,' Derek raged on. 'You're not getting any of my money. You shouldn't even have a stake in it. That husband of yours screwed me over.'

'By sleeping with your wife?' Cathy said, still nonplussed.

'For getting her to sign over half of my very expensive whisky to him and not signing it back to me as agreed,' he spat back. 'And you're not getting it! Like I said, it's prison and the angel's share for you now!'

'He did not!' Cathy cried, her heart beating so hard in her chest she thought she might faint. Yet her curiosity was getting the better of her. There were solicitor's letters in her home, lots of them. They'd been arriving for weeks. 'What's the angel's share?' she said unsurely, directing the question to Joanna-Rose.

'The vapours!' Derek raged.

'Ahh,' Joanna-Rose said. 'So that's why all there's a big hurry to bottle it, is it? You're worried there's not so much left.'

He scoffed, before turning away.

'I don't understand,' said Cathy, looking from him to her.

'Over the years, a portion of the whisky held inside a cask will evaporate at the rate of two percent a year,' Joanna-Rose explained. 'So, after fifty years, you could potentially lose half the whisky. The vapours will float out into the atmosphere to become what's called the angel's share. If this cask contains a particularly rare whisky, they might have to open it before the alcohol content begins to deplete, which makes for a far less lucrative return. And as Derek is looking jittery, my guess is we have our celebrity-facing-financial-ruin here very much by the short and curlies.'

'Why?' asked Cathy.

'Because to open and bottle it, they need the permission of all owners,' she said. 'And I think, from what Derek is saying here, that one of them might be you.'

'Pah,' Derek spat, turning around to face them again. 'That might be true if she wasn't about to be a convicted criminal.' He pointed an accusing finger at Cathy.

Joanna-Rose dipped her chin and regarded him over her spectacles. 'Who is your reading for this evening, Derek?'

He pursed his lips, taking a step away from her.

'Let me help you,' she said. 'Rich, influential people who will continue to pay you top dollar, until you die, for private psychic readings, am I right?' she asked, his annoyed face confirming that she was at least on the right track. 'Which is why you tried to steal the Jura Parish Church book of condolences, a rather incriminating act to be caught doing at this point in time, wouldn't you agree?'

'This is the last one, I tell you,' he said. 'There will be no more, at least for the time being. And there are no witnesses to what you claim except for you,' he said with a sniff. 'Who's going to believe three women who kidnapped me?'

'Who will pay cash for your readings, when you are revealed to be a big, fat, fraud?'

'I am not!' he snapped back.

'Smile for the camera,' Joanna-Rose reminded him, lifting up and patting her handbag. 'My mobile phone is here, Derek, tucked in with mother.'

Derek grimaced as Cathy looked at her, puzzled.

'And it has some very interesting film from last night on it, doesn't it Derek?' Joanna-Rose said, looking pleased.

Derek screwed up his face and put a fist to his chest. 'I... I have to sit down,' he said, toppling back to take a seat. He mopped his sweating brow with his sleeve, before looking up searchingly at Cathy. 'Is it only me that is a little perturbed at this woman claiming to have her mother in a handbag?' he said.

'I brought her here to see you,' Joanna-Rose replied dryly.

'I have shares in a cask of whisky?' Cathy asked Joanna-Rose.

Derek sucked his teeth, still unconvinced of her ignorance in the matter.

Joanna-Rose looked at her and nodded slowly, feeling both elation and pity for her friend at the same time. 'Derek here owns one share of a whisky I'd be willing to bet is extremely rare and lucrative,' she told Cathy. 'And, it would appear, thanks to Bob's dalliance with Libby Colquhoun, that there has been some arrangement which culminated in the signing over part-ownership from Libby to Bob.'

'She knows that already!' Derek barked, huffing loudly.

'Which means what?' Cathy asked.

'Which means,' Joanna-Rose replied, 'that *you* own the other half.'

Cathy paused, looking uncertainly from Derek to Joanna-Rose, her eyes stinging with new tears. When she spoke again, her voice sounded broken and sad. 'So,' she said. 'When you collapsed at your last show and began calling after me, it wasn't to give me a message from Bob then? It was it to tell me that Bob was sleeping with Libby for money.'

Joanna-Rose walked up to her friend and placed both hands on her shoulders. 'Cathy,' she said, shaking her. 'I suspect it was to stop you from claiming half of what is now yours.'

'Then why was he trying to kill himself?'

'I thought I'd lost you *and* the money, that's why,' Derek said at last. 'Never in a million years did I expect to ever see you again after you used your open ticket. I thought I was ruined.'

'You didn't know where Bob lived?' Joanna-Rose asked, with an incredulous expression.

'The bastard gave me a fake address,' Derek fumed. 'I couldn't find him! More proof he was just out to ruin me.' He wrung his hands and shook his head, chastising himself again for the fool he'd been. 'Look,' he said after a pause, speaking more calmly to them. 'I may as well tell you that ownership of the cask is all I have left. If it isn't opened soon, the whisky will be worth a lot less. Even if I have to share the profits, we have to bottle that whisky, now.'

Cathy's eyes flashed with anger. 'I don't want any part of it, you can have it all!'

Derek eyed her with suspicion, but nodded in agreement. 'Well okay, good,' he said. 'At last, someone with a little sense. It is my whisky, after all.'

Joanna-Rose held on to her friend's shoulders, shaking her again. 'Cathy,' she said. 'Whatever happened yesterday is for yesterday. You have a new tomorrow now! Take what you're given for Christ's sake. That whisky is your ticket out of trouble. It's time to get a little much-needed heat into that house of yours.'

'I don't want this man's filthy money,' she said. 'I bet he stole it anyway. Or cheated someone out of it.'

'She's right, I did,' he agreed quickly. 'It was an old client of mine. He bequeathed it to me after I had comforted him with messages from his late wife for years.'

'So you admit your readings are lies?' Joanna-Rose asked him.

Derek hesitated, before speaking again. 'I admit I may have had to elaborate under difficult conditions from time to time because of what is a very unpredictable psychic gift,' he said. 'I received it from a man who trusted me, perhaps a little unwisely. Which is exactly how Cathy's husband managed to acquire half of it.'

Cathy broke free from Joanna-Rose's grasp and put both hands to her ears. 'I don't want to hear anymore, please,' she pleaded. 'Just let him take the whisky, I don't want it.'

'Whisky? I'll have it,' Fleur called out, skipping in the doorway with a cheery grin, before noticing everyone's expressions. 'What did I miss?' she said.

Chapter Forty-One

The trip from the church to Minister MacFarlane's home in Michael's van was the quietest journey the three women had shared yet. Nobody spoke. Fleur was thinking of Charlie, Cathy was having a private, emotional battle with herself and Joanna-Rose was thinking of her mother.

Derek was a rogue and a fake psychic, there was nothing more for her to know about him. She was her mother's daughter. Her only saving grace from this disastrous meeting with Derek was the discovery he had tripped himself up in his own dealings, meaning he could help her friend live out the rest of her days in comfort, if only she would take the money. He was a man who would sell his own wife for a whisky cask. Her mother had been all Joanna-Rose had in the world and she missed her, even when being with her at the end meant she had to revert to talking to her as Barry when Alzheimer's rendered her unable to recall the woman Joanna-Rose was, instead of the son she used to be. It made her sad but she understood. Kathleen Barton's last days were clouded in fog, her mind gone long before her last breath. She hadn't known what she was doing.

Once upon a time, before the illness that took her mind, Kathleen had accepted and embraced Joanna-Rose as her daughter, though she had never stopped reminding her how lucky was to be in the loveless but functional relationship with Robert. Kathleen had asked Robert to take care of Joanna-Rose, that much she knew.

As they drew up to the minister's house, they saw a large 4x4 with blacked-out windows in the driveway.

'Goodness,' said Minister MacFarlane. 'We're late. The Viscount has sent his car for you already.'

'Oh, but I hoped to change,' said Derek, looking down at his ill-fitting clothes.

'No worries there, Derek,' the minister replied. 'We'll run in and grab a few things. I'm sure the driver won't mind waiting a moment.'

As the minister went to speak with the driver of the 4x4, Derek turned to the women and spoke quietly: 'Right,' he said. 'This is what we are going to do. Tonight, I will do the reading and, as it happens, now that Cathy is here it's the perfect opportunity for me to discuss the drawing of the cask. The deal is this. Sign it back over to me, I'll sell the lot to Viscount Fraser, who has already offered me £100,000 for it, and I will give you half. Fifty grand for your trouble. That's the deal.'

'Wait, what is this?' Fleur gasped in astonishment. 'Fifty grand for what?'

She stared open-mouthed at Cathy, who hushed her.

'There isn't much time to explain, Fleur,' said Joanna-Rose. 'But it turns out that Bob swindled Derek out of a share in the cask of whisky in that photo.'

'What? How?'

Seeing Minister MacFarlane walking back towards them, Joanna-Rose poked Cathy in the ribs, signalling for her to be quiet. 'I'll explain everything later,' she whispered.

'Okay, Derek, why don't we run on in and get you a quick wash and shave and in to some of my better clothes?' the minister said. 'And ladies, would you like to come in for a quick freshen up too?'

'No thank you,' Cathy replied for them all, sounding a little more panicked than she'd intended. 'We're just going to sit out here for a little while and wait, if that's okay?'

'Well, of course,' he replied, looking puzzled. 'But are you sure? It's getting a bit late and the weather is turning cool.'

'Yes it's fine, thank you,' said Joanna-Rose.

'Yes, fine,' repeated Fleur.

'What do you mean, Bob "swindled him" out of the cask?' Fleur repeated her question as the three women gathered by the sea's edge, away from the waiting car.

'Bob was employed by Derek to... to...' Cathy stopped, finding herself overcome with emotion.

'To win over Libby Colquhoun,' Joanna-Rose finished for her. 'With the legal help of Robert and Charlie, Derek acquired a cask of whisky from a dying old man. It is a very old whisky from the now closed, MacReeley's Distillery. Derek's told us it has to be bottled now, as its age means the alcohol content may be starting to diminish.'

'So what has this to do with Bob and Libby?' asked Fleur.

'Derek wanted to hide his investment from the taxman, as we know he has been doing with a lot of his money, so he signed the cask over to Libby,' Joanna-Rose explained.

'And Libby, having no idea how much it was worth, signed it over to Bob,' said Cathy.

'Why? Why would she do that?'

Cathy opened her mouth to speak but choked on her words.

'Because Derek paid Bob to sweeten her up, gaining her confidence and conning her out of it,' said Joanna-Rose.

Fleur put a sympathetic arm around Cathy's shoulder. 'I'm so sorry,' she soothed. 'This must be awful for you.'

'I… I can't begin to tell you how lost I am in all of this,' she replied with a sob. 'The more I hear of his dealings, the more I realise I didn't know my husband at all.'

'What I don't understand though, is why Derek would get Bob to have the cask signed over to him. Why didn't he just ask Libby himself if she had no idea of its worth?'

'Probably because she loathes him,' said Joanna-Rose. 'She wouldn't give him a pebble if he asked for it. Bob was to take her out, wine and dine her, and gain her trust, then ask about the cask. That's why Cathy had the photo. Derek gave it to Bob, who was to show it to Libby, telling her he read about the deal in the newspaper and was interested in the whisky as an enthusiast. Not caring too much about it at all, after a while she offered it to him as a gift.'

'But Derek wasn't expecting two things,' Cathy said. 'That Bob would begin seeing Libby and having a relationship for real, while he was still trying to win her back, and Bob dying before he could sign the cask back over to Derek,' she explained. 'Bob was to get fifty thousand pounds for his part in the deal. But it was never completed and as Bob is now dead, his share in the cask now belongs to me.'

'Only, given the fact he was about to kill himself when he thought he'd lost out on the entire cask, something tells me he's underplaying the casks true value,' Joanna-Rose said. 'We can't believe a thing that man says.'

'Result!' cried Fleur. 'Cathy, don't you know what this means? You're rich!'

Cathy looked nonplussed. 'I don't want the money! The fruits of my husband's sordid dealings? His affair? Oh no!'

'But you can keep your house! Pay off your bills!'

'Fleur, did you hear me? I don't want it!' she cried. 'I've agreed I'll sign it back, first thing tomorrow when we're back in Islay.'

Fleur looked from Cathy to Joanna-Rose, who shrugged her shoulders.

'I tried speaking to her,' Joanna-Rose said. 'But she's made up her mind.'

'You've got to be kidding,' said Fleur. 'That weasel has been a fraud all his life and, forgive me for saying this, Cathy, but Bob was *cheating* on you. He was sleeping with another woman, and one I might add who was being cheated by Derek too. Take something for yourself for once!'

'I won't,' Cathy replied. 'I don't care if I lose my house. What good are all my memories in there anyway? They're all fake. I just don't care about any of it anymore.' She put a hand to her temple, feeling a headache coming on. 'But you're right about one thing,' she continued. 'And I hadn't thought of it until now, but Libby was cheated by Derek too. The share in that cask belongs to her. Not Derek, not Bob and not me.'

'Oh, what?' Fleur began, sounding exasperated. 'What are you saying now?'

Cathy straightened and looked at Fleur, her eyes steely and determined. 'I'm saying there is just one right thing to do in all this mess,' she said. 'And when we get back to Islay, before the bottling, I'm contacting Libby.'

Chapter Forty-Two

The Fraser estate cut itself from the evening hue that cloaked all of Jura's high ground as their car approached. The women and Derek stepped out of the 4x4, which started away as soon as they'd done so, and made their way towards the sprawling, Victorian mansion before them.

'Is it a castle?' asked Fleur.

'No,' Derek replied.

'It's like a scene from a crime thriller,' Joanna-Rose observed.

'Yes, it is,' cried Fleur. 'All that's missing is forked lightning and a creaky front door that opens itself.'

'And a pale-faced, balding butler with a hump,' said Cathy.

Fleur stopped walking and looked at her. 'That's not a crime thriller, that's *The Rocky Horror Show*!'

'Ah Derek, how lovely to see you again!'

Everyone turned to the direction of the voice to see a slight, elderly woman hobbling towards them with the aid of an ornate, mahogany walking stick. She wore a tight, cornflower blue cashmere sweater dress and knee high boots. But what was most striking about the woman, aside from the smoky, Bridget-Bardotesque eye make-up, was her platinum-blonde hair, coiffured into an overly-high beehive, the top of which bounced precariously as she walked, threatening to tumble loose over her face at any moment. Her blood-red lipstick smile changed to a deep frown, as the petite Yorkshire Terriers following at her heels began growling and yapping a warning at the group.

'Oh do stop it, Pippy-LaBelle. And you too, Mistress Tanya. You should know better!' the woman snapped at the dogs, who stopped yapping at once but continued to growl suspiciously.

'Dorothea, you look radiant as always,' Derek said, taking her outstretched hand as she finally reached them. 'How long has it been?'

'Oh, too, too long,' she replied. 'Nobody has referred to me as radiant for, oh, at least two years.'

Derek looked surprised. 'It hasn't been that long, has it?'

Lady Fraser smiled. 'Indeed it has. We wondered what had happened to you.' She turned to appraise each of the women, one at a time, her eyes finally resting on Cathy's cleavage. 'So,' she continued, still staring at it. 'Are you going to introduce me to your friends?'

Cathy felt her neck flush as Derek began to introduce them. 'This is Cathy, my new assistant. This is Fleur.' He pointed to her with a welcoming grin that looked so insincere and creepy it made her scowl, when she knew she should be acting like an old friend. 'My new secretary. And, would you believe, this is Saorla Nardone.'

Lady Fraser's smile turned to an expression of astonishment. 'The playwright?'

Joanna-Rose smiled back, trying to keep her annoyance under check.

'The very same,' Derek said, looking so pleased Cathy imagined there may have been some actual pride in his voice.

'How wonderful. Lovely to meet you, Saorla!' exclaimed Lady Fraser, her voice raised so loud there was an echo in the valley around them, that the old lady didn't seem to notice. She turned to shake Joanna-Rose's hand. 'I've seen all of your plays. Absolutely adored "Where Friendships Are Forged".'

'Thank you,' Joanna-Rose replied with a smile. 'But Saorla Nardone is a pen name. I'm actually called -'

'So deep and so very, very touching,' Lady Fraser went on, seeming to not hear her. 'I suppose you'll be working on another one at the moment?'

Joanna-Rose opened her mouth to reply.

'Oh, you could mention of us and the house in it,' Lady Fraser continued. 'You'll love it here, lots of writerly inspiration for you.'

She took her place between Derek and Joanna-Rose and put an arm around each of them, before leading them towards the front door. Fleur raised her eyebrows at Cathy, as they trudged behind at the speed of an arthritic tortoise, thinking they might get in from the early evening chill at about midnight.

'You know,' Lady Fraser boomed, leaning in so heavily the handle of her walking stick dug into Joanna-Rose's side, 'my Great Uncle Angus wrote a play once.'

'Interesting,' said Joanna-Rose.

'Yes, it was. And hilarious of course. Great Uncle Angus was a hoot. Is your next piece going to be another comedy?'

'Actually, it's my biography,' Derek answered for her.

'Oh good heavens, a book? How exhausting.'

Joanna-Rose thought about telling her that writing plays was just as exhausting, but there seemed little point. Lady Fraser appeared to like to listen to herself more than anyone else.

'I was thinking of writing my memoirs, of course. But it's finding the time, you know. Impossible, what with the stalking and all.'

'Oh? Who have you got your eye on?' asked Fleur, making Joanna-Rose and Cathy chuckle. Lady Fraser didn't hear her.

'But then, if I had just thought of getting some assistants like you, dear Derek. Now that would help enormously. Horatio, Derek's here!' she shouted out, releasing her human leaning posts to rest on her walking stick, as they finally entered the grand hallway. She turned back to Derek. 'Robert and Jemima will be here presently,' she said, referring to the Prime Minister and his wife. 'They'll be arriving by helicopter, of course.'

'Up here?' Cathy asked. 'Where will they land?'

'We have a helipad, naturally,' Lady Fraser said to Derek, so loudly he had to lean away. 'What will we be doing with your assistants during the session?'

'These three?' he asked, looking bewildered. 'I thought they could come and listen in too?'

At that moment, Viscount Fraser appeared at the top of the stairs. 'Derek,' he boomed, his voice echoing and bouncing from the high ceilings. 'How great to see you here again.'

Lady Fraser leaned in to Derek and whispered, 'I'm sure Ms Nardone will have clearance, but I'm not so sure about the other two.'

'Oh, er...' Derek regarded Fleur and Cathy, who were both trying to look disinterested yet straining to listen in. 'I'm sure Robert won't mind.'

'He won't, but his people will. They've gotten very tetchy since the urine throwing incident at that community garden in Birmingham.'

'She thinks we're going to throw pee on the Prime Minister in the garden,' Cathy said under her breath to Fleur.

'You mean we're not?' Fleur asked, feigning a look of astonishment.

'Hello again, lovely ladies,' boomed Viscount Fraser, who had joined them at the bottom of the stairs at last. 'May we offer you a drink in the library?'

'I'm not sure where we're putting the ladies yet, Horatio,' Lady Fraser boomed at him. 'There are protocols, as you know.'

'Dorothea!' he said, tapping the old lady on the shoulder. 'Turn your hearing aid up!'

As she put a hand to her ear to fumble with the aid, a loud whistle screamed out of it, making them all cover their own ears. Grinning, Viscount Fraser motioned to a room on their right. A final twist bringing the whistling to a halt, Lady Fraser, Joanna-Rose and Derek swept past him into it, leaving Fleur and Cathy behind. They looked at each other, unsure of whether or not they should follow.

'There are some wonderful paintings on the wall in here,' Lady Fraser said, still as loudly as before. 'Let me show them to you, Ms Nardone.'

'Please, call me Joanna-Rose.'

At once, the question was answered, as Viscount Fraser's friendly face leaned back out of the doorway to beckon them in. 'This way, ladies,' he said, straining to look down Cathy's sweater as they passed.

'That's why Lady Posho doesn't want us,' Fleur said in Cathy's ear once they were out of earshot. 'It's because her husband might.'

Cathy screwed up her face. 'What?'

Fleur stopped and swept both arms across in an up-down brush of her own body. 'We're too sexy!'

The Viscount caught them up and winked at Cathy, who fanned her neck scarf out to cover her cleavage.

'So, how are you tonight, Viscount?' Fleur asked, leaning across to pull the scarf from her. 'It's rather hot in here, don't you think?' she said to Cathy, who glowered back at her.

The Viscount, however, was smiling wider than before. 'Wonderful, wonderful. The old ticker is still firing, even at my age. As are other things,' he winked and touched his nose, 'if you know what I mean,' he said with a wide grin. 'Now, can I get you ladies a wee drink? Whisky? Vodka?'

'Two whiskies,' said Fleur. 'Thank you.'

She curtseyed.

'What are you doing?' Cathy whispered, as he headed off to fetch their drinks.

Fleur opened her jacket, undid the two top buttons on her shirt, and stuck her chest out. 'Do you want to get in to meet the PM and his wife, or not?'

'Ladies,' Lady Fraser announced loudly. 'I'm afraid it has to be said that while you are both very welcome to a little drink and some snacks here in the library, the actual reading Derek does is to be a very, very secretive affair. We cannot have everyone listening in. So, I think it best that you both stay here when the Prime Minister arrives, at least for the reading part, if that is agreeable to you both?'

'Dorothea, you're shouting again!' Viscount Fraser said, appearing beside Cathy and Fleur with a drink for each of them.

Lady Fraser fiddled with her hearing aid.

'In here?' Cathy said, taking the offered drink and looking around at the floor-to-ceiling books, roaring fire, sumptuous, squashy armchairs and sheepskin rugs. She nodded. 'I think this will be just fine.'

Fleur motioned to the deer's head above the door. 'That what happened to the last old dear that tried to listen in?' she asked.

Lady Fraser, still twiddling with the thing behind her ear, didn't hear her.

'Oh Fleur, I can see I'll have to keep my eye on you,' Viscount Fraser said, giving her a nudge.

'Not from one of your deer's heads, I hope?'

As he leered at her, Cathy gave a sharp tug on Fleur's jumper, making her start.

'What?'

'Come and look at this,' Cathy said, pulling her away to the bookshelves. 'They have a copy of '*Bury My Heart at Wounded Knee*'. My dad had that book.'

'I bet there's an actual late wounded knee on the wall in here somewhere too,' Fleur said.

'Ooh, listen,' Lady Fraser called out.

There was the chucka, chucka sound of a helicopter in the distance and, on cue, the dogs outside in the hallway began to bark.

Fleur's mouth fell open. 'Well,' she said. 'Lady Fraser heard that right, at least.'

'Wonderful,' Lady Fraser shouted, earning a tsk from her son. 'That will be the Prime Minister and our Granddaughter. If you'd like to follow me, Derek. And you, Ms Nardone. It's time to make our way to the lounge to get everything prepared.' She stopped, noticing Viscount Fraser, who was leaning on a sideboard staring at Cathy, who looked on obliviously. 'Oh do come along, Horatio,' Lady Fraser said with a sigh. 'We have to have the ambience just right, as you know, and Derek hasn't even seen the room yet.'

'Yes, hurry along,' Fleur said, feigning a posh accent. 'You should all get there in a week.'

'The ambience?' Cathy said, giving Derek a thoughtful look. 'You mean you need low lighting for these readings?'

Derek opened his mouth to speak but Lady Fraser cut in ahead of him, surprising Fleur with the fact she had obviously heard her.

'Of course!' the old lady said, giving her a look of disdain. 'You'd think you would know that, being his assistant.'

Chapter Forty-Three

Fleur gazed out of the window, watching the helicopter as it flew over the roof of the house.

'Get away from there!' Cathy hissed, pulling her back and closing the curtains. 'We don't want them all thinking we're a pair of nosey parkers. Or worse, celebrity spotters.'

'Frankly, I couldn't care less,' said Fleur with a sniff of indifference. 'Who cares what they think? And who on earth told you the Prime Minister was a celebrity?'

Cathy shrugged. 'Oh, you know what I mean,' she said.

Fleur let out a sigh. 'Well, this will be a much more boring evening than I planned,' she said. 'Locked in the library away from all the important people.'

'You say "locked in a library" like it was a bad thing,' Cathy told her. 'Look at all these books! I can only dream of having a huge library like this.' She twirled around with her arms out, making Fleur think of Julie Andrews telling everyone the hills are alive in *The Sound of Music*. 'I have this recurring dream that I get rich,' Cathy went on. 'I've had it for years now, since I was a girl. I dream that I'm camping with some friends, when a plane crashes in the long grass, just yards from where we're sat toasting marshmallows.'

'That wasn't a dream, it was *Five Go To Billycock Hill*!'

'And I run towards the plane, but stop to avoid falling over a suitcase that's lying on the ground. So I bend down to open it, and -'

'Let me guess, it's stuffed full of money?'

'Yes! How did you know that?'

Fleur blinked. 'And you keep it? In the dream, I mean? Because you don't seem like the sort of person who would do that, to be honest. I mean, look at the cask of whisky. I can't believe you're just going to hand that over to Libby bloody Colquhoun.'

'I don't want any part of that money, Fleur,' Cathy snapped, her dream-world bubble well and truly popped. 'Can you please leave it alone?'

'Cathy, don't you see? This is your suitcase of money! It's yours. You've got to take it or you'll lose everything. You don't want that, do you?'

'Bob as good as stole Libby's share from Derek. Why would I want his stolen gains from his affair with that woman?'

'Why would you want to give that woman all the money?'

'Please just drop it!' Cathy cried, raising both hands to her temples in exasperation.

Fleur sighed, and began walking over to the door. 'Oh well, if you don't want to talk, I'm off to look around this big, posh house.'

'What are you doing?' Cathy said, her eyes wide as Fleur opened the door and peered out into the hallway.

'It's boring just sitting in here. Why can't we have a little look about? No one will know. They're all busy in a lounge that is too posh for minions like us, that's if they've reached it yet, waiting for Lazy Fraser.'

'You mean *Lady* Fraser,' Cathy corrected.

'I know what I mean. Come on.'

'It could be right across the hall, for all you know,' said Cathy, pushing the door closed.

'No, it isn't,' said Fleur, pulling it open again. 'Can you hear anyone in the hallway rushing out to greet the PM and his wife? No, they've all gone to the helipad, no doubt. Which could take a half a century. We can sneak upstairs while they're out.'

Cathy looked alarmed. 'Don't be ridiculous!' she said. 'You can't go snooping around the place. They're bound to catch us!'

'No, they won't,' Fleur said, signalling to her to look outside the door. ''There's no one in sight. Come on, we can make it to the staircase in lightning speed.'

'Fleur, stop!' Cathy whispered, as the other woman disappeared outside. Terrified, but equally curious, she looked about the library before shrugging and following suit.

As they began tiptoeing up the stairs, a sudden thought occurred to Cathy. 'What if they have children up there?'

'They're both in their seventies if they're a day,' Fleur replied. 'Come on, let's just have a little look about. We'll be back down before the séance thing is finished, I promise you.'

'I know I'll regret this,' said Cathy.

Before either of them could consider the matter any further, they heard loud voices coming from the back of the house as people came out into the hallway, making Cathy and Fleur bolt upstairs in double-quick time.

'I'll just go and show Matilda's handkerchief to Derek.'

The booming voice was Lady Fraser's. Fleur pointed to a large, ornate door in front of them and the pair dived towards it, disappearing inside.

'Whoa,' Fleur exclaimed, eyeing the enormous, four poster bed in the centre of the lamp-lit room, swathed in a deep, crimson bedspread. Thick, red velvet curtains were draped around it.

'Crikey,' whispered Cathy, looking wide-eyed around the room.

'It's like a tarts boudoir,' Fleur said.

'Fleur!' Cathy said, turning to shake her shoulders as the rattle of a walking stick on the staircase startled them both. 'Lady Fraser is coming to find a hanky. What if she's coming in here?'

'Chill out, woman. It'll take her ages,' Fleur said.

A loud buzzing sound, followed by a slow scraping rang out in the hallway.

Cathy looked at Fleur, her eye's filled with horror.

'Stair lift!' they said, together.

'Is it a very old handkerchief?' They heard Derek ask.

'They won't be coming in here,' whispered Fleur. 'Does this look like the bedroom of a woman in her eighties? No, this will be the room set up for the *Hello Magazine* shoot or something. Maybe we should leave them a little gift.'

As Cathy looked about the room for a hiding place, Fleur felt inside her jacket pocket, before spilling the contents out on to the bedside table with a satisfied grin.

The buzzing and scraping followed by pad of slow footsteps on the stone stairs got nearer, as did the voices. They sounded like they were at the top of the staircase now.

Cathy spied the bay window, draped in thick, red curtains to match the ones around the bed and dived behind them, beckoning Fleur to do the same.

The door clicked open.

'Cathy!'

'Shhh. They're coming,' Cathy hissed, making her way to the wall edge and holding back the curtain a little to peer out.

'But, you can see our feet!' Fleur said, more urgently.

Cathy's heart was in her mouth as she spied Lady Fraser entering the room.

'Shhh!' she whispered.

Fleur tapped on Cathy's shoulder, but she shrugged her off, hanging on to the curtain edge to watch as Derek followed Lady Fraser slowly in. When they finally reached the bed, he pushed her roughly on to it, so suddenly Cathy had to cover her mouth as a horrified gasp almost escaped her.

As Lady Fraser fell she rolled over to face him, her walking stick clattering to the floor. 'Oh Derek,' she roared, so loudly her voice bounced off all four walls. 'I've missed this!' And with that, she pulled him on top of her in a passionate embrace.

Replacing the curtain so she could no longer see, Cathy straightened up and turned to Fleur, who had a hand over her own mouth now, pressing so hard she was turning purple.

'Oh, ummm, mummmm,' was all they could hear, as the couple kissed. There was a rip of someone's clothing.

Cathy covered her ears.

'I thought you weren't going to come,' Lady Fraser yelled out.

Fleur took her hand from her mouth, breathing a sigh of relief. 'Oh, thank God,' she said. 'He's finished.'

'Darling, Dorothea,' Derek said. 'Please turn up your hearing aid, or someone downstairs will hear us!'

The women heard a swift, deafening whistle, confirming the old lady had done as instructed.

'I told you I'd be here,' Derek continued. 'It's just... things didn't quite go the way I'd planned.'

'We were supposed to be running away together!' Lady Fraser thundered.

'Shush, darling,' Derek said. 'Please, try to be quieter, my love. You see, I got caught out, by my assistant, Cathy. She found me on the beach. She saw me go into the water. What could I do? I was rumbled.'

Cathy and Fleur turned to stare at each other, both wide-eyed and open-mouthed.

'Oh no, it's all over,' Lady Fraser cried. 'Our escape to the Cayman Islands. I have my suitcase ready, hidden in the summerhouse.'

'Oh, my poor darling. We can't go, not yet.'

'You mean we still could?' This time her voice sounded quieter, and hopeful.

'Yes,' he replied. 'But the thing is, Dorothea, I'm going to need you to sign my share of the cask back to me.'

Cathy's neck bristled.

'But I thought we were just going to take the cash after the bottling?' Lady Fraser said, sounding surprised.

'Oh, Dorothea.'

There was a pause, before the sounds of more lip smacking. In a moment, Derek spoke again. 'It isn't as much money now as I was expecting,' she told her. 'There's been... a complication.'

Fleur nodded at her friend, the complication, giving her a thumbs up.

'Derek, six years I've waited for you. Six years!' Lady Fraser cried. 'All this time and Horatio's never suspected a thing, although I don't know how I hide it from him, really I don't. How can he not see the desire between us whenever you're here?'

Fleur turned to Cathy, held her stomach and pretended to be sick.

'And every time I think we can get away at last, something comes up. Surely there's enough money to pay those silly gambling debts by now?' Lady Fraser's voice was full of desperation.

'Oh God, Dorothea,' Derek sighed. 'You know I can't keep my hands off you in that tight, little blue dress. Don't you, you minx?'

There was a peel of over-loud laughter and more ripping of clothes, until Derek stopped and sighed, 'I have to have you; I do! But I really must insist we sort out the details on the cask tonight, my darling. The bottling has to happen now. The whisky is very old.'

'What does that matter?' she asked. 'It will just get more valuable. Can't we just leave tonight?'

'But we have no money,' he told her quickly. 'Horatio will cut you off as soon as he learns about us. We have to bottle the whisky first, or it could be worthless anyway because the alcohol content may be starting to deplete. Please, my love. I need you to sign this.'

There was a rustling of papers and Cathy peered around the curtain to see Derek lean over Lady Fraser to reach into his discarded jacket pocket.

'Cathy!' Fleur whispered, tapping her on the back.

'Shhh!' she said, batting her with an arm without turning round.

'But Cathy!' Fleur said, more urgently.

'Would you look at this,' Lady Fraser exclaimed, noticing for the first time two bottles of lubricant on the bedside table. She pushed Derek off and leaned over to pick one up, examining the label.

'What is it?' Derek asked.

'Looks like lubricant,' Lady Fraser replied, her eyes wide in shock. She turned to peer at him, as he took the bottle from her hand. 'Oh, please, Derek,' she said, her surprised expression turning to one of exasperation. 'Not that game again.'

'Thank you, thank you, my darling!' Derek replied, jumping on her as she burst into girl-like giggles. 'Turn over!' he barked.

Fleur gasped. 'Dirty old bugger,' she said aloud.

Cathy gasped too, as, alerted to the sound, Derek and Lady Fraser stopped canoodling and spotted Fleur standing in the middle of the bay window, the curtain pole hanging off on one side and the left curtain on the floor at her feet. Cathy released the bit of curtain she was holding, noticing for the first time that only the right hand side – the bit she was holding - had stayed fixed to the rail, so she had been concealing merely her face. Her body had been in full view of the room; as was Fleur.

'I tried to tell you,' Fleur said with a shrug.

'Oh... my... God!' Derek gasped, still straddling the old woman.

'What are you both doing?' said Lady Fraser breathily, pushing Derek off as, red-faced and breathless, she began making furtive attempts to button her blouse up.

'We might ask you two the same,' snapped Fleur.

Chapter Forty-Four

'It was such a pleasure to meet the Prime Minister himself,' Cathy beamed, as the four stared at the morning mist covered Isle of Jura from their windows.

The group were sat in Cathy's car, on the ferry, heading back to Islay.

'And so kind of Lady Fraser to agree to let us stay the night, too,' Cathy added with a wry smile.

Derek scowled.

'It was,' agreed Fleur, casting a flirtatious smile at her favourite ferryman, who winked back. She patted the breast pocket of her coat with a satisfied grin and turned to Derek. 'And how amazing that you knew all that stuff about his wife's late aunt Matilda, while simultaneously, on the other side of the island, Minister MacFarlane was searching for his missing book of condolences.'

'Which we found right in the bushes where we accidentally left it,' said Joanna-Rose. 'About ten minutes after you just had to go use the toilet in the church.'

'I *did* need the toilet,' said Derek. 'And anyway, how was I to know you had left it out there? Fleur said she had put it back.'

'And you were so relieved to discover I'd forgotten, weren't you?' remarked Fleur. 'You're a fake, Derek Montrose. Always have been, always will be.'

'Well, I've well and truly paid for it now, haven't I?' he grumbled, turning away from her and folding his arms.

Fleur look round to give a wave to her admirer, and said, 'I love you.'

Derek turned wide-eyed to stare at her. 'What?'

'Not you,' she said, pointing to the ferryman, 'him.'

'Thank God,' Derek grumbled, pulling his jacket more tightly around him and looking back out of his window. 'Well, you can all believe what you want to believe, I don't care,' he said, his eyes narrowing as he squeezed the wad of cold cash in his right pocket. 'I didn't get to where I am today by stealing a book of condolences. I have the gift.'

'So how come we caught you sneaking it out then?' asked Fleur.

'I told you -' Derek began.

'Yes, you told us you have long dead relatives on Jura you wanted to read up on. Funny that, because for one thing I'd have thought you could just go into a dark room and speak to them direct and for another, I get the distinct impression you go over to Jura rather a lot,' said Fleur, casting him a knowing look.

'I've never been in the boot of a car before.'

'You're welcome. Please travel with us again anytime for more original and quirky experiences.'

'Can you two just stop bickering for five minutes?' said Cathy. 'I'm getting a headache. Listen, Derek,' she added more solemnly, turning round in her seat. 'There's something I need to tell you.'

Fleur's eyes widened. 'Now?' she said.

'Now,' Cathy replied. She looked at the old man. 'There's somebody waiting for us on the other side.'

'Oh, he knows all about that,' Fleur said with a smirk. 'He's got the gift, remember?'

'I mean on Islay,' Cathy continued, eyeing Derek in her rear-view mirror. 'It's Libby.'

Derek sat bolt upright in his seat, staring at her with hopeful eyes. 'She is?'

'Yes, but it's not what you might think.'

'Tell him what you did, Cathy,' Fleur told her. 'Tell him what you've gone and done with your suitcase of money after all these years of chasing it.'

'What?' said Derek, sitting bolt upright.

'I'm going to tell her about the cask.'

'You what?' He threw himself back against the seat, before leaning forward again to put his head in his hands.

His shout had made the people in the next car look at them and Cathy felt her neck redden.

'Why… would you?' he stammered.

'It's the right thing to do,' she told him.

Derek looked up at her. 'The woman's a cheat!' he raged. 'She doesn't deserve a penny of my money!'

'Really?'

Catching Cathy's accusatory glance in her rear-view mirror, he swallowed hard. 'How?' he said, tugging nervously at his shirt collar. 'How will you even contact her?'

Cathy shrugged. 'I already have,' she told him.

'How?'

'It was easy,' she said. 'I just Googled her and then contacted her agent. When I said it was something about you and money -'

'She replied right away,' Joanna-Rose finished for her.

'So you were in on this too?' Derek said to her, his eyes wide and angry. 'Is that what you came to do, ruin me? I might have known.'

'Don't take it out on Joanna-Rose, this has nothing to do with her,' Cathy told him. 'It was my idea and mine alone. You and Bob cheated the cask out of Libby. Whatever she's done, she doesn't deserve that.'

'I had a son, and now I have... I have... a thing. What do you call yourself?' he went on.

'A thing?' said Fleur. 'What the hell is that supposed to mean?'

Joanna-Rose looked stung, but just for a moment. At once, she rolled down her window, straightened herself up in her seat and turned around to face Derek. 'I'm not a thing, as you and so many before you have so gracefully put it. I'm a post-operative, transgender woman,' she told him. 'Can you bring yourself to say that, Derek? Like it isn't some kind of disease? And I'm proud! Not weird, proud! Not a freak, proud. I'm proud of who and what I am. I'm living proof that it's okay to look to the person you feel you are within yourself and bring her out. Can you even imagine how liberating that is?'

He didn't answer.

'No, of course you can't,' she snapped. 'Because the great, Derek Montrose has been living a big, fake life forever. I pity you, I really do.'

'You? Pity me?' He looked her up and down and tutted. 'I'm not the bloke in the dress, in desperate need of psychotherapy. Really, if you want my money, take it and get yourself some help.'

Cathy let out a gasp of horror.

'I'm sick of your hate,' Joanna-Rose said to him, turning back to face the windscreen with a heavy sigh. 'You, the people who put these scars on my hand,' she raised her left hand idly. 'The schoolkids who kicked me until I passed out because they thought I was *in need of help* as you put it.'

Cathy patted Joanna-Rose's knee and gave her a sympathetic glance.

Watching the exchange, Derek began, 'I didn't know...'

'You don't know half as much as you've been making out for all these years, Derek Montrose. Or should I call you, Mr Compassion? A dying old man left you a cask of very old and expensive whisky because of your kindness and humanity, yet you refer to *me* as a thing.'

'Who probably isn't even my son,' he retorted.

Fleur, who had been watching and listening without a word until that moment, asked quietly, 'You're a transgender woman?'

Everyone fell silent as the ferry began to slow, their attentions turned to the ferrymen on and offshore, going about the business of preparing for passengers to disembark. As Cathy started the engine, still nobody inside the car spoke.

Rolling down her window, Fleur threw a screwed up piece of paper at her ferryman as they passed. He tipped his hardhat at her in thanks, before stooping to pick it up.

'Well,' she said, rolling the car window back up and breaking the silence between them all at last. 'That is brilliant. I mean, Joanna-Rose, you can't tell at all!'

'Oh hush, Fleur,' Cathy butted in, afraid of what she might say next. She turned the car up the hill and drove away from the ferry port.

'No, I mean it,' Fleur continued, still beaming at the prospect of a date in the near future. 'You're a woman. Who needs to know anything else? And this worm,' her smile fell as she pointed to Derek. 'Doesn't deserve to have you in his life, even if you are his son.'

Cathy stole a sharp look at her in the mirror.

'Daughter,' Fleur corrected herself quickly.

'She's not my son,' Derek said, looking exasperated. 'He just thinks I've got something she can put a claim to.'

'She,' Cathy corrected. 'Not he. Not he, then she. *She*. Why is this so hard for you?'

'I don't need anything from you, I have enough of my own money,' Joanna-Rose told him. 'I'm Saorla Nardone, remember? Which reminds me...' She turned around in her seat again to face him, her eyes flashing accusingly. 'Who told you, Derek?'

He froze. 'Erm... who told me what?'

Cathy took a sharp intake of breath and stared over at Joanna-Rose, before slowing the car to pull into a passing place. Bringing the vehicle to a standstill, she turned her attentions to Derek, who was sat, dumbstruck. 'Oh, yes,' she said to him. 'Who *did* tell you?'

Fleur tutted and threw up her hands in annoyance, and said, 'Who told him what?'

'Who told you I was Saorla Nardone?' Joanna-Rose said to Derek. 'It wasn't me,' she looked at Cathy, 'was it you?'

Cathy shook her head.

'Well... it was... her,' Derek stammered, pointing to Fleur, who looked at Joanna-Rose and shook her head too.

Facing the front again, Joanna-Rose picked up her carpet bag and pulled it to her in a tight hug. 'Oh, mum,' she said, as a lone tear trickled down her cheek. 'It was you, wasn't it?'

Cathy swallowed and put a sympathetic arm on her shoulder, before turning to Derek. 'How long have you known?' she asked.

He chewed his lip and stared wordlessly back at her. Fleur stared at both of the women, looking even more confused.

'You've known about me all along, haven't you?' Joanna-Rose said to him, without turning back round. 'But you were ashamed. Let me guess, afraid of bad publicity?'

'More like afraid of the child support payments,' Cathy said.

'I paid them,' Derek snapped, so suddenly he made all three women start. 'I paid them for years. And then, when she was old enough, I paid... I paid...' He stopped as Joanna-Rose turned to meet his gaze again. He looked away, pursing his lips.

'You paid my mother not to tell me? To keep me quiet?' she said.

'No,' he snapped back. 'She would never have agreed to that. It was something else. I needed to be absolutely certain you wouldn't just appear without warning, right at the height of my career. So I had to find someone I trusted, someone who would find out the moment Kathleen decided to tell you, in case you took it upon yourself to come looking for me. So -'

'Oh my God!' Joanna-Rose released her tight grip on the bag and put her hands over her mouth.

Cathy drew in her breath, put both arms on the steering wheel to steady her and closed her eyes. It was Fleur that finished Derek's story for all of them.

"You absolute pig of a man,' she said. 'You paid Robert to watch over her.'

Chapter Forty-Five

Having enjoyed a feast of delicious baked potatoes with haggis and red onion marmalade from The Old Kiln café, the three women sat with a tray of fine whiskies on a huge, flat rock, looking over the Irish Sea behind Ardbeg Distillery.

'Slainte Math!' said Fleur, as they each raised their glasses and washed a wonderful, Scottish lunch down with the smokiest drams any of them had ever tasted.

'To new beginnings,' said Cathy, her eyes watering from the shock of quickly swallowed whisky. She shuddered.

Joanna-Rose coughed and looked at her empty glass. 'Boy, that was a peaty one, even for me,' she said.

Fleur licked her lips and reached down for a second dram from the tray. 'What time are we meeting Libby?' she asked Cathy.

'In just over an hour,' she replied, looking at her watch and taking a slow breath in, overwhelmed by the sudden knot in her stomach. She took another, more reluctant sip from her whisky.

'Where exactly?' Joanna-Rose said.

'The car park beside the beach at Machir Bay,' she said at last.

'So you're determined to go through with this?' Fleur said, turning her head to look up the road before sighing at the thought of how far up the road the car was. She was too full of whisky and baked potatoes for running.

'You're going to give away your one chance for a better future to some woman you've never even met?' Joanna-Rose said.

'One who has cheated as much as Derek has, I might remind you,' added Fleur, stretching out her arms before reaching, unnoticed, behind Cathy for her car keys.

Cathy looked out at the calm waters, twinkling in the late morning sunlight, closed her eyes and breathed in fresh, cool, Islay air. It was salt, sea, lush, green grass and peat – a heady combination. 'Do you suppose we should give Derek some lunch?' she asked.

'I'll take something back for him,' Fleur said, screwing up her nose before casually stuffing Cathy's keys in her pocket.

'No need for anyone to go out of their way for him,' Joanna-Rose agreed. 'He can stay where he is for the time being.'

Cathy looked down at her hands and sighed. 'I have to tell her,' she said.

'In that case,' Fleur said, with a nod to Joanna-Rose as they began getting to their feet. 'Then I'm sorry to do this to you, Cathy, but it's for your own good.'

Puzzled for the briefest of moments, Cathy watched her friends run away before a realisation dawned. She got to her feet.

'Wait!'

Neither of them knew where it was, so it had been decided that Joanna-Rose would drive while Fleur read the map, as they made their hurried way to Machir Bay without Cathy.

'You'll have to slow down, the roads are quite bumpy,' Fleur complained, smoothing the paper map out on her lap and leaning in to read it. As the car began to slow, she pointed to a left turn at the crossroads, which the other woman steered them into. 'So,' Fleur said after a moment. 'Why have you never made any friends before?'

'Well, I did have some friends, but the people I spent any significant amount of time with before now were just on the internet,' Joanna-Rose explained. 'I communicated with them through a variety of pseudonymous personas, not revealing my true self or trusting anyone, and most often while I was drunk and should have been writing.'

'What about your writing?' Fleur asked. 'Didn't that make you have to socialise a little?'

The other woman shook her head sadly. 'I hadn't written a word that made any sense since Robert died. Can you believe that? I'm amazed my poor agent has stuck by me.' She pulled Cathy's car into a passing place, as a green Volkswagen went by, its occupants waving gratefully at them. 'But that was until I saw this island and then Jura. Now I can't stop! Getting outdoors to meet you and Cathy was a first, and as you know this was brought about by copious amounts of alcohol. Only in the widow's forum on Facebook was I using an account under my real name. I suppose this was my way of reaching out to normal life again.'

'So, are you Joanna-Rose Hepple then? I mean, is that your real name?' asked Fleur.

'Yes, I changed it to Robert's by deed poll.'

'And do you have relationships online?'

'I've had a few, yes. But I'm in love with Isaac, my gardener, would you believe. Someone whom I always felt I could never have.'

'That might not be true.'

'I don't know for sure,' Joanna-Rose agreed. 'But one thing I know is it's hard to reveal your feelings out in the real world to a straight man, unless you lie about who you are and I'm not going to do that, it isn't fair. No, it has to be honest or nothing. The thing is, you never know how somebody is going to react. Finding people online is easier for someone of my age. I'm too old now for the club scene.'

'Why not just tell him who you are first?' Fleur suggested. 'Not the "you love him" bit, just the truth about you. You'll see from his reaction how that makes him feel, and if he seems okay with it, tell him!'

It's not meant to be,' Joanna-Rose said. 'He's like... I don't know, *the sun.* And I'm the moon.'

'Exactly,' Fleur reasoned, without a hint of irony. 'It's the perfect partnership. When you come out, he will go down.' She stopped; her brow furrowing as she thought about what she'd just said again.

Joanna-Rose's eyes widened.

'Oh... err... wait. That came out wrong,' Fleur stammered. 'Can we... how about... err, you tell me how this all started for you? I'd like to be able to understand. Not the Isaac thing. You. How you went from Barry to Joanna-Rose.'

'I began crossdressing in my mother's clothes before I hit puberty,' Joanna-Rose replied, relieved to be back on subject. 'I mean, I've never been what you might call a flamboyant type. I don't even own any jewellery, nothing pretty or dazzling that might bring me more attention,' she said. 'But I assumed at first that my desire to wear women's clothing was a sexual thing. In the very beginning I fetishized it.'

'Fetishized?'

'I thought it was a kink. My thing, if you like,' she explained. 'But my mother found me doing this one day and never said a word after it. She wasn't angry or ashamed, she just went with it from the start. She was a pretty amazing woman, by all accounts. So then I began to feel okay about it and I experimented outside of the house, wearing high heels and make-up to school. Then I was labelled a freak, bullied mercilessly until... well... you know the rest. And the thing is, when people label you enough, you start to make it fit. I admit I've lived a solitary existence ever since that beating.' Despite herself, Joanna-Rose chuckled. 'Being a writer was the perfect career until I found I couldn't do it anymore.'

Fleur swallowed hard. 'Joanna-Rose, I've got to tell you, the world needs more people like you, helping them to understand. Because I'm not going to lie, I didn't understand at all before now.'

'No, thank you,' Joanna-Rose replied with a wry smile. 'It's nice to have another someone that isn't ashamed of me.'

'Oh, don't thank me,' Fleur said. 'I think you'd have a lot more friends completely accepting of you if you'd just ventured out more, to be honest. And as for me, well, in the past, I have to admit I haven't understood such things. I've been guilty of the point and stare thing – of mocking things that I can't comprehend. I think I'm like a lot of people, the result of having grown up in a culture and age that didn't understand. I always thought these things were a choice, rather than something people are born with, if you see what I mean. But sitting here now, listening to you, knowing a little more about your life and hearing you describe growing up and struggling alone with all your feelings, I feel... Well, frankly I'm ashamed of myself and society, not you.'

'I'm touched, Fleur. Thank you for saying that. If I've educated one person today then my life was worthwhile.'

'Your life has always been worthwhile,' Fleur responded, patting her on her arm. 'You're making things that have touched other lives with your writing. Hopefully, you'll go on touching other lives. The two most important things to be in life are your true self and a teacher.'

'But I'm not a teacher.'

'In ten minutes, you have taught me more about what it means to be transgender than I have ever been told or bothered to find out for myself. And this old woman was once a silly, misguided teenage girl who ran screaming every time a Boy George record came on the radio.'

'Screaming?' Joanna-Rose said with a smirk. 'Really?'

Fleur nodded, her cheeks flushing at the memory. 'Yes, we all did. "Turn that freak show off! Get Duran Duran back on!"' she said, imitating her teenage self. 'I'm ashamed, Joanna-Rose, I really am. But I'm so glad to have been enlightened as an older, more mature person and to meet you, one of life's teachers.'

'What a lovely thing to say,' said Joanna-Rose, putting a hand on Fleur's knee. 'You've made me feel all warm and fuzzy.'

'So, is it strictly men you go for?' Fleur said, looking down at her knee and bursting her friend's warm, fuzzy bubble.

'Yes, it is,' Joanna-Rose replied with a laugh. 'You don't need to worry.'

'Oh I'm not worried,' Fleur told her quickly. 'It's just... well, I wondered, that's all. Relationships must be so hard for you to find. No wonder you turned to the drink.'

Joanna-Rose looked at her with surprised eyes. 'I haven't had much to drink since we came here,' she said.

'And you don't have the G and T's?' Fleur asked.

Joanna-Rose frowned. 'Don't you mean the DTs?'

'That's it,' Fleur replied with a smirk. 'And you've never gone for methylated spirits or anything? I mean, when you can't get hold of anything else?'

The other woman laughed aloud. 'I admit I think about drink a lot, but I'm not pulling my hair out or going on a desperate, secretive search for one when my supply runs dry. Especially any that include the garages and kitchen cabinets,' she said. 'So I think that's a sign it's at least still under my control. I've just been using it as a crutch, I suppose. But all that is going to change now. I need to learn to handle life a bit better, alone.' She looked in the rear-view mirror at her carpet bag on the back seat.

'You're not alone anymore,' said Fleur. 'You've got me and Cathy now. And maybe a new man on the horizon, if you play your cards right. Because you deserve love, Joanna-Rose, honestly you do. Why the hell you agreed to shack up with a man that didn't love you, I'll never know. I mean, after everything you've lived through. I don't get it. You seem much stronger than that to me.'

'Robert did help me, you know,' Joanna-Rose explained. 'He encouraged me to transition, which I eventually did with his full support when I was thirty. I guess I have that to thank my father for.'

'Do you think Robert was, perhaps, a substitute father?'

Joanna-Rose blinked, surprised at Fleur's question. The thought had never crossed her mind before. 'Maybe,' she admitted, after thinking for a second. 'I mean, it wasn't exactly love at first sight. I wasn't interested in him when my mother introduced us. Then we became friends, and after a time I found I was able to trust him enough to reveal everything about me and to my amazement – because I'd never told anyone else in my life till then - he just accepted it. Sadly we all know why now, though.'

'What a lonely life,' Fleur said. 'Never knowing real love.'

'I loved my mother,' Joanna-Rose said.

She pulled into the car park at Machir Bay and brought the car to a stop beside a gleaming, white Ferrari. In it, wearing enormous, round sunglasses that made Fleur think of a giant bee, sat Libby Colquhoun. Spotting them, she opened her car door and stepped out, flashing long, over-tanned legs from the split in her bright, white skirt as she walked. Teasing flowing, blonde locks from her eyes as the wind drove them whipping across her face, she stooped to look in Cathy's car and waved. Fleur opened her window and stretched a hand out in greeting as she approached, her gaze falling immediately to the woman's feet, and the bright, red pair of chunky Crocs sandals she was wearing. Before now, Fleur had pictured her as a petite-yet-towering stilettos kind of woman.

'Hello Libby,' Joanna-Rose said, getting out of the car and waving a hand to her. 'I'm not stopping to chat. My mother and I are off for a walk on the beach.' She lifted her carpet bag and waved it at her. Then, giving Fleur a knowing glance as she walked away, she said, 'I'll leave you and Cathy here alone to talk.'

Fleur got out of the car. 'So, come on,' she said, placing an arm around Libby's shoulders, momentarily overcome by the strong scent of Chanel as together they watched Joanna-Rose disappear over the sand dunes, to the beach below. 'How does it feel, marrying a really old man for his money?'

'I... did... not...' she gasped, pulling away and looking appalled at the suggestion.

'Oh yes you did.'

'I have stayed with Derek for fifteen years,' Libby argued. 'And have endured his rages, the drinking, the heavy schedule -'

'All of which you thought would send him to an early grave,' Fleur said. 'Bit of a disappointment, I suppose, Libby? May I call you Libby?' she added, before continuing on without waiting for a reply. 'But then, you've had a string of lovers to keep you amused while you wait, haven't you, Libby?'

'A woman has needs,' the woman retorted with a sniff of indifference.

'Perhaps you can make the results of your "needs" up to Bob Harper's widow now by accepting her very generous offer. Extremely generous, given that you were sleeping with her... *my* husband,' Fleur said, inwardly cursing herself for her mistake.

Libby stiffened, tilted her chin and peered at Fleur over her sunglasses. 'Sleeping with?'

'Oh, don't bother denying it,' Fleur snapped. 'Derek told us – me – the whole, sordid story.'

Libby blinked, her puzzlement apparent. Then, after a moment, she sighed. 'Well, of course he did,' she said at last. 'He must be planning to make out I was unfaithful, because then I don't get a bean. Damn prenuptial agreement.'

'You weren't unfaithful?' Fleur said, unable to hide the surprised tone in her voice.

'No! But I guess you'll read the papers like everyone else and jump to your own conclusions about me, though,' she said, turning her hands over to examine her fingernails.

'Libby, I've seen pictures of you out and about with all kinds of men, are you really trying to have me believe you've been a saint? Come on, this is just you and me here talking.'

Libby eyed Fleur suspiciously, and then, seeming to think better about arguing, her expression changed. 'Okay, well sure, I dabbled with a few men,' she conceded. 'But not Bob from the Distillery. I mean, no offence and all that, but he wasn't really my type.'

Fleur stood up straight and turned to face her fully on. 'Libby, are you saying you didn't have a relationship with Bob at all?' she asked.

A loud thudding sound came from the boot of the car. Fleur ignored it.

Libby nodded. 'That's what I'm saying. He got in touch to advise me on the best course of action regarding the sale of my share of that useless cask of whisky and that is all. He didn't tell you all of this?'

Fleur shook her head.

'He said he was from the distillery and they were getting in touch with all owners who hadn't paid warehouse rental, or something,' Libby continued, starting to twist round to look at the car as the thudding got louder.

'So you just signed it over to Bob?' Fleur said, pulling Libby back around to face her.

'Sure, why not? I got five hundred pounds for it! I was happy to sell. What do I want with a barrel load of old whisky? I hate whisky.'

The thud turned into some scrapes, bangs and muffled howls.

'What is that noise?' Libby asked, turning again to look behind her. 'It seems to be coming from your car.'

'I think the exhaust is falling off,' Fleur told her.

Libby turned back and nodded, still unsure as the rumbling and commotion behind her got worse. 'You know, it's just like Derek to accuse me of having some sort of affair with Bob,' she said. 'He will do anything to stop me suing him for half the house. Was it him that told you that?'

'Five hundred pounds for the cask, you say?' asked Fleur, ignoring her question and scratching her chin thoughtfully.

At once, Libby's expression changed from puzzled to smug. 'Yes, five hundred pounds,' she said. 'I thought that was pretty good, seeing as a bottle in the supermarket is only about thirty.'

'Libby,' Fleur said, looking incredulous. 'How many bottles do you suppose there are in a cask?'

More thuds and muffled sounds ensued.

'Erm, aren't you going to check that?' Libby asked, pointing at the car.

'In a minute,' said Fleur. 'So, what do you think?'

'About four?' she said, adding, 'You know, I think the whole car is shaking. That's not right for a loose exhaust, is it? Is there -'

'Four, yes, that's err... right,' Fleur agreed before Libby could finish her sentence. 'One hundred and twenty pounds. How clever of you to make a three hundred and eighty pound profit.' She said the last part through gritted, could-not-believe-the-stupidity teeth. 'Now, would you like to make another one?'

'Another three hundred and eighty pounds? Well, given that I stand to make a cool million or more from my divorce settlement if I can show his infidelity claim up for the complete lie that it is, I hardly think it's worth it, is it? Is that all you brought me here for?'

'Exactly!' replied Fleur. 'You're right. It's not worth it, especially knowing what we know. I think we've finished our business, in that case.'

The thudding in the car continued, along with some muffled cries.

Astonished, Libby stared at Fleur. 'Someone just said, "Let me out",' she told her. 'I know I heard it.' She started to back away, looking terrified. 'Is this a kidnapping?' she said.

Fleur held her hands up before leaning forward to catch Libby's hands. 'No, no,' she reassured her. 'Well, not of you anyway. You see, I have some inside information on Derek to help you with that infidelity claim he's making to stop you getting your full divorce entitlement.'

'Inside information?' she said, unable to take her eyes off the now rocking car. 'At this moment in time, I'm still his wife. How much inside information do you suppose I don't have?'

Fleur grinned to herself. 'Oh, plenty,' she said, rubbing her hands together with glee.

The thudding and scraping stopped. But they heard a distinctive, 'AWW!'

'Erm...,' Libby said. 'If you don't mind my asking, who have you got in the boot of that car?'

'Derek,' Fleur replied with a satisfied grin.

Libby took off her sunglasses and stared, wide-eyed at her. '*My* Derek?'

'What if I was to tell you that your Derek was sleeping around too,' Fleur said, 'For six years.'

Libby shook her head. 'I wouldn't believe you,' she said. 'Derek adores me.'

'He also adores Lady Fraser.'

To Fleur's surprise, Libby began to laugh. 'Oh no, no, no,' she roared, leaning on her car for support as she went over on a stiletto in her state of mirth. 'He wasn't sleeping with Dorothea,' she said. 'He was conning her. I knew all about it. He was sweetening her up, telling her lies about paying off some debts before they could leave their spouses for each other. She was laundering money for him.'

'How?'

'I don't know,' Libby replied. 'Selling him things that he paid cash for and providing largely inflated receipts, that kind of thing.'

Fleur walked up to Cathy's car, with Derek still thudding on the inside of the boot and gave it a good, hard, whack. 'And you don't believe he was having sex with her?' she said, to Libby.

The other woman stopped laughing, looking from Fleur's face to the car boot. 'No,' she said after a pause. 'I don't.'

'What if I told you I saw them?' Fleur said. 'What if I told you a quick call to Lady Fraser to tell her all you have just told me would confirm it all?'

She clicked the button on the car boot, and pulled it open.

Chapter Forty-Six

'I like to imagine you're young again, wherever you are now,' Joanna-Rose told her oversized carpet bag, as she sat on a rock beside it. Her voice seemed reduced to almost a whisper against the rolling, crashing waves of Machir Bay. 'You were beautiful, mum. That's why everybody wanted to take your photo. You shone in every one of them.'

She picked up a stone and tossed it at the ocean, before looking back at the bag. 'I know why you didn't tell me about him,' she said, 'You thought he would hurt me, didn't you?'

A dog barked and she looked up to see a couple on the beach further down, chasing a black puppy all the way into the surf. Joanna-Rose pulled her scarf tighter around her throat and blew out her cheeks. 'Rather them than me,' she said, removing her shoes. 'I might take a short paddle, just for you, mum. But it's a bit cold for a swim.'

'We always loved a swim, have you forgotten?'

Startled, Joanna-Rose looked around, but found herself alone.

'What did you say?' she asked aloud. 'Mum?'

There was no reply, the only sound being the wind in her ears and waves crashing on the sand.

Joanna-Rose stood up, bending over to pick up her bag, before walking to the shoreline and looking down at her bare feet. Shivering in the wind, she stooped to open the bag and pulled out a large, plain, brown plastic jar that looked as though it could have held something as simple as three litres of oil. She hugged it in the crook of one arm, running a finger from her free hand over the first line of text on the label, which read, KATHLEEN BARTON.

'My brother and I used to swim here,' Kathleen said, watching Barry splash through the shallow waters of the river's edge. It was a sunny day, and all about him, children from the estate were running wild, laughing and screaming as they kicked freezing-cold water at one another.

'Did you?' Barry replied, his eyes wide with surprise.

'Of course,' she said with a laugh. 'I wasn't always this old, you know.'

'But, parents don't like the river,' he said, pointing at the mums and dads watching from the riverbank. 'They say it's too cold.'

'Cold, is it?' she said, laughing aloud. And with that she stood up, took off her shoes and, tucking her skirt into her knickers, padded through the water before stooping down to give him a hug. 'Barry,' she told him, ruffling his hair affectionately. 'Acting the way people expect you to is rarely very exciting.'

Joanna-Rose thought of her beautiful, voracious, full-of-life mother, whom she'd kept at home and then carried with her since the day after the cremation. She knew why she hadn't been able to decide where to scatter her ashes. She had been unable to let her go. With a heavy heart, she twisted off the lid of the jar. 'I don't remember you carrying me home that day, mum,' she said out loud. 'I only know that you did. But then, you always did.'

She tried to imagine that day, as what must have been a terrified and horrified Kathleen Barton ran down the street for home, carrying the unconscious body of her only child, covered with blood and still wearing the non-conformist, bright, red stiletto heels that had so offended his classmates. Nobody came to her aid. Not one person offered to help carry the boy, to call the police, or even an ambulance. Later, not a soul came forward to name the perpetrators, even though the attack, in broad daylight and on a regular route home for schoolchildren, must have been witnessed by someone. With Barry Barton's removal to social outcast in the small village where they lived, Kathleen Barton's had soon followed.

When she had awoken from surgery, three days later, Joanna-Rose could remember promising to never wear the red shoes again. Nothing, she'd decided, was worth being an outsider for.

Her mother's reply was a simple one, yet had resonated in her child's heart ever since: 'You must never simply *wear* those beautiful, rose-red shoes, Barry. I want you to dance in them.'

Joanna-Rose had been home taught for the next four years. And from that day to this, she realised, wiping a now heavy flow of tears from her eyes with her sleeve, she had never danced in her rose-red shoes. She'd been living in exile. 'I'd do it for you now, mum,' she said softly, into the wind.

'ARGHHHHHHH! What was that?'

Alerted by the shouting, Joanna-Rose spun round to see Derek limping over the dunes towards her, with Libby in hot pursuit, waving a thick, red sandal in one hand, aiming it at his head.

'You sneak!' Libby shouted, 'you snake in the grass! I HATE YOU!'

The heel of the second, heavy sandal bounced off his bald bonce with a clunk, as he ran a little further before tumbling into the water in front of Joanna-Rose in an exhausted heap. 'I can't run any more,' he said to her, clutching his chest and gasping for air. 'I'm finished. Help me, please.'

Before Joanna-Rose could reply, he was up and off again, with Libby giving chase, hitting him all the way as he limped down along water's edge, trying – and failing – to avoid the crashing waves.

Blinking in the bright sunlight, she watched the pair charge further away, as did the couple with the excitable black puppy who, unbeknownst to Joanna-Rose, were now walking only a few feet away. Joanna-Rose smiled at the pair as they laughed aloud at all the furore, before her eyes were drawn to Libby's discarded Crocs, and, putting down the plastic jar, she walked over to collect them. They were rose-red, and sturdy; definitely waterproof. She turned them over to check the size. Maybe a size smaller than she was, but still...

'One last paddle, mum,' Joanna-Rose said, as on a sunny, autumn day, through the ice-cold waves and in view of two bemused dog walkers, she twirled round and around with her skirt tucked into her knickers, scattering the cinders of Kathleen Barton to the brisk, Scottish wind and the slate-blue waters of Machir Bay. Because this was where she had, at last, learned to dance.

Chapter Forty-Seven

'A private seller has released a rare, 50-year-old single cask whisky from MacReeley's Distillery, described as the finest cask that has ever been produced in Scotland. The bottles will be available to buy online exclusively and are expected to be snapped up by whisky enthusiasts and collectors within hours.'

'Wow,' said Cathy, as she stood looking over Fleur's shoulder at the article on the internet. 'Derek said there would be twenty or thirty bottles.'

'And what was it he said Viscount Fraser was buying for? One hundred thousand pounds for the cask? How much is that a bottle?'

'Maybe three to five thousand a bottle. Blimey, who'd pay that for a bottle of whisky?' Cathy said.

'Like the article says, enthusiasts and collectors. This is big business, you know.'

'I know, but five thousand pounds! That's ten months mortgage payments to me.'

Fleur made to close the laptop, before spying a Facebook alert at the bottom of the screen.

'Ooh, it's that old boyfriend of yours, Martin,' said Fleur, clicking to open it before Cathy could stop her.

'Don't... oh Fleur, you mustn't read that!'

'He says, "Are you still coming tonight?"' Fleur spun round to look at her. 'Are you still coming tonight? Have you arranged to meet him, after all?'

'No. Well, yes, but it was because I was angry.'

'You did this while we were in Jura?'

'Yes.'

'Crikey, well done you for getting a phone signal. I almost fell off the stairs up to the Laird's Loft trying to read a weather report on the BBC website.'

'Yes, okay, I did it but that was then and this is now. I thought Bob had been cheating on me, but, as it turns out he wasn't so I won't be going to meet Martin. Can you make my excuses for me?'

'I will not!' Fleur retorted. 'Cathy, don't you see? This is another suitcase full of money. You've got to grab it! Do you think Bob would want you to be lonely and sad for all of your days?'

'I don't think he'd want me to be, but I can't help that I am,' Cathy sniffed.

'Okay, he kind of helped Derek rip off his ex for a price, but I can see how the money would have enticed him, coupled with the fact that both of them are pretty bad people,' said Fleur. 'And as it turns out, his decision has helped you more than he could ever have realised it would. In fact, I've got to say, I'd have done it too. But he seems like he was a nice, loving husband so I can understand why it's hard to let him go. But why the prolonged, enforced misery?' Fleur asked.

Cathy relaxed back in her chair, screwed her eyes shut and exhaled noisily. 'It's not enforced, it's very real. You see, I can still see the terror in his eyes,' she said.

'You mean, when he died?'

'Yes,' Cathy admitted. 'It was the worst, most horrible day of my life and no matter how I try, I can't get the pictures out of my mind. I relive that day over and over. I can't bear it.'

'Oh Cathy, I'm so sorry. But tell me something, will you?'

'What?'

Fleur took a long breath inward. 'Do you think the length of your grief is a reflection of how much you loved him?'

'I don't know,' said Cathy. 'I've never thought about it like that. Maybe, I suppose. But when I think of those last moments, as I do all the time, I think how much he must have suffered and I can hardly breathe, it hurts me so much.'

'So stop thinking about it,' Fleur said.

Despite herself, Cathy let out a sarcastic laugh. 'Yes, that's it, it's that easy. Why didn't I think of that? Just stop thinking about it!' She hit her forehead with her palm.

Fleur caught both her hands in hers. 'Cathy,' she said, looking straight into her eyes. 'You had twenty, wonderful years with Bob. He was, as you've told me enough times, a lively, interesting man who was full of get up and go. And here you are, almost two years after his death, still loving him so much it's clear to me you must have had the most fantastic marriage. Yet, when you're remembering him – your rock, the love of your life – the mental highlight reel you choose to play is that one?'

Cathy caught her breath, her eyes filled with the new light of recognition. 'Yes,' she acknowledged.

Fleur sighed. 'Do you think if you could have had a message from the other side, that Bob would have asked you to be miserable and alone every day for the rest of your life?' she asked.

'I don't think he would have told me to go out with my ex, that's for sure.'

'How do you know?' Fleur replied. 'How do you know he's not in a field full of daisies, singing Hallelujah with a whole, new barrel of whisky at his feet, thinking this death malarkey is fabulous and not giving you a thought?'

'I don't. But I hope that isn't true.'

'Why? Because at the end of your days, you'll find out you wasted all the years after his death being sad while he was rejoicing? Does real love require both parties to be wretched and desolate until they meet again? Doesn't Bob's sudden, untimely death make you want to get out and experience everything?'

'I suppose...'

'Don't you want to get back on the horse before you've forgotten what your saddle's for?'

Cathy's thoughtful expression turned to irritation. 'Fleur, I'm not going to go out with Martin and that's that.'

Fleur frowned. 'Well, I'm out,' she said.

'And anyway, you are forgetting one vital element in this whole thing,' Cathy continued. 'Martin dumped me, quite brutally as it happens. I was heartbroken and it took me several years to get over it.'

'So go out for dinner then dump *his* sorry backside this time,' Fleur said, before stopping. 'Years?' she said, sounding taken aback. 'Really?'

'Yes, really. I was young and I thought he was the great love of my life. When I read he'd married someone else not long after he dumped me, I was distraught. I thought that was *my* life. She was living in the world I was supposed to have had!'

'For how long were you thinking about this?'

Cathy shuffled uncomfortably in her chair. 'About twenty years,' she admitted. 'I was still thinking about Martin from time to time after I met Bob, if I'm honest. Oh Fleur, there was even a night when Bob and I had a row and I had a lot to drink. It was before we were married.'

Fleur's eyes widened. 'And what happened?'

'I got my bike from the shed and rode all the way to the house where I knew Martin was living. It was 2am.'

'What did you do?'

'I just sat there, mesmerized. It was stupid and I was completely drunk. God, I shudder to think that anyone might have looked out of a window and seen me there.'

'Jesus, Cathy, that's not love, it's obsession.'

'I know,' she agreed. 'Don't you think I've grown enough to realise that? It wasn't Martin I was sad about though. It took a long time for me to get it, but I do now. It was the rejection. I held the pain of it for twenty years, but I was not and am not now in love with Martin anymore.'

'But admit it,' Fleur replied. 'You must be a little curious, or you would never have agreed to meet him.'

'Okay, so I'm curious,' said Cathy. 'But that's all it is. If I went to meet him it would just be because I want him to have had a terrible life without me. I want him to have spent years wondering "what if". That's all this is. I don't have any romantic feelings for him.'

'How do you know that unless you go and see him?'

'Because I'm in love with my husband,' came the quick reply.

'Your late husband,' Fleur said. 'Cathy, Bob's gone, but you're still here. Aren't you going to allow yourself to have a life now? What if Martin still loves you?'

'I do have a life.'

'No, you don't,' Fleur told her. 'You have an *existence* and you aren't managing that very well, are you?' She nodded towards the pile of letters and bills still on the desk.

'It might all be sorted out when the whisky sells,' Cathy said.

'Thanks to Joanna-Rose and I convincing you that neither Derek nor that Libby are worth giving up a fortune for. They deserve each other. Hey, do you think Derek might do time for all his dodgy dealings? It would serve him right too.'

'I don't know,' Cathy said. 'But I can't thank you and Joanna-Rose enough. Nor can I stop thinking of Libby's disappointed face when she realises there is nothing left of Derek's fortune for her to win with all that information you gave her on *his* cheating ways. What a pair,' she said, shaking her head. 'So,' she added with a smile, 'what about you?'

Fleur sat up straight 'Me?'

'Yes, you. When are you going to go back to your house and start clearing it out to live in again? Do you think I'm not aware the builders left weeks ago?'

'No, they didn't,' Fleur said quickly. 'And anyway, how do you know?'

I just happened to drive by yesterday and saw the scaffolding is gone and nobody's working there,' Cathy said. 'So, naturally, I took a look in the lounge window and, guess what? Your floor is fixed. That is, apart from all the trash around the place. Honestly, have you been auditioning for *Britain's Worst Hoarders?*'

Fleur's mouth fell open and she stared at Cathy, who straightaway began to feel guilty.

'Oh Fleur, it's okay if you don't want to go back home. I understand that you're lonely,' she told her.

'Who said I was lonely?'

'Everything about your house,' Cathy replied, giving her a sympathetic smile. 'Do you suppose if you start to pick all the rubbish up and clean you'll see just how big and empty the place is without Charlie?'

Fleur opened her mouth again looking like she was about to protest, but sighed instead. 'Yes.'

Cathy almost fell off her chair. 'What? I'm right?' she said. 'Wow, I'm psychic!'

'Now take fifty quid off me and tell me my dead grannie said Philip needs me,' Fleur said.

'Which he most likely does now you come to mention it. Anyway, I thought you said you had a daughter?'

Fleur's face fell and she sighed. 'I do.'

'So you're not alone then,' said Cathy. 'Why don't you call her?'

'Because I told you, she doesn't want to know me anymore.'

'Why?'

'I thought we were psychoanalysing you today, not me?' Fleur argued.

'Why?'

Fleur blew out her cheeks and slumped back in her chair. 'Because she thinks I didn't care about her father,' she said finally.

'Why on earth would she think that?'

'Because I didn't go to his funeral,' Fleur replied. 'I was angry with God and I just couldn't go, it's as simple as that. I couldn't stand in that church thanking God for Charlie's life and his death.'

'And you're not angry now?' Cathy said, noting the picture of Jesus that had been hung back on her wall that morning by Fleur.

'No, I'm not now,' Fleur said, seeing the direction of Cathy's gaze. 'Nor his son.' She nodded at the picture. 'Minister MacFarlane helped me some with my "spiritual" stuff and anyway, it turns out God is another imperfect being, just like the rest of us.'

'So, why don't you pick up the phone and explain all this to, what's her name?'

'Mandy.'

'Why don't you tell this to Mandy?'

'Because she'll slam the phone down on me and it will hurt too much. She isn't my daughter you know, she's Charlie's.'

'But you've been there for her up till her father's death?'

Fleur nodded. 'She did phone me in Jura, but I couldn't call her back,' she admitted. 'I ran all over the place, but I couldn't get a bloody signal.'

'So she wants to talk to you then,' Cathy said. 'And my guess is she needs you now as much as she needed you then. We all need our mothers, no matter how old we get. I still miss mine,' Cathy said.

'I don't know, I don't even remember mine,' Fleur began, staring down at Cathy's laptop before looking up again at her friend with mischief in her eyes. 'I tell you what,' she said more brightly. 'We'll make a deal to improve all our lives for the better. I'll call Mandy if you leave this damn, miserable, all-widows-together Facebook page with me and join a something that's a bit more exciting. What do you think of Tinder?'

'Oh no,' said Cathy. 'No, no, NO!'

Chapter Forty-Eight

'Have you seen the result?'

'Hello, Joanna-Rose, how are you?' Cathy asked, as the other woman pushed passed her into the house.

'The auction, Cathy!' she exclaimed. 'Have you read about it? I was watching all night!'

Cathy closed the door behind her and leaned in to sniff her friend's breath. 'Have you been drinking again?'

'No,' Joanna-Rose replied. 'I've not touched a drop in four weeks and neither do I own a wine cellar anymore. I've sold the lot and guess what?'

'What?'

The question had come from Fleur, who had wandered out of the living room, toenail clippers in hand, to see what all the commotion was about.

'I've finished my play!'

'Oh Joanna-Rose, that's wonderful news! Oh Fleur,' Cathy said, turning back to her. 'She's writing again!'

'I know. I'm here too. I heard her.'

'How did this happen?' Cathy asked.

'I don't know. All that fresh sea air, the drama, the excitement...'

'The kidnapping,' said Fleur.

Joanna-Rose rolled her eyes. 'It's true,' she said. 'It's all in there. But wait, wait wait! That's not what I came to tell you. It's something far, far more exciting.'

'You told Isaac how you feel?' asked Fleur.

'No,' Joanna-Rose admitted. 'Although, I have told him all about my past.'

'And what did he say?'

'Listen, you've got to let me get this out -' said Joanna-Rose.

'Ooh, that's a little bit presumptuous of him,' Fleur said, sucking in her cheeks. 'But still, a result don't you think?'

'No, I don't mean Isaac. He said nothing, that's what he said. But that's not what I came to tell you about. I -'

'He said nothing?' Fleur gasped. 'Didn't you have the, "I'm the moon and you are the sun," talk at all?'

'Fleur will you stop and listen for a minute!' Joanna-Rose shouted out in frustration. 'It's about the whisky auction.'

'Oh, that,' said Cathy. 'We couldn't get in to watch. You have to be a club member.'

'A simple online form which I bothered to complete,' said Joanna-Rose with a grin. 'I watched the whole thing.'

Fleur and Cathy leaned in.

'And?' said Cathy.

'Will she be able to clear her mortgage arrears on this place?' Fleur asked.

Joanna-Rose took both Cathy's hands in hers and spun her round and around. 'Oh Cathy, what's a mortgage?' She beamed.

'I hardly think this is the time for rubbing her nose in *your* wealth,' Fleur snapped.

'Cathy,' Joanna-Rose went on. 'Say goodbye to your mortgage. Say goodbye to this house if you like. You're moving up in the world.'

Cathy's eyes widened. 'How?'

'What did the cask fetch?' asked Fleur.

'Nine hundred thousand pounds!'

Cathy stopped dancing and her mouth fell open.

'For thirty bottles?' said Fleur.

'Thirty? Try a hundred!'

'Why that lying little…' Fleur began, thinking it was time for her to give Derek another beating with a giant bible.

'Do you know what this means?' Cathy asked Fleur.

'We're going shopping?'

'I'm rich,' squealed Cathy, jumping again with Joanna-Rose, taking them in to her living room. 'I'm bloody rich! Do you hear that, Jesus? I've got four hundred and fifty thousand pounds,' she sang to the picture on the wall.

'Correction,' Joanna-Rose told her. 'You have nine hundred thousand pounds, Cathy.'

'I do?'

'It seems Lady Fraser was only too happy to relinquish her share,' Joanna-Rose told her. 'Perhaps because Libby told her Derek was only using her, or perhaps in case the whole sordid matter got back to her husband when the details of the sale came out in public. The auction has made all of the papers, you know.'

'Which someone warned her might happen too,' Fleur added, with a grin that let the other two know who had.

'I have nine hundred thousand pounds,' Cathy said, almost to herself.

'Nine hundred thousand pounds,' Fleur repeated, following them in and making a quick mental calculation in her head. 'That's nine thousand pounds a bottle.'

'I know,' Cathy squealed, clapping her hands together. 'And to think, there's another one here somewhere too, according to Derek.'

'There is?'

'Yes,' she replied. 'He said they drew a single bottle at the time of the purchase. That's what they're drinking in the picture. He said he gave it to Bob as part payment for swindling Libby.'

'After we agreed to let him go without telling the papers what a fake he is,' Joanna-Rose reminded her.

'And you think it's here, in the house?'

Cathy nodded. 'I'm sure of it. He has such a love for collecting the stuff, it's bound to be in there somewhere. A special... blend...' she stopped.

Fleur swallowed, as both their eyes fell on the empty bottle still on the sideboard that the women had drunk before leaving for Islay.

'I... I had no idea...' Fleur began.

'I can't believe you!' Cathy shouted, chasing her out into the hallway.

'But you still have nine hundred thousand pounds?' Joanna-Rose called after them.

Chapter Forty-Nine

'Oh, it's you, Cathy. Sorry, we're a little late opening up after lunch. We were doing a small stock take.'

'Really? We have small stock?' Cathy's eyes narrowed as she spied Jodi rearranging her hair and straightening her blouse through the gap in the door that led to the back office. 'And what did you find? Everything in order, I hope?'

Joan nodded. 'Naturally. I run a very tight ship, as you know.'

'Good, well, can you pass me the keys, please?'

'The keys?' said Joan, looking annoyed. 'What on earth do you want those for? Look, Jodi and I are very busy here and your incessant banging for the last ten minutes was very off-putting.'

'*My* incessant banging?'

'Yes, on the door,' she replied. 'We thought you were a customer that wouldn't go away.'

'Joan,' Cathy said, putting a hand on the other woman's shoulders while reaching for the shop keys with the other. 'How long have you been having sex with your niece?'

Joan's face turned crimson as she released the keys in shock. 'What on earth...' she began.

'She's not your niece though, is she Eric?'

As Cathy spoke, she turned around and beckoned to Joan's husband, who stood in the doorway.

'It's okay, Eric,' she said. 'It appears your wife and her lover have finished their liaison, all captured by the office CCTV no doubt, should you need to check my facts.'

Jodi looked up at it in alarm. 'Have you been keeping films of us, Joan?' she asked.

'I... don't... keep them,' Joan stammered under her breath, before calling out, 'Eric, this is all an awful misunderstanding. Cathy doesn't know what she's saying. She's been though a terrible time, what with losing Bob and everything.' She attempted to hustle Cathy towards the door as he was entering the shop, but Cathy stood firm.

'It's your turn to go out, Joan,' she said, shaking the keys in the other woman's face. 'You and Jodi can leave now, please.'

'What?' Joan said, her face incredulous. 'You can't do that. I'll be calling the franchisee. We'll see who's putting who out here. You're off your head.'

'Why don't you just talk to me to my face?' Cathy said, with a wide grin. She took a letter from her pocket and waved it in front of Joan, before placing it in her palm. 'It's all there in writing for you. I'm the new owner and you are the new ex-employees, sacked for gross misconduct, effective immediately. Now, Eric,' she said, addressing Joan's husband who was now stood behind her, his expression grim. 'Would you like to come into my office to view some CCTV footage?'

'The CCTV footage was a mean stroke for you though, Cathy,' Joanna-Rose said, dropping another grape into Isaac's mouth, which he devoured a little too noisily, making her howl with laughter.

'Is someone there with you?' Cathy asked.

There was more laughter. Cathy took the phone away from her ear and shook it.

'Hello? Joanna-Rose? I think there's some interference on the line. All I can hear is a crackling noise.'

'Isaac,' Joanna-Rose said. 'Not on the bag of grapes! If this is how they make wine, I might have to start drinking it again.'

Chapter Fifty

There was another two weeks to go, she was sure of it. No need to check the calendar, the due date was etched on her brain; the second of February, two weeks from today.

'Ooh, I need her,' she yelped at him. 'Please! Try the number again.'

He stopped rubbing her back and reached in his trouser pocket for his phone.

'I dialled three times already,' he told her. 'She's not answering. Don't you think we should just go to the hospital now?'

'Not without her,' she insisted. 'I need her to be there with me. She promised!'

He sighed, feeling helpless as his wife let out a long, low moan. The pains were getting closer together. He dialled the number again.

'Bloody phone!' Fleur shouted at the light in her darkness. 'Philip!' she shouted. 'Bring it to me! Fetch, Philip, fetch!'

Philip looked down at her and yawned.

'It's there, right at your feet!' she told him.

It buzzed again, making him sniff at it in curiosity. It was just enough to push it over the edge and, as if by the hand of some unseen power, right into her lap.

'Hello? Is that you, Cathy? Can you send help? I'm stuck in another bloody hole. It's the kitchen this time!'

Cathy stared at her phone in disbelief. Surely this couldn't be happening a second time? Before she could give it any more thought, her mobile lit up again.

'Hello, Joanna-Rose,' she answered quietly, her mind still on deciding a solution for Fleur.

'Whatever's the matter, Cathy?' the other woman asked. 'You sound worried.'

Cathy swallowed hard, an image of shattering glass entering her mind. 'Fleur needs help again,' she replied. 'Does that man of yours have a big ladder?'

'Please,' she said, her breaths coming quicker now. 'Try her again!'

He shook his head. 'But I told you, darling, she's -'

'TRY HER AGAIN!'

Fleur's phone lit up the darkness and she scowled at it, not recognising the number. 'Bloody bank,' she complained.

'USE MY PHONE!' She was crying now, and threw her mobile at him before leaning on the windowsill, crying out as another wave of pain descended on her. 'She won't know your number,' she yelled. 'CALL HER AGAIN!'

Twenty minutes later, Michael Smith turned to his sweating, pain-riddled wife and frowned.

'Mandy,' he said. 'We're going to the hospital now and I'll have no more arguments. The new grannie is on her way, don't worry. She'll be meeting us there. Cathy and Joanna-Rose have gone to get her, with a...' He paused, shaking his head as he recalled the finer details of his conversation with Fleur. 'Well,' he said finally, 'with a fire crew, to be honest.'

Epilogue

'What should we say?' Cathy said, scratching her head and staring blankly at her mobile phone.

'Hot, sexy fishwife seeks catch of the day?' Fleur suggested.

'Be serious,' Cathy replied, looking embarrassed. 'This Tinder app thing was *your* idea.'

'You wouldn't have had to join, if you'd gone out with your first love, like I told you to.'

Cathy shook her head in exasperation. 'I don't know how many times I've told you,' she said. 'I have no desire to meet him, ever. He's a loser that belongs to yesterday.'

'Did you tell him that?'

'Yes. Well... not in those exact words, but -' she looked down at her phone and tapped on the screen. 'I've made my peace with the past, that's all. As you have with God, I'm pleased to see,' she said, without looking up.

Fleur eyed the new addition to the wall above her television – a simple crucifix. 'Oh, that,' she said. 'I found it under the dust. Now, let me look at your nominations for Mr Tomorrow.' She leaned over Cathy's shoulder to read with her, just as the doorbell rang. Philip immediately pounced on to the sofa in fright.

Cathy looked up at the cat, as he set about washing his ears as if nothing had happened. 'Is it safe to move that quickly in here?' she asked, before surveying her friend's newly cleaned living room floor.

'The floors are all fixed now,' the older woman said with a scowl, as she headed out to get the door.

'I'll go get the gift,' Cathy called after her, with a chuckle.

Joanna-Rose entered Fleur's lounge to find Cathy popping open a bottle of Bucks Fizz.

'CONGRATULATIONS!' her two friends sang out in chorus.

'Ooh, what a nice surprise,' she said, her eyes glistening as she grasped the glass Fleur held out to her and took it to Cathy. 'Low alcohol, I hope?' she asked.

'Of course,' replied Cathy, filling her glass with the orange-coloured bubbly. 'Well done on finishing the play! We're so proud of you!'

'Now drink up and get on with your next masterpiece,' Fleur added with a grin, passing her a small, black box with a red ribbon around it. 'And never be alone while you're writing it.'

'For me?' Joanna-Rose said.

Fleur nodded.

She took the box from Fleur and slowly lifted the lid, to find a silver locket engraved with an imprint of a pair of Crocs, which were a bright and shiny, cherry red. She smiled, as the memory of her mother's last - and her own first - dance in the Irish Sea came to mind.

'As long as you have us, you'll never be alone again,' Cathy said with a kind smile, as Joanna-Rose opened the locket. 'But we also thought you might like to keep Kathleen with you.'

'In something prettier and more delicate than a carpet bag,' Fleur added.

'It has a tiny urn inside of it,' Cathy explained, as Joanna-Rose lifted the locked to examine it more closely. 'Fleur took the liberty of salvaging some of the last ashes from the jar. We hoped you wouldn't mind.'

Joanna-Rose's eyes filled with happy tears. 'Mind? No! It's wonderful,' she cried. She closed the locket and let Cathy help her fasten it around her neck. 'You know,' she said, wiping her eyes and smiling down at the necklace. 'I think you silly sods have literally saved my life.'

'If bereavement has taught me anything, it's that people don't let themselves have enough silliness in their lives,' Cathy told her, with a coy look at Fleur.

Fleur gasped. 'A common regret of the dying! You remembered!' she said with a grin. 'Dare to never lose the silly side of yourself. And don't worry,' she added, putting an arm around both of her friends, pulling them all closer. 'I'm here to keep you sweet on that one.'

'You can say that again,' Cathy agreed.

'So, when can we go and do some more silly stuff in Jura?' Fleur asked, looking at them both with a hopeful, mischievous expression. 'It'll help Joanna-Rose write, we can take the long walk right up to George Orwell's door this time and oh,' she added, looking at Cathy with a twinkle in her eye, 'there's a certain ferryman I'd like you to throw in your boot for me.'

Joanna-Rose's eyes widened. 'There is?'

'His name's Jimmy,' Cathy told her, with a wry smile.

'Life is so good,' Fleur said, skipping over to the sideboard to pick up Charlie's sporran, 'I think it's time for a boogie.' She nodded to Joanna-Rose, 'I expect you'll be a very keen dancer, by now.' She opened the pouch and took out her phone and her earphones.

'Well, your iSporran's no good to us,' Joanna-Rose said. 'Only you can hear the music.'

'Praise be to God,' Cathy added.

'You think?' Reaching a hand back into Charlie's sporran, Fleur pulled out two more sets of earphones and a multi headphone splitter, and held them aloft.

Cathy groaned.

Joanna-Rose raised her eyes to the ceiling and then, shaking her head, reached for the offered earphones. 'Dare to never lose the silly side of myself, you say?' she said, with a chuckle.

The pair looked at Cathy.

'Aww,' she groaned, holding out a reluctant hand to receive a set of earphones. 'Okay,' she said. 'But only if you're absolutely sure this floor is safe.'

The author would like to add, she can't promise that it was.

By the same author

THE NEW MRS D

After Shirley Valentine, after The First Wives Club and hot on the naked heels of Calendar Girls... there was The New Mrs D!

'Wine-spittingly, chocolate-chokingly brilliant! Hill is the Tom Sharpe of her era! Genuinely laugh out loud funny with great writing and a plot to keep you hooked. Buy it, read it - but if like me you are of a certain age, do so with an empty bladder.' – Amanda Prowse, author of the No Greater Love series.

Four days into their honeymoon in Greece, Bernice and David Dando have yet to consummate their marriage and after having accepted his almost non-existent desire for sex throughout the relationship, Bernice finally discovers the reason; he is addicted to porn. Learning that the love of her life chooses the cheap thrill of fantasy over her is devastating but then, 'every man does it; it's just looking, right?' If she leaves the relationship because of virtual adultery, will she be labelled as pathological, overreacting, or even worse, frigid?

When funny, feisty, forty-something Bernice plans the adventure trip of a lifetime, she doesn't expect to be spending it alone. But as it turns out, unintentionally contributing to a Greek fish explosion, nude karaoke and hilarious misadventures with volcanoes are exactly what she needs to stop fretting about errant husbands and really start living. But when Mr D tries to win her back, Bernice has a decision to make: is this a holiday from her humdrum life, or the start of a whole new adventure?

"The New Mrs D is a refreshing, sharp-witted and empowering romp that reflects real life, delves into unspoken about subjects and slaps the reader in the face with honesty." Fleur Ferris, author.

The New Mrs D is a story about one woman's midlife awakening... on her honeymoon alone.

Acknowledgements

Every author needs author friends. So, thank you to my super-supportive writer pals: Fleur Ferris, Fiona Gibson and Amanda Prowse – all of whom are always terribly busy being brilliant, yet find time to offer me the kindest words of encouragement, advice, the occasional 'don't do it!' and for reading the things I write.

To Martin and Raymond Armstrong of WhiskyBroker Ltd UK, who kindly provided me with a world of advice on the perks and technicalities of whisky collecting, for which I am eternally grateful. I would like to say that I did the very best that I could.

To Helen and Stephen Rooney. True friends would allow me to randomly message them all hours of the day and night with chemistry and accountancy related questions, which you did. You guys have supported me ever since the day this madness began. Thank you.

To Flora Napier of Blueprint Editing, Edinburgh, for always being my right-hand woman. Both my novels have begun and ended with you. Thank you for being so supportive.

To the book doctor, Debi Alper, who took my first draft and helped me polish it so hard, I could see my face in it. You are a miracle worker.

To Carol Bain, the very first reader of this work, who came along right when I needed her, in the most magical way, and kindly gave her time to tell me what sucked about it so that I could try to do better before pressing publish. I am eternally grateful, especially because it was all for the price of a Woo Woo.

Thanks to Will Stockham, whose amazing company first took me to Islay for a whisky tour back in the days when I was pronouncing it 'Is-Lay' instead of 'Isle-Lah', making me fall madly in love with the island *and* the scotch.

To my family, who drop what they are doing to cheer me on, never questioning where all of this might lead. You usually leave it there for me to pick up, but still, I love and appreciate you all.

To my mother, who left us at the crucial moment, when I was putting the finishing touches to a story about bereavement. Your influence lives on in us all. See you on the other side, mum.

And finally, to the wonderful people of Islay and Jura, who didn't know I was writing about them and the incredibly beautiful part of the world they inhabit.

About The Author

Heather Hill - comedy writer and mum of five (not the band) lives in Scotland and is one of a rare kind; the rare kind being one of the 0.5% of females that is ever-so-slightly colour blind. She is known to have been prevented from leaving the house with blue eyebrows on at least one occasion.

Heather started out writing lines for comedians in the Aberdeen, Glasgow & Edinburgh live comedy circuit, before embarking on a novel writing career. Her debut British comedy eBook, 'The New Mrs D', was an Amazon No1 bestseller before the paperback was published by Fledgling Press, Edinburgh in Spring 2015.

For news of new publications, you can subscribe to her newsletter at: http://bit.do/HHMAIL.
You can connect with Heather online by visiting her blog at www.heatherhillauthor.com. Or catch her on Twitter & Instagram, where she is often found sharing photos of her breakfast. Follow Heather - and her breakfast - @hell4heather or on Instagram @heatherhillauthor

Printed in Great Britain
by Amazon